For Jim and M[...]
Long, long [...]
friends and colleagues. With
all best wishes –

Virgil Scott
Feb. 1958

YO-AFZ-622

THE SAVAGE AFFAIR

Also by Virgil Scott

THE DEAD TREE GIVES NO SHELTER
THE HICKORY STICK

The Savage Affair
by Virgil Scott

HARCOURT, BRACE AND COMPANY 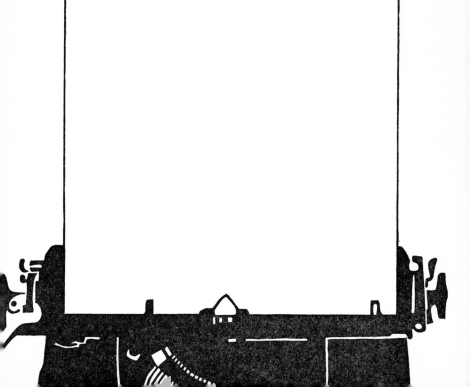 NEW YORK

© 1958 by Virgil Scott

All rights reserved. No part of this book may be reproduced in any form or by any mechanical means, including mimeograph and tape recorder, without permission in writing from the publisher. first edition

Library of Congress Catalog Card Number: 58-5475

Printed in the United States of America

To Naomi and Julian

Hyatt Engel   I

1 IN THE BEGINNING IT LOOKED like a routine assignment. I can see now that it wasn't, but I mention this fact because when you come right down to it, none of us had access to any crystal ball. Not Kay, who managed Savage's account in a way that ought to have kept worry away from his door for at least a few years; not Mattson, who had an investment to protect and whose business it was to feel trouble brewing; not Jean Reynolds, who, to phrase a Madison Avenue rumor delicately, was closer to him than the rest of us. Not even Alice, who there at the end may have been viewing the scene from a difficult angle, but who nevertheless had lived with Michael long enough to have developed some sensitivity to his inner tensions. These were the ones with the ringside seats, and so all I am trying to say is that what we needed was a vision which was adjusted to the gloom that is underneath the roiled surface, and none of us had it.

My mind can work this way now. The last news dispatch is in now, and the last caption has been pasted beneath the last photograph, and it is easy now to let hindsight go to work. It is after the fact now and Monday afternoon, a time when your mind has an inclination to nudge around at the whys because by Monday afternoon the magazine has been put to bed and the high-speed presses are spinning out the verbal patterns somewhere else and the lights here in the editorial offices have been flicked off and you stand alone in the shadows and the quiet. But seven months ago, when I came into this story, it was

3

a Wednesday morning, and when you work on *Insight*, Wednesday morning is no time for idle speculation because that is when the wheels start to go around.

My apartment then was on West Twelfth in one of those converted brownstones with gothic doorways and ceilings ten feet high. There had been one of those spontaneous gatherings in a bar the night before, which no doubt accounts for the way I felt that morning. I didn't have a hangover exactly, but there was a flat, tired, stale taste in my mouth that toothpaste wouldn't cut, and a thickness behind my eyes for which neither a cold shower nor black coffee was the right antidote, and when I came out of the house, I was wondering why I hadn't gone straight home to bed the night before.

I stood out there on the grey cement stoop, with the gothic door behind me and under my hand the wrought-iron railing which was my landlord's concession to a world in transition, and dissipated sixty seconds trying to answer that one, and then I squandered another minute on the problem of the twenty-odd blocks between there and work. I considered the mid-August haze at the skyline and thought about the conference coming up with Jim O'Brien and thought about walking to work. I had been a New Yorker long enough now to have acquired the native horror of distances, but the way I felt right then, walking seemed like the intelligent thing to do.

I felt better when I got to the office, though I knew it wasn't just the walk that had done it; twenty blocks back in Conneaut, Ohio, wouldn't have bought me anything but fatigue. But walking up Fifth Avenue at eight-thirty in the morning is something else again. You walk up Fifth, and you catch whatever it is a person catches in this town from all the people who may not know where they are going but who do know when and how they are going to get there, and so, when I pushed through the bronze doors of the *Insight* building, I felt better. I was sweating a little, and my head was clear, and I was beginning to get that feeling of being tightly stretched, like a wire. There would probably be a relapse around noon, and I would go out to lunch with Dave Goldstein and Bill Servat and Helen Stone and drink too many of Mario's dry Martinis trying to get that

4

feeling back, but in the meantime I felt close to the way you are supposed to feel when it is the beginning of your week and you are on the staff of a news magazine.

When I came into the lobby, George was leaning against the wall outside the elevator that ran exclusively up to the *Insight* offices, from sixteen to twenty. George had a face that had gone seven tough rounds with life, including some rough treatment in the clinches, and as I stepped into the elevator, he made a noble but tragic effort to smile at me.

"Morning, Mr. Engel," he said.

"George," I said, "do you have to smile this early in the morning?"

"Just trying to be cheerful," he said. "The way it tells you to in the manual." He straightened up and followed me into the elevator. "You're a little late this morning," he said. George made sixty a week, and I had a theory that he resented those of us who made more and that is why he was always reminding us that our jobs were in danger. "Tough night?" he said hopefully.

"Not particularly. Mr. O'Brien come in yet?"

"Not yet."

"Well," I said, "do me a favor. Push that button before he does."

"Mr. O'Brien didn't," he said. "But Mr. Ulrich did."

I didn't say anything. Ulrich was the principal owner and publisher of *Insight*, and his office was on the twentieth floor, and I couldn't see what he had to do with the situation.

"Came in at eight-thirty," George said. "Got off at seventeen."

"George," I said, "will you kindly push that goddam button?"

"Sure, Mr. Engel." He pushed the button. Then he looked around at me. "You ought to relax, Mr. Engel," he said. "You'll have ulcers before you're forty if you don't learn how to relax."

I leaned against the rail at the back of the cage and looked at the toe of my right shoe. I was thinking that I needed a shine, and then I was wondering why Ulrich had decided to grace our department with his presence this morning. It wasn't anything routine, you could depend on that, because Ulrich didn't operate that way. Because if Ulrich had something run-of-the-mill on his mind, he had his secretary call you, and you went up to twenty and sat down before a desk which was bigger by ten square feet than the cubicle I called my office, and Ulrich told you what he wanted.

So the reason Ulrich had gotten off at seventeen was that something had gone wrong. The trouble could have been anything from his second wife to a sloppy second paragraph, but if he had gotten off at our floor, it meant that whatever cog had slipped had been in our department. In which case God had better come to the aid of whoever Ulrich succeeded in trapping this morning.

"Seventeen, Mr. Engel," George said.

I started out of the cage. George had his eyes on the side of my face. "Take my advice, Mr. Engel," he said. "Relax. What have you got to lose?"

"Cigarette money," I said. "And a bright future."

Goldstein was fond of saying that the reception room on the seventeenth floor reminded him of the outer office of a dental surgeon who overcharged, but Goldstein usually said the first thing that flicked into his mind, and personally I thought it looked exactly as it was intended to look, like the reception room of a national magazine. There were leaded-glass bookshelves in two of the corners, containing a complete file of *Insight* bound in hand-tooled leather; on the walls were framed copies of a half-dozen of our more sensational critical pieces; there were overstuffed chairs and davenports done in red leather; and at the far end of the room was the receptionist's desk. To the right of that was the door into O'Brien's office, and to the left the door into what Goldstein called the servants' quarters.

As I stepped off the elevator, Janet, our receptionist, smiled brightly and said, "Good morning, Mr. Engel," but I didn't smile back. All those books on how to be an executive at twenty-five thousand a year tell you that a smile is the way to begin a day, but my mind was on Ulrich at the moment, and anyway, Janet wasn't the kind of a girl who inspired smiles

6

from the heart. The writers at *Insight* had to take what personnel sent down to them in the way of help, but O'Brien didn't, and whenever he hired a girl, I always wondered why they had to look like they had been picked at random from off the substitute list for the public school system. So I just nodded vaguely as I crossed the reception room and hoped I could get through the door before she could remind me of my appointment with O'Brien at ten-thirty.

I didn't quite make it. "Oh, Mr. Engel," she said as I got to the door. I turned with my hand on the knob.

"A Mr. Camden called," she said. "At eight-thirty."

"Camden. Camden." The name didn't ring any ring. "Did he say what he wanted?"

"Not exactly," Janet said. "Just that he was at the Statler, and as soon as you came in you should get in touch with him, and not to make any other plans for tonight because he wanted to have dinner with you."

Camden, I thought, Camden; and then it came to me. Oh, my God, I thought, Walt Camden. "If he calls back, tell him I'm tied up, will you, Janet? Tell him I'd sure like to see him, but this is our big day around here, and I'm scheduled right on through the night. Be sure to get that 'sure' in when you tell him. He doesn't think you're sincere unless you get a 'sure' in somewhere."

"I'll tell him," she said, "but I'm not very good at lying over the phone, Mr. Engel."

"Goddam it, Janet," I said, "lying is part of your job."

She transferred her attention to a fingernail. "All right, Mr. Engel. I'll tell him."

I wondered if she was going to start to cry. Then I thought briefly of what the psychologists call misplaced antagonism or scapegoating or something, and felt ashamed of myself. After all, it wasn't Janet's fault that I had started the day without enough sleep behind me, and that George had needled me on the way up, and that Ulrich had picked today to come visiting, and that Janet had the kind of hair and teeth she had.

"Look, honey," I said, "Walt Camden is a real-estate dealer in Ashtabula, and he's in town on the kind of business trip small-town realtors go on every six months, and what he has in mind for tonight is a free dinner followed by the third girl on the left over at the Copacabana, and he thinks I can manage it because I'm the fraternity brother who came to the big city and made good." I stopped for a breath. She was still looking at her fingernail. "All right," I said wearily. "The hell with it. If he calls again, put him through."

She looked up and smiled. Then she dropped her eyes to her calendar pad. "You won't forget your appointment with Mr. O'Brien?" she said. "At ten-thirty?"

I tried to calculate how many weeks Janet had been with us. Thirty, at least, in the course of which she had reminded me thirty Wednesday mornings that I had an appointment with O'Brien. "I won't forget," I said.

"Should I call you?"

"No. I'm not going anywhere. I'll just check with you at regular intervals." I pushed through the door and started down the hall toward my office.

As soon as I opened the door, I gathered that everyone in the department had beaten me to work. When I passed Helen Stone's office, she was saying into the phone, no, she couldn't make it tonight, maybe another time, darling, but tonight was simply impossible; and down the corridor I could hear Bill Servat pecking sporadically at his typewriter; and when I stopped in Goldstein's doorway, he was hulked down in the swivel chair, with his back to me and his feet on the desk and his eyes behind the thick glasses no doubt looking gloomily into the middle distance. Usually this punctuality wouldn't have bothered me because as long as you did your job, you weren't expected to punch a time clock. But that day I had a feeling that I should have been in when Ulrich got off at seventeen. Probably Ulrich wasn't interested in the writer who handled the book page, but still I had that feeling.

Goldstein must have sensed me watching him from the door. Anyway, he reluctantly uncrossed his ankles, dropped his feet, swung around, and peered across the cubicle at me.

"Well, well," he said. "Another wanderer in the wasteland.

8

Come on in and park your tail and hang around for doom, Hyatt."

I found myself wondering, as I crossed the office, if Goldstein had been Ulrich's reason for getting off at seventeen that morning. "What doom?" I said.

"Just any doom," Goldstein said. "Nuclear fission applied to 42nd and Broadway, or arteriosclerosis, or just a job on *Insight.*" He tilted back in his chair and peered up at me. "Tell me, Hyatt," he said, "do you *really* like this job? Are you *happy* with us?"

"You know something?" I said. "If you keep talking like that long enough, Dave, you're going to start believing yourself. Then where will you be?"

Helen Stone stuck her head in the door. Helen had ash-blonde hair which, so far as I could judge, owed only a minor debt to rinses, and this month she was wearing it shoulder length. The hair-do belonged on a Middle Western campus, but otherwise she looked like the provincial's conception of a New York career woman. "This isn't private, is it?" she said.

"No," I said. "We're glad you dropped in, Helen. Dave's polling the staff this morning. He wants to ask you if you like your job." I sat down on the edge of Goldstein's desk. "What time did you get here this morning?" I asked him.

"I slept here," Goldstein said. "I spent the night curled up on that goddam desk. Why, Hyatt?"

"Nothing. Just idle curiosity."

Goldstein's eyes drifted across to Helen. "Hyatt," he said, "has been with us a while. Hyatt has been around long enough to know you don't go around leading with your right." His eyes drifted back to mine. For an instant there they almost blinked, and then they didn't. "Fact is," he said, "I was half-asleep when he came down the hall this morning. I got the impression he was looking for you, Hyatt."

"I don't suppose you got any impression about what he wanted to see me about?"

"No. Just the impression that he was looking for you."

9

I looked at Helen.

"Don't ask me," she said. "You boys lost me five minutes ago. Who was going down the corridor looking for whom?"

"Nobody," I said. I got to my feet. "I'd better be getting to my office. I've got some stuff to clean up before ten-thirty."

I eased past Helen and went down the hall to my office. The office looked just the way it had when I had left it Monday night. In another hour the morning mail would come in, and by mid-afternoon the place would be littered with fifteen or twenty items from the publishers' fall lists. But now there were only the books in the cases around the walls, and the covered typewriter at my right hand, and in the small bookshelf on my left, within easy reach, the neat rows of the *Cumulative Book Index* and *Publishers' Weekly*, and on the desk nothing but some sharpened pencils and, between the bronze book ends, three copies of the *North Star Review*. Now the place looked the way I like an office to look, and I sat down and leaned back and told myself I ought to take George's advice and relax. Because the chances were that Ulrich hadn't wanted to see me at all, that that had been part of the ribbing too, along with Goldstein's story about sleeping on his desk last night.

I told myself that, and then I put a foot on the edge of the desk and looked at the three copies of the *North Star Review* and remembered the spring when those three magazines had gotten me this job.

Once there had been a picture beside the magazines, but that had been a long time ago. It had been three years now since the girl who had sat for the portrait had gone back to Minneapolis and gotten herself married to a college instructor, and almost that long since I laid the picture to rest in the bottom drawer of my desk. It was, in fact, so long ago that I didn't miss the picture any more when I sat down at my desk, but this morning for some reason I found myself trying to remember how Rachel had looked in it. She had been only nineteen when the picture was taken, and I remembered that she had been wearing a tan spring coat, and I could still see her hair, so black it looked blue under artificial light. But that was all of her that I could bring back, and for just a moment I played with an impulse to lean and resurrect the picture from the darkness of my bottom drawer and refresh my memory.

Only I didn't. Instead I jerked my mind off Rachel and back onto the *North Star Review*.

Seventeen of us had been responsible for that magazine. Most of us had been graduate students, and all of us had been young and ambitious and unpublished. It had been Charles Seliak's idea originally, and that fall we scraped together three thousand dollars and saw three issues through the presses. It had been the usual collection of little-magazine stuff—some abstractionist poetry, and a trio of static short stories, and an incomprehensible article on Faulkner, and three chapters of a novel (in progress) by Hyatt Engel. For I had been ambitious in those days. I had had dreams back then of writing the Great American Novel. Then we discovered that three thousand wasn't enough to keep a magazine going, not even a little one. Not that I mourned the passing of the venture. Because by spring my novel was still in progress, and in the meantime O'Brien had picked up a copy of the *Review* somewhere and seen some samples of my critical prose and I was on my way to New York.

I thought about that year in Minneapolis, and about that first summer in New York; how Rachel had followed me here, and the apartment we had had in the Village, and all the times I had asked her to marry me; I thought, too, about all the quarrels we had had over this job, and over where I was going and how I was betraying an early promise or something. And suddenly I wondered what it would have been like to have written a good novel. I don't mean I had regrets; I knew what writers made on books, even relatively successful books. But just for a moment I wondered what it might have been like if I had gone the way Rachel had wanted me to go. Probably, I thought, I would be back in Minnesota now, teaching sophomore journalism for four thousand a year, and that novel still in progress because I would have learned by now that there wasn't any such thing as the Great American Novel. But very

11

briefly I wondered whether, if I were back there now, it would be this kind of a morning. Very briefly I wondered if back there an Ulrich ever got off at seventeen.

Then I shrugged and glanced at my watch. I had only thirty minutes before my appointment with O'Brien, and I straightened up and reached for my middle drawer and the folder for next week's book page. By the time I had my fingers on it, I had squeezed the past out of my memory. I had tidied up my mind. I had put first things first.

There had been a day when I would have had a time managing that, when I would have had to wrestle. But not any more. Now it was easy. Now there wasn't anything to it at all.

𝟚 WHEN I OPENED HIS DOOR
O'Brien was leaning back in his chair, one knee braced against
the edge of his desk, his hands locked behind his head, and a
forgotten cigarette smoldering in the ashtray. He didn't see me
right away—or else he didn't choose to let me know he saw
me—and I stood there a spell and searched his owlish, tender-
skinned face for a sign of what had been going on this morning.
Only there wasn't any sign. His expression was his own, and all
I could make of it was that he reminded me of a history
teacher I had had back in high school. The history teacher had
had a little less chin and a lot more hair than O'Brien, but the
resemblance was there.

I stood still until his eyes shifted and acknowledged my
presence. Then I nodded, walked across the office, and laid
the sacrificial offering for the week deferentially in front of
him.

He blinked up at me. "Well, Hyatt," he said. "Another
Wednesday morning, eh?"

I dropped into the chair across the desk. "That's right," I
said. "Another day, another dollar, Jim."

He blinked again. Then he drew the folder to him and flipped
it open.

"You asked me to set up a schedule for the next three
months," I said. "Before we found ourselves in the middle of
the season with no allowance for a major item."

He nodded, his eyes on the outline. "The Savage item," he

13

said. "You might move it back a couple issues. Give the book a chance to catch on before we ride with it." He flipped a page and ran an eye down my titles for the "Briefly Mentioned" section. Then he leaned back in his chair. "Which brings us to this week," he said.

"I dropped the Johnson review on your desk when I left Monday."

"I read it." He fumbled in his shirt pocket and came out with a cigarette. I got out my lighter and leaned, and he worked on it long enough to be sure it was lit and then laid it in the ashtray to go the way of the other one. "We're going to forget the Johnson," he said.

"Why?" I asked.

He shrugged. "Say it doesn't ring a bell. Say it hasn't resonance."

That was O'Brien's favorite criticism. He was always saying that a review didn't have resonance. None of us knew what he meant by it, but you didn't ask him to draw you a picture because a writer on *Insight* was supposed to have a feel for something like that. It was what they paid you a hundred a week for. But this time I knew it was a lie. We had bought a dozen reviews from Charley Seliak in the three years I'd been here, and this one was as good as any of them.

"I thought it was good," I said.

"All right. Let's say the novel isn't big enough to earn a lead spot."

"I thought it was a pretty fair novel, too. I don't see Johnson having to do any apologizing for it."

His eyes refused to have anything to do with mine. They came in from the right, hesitated a minute, and then slid on by. They had a myopic quality, and I thought I caught something like sadness or bitterness in them. But maybe not. Maybe it was only a tired knowledge of the nature of Wednesday mornings. "Let's let it go at that, Hyatt," he said.

"Just a minute." I leaned forward an inch or so, concentrating on the eyes, trying to catch hold of them. "I realize the novel is political," I said. "It takes the Constitution seriously, which no doubt means that certain elements in our population will see tinges of pink in it. That's why I asked you about running it. At which time you very emphatically insisted that the political position of a writer was one thing we didn't have to worry about—"

"I didn't say that, Hyatt. What I said was that I couldn't commit myself until I'd seen the review."

"What you said was, if the review came up to our *critical* standards—" I waved a hand helplessly. "Look, Jim, I committed myself on this. I asked Charley Seliak to do the review. I told Charley we were paying sixty dollars for lead reviews this year. If we relegate this to the 'Briefly Mentioned'—"

"We aren't going to relegate it to the 'Briefly Mentioned.'"

"Well, then, what the hell are we going to do with it, Jim?"

"We never heard of the novel," he said. "The first time we even knew it existed was when we saw it on a table over at Brentano's."

"Listen, Jim," I said, and now I was concentrating on keeping my voice sweet and reasonable and conciliatory, on keeping it very goddam patient, as befitted a writer who was also A Young Man Who Wanted To Get Ahead. "Listen," I said, "Murell Associates may be a new firm, but P. J. Murell isn't exactly a stranger in this town. He isn't some fly-by-night. You pull a trick like this, he's liable to be unhappy, unhappy enough to unburden his sorrow to a lot of people who buy adver—"

"That's a chance we have to take," he said.

"All right," I said wearily. I settled back in the chair and gave up the game with the eyes. "And what do I tell Charley?"

He shrugged. "You can think of something, Hyatt."

Which was the God's truth, I thought, and what I could think of was the probable financial situation at the Seliak household. It was no doubt Charley's own fault—no one had forced him to stay on at the University, he had had a chance to go into advertising, where a man made a salary he paid income tax on. But I knew what it was like to send something off by registered mail, and then spend a week figuring what

15

you were going to do with sixty extra dollars, only to find out that it had all been a mistake. I knew because I had been there myself.

I studied O'Brien's expression and knew it was plain foolishness to keep up the struggle, and kept on struggling anyway for reasons so obscure I didn't even know what they were myself. "The trouble is," I said, "Charley's probably spent that sixty dollars already."

"That," O'Brien said, "is tough. He's free-lanced long enough; he ought to know better."

I looked down at my hand. Lying against the brown arm of the chair, it looked white and dead, like something that had been too long out of the sun. "It's only a lousy sixty dollars," I said. "What's sixty dollars to us? Dinner for a couple of businessmen who drop in on advertising. One item in the expense account of a foreign correspondent. But to Charley maybe it's getting caught up on bills for the first time since Christmas. Or the first decent suit in a couple of years. Or the first night out with your wife since Christ knows when." My hand came off the arm of the chair, out in front of my face somewhere. "Maybe you could put it through anyway, Jim."

"Now, Hyatt," O'Brien said gently, "you know better than that. Don't you?"

"Yes. I suppose I do."

"You know what they're like up in disbursements. I sign a voucher for a piece of free-lance copy we don't use, Ringgold's on my line first thing the beginning of next month, asking me are we running a business this year or the Ford Foundation, telling me that when the boss lets him know we're subsidizing college instructors, *then* they'll start paying Hyatt Engel's old roommates for—"

"All right," I said. "So what do I tell Charley? Explain to him how they are up in disbursements? Or do I just say it was a good review of a good novel, but I couldn't move it across your desk? For some reason you choose to keep secret?"

"Look, Hyatt," he said, and his voice was still patient, but the danger signs were beginning to show, the touch of pink in the smooth, almost beardless cheeks, the white in the lips,

16

"Look, I just work here, too. I'm just one of those sad little men who congregate in Ulrich's office on Friday afternoon instead of Thursday morning. I run a department that rates somewhere between 'Science' and a catch-all like Levinski's, and I don't have a goddam thing to say about policy."

"All right," I said.

His eyes stopped drifting. They rose from the desk and hooked into mine, and his voice was still soft but it couldn't be called patient any more. "Maybe you're unhappy with us lately, Hyatt," he said. "Maybe you're like some others I could name, you'd feel more at home among the anti-McCarthy element over at *Time*."

"No," I said. "I'm not unhappy, Jim. Not unhappy enough. Or if I am, it's because I don't like being encouraged to crawl out on a limb and then wake up and find I've been abandoned."

"Oh, for Chrissake, Hyatt, come off it."

"Sure," I said.

He studied my face a moment. "Look, Hyatt," he said, "I'm sorry about this. But there isn't a thing I can do about it."

"Sure there isn't," I said.

"Once you settle on a policy," he said, "you have to stick to it."

"I know."

"You know," he said. "Like hell you know. You don't know a goddam thing. Except the crud they spoon-fed you at that college of journalism you attended, with its one lousy teletype machine and the teacher some square they hired off the Strong-ville *Record and Courier*." He looked at an indeterminate spot a little above and behind my head. "Read this week's issue yet?" he asked, his voice suddenly quiet and cold.

"The book page."

"Read some more of this week's issue. Read 'Education' this week. The story about the impending Campus Witch Hunts. Very enlightening."

I could just bet it was, I thought. I could just bet that that story was a flash of light illuminating the political darkness of our time.

"The boss didn't read that story, either," he said. "Not until

17

it was in print. Nobody gave him the chance. Donaldson put the magazine to bed Monday night."

"So?" I said.

"So it's like Tia Juana up there this morning. Very wide open. The scramble for the inside rail is a wonder to behold. Because Donaldson is right now sitting in his office, having been given the opportunity to accept a technical discharge by noon today. The boss gave him that long because they need it in accounting to figure up his severance pay."

"So that's what tore loose this morning," I said.

"That's what tore loose," he said.

"I don't suppose," I said, "that that's why Ulrich stopped off here this morning? To invite you upstairs?"

"You're beginning to get the picture," O'Brien said. "The boss isn't kidding when he says you're either for him or against him."

"I guess he isn't." My mind was suddenly only half on this conversation, for I was wondering who was going to move into this office when O'Brien moved upstairs.

"In short," O'Brien said, "I can't see this as exactly the time to be running a favorable review of what Ulrich might consider a left-wing novel."

"No," I said.

"Maybe he wouldn't care," O'Brien said. "Maybe he wouldn't even notice. But I'm not taking the gamble."

Goldstein was the logical one, I thought; Goldstein was as good as any of us, and he had seniority. On the other hand—

"Are you by any chance listening to me?" O'Brien said.

"Yes. Sure I'm listening to you, Jim."

He slid down another two inches in his chair. "Your trouble is, you worry too much. About other people. About the Charley Seliaks in this world. If you're ever going to be anything but a writer in this organization, you're going to have to get over that, Hyatt."

"I suppose I am," I said. On the other hand, I was thinking, there had always been friction between Goldstein and O'Brien, and—

"In the remote and improbable event that you should ever

18

be moved into this job of mine," O'Brien said, "you can bet your sweet life you're going to have to get over it."

I dropped my eyes. "So what do we use for a lead this week?"

"Anything," O'Brien said. "Just so it's safe. And quick. Something you can knock out inside thirty-six hours."

"That soon?"

"If not sooner." His eyes had that tentative look eyes get when you are being interviewed, when they are trying to size you up. "Because I've got another job you'll want to be getting at before the week's out."

"What other job?" If not Goldstein, then me, I thought. Because Bill Servat is over his head already, and Helen Stone is the wrong sex. Unless they transfer somebody from some other department. "What kind of a job, Jim?"

His eyes stayed on mine another long minute. "I was just wondering," he said, "how you'd like a crack at a cover story."

I could hear the three of them in Helen's office when I opened the door into the corridor. They were in there waiting for me, the way they always waited for me on Wednesday morning, because I always saw O'Brien in the morning and they saw him in the afternoon, and so, in the course of three years I had become a kind of advance scout. We always pretended, when I got back from the morning session with O'Brien, that they were just hanging around so we could all go to lunch together, but we all recognized this as a convenient fiction.

Dave was doing the talking when I came into the doorway; then he looked past Helen and Bill and saw me.

"Well," he said, "I was beginning to think you were closeted in there for the day. Either that or you were no longer with us." He glanced at his watch. "Are we going to lunch or aren't we? I'm due back at one."

"All right," I said. "Mario's?"

"Naturally Mario's. Where the hell else do we ever go except Mario's?"

"I only asked," I said, "because I've got to make a call first. Why don't you three go ahead?"

"They've got phones at Mario's," Dave said. "You can find out somebody's out to lunch from there just as easy as you can from here. Anyway, what's so important it can't wait until afternoon?"

"I've got to call an editor," I said. "If it's any of your goddam business, Dave."

It didn't phase him for any longer than it took me to breathe in and breathe out again. "You know better than that, Hyatt," he said. "Every editor in this town leaves for lunch at eleven-thirty and gets back at three." He looked sidewise at me. "You aren't looking for another job, are you?"

"Oh, for heaven's sake, Dave," Helen said, "quit arguing and let him make his call." She looked at me. "I'll stick around and walk over with you," she said. "I don't have to be back until three."

"All right." I ducked out of the doorway and went on down to my office and asked Janet to put me through to Mattson and Company. The girl over there told me that both Mr. Mattson and Jean Reynolds, Savage's editor, were out to lunch, and that Kay Anderson was Savage's agent. I hung up and put a call through to Kay Anderson. She wasn't there either, but they told me she'd probably be back by one-thirty, and did I want an appointment? I said yes. I hung up, opened my drawer, and started looking for the *Insight* directory.

My phone rang before I could find it. It was Janet to tell me Mr. Camden was calling again and should she put him through? I had forgotten about Walt.

"No," I said. "Tell him I'm out to lunch. Tell him I won't be back all afternoon, and you don't know where to find me." I waited a moment. "Which is the God's truth," I said. "For a fact."

"All right, Mr. Engel." She didn't sound convinced. "Supposing somebody else wants to get hold of you?"

"I'll be at Mario's until one. After that I'll keep in touch. Every hour on the hour."

"All right, Mr. Engel," she said.

I hung up and leaned back in my chair. Helen was standing in my doorway.

"Christ, what a morning," I said.

"That's the way of some mornings," she said.

"Give me another couple minutes." I dialed accounting and asked for Jack Beardsley. "Hyatt," I said, when his voice came through. "Would you do me a favor, Jack?"

"Maybe. If I can, Hyatt."

"What I was wondering," I said, "could you send somebody a company check? For sixty dollars? If I covered it?"

He thought it over. "I don't see how, Hyatt," he said. "We've got no way of accounting for—"

"I thought maybe you could void the stub, and tear up the check—"

He laughed. "You don't know much about accounting, do you?"

"Okay," I said. "I just thought I'd ask."

I hung up. Helen was frowning at me. "What are you up to now?" she asked.

"Trying to buy a conscience." I got onto my feet. "Only they don't seem to be for sale. Not for sixty dollars, anyway."

"You know," she said, "you're very enigmatic today, Hyatt. Not once this morning have I had the faintest idea what you're talking about."

"Haven't you?" I came around the desk. "I don't suppose," I said, "that you'd know anything about writing one of those Personality-in-the-News stories?"

"Not much. Why?"

"Never mind," I said. "Maybe it will come to me."

When we got to Mario's, Bill and Dave had trapped a booth down at the far end, within whispering distance of the bar. They were playing with empty cocktail glasses and looking the way people look when they are waiting for somebody. I steered Helen toward them, through the red leather and the chrome and the shellacked knotty pine.

Dave gloomily watched me slide into the booth. "There was a call for you," he said.

"Here? A call here?"

"No," he said. "At the corner of 42nd and Fifth. The public

21

phone was ringing when we went by, and I answered it, and what the hell do you know, it was for you."

I let my eyes rest on his another five seconds. Then I looked at Bill. "Did anybody order for us?" I said.

"An omelette," Bill said. "And a Martini. How was he, Hyatt? Was he his usual self today?"

I looked at him and recognized the taste of pity faintly on my tongue. Bill Servat was a kind of minor Jack-of-all-trades at *Insight*, sometimes writing music reviews for us, sometimes the religious page for Levinski. He had a long, serious, scholarly face, and life was an insoluble problem for him. He had no business in a competitive world, and I wasted several minutes a week tasting pity for Bill Servat. "I don't know," I said. "What do you mean, his usual self, Bill?"

He spread his hands. "You know. Was it one of his good days? Or is today his day for delivering his lecture on the fine points of English syntax?"

"Well, he didn't let the Johnson review get by him, if that tells you anything."

"Why not?" Goldstein said.

"No resonance. It didn't ring a bell. He wants the copy to ring a bell this week."

"Oh, Lord," Bill groaned. "One of those days."

The waiter materialized silently out of the subdued light and set a Martini in front of me and another in front of Helen. "Call for you, Mr. Engel," he said.

"All right. I'll take it back in the booth." I slid out from behind the table and walked to the rear. "Yes?" I said into the phone.

"Hyatt?" The voice sounded deep and vaguely familiar.

"Yes. Who—"

"You're a hard man to get hold of. How the hell are you, Hyatt?"

I remembered, then. And damn her, I thought. "Oh," I said. "It's you, Walt."

"Now, Hyatt, is that any way to greet an old friend?"

"I didn't mean that the way it sounded," I said. You can forgive teeth like hers, I thought, and that hair, but this is

22

something else, and if I ever get a crack at the running of the department— "How are you, Walt?"

"Fine," he boomed. "Great. Full of vinegar and you know what."

"I'm glad to hear it," I said. "What are you doing in town?"

"We've got a little convention going on down here. We're tearing a damn hotel apart. Whyn't you come on over?"

"I wish I could, Walt."

There was a moment of meditation, and I wondered if Walt had changed with the years, if maybe that was going to be all there was to this. Then he said, "What I called you about, what are you doing tonight?" and I knew it wasn't.

"Well," I said, "I'm afraid I'm tied up, Walt."

"Well, untie yourself, boy. Because you and me, we're going out on the town."

"I wish I could, Walt. I'd sure like to. But you know how it is."

"Hell," Walt said, "bring her along. You're single and I'm broad-minded. Fact is, if you've got another interesting number in that little black book of yours, bring her along, too."

"I haven't got a little black book," I said.

Walt laughed. "I'll bet."

"It's the God's truth. You'd do a lot better just to run up to Radio City and hire one of those guides up there. They know this town better than I do. For a fact."

"Still the same old card, hey, Hy?"

"Maybe if you're staying over," I said, hoping to God he wasn't. "Maybe by Friday—"

"Now listen, chum," he said, "you know damn well I'm going back tomorrow because I told your secretary, and if you want to know what I think, it's my impression you're trying to give an old friend the brushoff."

"No, I'm not," I said wearily. "It's just that Wednesday's a very complicated day over here. It's the first—"

"Sure," Walt said. "I know how it is, chum."

"I'd sure like to see you, Walt, but you can understand the situation."

"Sure," Walt said.

23

I looked at my watch. "I'm going to have to break this off," I said. "I've got a one-thirty appointment, and I haven't had any lunch—"

"Sure," Walt said. "Go ahead. All I wanted was to say hello before I left town."

"I'm glad you did."

"All I wanted," Walt said, "was to give you the opportunity of giving an old friend the business."

"Goddam it, Walt," I said, "I am not giving you the business. I have to do a lead review inside of thirty-six hours on a book I haven't even read yet, and I was just this morning assigned a cover story that I have to get to work on because you might say my future hinges on it, and if I can find two hours in the next seventy-two somewhere, I am going to have to get some sleep because I may be taking a plane out of here Saturday. If you want to call this giving you the business, Walt, all right, I'm giving—"

"There's no call to get sore, Hy. All I wanted to do was say hello."

"Well," I said, "you've said it now, Walt."

I hung up. I felt vaguely like a bastard, and I felt tired and irritated, and my mind flicked briefly onto Janet, who wasn't any good at lying over a phone, and then I was hoping, I was really hoping, that I would get O'Brien's job instead of Dave Goldstein.

I walked back to the table and slid in beside Helen. The chill was off my Martini by now, but I drank it. "If I ever find myself in a position to do anything," I said, "something is going to be done about the receptionist on our floor. First thing."

"Why?" Helen said. "Who was that, Hyatt?"

"An old college chum," I said. "A voice out of my past to make me repent of the sins of my youth, and I don't suppose any of you know any girls who would be interested in being pawed tonight by a realtor from Conneaut named Walter Camden."

"The hell with Walter Camden," Dave said. "At the moment Walter Camden's problems curiously fail to interest me."

24

The waiter came over again. "Another one, Mr. Engel?" he asked.

"Yes. And turn up the heat under that omelette. I have to be out of here by one-fifteen." I looked around at them. "All right," I said. "None of you know any girls. So would any of you have any tips on how you go at writing one of those Personality-in-the-News things?"

"That's the second time you've asked that," Helen said. "But why? That's Harry Levinski's department."

"And if you're thinking what I think you're thinking, Hyatt," Dave said, "you're off in the clouds. It's a well-known fact that Harry's department is already over-staffed—"

"I don't think I'm thinking what you think I'm thinking, Dave," I said.

Dave's eyes left mine, and the waiter was there again with our omelettes and a tray of garlic bread and my second drink. I watched the waiter's hands a minute and then I looked at Dave again. His face was beginning to look fine drawn, as if tiny wires underneath the surface were holding it together. "That's my next assignment," I said. "A personality. On a new literary find. One of Frank Mattson's discoveries. Name of Michael Savage. His first novel is National Book Club for October and the property of Century Film Productions before the ink is dry on the galleys." I sank a fork into the omelette. "Like O'Brien says, it's a natural. Barring the assassination of the President, or World War III, or a lynching in Mississippi, it might even turn out to be a cover story."

"You're doing this," Dave said, "on top of the book page? They must be grooming you for something, Hyatt."

"They might be. You never know. Though I guess you're doing the book page for a couple weeks, Dave."

"Oh. I didn't know that. Supposing I don't want to do the book page, Hyatt?"

"I think you will. Once O'Brien explains the situation to you."

"What situation?" Bill asked.

I looked at Bill Servat briefly, and then I looked away again.

25

This had very little if anything to do with Bill Servat. "Has anybody read 'Education' this week?" I said.

"Yes," Dave said. "This morning. I was wondering what that story was doing in *Insight*."

"Donaldson put the magazine to bed Monday night," I said. "I gather he wanted the story in."

"And?"

"Donaldson collected his severance pay about thirty minutes ago. If they've stayed on schedule over there."

"So that's what everything's all about this morning," Dave said.

"Partly," I said. "The rest of it being, O'Brien's been invited upstairs."

"O'Brien has?" Dave looked down at his hands. "Oh," he said.

"Yes," I said. "So my guess is, you'll agree to do the book page. Since you can no doubt now see the same picture I'm looking at."

"I can see it, all right," Dave said. "The sons-of-bitches are cute, aren't they? Playing us off that way."

"Well," I said, "I guess it's one way to separate the milk from the cream. Unless there's nothing to it. Because it could be just coincidence."

"Coincidence," Dave said. "Coincidence." He was drawing pictures on the tablecloth with his fork. "That O'Brien. He thinks he's a very devious character." He stopped drawing pictures and brought his eyes back up to mine. "So they've organized a rat race. So what are you going to do about it, Hyatt?"

"I'm going to give it that old college try. Naturally. What else?"

"You wouldn't have to, you know."

"I know," I said. "I don't even have to work on *Insight*. I've got a job waiting for me on the Springfield *Ledger-Post* anytime I say the word. Thirty-five dollars a week."

"Neither of us would have to," he said. "We could refuse to cooperate. Just not budge our butts off the starting line." He grinned at me. "If you should spend a couple weeks finding out there isn't any story on Michael Savage, I could maybe see my way clear to lousing up some book reviews."

"No thanks, Dave. Thanks just the same, but no thanks."

"Why not?"

"Because I want that job," I said.

"So do I want the job. But I'm willing to pay only so much for it." He leaned. "How much are you willing to pay, Hyatt?"

"Any amount within reason. Say my right arm up to about here."

"How much?" he said.

"Goddam it, Dave, this is the way the world's organized, and when are you going to stop being a bloody romantic?"

"How much, Hyatt?" he said.

"All right," I said. "All right. Listen. I was four years in the South Pacific fighting for—"

"Go ahead," Dave said. "Give us all of it. Tell us how your old man was a section hand on the B & O, and how you got screwed out of that scholarship because you were wrong side of the tracks, and how you waited table at a fraternity house to get through college." He looked at his hands; they were lying open in front of him now, but somehow you could tell they weren't relaxed. "I'm a Jew from the lower East Side, but go ahead—tell us all about your life and hard times, Hyatt."

"No," I said. "You tell it today, Dave. You do it better than I do."

"I have to hand it to you, Hyatt," he said. "I don't know where you're headed, but you are sure going to get there."

I looked at the clock behind the bar and then pushed my plate away from me. "I've got to be shoving," I said. "I'm supposed to be at 43rd and Fifth by one-thirty." I laid a five on the table. "That ought to cover my piece of the check."

"I'll see you get your change," Dave said. "Exactly."

I looked down at him. "What do you want, Dave? To win by default? Ride in on seniority?"

His eyes came up to mine, fast. "I hadn't even thought of it that way," he said.

I looked at his expression and guessed that he hadn't. Dave was the kind who wouldn't. But I said it anyway.

27

"The hell you hadn't," I said.

Outside it was very pleasant. The sun was bright but not a glitter, and the sidewalks were full of men in summer suits and women in print dresses. I stood out there in the warmth and fumbled for a cigarette and thought about what a fine day it was, and about me and Dave, and about O'Brien moving upstairs. And the hell with Dave, I thought; let him feel that way if he wants to. It's going to be interesting, I thought, if he beats me out of this job, but until he does, the hell with Dave Goldstein, and I lit my cigarette and pulled my hat down an inch and started walking north, in the direction of 43rd, in the sunlight.

3 IT WAS ONE-TWENTY WHEN I
stepped off the elevator into the offices of Anderson and
Carew, literary agents. I leaned on the counter that protected
the girl at the switchboard from the outside world and waited
for her to look around and decide whether I was anybody important or not. She took her time about it. She looked like one
of those small-town girls who are always coming to the Big City
and Making Good, and when she did acknowledge my presence, she looked at my suit and tie, not my face, for that is
how they do it in places like this. Then she asked if I was the
man from *Insight*, and I said I was, and she said Miss Anderson wasn't back yet but I could wait in her office. She led me
down a passage made of veneered panels and frosted glass and
opened a door. Then she went away.

It was the office of a literary agent. All the offices of the people in this business—the publishers, the magazine editors, the
book reviewers—look pretty much alike, and yet there is a subtle difference, and this was the office of a literary agent. There
were first the pictures on the wall, all photographs, all autographed with declarations of affection or sincerity or indebted-
ness; there was the desk which, except for the litter on it,
could have been transported from my office during the lunch
hour; there were the bookcases, filled with volumes which had
apparently been collected at random unless you knew that
they were all autographed, too. It was the office of a literary

agent, and it had a subtle character of its own, like forty-dollar perfume.

I went in, sat down in the chair facing Kay Anderson's desk, leaned back, and studied one of the photographs on the wall. It was a photograph of a novelist who had won a Pulitzer a few years back, and it was inscribed "To Kay, who stuck with me." For an instant I thought of the novel I had started once and wondered what you had to be born with in order to write a Pulitzer Prize novel. Then I found myself adding up the reward Kay had realized for sticking with this one. It was enough, I thought, to revive your faith in poetic justice. Speculation had it that the book had grossed something in the neighborhood of two hundred thousand, and ten percent of that was a fair enough figure for sticking with somebody. I could find it in my heart to stick with somebody for that, I thought, and maybe Rachel had been right. Maybe I should have remained a graduate student at a hundred a month and finished a novel.

I uncrossed my legs, shifted my weight, and let my eyes fall to Kay Anderson's desk. It was a hell of a messy desk. There was a bright, new, yellow book in the middle of it, serving as a paperweight, and I tried reading its jacket upsidedown. But the angle or the distance was wrong, and so I got to my feet and walked around behind the desk.

It was Michael Savage's new book. The lettering "SOME DIE ON THE VINE, a novel by MICHAEL SAVAGE," looked very black against the blank, mint-new yellow of the jacket. I sat down behind the desk and opened the book to the front blurb, which said that this was a story of ten years in the life of a boy and young man, a study of the relationship between an ambitious youth and a father who was a failure. The novel was a contrast in values, the blurb said, and it told a gripping story, but it was saved from slickness because it also contained other levels. Which was inevitable, I thought. The vocabulary of the little magazine had come into its own since the war, and now all the promotion people were talking about levels.

I closed the book without turning to the picture and biographical sketch on the back flap. I didn't have to turn to it because I knew what Michael Savage would look like and I knew what the sketch would say. I read forty of those things a month, and there wouldn't be anything in this one either that you could use in an *Insight* personality story.

Underneath the book was a document, some kind of a legal form. I caught the words *Century Film Productions* and realized I was looking at a movie contract. I had never seen one before, and I had wondered most of my adult life about those figures you are always reading in the newspapers. I pushed the book aside and ran my eye down the first page of the contract. There wasn't anything there that told me what I wanted to know, nor anything on page two, and as I flipped that page, I decided that this must be why you paid an agent ten percent. There was some very fancy phrasing in that document, most of it having to do with the rights the author gave the studio in return for one dollar and other valuable considerations.

I found what I was looking for on page six, which was that Michael Savage was going to get fifty thousand dollars for screen rights to *Some Die on the Vine*. A figure, I thought, as I replaced the pages and looked up and across the office, that would no doubt get doubled in the newspaper stories.

She was standing in the doorway, watching me.

She was a tall woman with gray hair, and if I was any judge, the gray was a lie because otherwise she could have passed for thirty-five. She was wearing a black linen dress, and she looked very cool and poised and self-assured, almost amused, standing there in the door.

"Hello," she said.

I said hello.

"Are you in the habit of reading other people's mail?" She had a low, controlled voice, but there wasn't any huskiness in it. Instead it was almost bell-like.

"I've never seen a movie contract before," I said.

"Well, go right ahead. Don't let me interrupt."

"No. I found out what I wanted to find out."

She was studying me, filing me away in some classification

in her mind. "You're a cool son-of-a-bitch," she said pleasantly. "I'll bet you fit right in over there at *Insight*."

I moved Savage's book an inch to the left. "I don't suppose an apology would buy me anything," I said.

She moved into the room without answering me. She was a tall woman and long-legged; a little brittle, the way some expensive women in New York look, but very handsome. Except that there was something different somewhere. Something, her brief hair style maybe, made the difference between femininity and just female. And, I'll bet she is like ice in a slow thaw, I thought, which is the coldest goddam cold there is. She isn't a person, I thought, she is a machine that has conveniently assumed human form for the sake of doing a job.

I made a move to desert her chair but she waved me back. "Never mind," she said. "I'll sit here. Maybe you'll want to use the desk. To take notes. If you do, just push that stuff out of the way. There's paper in the upper right-hand drawer. Though you probably know that already."

I grinned. "I am only capable of certain lengths," I said.

"I am relieved to hear it," she said. "I've wondered for a long time how Harry got all his information. I'm beginning to understand."

"I'm not in Harry Levinski's department. I belong to O'Brien. I do the book reviews."

"Oh." She turned a little in her chair and smoothed down her skirt. "Well, go ahead and ask me some questions, Mr. Engel."

"I might as well level with you," I said. "I've never done one of these biographical things before, and I'm hoping you people who know Savage can give me some ideas."

"Well, you might start at the beginning." She nodded in the general direction of the book. "Read it yet?"

"I just got this assignment this morning."

"How about the jacket? The biographical sketch?"

"No. I don't have to. I know what it says."

"Tell me," she said. "What does it say, Mr. Engel?"

I picked up a pencil and started a doodle on her appointment pad while I organized a thumbnail sketch. "Michael Savage," I said, "is twenty-nine years old, married, two children. He lives in a modest six-room house in Minneapolis and drives a beat-up '38 Chevvie. He wrote his first novel at the age of seven and burned it a year later, an act which required courage but was no doubt judicious. In twenty-nine years he has worked at seventeen jobs ranging from farming to copywriting. During the war he was a second lieutenant, and for the sake of the promotion people, I hope he was in on Sicily, Salerno, Cassino, Anzio, the fall of Rome and the liberation of Paris. It took him eight years to write *Some Die on the Vine*, and with this, his first published novel, he bids fair to join the front ranks of major American novelists."

I tried glancing at her without lifting my head. What I did was lift my eyes straight into hers.

"I'd suggest," she said, "that you start with the jacket, Mr. Engel." She fumbled in her handbag, located a cigarette and lit it. She smoked the way a man smokes, as if she were interested in the results, not the technique. "Michael Savage," she said, "is thirty-six, not twenty-nine. He has four children. During the war he was 4-F and taught ASTP at the University. Outside of writing, the only thing he's ever done is teach, and last year he quit his job and sold his house and car and wrote *Vine*, which technically is his second novel, not his first, though *The Alley* is very short, a novelette actually. According to his last letter, he is at the moment driving a Cadillac and has acquired an abandoned castle ten miles into the Minnesota hinterland." She smiled gently. "You were right about the novel, though. As Frank Mattson put it, this man can go far."

I drew a large H on her appointment pad and then appended an E. I started to draw an arrow through the joined letters and then changed my mind and stabbed them with a broad-shafted knife instead. She watched the symbolic act. I couldn't detect a great deal of interest in her expression.

"I don't know much about these biographies," I said. "But I'm guessing that what the story lacks so far is involvement. The general reader isn't going to get sent anywhere by that story."

"This means something to you," she said. "Doesn't it?"

"Yes," I said. "This means something to me." The point on the pencil broke. I laid it carefully on the desk beside the pad. "Maybe you could suggest another angle."

"It's your hide. You lug it to market."

"An *Insight* personality," I said, "usually follows a formula. The lead is a thumbnail biography. The body quotes what the subject has pungently to say about our gadget civilization and the century of the common man. The ending gives the essence of his theories about art or business or war or whatever the hell it is he does. But maybe I could do something different in this one. Like explain in four thousand words what it is that makes a writer tick." I leaned. "Tell me, what do you think makes the wheels go round in Michael Savage?"

She smiled. "If I knew, I'd probably be paying a lot more income tax than I am."

"Take a stab at it," I suggested. "What's he like? What impression do you get?"

"Well, he takes his writing pretty seriously. I think it's the only thing he ever wanted to do." She ground out her cigarette. "Ever know a compulsive worker, Mr. Engel?"

"One or two."

"Michael's one. He started another book the same week he finished V*ine*. I gather from his letters that it's giving him trouble. Normally he writes very fast—did *The Alley* in three months and V*ine* in less than a year. Probably because he was writing about himself. But now he's tired, and he ought to be off on a vacation somewhere. But he won't listen to advice."

That wasn't much help, and I looked gloomily at her. The alcohol from lunch was beginning to go out of me, and I was feeling the way you do in the middle of an afternoon. "Go on," I said.

"That's all. Except that when I see him, I hope I can talk some sense into him. In his last letter, he had a paragraph about being a one-book writer." She nodded toward the book again. "You might try reading it. It might give you an idea."

"I guess I will," I said. "I guess maybe that's the first step. Mind if I use your phone?"

She nodded, and I picked up the phone and asked for the Murray Hill number that belonged to Savage's publisher. The girl over there said that Mr. Mattson wasn't back from lunch yet but Jean Reynolds was, and I waited while she made the connection, and then it was another voice on the line. It was a voice you could call young and warm and somehow lovely, and I permitted an imaginary picture of Jean Reynolds to form in my mind while I gave her a thumbnail sketch of what it was I wanted to see her about. Then I hung up and looked at Kay again. She smiled sympathetically. "Maybe Jean will have an idea," she said. "Or Michael. He's due in sometime this evening, you know."

"No," I said. "I didn't know."

"Yes." There was a look of serene and withdrawn indifference on her face, and I thought, there is more she could tell you but she won't. Because you are an *Insight* man and she caught you reading a movie contract on her desk. You had better have more luck over at Mattson and Company, I thought, because you are sure as God not going to get anything that will read out of this one.

I got to my feet. "If anything else should come to you," I said, "you might let me know."

"Naturally."

"After all," I said, "you have some interest in this trip to the fair, too. A story in *Insight* could sell quite a few copies."

"I imagine it could," she said.

I walked across the office and retrieved my hat. I turned at the door. She had gotten up and was walking around her desk, and she didn't glance my way. I put on my hat and walked down the corridor and past the small-town girl who had come to the Big City and Made Good and rang for the elevator.

Maybe in ten years or so I will forget the first moment I saw Jean Reynolds. But I haven't forgotten yet. Because it was like the minute you step out of the stall and turn the shower handle all the way to cold and then step back in. She was typing when I came into her office, and then she stopped and got up and started around the desk. She didn't take more than three steps, but it was enough to let me know how she walked, and then she stopped and leaned forward a little, and it was as if I had come into the student union just at dusk and she had gotten up from one of those big, blue davenports and started across the lounge. Or as if this were three years ago, and she had come out of the kitchen as I walked into our apartment, and for an instant I felt something tight and sad and not-quite-forgotten in me.

"Come in," she said. "I've been expecting you." Even her voice was the same, and I had the illogical feeling that her name wasn't Jean Reynolds, that she had never gone back home and married a college instructor, that she had been here all the time, a few blocks from the *Insight* building.

She crossed the office and extended her hand, but I didn't take it. She held the hand there in space a moment; then she raised it slowly and touched her hair. "Is something the matter?" she asked.

"No."

"A smudge, maybe? I'm always getting carbon smudges on my face."

"It's just that you look like someone else."

She didn't, of course. Now that I had time for a second look, I could see that there were only the similarities you sometimes see between sisters. She was the same size as Rachel, and her hair was very dark (it even glinted blue where the light from the window behind her glanced across it), and there were those fagile, graceful lines in her face which you do not often see in Occidental women. And there was the voice, clean and a little thin but with a suggestion of warmth, of passion, underneath it. But her mouth was wider than Rachel's, and her face was closer to oval than heart-shaped, and her eyes were brighter. And Rachel had not worn her hair like this. Rachel parted hers in the middle and combed it back and kept it in place with two barrettes.

Jean Reynolds stood there, one hip touching the edge of the desk, and watched me. "She must be quite a memory," she said.

"She was a long time ago."

36

"Do we really look that much alike?"

"No. You were against the window and the sun was in my eyes."

She laughed lightly, without embarrassment. "Well, are you going to interview me from the door?"

There was a manuscript on her desk and a page in her typewriter. "If you're in the middle of something," I said, "go ahead and finish it."

"It can wait." She smiled, a smile that sifted up into her eyes and softened them.

"Well," I said, "if you don't have to go on with that, maybe we could go somewhere else."

"Maybe. Where did you have in mind?"

"Maybe I could buy you a drink."

She glanced at her watch. "I guess you could," she said.

On the way down in the elevator, she leaned against the rail and tried to make conversation. "I don't know how much help I can be to you, Mr. Engel," she said. "Did Kay have anything to offer?"

"Not much. Just some vital statistics."

"Didn't she tell you how Michael ought to stay away from New York? Because our values might get to him?"

She was wearing a smile I couldn't read. "No," I said.

"Kay subscribes to the grass-roots theory. She thinks the only people who can't get hurt by this town are advertising men and fight promoters."

"She didn't mention that. Just that he's thirty-six and was 4-F. And what can an interviewer do with that?"

"He did try to enlist, you know. Every branch. But he's got flat feet."

Oh, God, I thought, flat feet yet.

I followed her out onto the street. It was mid-afternoon, and a light breeze was skimming Manhattan. The cabs were beginning to come to life again after the early afternoon slump, and secretaries in light dresses and no hats were hurrying back to work from their coffee breaks.

"He really is small town, I guess," she said. "You could use him in a tragedy. If you subscribed to Rousseau."

37

She put her hand lightly on my arm as we crossed 41st, and I thought of those afternoons three years ago when Rachel and I used to walk around the Village, and you would see the lonely kids in the alleys, batting tennis balls against the blank brick walls, and in Washington Square Park the five-year-olds milling around while their mothers sat on the benches. Sometimes we would go into one of those bars down there, with the cracked mirrors and the glasses that were never quite clean and the sad, ragged, aging men, and drink a beer.

"The noble Savage," Jean said.

I came back from another world and looked at her.

"It's a pun," she said. "The noble Savage. Rousseau. Get it?"

"I have a suggestion," I said. "Let's not talk about Michael Savage any more."

She dwelt on that a moment. "I thought that's what you wanted to talk about."

"It was. But not any more. Not until we've had a drink."

"All right." She turned her face up to mine. The breeze was blowing lightly through her hair, and I could trace the delicate bone structure of her cheek line, and I thought, I have run my fingertips lightly down that line. "What should we talk about, Mr. Engel?" she said.

"We could talk about what a fine day it is."

"All right. It's a fine day, isn't it, Mr. Engel?"

"Yes," I said. "It's a wonderful day."

"It's usually sweltering in August. But this year has been unusual, hasn't it?"

She was laughing at me but I didn't care.

The lounge at the Biltmore was out of the early afternoon slump, too—beginning to fill up with those temporarily-without-escort kind of women you see in hotel bars, and with college kids, and with businessmen still working on clients. The waiter led us to a place away from the clatter and took our orders and went away. Jean followed his progress back to the bar, and I studied the side of her face.

"You're pretty young," I said, "to be an editor."

38

"And you're pretty young to be a VIP over at *Insight.*"

"I'm thirty-four, and I'm not a VIP. Just a writer."

"I'm twenty-nine, and a junior editor. And if you think you're low on the ladder, let me tell you about my job."

"It's a Mattson policy, I suppose," I said, "to assign National Book Club selections to junior editors."

"That was a special case," she said. "That was luck."

I leaned back against the leather and watched her taste her drink. She didn't have long fingers, but they were slender enough to give you the illusion.

"Frank Mattson located the manuscript," she said. "That was almost two years ago. Michael was teaching at the University, and we'd just started a college text department, and Frank went out there on a scouting trip and got Michael under contract for a textbook. That was how it started. Then Michael just up and quit his job one day. The next day he wrote Frank and said he wasn't going to finish that textbook, and he didn't know what to do about the advance Frank had given him because it was spent already. But Frank knew about this novel and made some kind of a proposition. I don't know much about that part of it. Except that Tom Rogers had published that first novelette of Michael's and lost money on it, and he had an option on *Vine,* and somehow they talked Tom into releasing him. I knew Michael never felt right about that part of it."

"And then," I said, "Mattson took this manuscript he had been finagling a year to get his hands onto, brought it into the office of Jean Reynolds, age twenty-nine and a junior editor, and laid it on her desk."

"Yes," she said.

"Why?"

She shrugged. "Maybe because Frank wanted to see what I could do with something important. Maybe because they just didn't think it would be this big. Maybe because Guy Averill was swamped at the time. Or maybe because Guy is a male and fifty-three and I'm twenty-nine and a girl. I don't know."

I leaned on that. "I know there's competition for manuscripts," I said. "But I didn't know it was this fierce. Do all publishers select editors on that basis?"

She didn't realize what she'd said for a minute. Then she did, and her eyes darkened, and her hand started for her mouth. "I didn't mean that the way it sounded," she said.

"Because if so, they sure expect considerable for their lousy eighty-five a week, don't they?"

"Now, look here, don't go putting words—"

"All right," I said. "Forget I said anything. Strike that from the record." I picked up my drink and killed it, quickly and neatly, and then set the empty glass down, carefully and precisely. "I think I know how a kid feels," I said, "who has an impulse to throw a rock through a plate-glass window. I think I could also do with another drink. How about you?"

"I think I'd better be on my way. This isn't getting any galleys read."

And you have certainly conducted this afternoon with brilliance, I thought; you have certainly followed all the prescribed recommendations of Journalism 202: *The Technique of the Interview*. "I guess this is my day for making enemies."

"I'll give you credit," she said. "You seem to have a talent for it."

"I didn't mean what I said. It's just that there was a girl once, and when I walked into your office today, I thought— Anyway, it got to me, that remark about Mattson assigning you to Savage because you were a pretty girl."

"I didn't say pretty."

"I know," I said. "I added that."

There was a tolerant amusement in her eyes now. "What exactly did you want to know? About Michael, I mean?"

"I don't know. I've never done one of these articles, and I don't know anything about how you go at them. If this were your baby, how do you think you'd handle it?"

She shrugged. "I suppose I'd be obvious. I'd tell people about the house and car he's just bought, and about his hobbies, and whether he composes on a typewriter or in long-

40

hand. And how much money he'll make on *Vine*. That's what people want to know, isn't it?"

"I don't know what people want to know. All I know is, I don't want to be obvious."

"Or how he quit a safe job and sold his house and car and lived on practically nothing while he wrote the book. Couldn't you work that mine?"

"What I want is something different. What I want to capture is the reason Michael Savage ticks."

"I wouldn't mind the answer to that myself," she said.

Our waiter materialized and laid the check very discreetly face down at my elbow, and I put a bill on the tray without taking my eyes off her. She has a lovely mouth, I was thinking. I had always wondered what had been the matter with Rachel's mouth, and now I knew. It should have been a shade wider. "If you shouldn't happen to be doing anything for dinner tonight," I said, "I know a place on East 43rd. Orthodox but quiet. The tourists haven't discovered it yet."

"I'm having dinner with Michael tonight."

I watched the waiter set down the tray with my change. "How long will he be in town?"

"Three days."

"And I suppose," I said carefully, "that three would make a crowd tonight."

She thought about that a while. "Not necessarily," she said, without noticeable conviction. "Except he isn't due in until eight-seventeen. It would make it pretty late."

"Why couldn't I pick you up around eight? We could go over there, get a table and then call him. At his hotel." I waited a minute. "I shouldn't have to remind you," I said, "that a lead story in *Insight* could sell quite a few copies."

"All right. I guess it would be all right." She made a move to get up.

"One more thing," I said. "There's going to be an opening over at *Insight*. My boss is moving upstairs. In case I should get his job, I'm going to be in the market for somebody who can run a book page."

41

"I'm afraid not," she said.

"I don't know what you're making at Mattson, but this would start at ninety-five. And raises come fast over there."

"I don't think," she said, "that I'd be interested in a job over there at two hundred. I've heard stories about what it's like at *Insight*."

"They were probably exaggerated."

"I'm sure they were."

"All right," I said. "Never mind. I just thought I'd mention it."

She stood up and I followed her out. I walked back to her office with her. Then, on the corner of 38th, I stood in the sun and lit a cigarette. I had four hours to kill. I thought about a movie, but instead I hailed a cab and gave the driver my address. I could use up an hour in the shower, I thought, and then I was going to mix myself a tall drink, and after that maybe I would take a walk through the Village.

Michael Savage   I

4   THEY GOT TO THE STATION
with only eight minutes to spare, and when Michael slid out
of the car and went around and unlocked the trunk, he could
feel in his shoulders and stomach that tension you get when
you aren't sure you are going to make a train. He got his bag
and brief case out of the trunk and came back to her open
door. "You don't have to get out," he said. "I'm going to have
to run for it."

"You've got your tickets?" Alice asked. "And your traveler's
checks?"

"Yes." I've got everything."

"Well, have a good time."

"That's not what I'm going for." His eyes slid away from
hers; he felt the embarrassment that comes when you are
sparring with the saying of good-bye. "Say good-bye to the
kids for me," he said. "When Alan gets up, tell him I'll bring
him back a tommy gun. One that really shoots."

"I won't tell him anything of the kind. And I hope you
don't."

"Well," he said, "an electric train, then."

"Michael," she said, "there is absolutely no point in loading
yourself down with a lot of things you can buy right here. Anyway, he's too young for an electric train." Her eyes fell to the
wheel of the car. "Don't get me anything, either. Not after
this car."

"We're rich now," he said. "We have to spend our money

45

on something. You just can't let it accumulate." He glanced at his watch. He still had six minutes. "Besides," he said, "I've wondered for thirteen years how you'd look in a black nightgown and a filmy negligee."

"I can tell you," she said. "I'd look silly. Just like I do in this car."

"You don't look silly. You look fine."

"I'm serious, Michael. I'm getting scared. We've been spending it like water. We haven't got *that* much."

"When it runs out I'll write another book." He leaned over and kissed her.

"Telegraph me when you get there," she said.

"The very minute. And drive carefully on the way back. This is too young to deserve a dented fender." He took a last look at the clean, conservative lines of the Packard convertible he had bought her for her birthday two weeks before. Then he picked up his bag and briefcase and hurried into the station and down the steps to the platform. Walking down the line of coaches, he slitted his eyes against the puffs of dust and felt inside him the tiny, electric coils of excitement and anticipation he always got when he was starting on a trip.

His seat on the "400" was on the aisle, which meant that the light would be bad for reading, and he thought that he really should have flown in spite of Alice's objections. There would be a compartment after Chicago, but Chicago was a long way when your seat was on the aisle. Not that there weren't advantages to traveling by train. You spent most of your mornings in the diner and most of your afternoons and evenings in the club car, and he always had the feeling, starting out like this, that this trip he might meet somebody very interesting.

In a minute, he thought, the train will pull out and I will go into the diner. He wondered if anybody else would be eating breakfast alone. Across the aisle and up three rows a girl was reading a magazine. She was a blonde and from his angled view she seemed young and well-dressed and pretty. If this were the Superchief and life were a Wakeman novel, he thought, when the train pulled out I would go into the diner,

46

and they would seat me at her table, and before we finished our coffee we would know that our destiny was to wind up in bed together. Then the girl turned around, and she wasn't very pretty after all, and for the second or third time this morning he wished, briefly and wearily, that Alice were making the trip with him.

It turned out to be a boring, tiring ride, but when they came into Grand Central, the tiredness left him. He had slept badly the night before, and at Buffalo he had thought, I am going straight to bed when I get there and sleep until noon tomorrow, and in Albany he had thought, I am going to take a plane back, I am not going through this again. But when the train slid into that final tunnel, the tiredness left him, and when he stepped off onto the platform, he could feel the quivers of excitement, like springs uncoiling, in his abdomen.

The train had been late, and cabs were at a premium, and it was almost nine when he followed the porter into his hotel. In his room he waited impatiently while the bellhop opened the window and turned on all the lights and checked the bathroom for towels and soap and then asked if there was anything else.

"No," he said. He gave him a half a dollar, and the boy eased out of the room and closed the door.

He stood in the middle of the lighted room, and the loneliness spilled in around him. That was always the way it was. After thirty-three hours on a train you ought to be tired enough to want to go to bed, but always there was the excitement when you stepped off the train, and coming into the hotel you felt as if you never wanted to sleep again. But then the door closed and you were alone with the lights and the quiet and the loneliness.

He opened his bag, found Jean's letter, and skimmed through it for her number. The girl at the switchboard let her phone ring eight or nine times and then said there wasn't any answer. When he hung up, he could feel disappointment like a toothache in him.

Well, he thought, I guess I can take a bath now.

The phone rang while he was sitting there.

"Michael," Jean said. "I've been trying to get you for an hour."

"The train was late."

"Nice trip?"

"Terrible trip. Very long. Very dull. No beautiful girls with foreign accents. The movies are a lie."

She laughed. "Had dinner?"

"On the train. What passed for one."

"We're at a place on 43rd," she said. "Want to grab a taxi?"

"We? Would I be in the way?"

"No. It's a man from *Insight*. He wants a talk with you. They're going to do a story on you."

She gave him the name and address of the restaurant. He dropped the phone on the cradle. Then he stripped and went into the bathroom and stepped under the shower. His skin felt dry and gritty from the train ride, and under the warm spray he could feel the muscles in his shoulders and back relaxing, and suddenly he did not feel lonely at all any more.

The place on 43rd was as cramped as a Middle Western bus terminal, with eight or nine intimate tables and a bar built out of wine casks, and pen-and-ink nudes on the walls to lend atmosphere. He didn't see Jean at first, and then she waved to him from one of the tables. A waiter was clearing the table when he got to it.

"Hello, Michael," she said. "This is Mr. Engel. From *Insight*. He runs the book page over there, and he's going to do a story on you."

The man got partly to his feet and put out a hand. He was a lean, blond man with a thin mouth and a straight nose and nervous fingers. "They tell me you've written a book," he said.

"Have they?" Michael said. "Who's they?"

"I don't know," Engel said. "It's just something you hear around town."

Jean was smiling up at him. "What'll it be to eat, Michael?" she asked. "The lobster is out of this world."

"I'm not very hungry. How about just a club sandwich?"

48

She nodded at the waiter. "What to drink?"

"A glass of milk."

"My God," Engel said.

Michael grinned into Engel's eyes, and Engel grinned back. Then Michael turned his head and looked at Jean. Her hair glinted blue-black in the light, and her shoulders and neck looked creamy against the black dress, and he was thinking that other men's eyes would follow you if you walked into a crowded restaurant with her. "You look beautiful tonight," he said. "It was lonely up there in that room, and you look beautiful tonight."

"Do I? I'm glad, Michael."

"You're the only woman of my acquaintance," he said, "who can wear a dress that's cut as low as that and still keep a man's eyes on your face."

"I want a minute to study that," she said. "I'm not sure it's a compliment."

"I thought," Engel said, "you said he was shy."

"He was. Maybe he's outgrowing it."

The waiter set his sandwich and milk in front of him, and Engel looked wonderingly across the table at the milk, as if he had heard all his life that this product existed but had never seen any until this moment. "They tell me you're from Minneapolis," he said. "I went to school there."

"Did you?" Michael said. "When?"

"Forty-six," Engel said. "I've still got some friends there. Maybe you know some of them."

"Maybe."

"Rachel Abrams?" Engel said. "That's not her name now. She married somebody in sociology. Conners, Connell, something like that."

Michael shook his head. "It's a big place," he said.

"Charley Seliak," Engel said. "You ought to know Charley Seliak."

"Yes, I know Charley."

"Do you? How is Charley?"

"Fine," Michael said. "He's got a new collection of poetry coming out."

"Has he? That's fine." Engel twisted the wine glass in front of him, and the conversation died in the middle of the table. During the moment of silence to observe its passing, Michael suddenly felt like Prufrock coming down the stairs with the bald spot in the middle of his head.

His hand was lying on the table, and Jean reached out and put her hand over it. "Well, Michael," she said, "how's the new book going?"

"Great," he said. "I've written a hundred and forty pages since February. My average is a third of a page a day. That comes to twenty words an hour. I know because I average it up. Every Sunday night."

"Well," she said, "you have to keep slugging." She paused. "I hope," she said, speaking slowly and precisely, as if feeling her way, "I hope you brought it along."

"I don't think," he said, "that I want to go showing those pages around. Not yet." He was conscious of her hand on his, and he was also thinking that he had been here only fifteen minutes and already she was beginning to sound like her letters. Since March she had been writing him monthly, asking him how the new novel was going, asking him if he had anything he wanted to show her yet. He supposed it was part of her job to keep writers at it, but there had been the days when he had come into lunch from five hours of fruitless work and found a letter from her and felt like ripping it across without opening it. "I don't know why it won't move," he said. "It wasn't like this with V*ine*."

"I know why," she said. "You need a rest, that's why."

"Maybe," he said. "Or maybe I can't write about anybody but myself, and I've written that novel. Maybe that's why I feel like I'm faking this one." He pulled his hand from under hers and carefully extracted the plastic pick that held his sandwich together. "The hell with my novel," he said. "Let's not bore each other with my novel. What's the program while I'm here?"

"We'll manage to keep you busy," she said, and outlined the program: the job the National Book Club wanted him to do, a tape to cut for a local radio station, an appointment with the firm lawyer, the advance autographing, and all the forms to fill out for all the remote and improbable awards. "And Kay called this afternoon," she added. "The movie contracts are ready to sign. She also said they might ask you to work on the script."

"I don't know anything about writing scripts."

"Out on the Coast knowing something about something is beside the point." She shook a cigarette out of the pack lying in the middle of the table, and Engel leaned over and held a flame to it. "And tomorrow night," she said, "we're invited to a party. If you want to go to a party."

"A party's fine," he said, feeling the relief because he was not going to be alone tomorrow night, wondering, behind the relief, if she was dragging him along to a place where he wasn't really wanted. He said, "But I don't want you to feel you have to entertain me every minute I'm here."

"I know I don't have to," she said. "I just want to."

He smiled gratefully at her and then turned his attention to Engel. "What about this story?"

Engel put his elbows on the table and hunched his shoulders. "I'm supposed to write a cover story about you," he said. "If there's a cover story in you. And if I can put a finger on it." His hand started toward his inside pocket and then stopped, and Michael thought, Introductory Journalism, Rule 7: *Never take notes at the start of an interview.* "I've collected some vital statistics," Engel said. "But nothing that resembles anything except a paragraph in *Who's Who.* You'd have made my job a lot easier if you'd been born ten years later. Or had been in the first wave at Iwo Jima."

"I imagine I would have," Michael said, and he felt suddenly the old, familiar, defensive stab of anger that came when somebody made a remark like that. And I wonder what he did during the war, he thought. Judging from that remark, he thought, one thing the son-of-a-bitch did not do was spend the years standing naked in the naked lines in the recruiting centers. "I was in the ASTP," he said. "Maybe you can play around with that. Because they used to send us weekly mimeographed releases. All about how we, too, were doing our bit."

"I'm sorry," Engel said. "I shouldn't have said that."

"It's all right," Michael said. "Forget it." The anger drained out of him, leaving in its place only the faint, tired dregs of bitterness. "Believe me," he said, "I wish I had been in it. I could have used that experience."

"Why?" Engel said. "You didn't miss anything."

"I'll trade you," Michael said, thinking of those years, thinking of what Hemingway had said somewhere about this being one of the necessary experiences, thinking of the quarrel with Alice when he told her he wanted to enlist, thinking of the ASTP's who couldn't see what learning English grammar had to do with survival along the hedgerows of Normandy, thinking of the years after the war and the returning veterans and the stories about occupied Rome and occupied Berlin and occupied Tokyo and how they looked at you because you sported no ruptured duck in your lapel. "I'll trade you even," he said. "Your four years for mine."

"I wish we could make a deal," Engel said. "I was a T/5 in the Pacific Theater. Malarial survey. The only thing I got out of it was mosquito bites." He put his elbows on the table and hunched his shoulders. "Forget the war," he said. "Tell me about success. Tell me about this new house."

"It was a big summer place," Michael said. "We bought it for a song and then spent a fortune winterizing it. So I'm already twenty thousand dollars into my publisher, and there's a mortgage on the place, and Alice is worried about the money we're spending like water." Engel had a habit of looking at you without raising his head. He did it now, and Michael had the disadvantage of a difficult angle but he could still read the expression. "I don't guess that's what you want, either," he said.

"No, not exactly."

"If I just had some idea—"

"I don't know myself," Engel said. "I've never done one of these things before. I was hoping that if I could just get you

52

talking, maybe something would hit me. Only it seems you're an uncommunicative bastard."

"I've got nothing to say," Michael said. "I grew up in a dull, middle-class home, the product of dull, middle-class parents. I went to college and got married, and then I went to graduate school because I'd married a girl who had to play it safe. Then I wrote a book." He spread his hands. "That's the pattern. That's all the story there is, and talking about it is like writing a letter home only because you haven't written a letter home yet this month."

Engel raised his head, and now his face was tight and tired and a little frightened, like the face of a kid up on his first delinquency charge. "Drama is not a necessary ingredient," he said. "What I have in mind is to vary the formula. What I am after is what it is that makes a writer tick."

"That sounds like a large order," Jean said. "Especially at this time of night."

"Over where I work," Engel said, "they are in the habit of large orders. They aren't a bit bashful." His eyes flicked out into the room. "Our waiter is on his way," he said. "Does anybody want any dessert?"

Michael shook his head. "Let me get the check," he said.

"You have four kids. Which *Insight* hasn't. And I'm on an expense account. So let's cheat the government out of it." Engel glanced at the check indifferently and laid a bill on the tray. "Maybe the atmosphere in here is wrong," he said, looking at Jean, asking permission with his eyes. "Maybe he'd talk better somewhere else. Maybe if I got him drunk—"

"It's after eleven," Jean said, "and he's been on a train for two days. I think tomorrow or maybe Friday—"

"I've got a better idea," Michael said. "I'm going back Sunday. And I hate traveling alone. Want to come along?"

"All right," Engel said.

"I'll wire Alice you're coming," Michael said.

"I don't want to be putting anybody to a lot of trouble," Engel said. "I can put up at a hotel."

"Alice loves company. Breaks the monotony of her days."

He grinned at Engel. "Personally," he said, "I don't envy you your job, Engel. Not if the subjects are all like me."

Engel shrugged. "It's a living. They pay you the first and sixteenth of every month."

"Well," Michael said, "relax. We'll get you a story. It may take us a week of solid work, but we'll find you a story somewhere."

Jean had moved since he had been here last, into an apartment in the Nineties just off Fifth. When the cab pulled up, she asked if he were awfully tired. When he said no, she asked if he'd like to come up for a drink, and he followed her into the building. Inside her apartment, he loosened his tie and sat down on her sectional davenport and watched her cross the room and disappear into her kitchenette. For a moment he had the illogical feeling that he was not in a strange woman's New York apartment, that instead he was home and a tough day behind him. Then that illusion was gone and he was thinking that he had never seen a woman walk as gracefully as she, that she must have gone to one of those dramatic schools where they practice with dictionaries on their heads.

He looked up at her and smiled when she came back in and handed him his drink. "Did you ever go to dramatic school, Jean?" he said.

"No, why?"

"If you didn't, where did you learn to walk like that?"

"I don't know. Like what?"

"Like Audrey Hepburn must walk across a stage. I've never seen her on the stage, but I imagine that's how she does it."

She sat down beside him. "I used to practice secretly," she said. "When I was twelve. In front of a mirror." Her eyes circled the room. "Do you like this place, Michael?"

"It's very nice." As far as he could tell, all New York apartments looked pretty much alike. They always had two rooms and a utility kitchen; if they were pre-World War I, they had high ceilings and flowered wallpaper, and if they were modern, they had asphalt tile floors and painted walls, and this apartment had asphalt tile floors. "It's very attractive," he said.

He tasted his drink, and for a minute there was the silence you get when two people have run out of apartments to talk about. Then she said, "I'm sorry about tonight. But he said he had to get this story."

"It's all right," he said. "What I mainly wanted was company." He looked down at his drink. "This is a lonesome town. When you are alone, it is."

"Tomorrow night will be different. I'll spend tomorrow night protecting you from the wolves."

He looked at her. She was leaning slightly toward him, and her eyes were smiling, and he wondered, as he had wondered on other trips to New York, what she would do if he should suddenly close the gap and kiss her. Those other times he had had the feeling that she would push him away and tell him quietly and evenly that perhaps he had better go now. But right at this moment he did not think that that is what she would do. "I felt sorry for Engel," he said. "I gather the heat is on him."

"At *Insight* the heat is always on. Only don't feel too sorry for him. Don't ever let him get you drunk."

"He didn't strike me as that kind. He seemed like a pretty decent guy."

"Maybe he is. But he is also an *Insight* man."

He studied her expression another moment and then transferred his attention to his unfinished drink. "I'll finish this," he said, "and then I'd better be on my way."

"Not yet. I didn't mean you had to go before you even got your hat off."

"I'd better. You're tired and so am I. Besides, you're a very distracting woman."

She chose to ignore that. "How about just one more?" she said. "For the road?"

"This is my second drink today." He stood up. "If I have a third one, I won't be worth a damn tomorrow. The stuff upsets my stomach." He watched her move her feet from under her and get up and face him. She had kicked her shoes off, and her head came barely to his chin. She seemed sud-

55

denly very small and fragile, like a child who ought to be protected.

She followed him to the door. He turned at the door and looked down at her, and suddenly he wondered what he would do if he knew absolutely that he could lean over and kiss her and no repercussions, nothing essentially spoiled. For the first time in his life he knew what it was to really want another woman than Alice. He had been married thirteen years, he thought, and there had never been any other woman except Alice, and they joked about this sort of thing happening to you when you were approaching middle age. Only it wasn't any joke, he thought, and looking down into Jean's eyes, he wished again that Alice had come along with him on this trip, that he didn't have to go back to that empty room.

"How am I distracting?" she said.

"Some other time," he said. "When it's daylight, and we aren't alone in your apartment." He stepped through the doorway. "It can be a very lonely town," he said.

In his hotel room he took off his coat and tossed it on the bed. Well, he thought, there is no point in going to bed now. There is no point to lying in the dark and thinking about how the novel wasn't going, or about Jean standing in her doorway in her stocking feet, telling him he didn't have to go home yet, or about Alice back in Minneapolis waiting for the week to come to an end. I wonder what it would be like, he thought, to come home to a woman to whom you have been unfaithful. Alice would have been proud of me tonight; she would have been highly satisfied with the way I got to my feet at exactly the psychologically dangerous moment. He thought of all the years Alice had put up with his moods and his income, and about the children, and about what Alice's face would look like if he were ever unfaithful and she found it out.

And I should have brought her along, he thought. I should have insisted. Maybe it would be different, he thought, if we were together right now, in a twenty-dollar-a-day hotel room, at one o'clock in the morning, with the murmur of traffic on the street below and the evening behind us. Maybe the thirteen years would not lie so indifferently between us if she had come along.

He got the Marquand novel out of his briefcase, and then he put the book back. Because he suddenly remembered, for no reason he could think of, something that had happened at a party a few years back. A girl had said, unexpectedly and drunkenly, "Oh, the hell with this, let's talk about sex," and right after that he had gotten into an argument with Jake Eberle. He was always getting into arguments with Jake, and that night he had almost swung on him. Now, as he stood there, it seemed to him that he might be able to do something with that memory.

He picked up the phone. "Listen," he said to the thin, polite, distant, feminine voice, "do you suppose you could locate a typewriter?"

"Beg pardon?" the girl said.

"A typewriter."

"I'll connect you with the night clerk."

He smoked three cigarettes before the boy knocked on his door, came in, and set the machine on his desk. He had a sheet of paper in it before the boy was out of the room; later, he did not even remember hearing the door close.

His mind was working very fast and very efficiently, all the details of that night crowding into it. He finished one page and then another, and this time he did not run into any stone wall. When he finally got into bed and switched off the light, there were seventeen pages on the desk beside the machine. It was a rough sketch, it had nothing to do with *The Suburb*, but he thought he could do something with it, and he thought, Oh, Christ, let it read well tomorrow morning, let it be like this again, let the dry spell be over now. His back and shoulders throbbed dully, and he thought, I am going to be groggy tomorrow and it will no doubt be a long day. But just the same it lay like something warm inside him when he dropped off to sleep, the knowledge of the thin pile of pages lying there on the desk beside the typewriter in the dark.

5 THAT SECOND NIGHT JEAN fixed dinner for them in her apartment. After dinner they lingered over cigarettes and a glass of Armagnac, and so it was after ten when they got to Betty Grigsby's party on 67th Street. Now it was after twelve, and Jean had excused herself and gone into the bathroom, and he was standing alone in the archway with a drink in his hand.

It was one of those apartments with a lot of sectional furniture and rooms flowing into each other. For two hours everybody had been working very hard at having a good time, but now the party was finally loosening up. Now the tall man in front of the living-room window was talking loudly to a single disinterested girl, and the group clogging the kitchen doorway was verging on boisterousness. On the davenport at Michael's left, the girl in the Hungarian peasant's costume was trying to hypnotize the fat, red-faced man who designed book jackets, and the only two people who were still on the edge of all the smoke and conversation were Michael and the gaunt, dyspeptic-looking man across the room in front of the imitation stone fireplace.

"It's a natural," someone in the cluster at the kitchen door was shouting. "It's an absolutely unique idea!"

"It's economically catastrophic," someone else said. "There's no security in it, Bill."

"That's the trouble with this country today," Bill said.

58

"Everybody wants security, nobody is willing to gamble. The pioneer spirit is dead in us."

Michael thought about the passages he had read which purported to be journalistic portrayals of New York parties, and about Frank Mattson telling him at lunch today that he, Michael, had read too many books about New York.

"Jim, darling," the girl on the davenport said, "the secret is relaxation. Just concentrate on forgetting your immediate surroundings."

"How can I?" the fat man said. "With you doing that to me, how can I?"

"Listen," the girl said, "this is a psychological experiment. Get it out of your head that there's anything sexual about it."

A woman with a long face and bony hips and breasts she had picked up in one of the better Fifth Avenue shops broke away from the cluster at the kitchen door and walked toward Michael in the careful, concentrated manner of the near blind or the consciously drunk. "Where's your girl friend, friend?" she asked.

"Powdering her nose, I guess."

"Do I know you?"

"I don't think so."

"Well," the woman said, speaking loudly against a burst of laughter from the group at the kitchen door, "wouldn't you like to take me away from all this? I have a sudden desire to retire from the scene with a new face."

Michael smiled at her. "There doesn't seem to be any place that's exactly private," he said.

"I personally know," the woman said, trying to keep her eyes focused on Michael's, "that Betty pays a hundred and eighty a month for this apartment and they can't even put a door on the bedroom. Don't you think that for a hundred and eighty a month they could at least put a door on the bedroom? Does that seem to be asking too goddam much?"

Michael felt a hand on his arm. He looked around and found that Jean was beside him. "I see you've met Beth," she said, coldly. "How are you, Beth?"

"You know how I am," Beth said. "You've got eyes. I'm drunk."

"How's Roger?" Jean said.

"He's over by the window. He's talking about how this time he wants his picture on the jacket. Can't you hear him, for Christ's sake?"

Jean looked brightly into Michael's eyes. "Are you getting tired of this yet?" she said.

"Not yet."

"Well, when you do, just let me know."

"Jean," Beth said, "would you happen to know anywhere in this apartment where somebody could find a little privacy?"

"I haven't given the matter any serious thought, Beth," Jean said. Her voice was very polite, very distant. "Have you tried the bathroom?"

Beth's eyes swam back to Michael. "Jean disapproves of me," she said. "Jean has lived most of her adult life in this town, but Jean is a highly moral girl, and she thinks I'm a tramp."

"Michael," Jean said, "shouldn't we sort of drift across the room and—"

"Yes," Beth said. "Why don't you, Michael? Why don't you go over and listen to my husband?" Her eyes were a clear blue, and underneath the surface they could have been filled with tears, or maybe it was just an alcoholic haze. "His name is Roger McKay," she said. "Roger is a writer. Very psychological. Very *avant-garde*. He refers to it as integrity." Her forehead was creased in an effort to keep her eyes steadily on his; then she gave up the struggle, dropped her head, and began to twist her plain gold wedding band. "Very goddam subtle and symbolic," she said. "Three years ago nobody except a vanity publisher would give him a second reading, and he used to talk about how commercialization was the cancer of American art. Then a first-rate publisher gave him a contract, and now he wants his picture on the jacket." She brought her head up, and Michael's eyes wavered, the way they would have if he had walked without knocking into her

60

bedroom and found her standing there without any clothes on. "I was very proud of Roger once," she said. "I used to think he was a genius. Then he got his name on a book, and we moved to this town, and the trouble with this town—" Her voice trailed off while she tried to put her finger on the trouble with this town. "Never mind," she said. "It was a brash impulse, and excuse me very much." She turned away from them and started across the room. Even with her back to him, Michael could tell that she was walking with an intense and terrible concentration.

Jean touched his arm lightly. "Let's go over and rescue Peggy Curan from Roger," she said.

"I am not asking them for any ten-thousand-dollar advance," the man at the window was saying when Michael and Jean came across the room toward him. He was unusually tall, at least six four, and obese, so that he looked not only huge but excessive. "I am perfectly willing to let the hacks with the costume pieces wade in the book-club gravy," he said to the small, dark, amused girl who constituted his audience at the moment. "I am satisfied with the crumbs under the table."

"Roger," the girl said, "aren't your metaphors getting out of hand?"

Roger glared at her. "Do you think I'm unreasonable? Is that the impression you get, Peggy?"

"Hello, Roger," Jean said. "What seems to be the trouble?"

"Listen, Jean," Roger said, "if I came over to Mattson with my next one, do you suppose Frank would maybe gamble on a couple of column inches in the *Saturday Review?*"

"I don't know, Roger," Jean said reasonably. "Buying advertising is like shooting crap. When you spend all that money, you want a fifty-fifty chance." She smiled at him. "You can't have your cake and eat it, too. Maybe you ought to go commercial on the next one, Roger. Just concentrate on telling a story."

Roger spread his hands. "The story of my life," he said. "And would anybody like to know what the soul peddlers mean when they tell you to 'just tell a story'? They mean softening all the villains, cutting out all the cracks about bankers, lawyers, capitalists, workers, the clergy, and Walter Reuther, and italicizing all the subtleties. Then, if you do all that and they still can't sell you down the river to the National Book Club, maybe they can make a serial deal with the *Post*."

Michael wondered if this was the way they talked when they were unsuccessful, and then he was remembering all the people he had known in the English departments, the unpublished novelists who told you how they refused to pander to popular taste, the short story writers who accumulated rejection slips and talked learnedly about the effects of advertising on magazine fiction, the savants who published articles on Joyce and Kafka and who expounded (without bothering to read any novels) on prostitution in contemporary literature. He did not feel sorry for Roger McKay, but he wondered briefly if he would be acting like this if he were in Roger's shoes.

The small, dark girl turned and looked up at him and smiled. "Hello," she said. "I'm Peggy Curan, and I suppose you'd be Michael Savage."

He said he was.

"Betty said Jean was bringing you," she said, and then the gaunt, moody man separated himself from the fireplace and came toward them. "Are you having fun, friend?" he asked.

It sounded like a rhetorical question to Michael, but he made a stab at an answer. "It's quite a party," he said.

"This is Michael Savage, Carl," Peggy Curan said. "His novel—"

"I know who he is." He had deep-set eyes, a gray, sad face and a voice to match. "So they peddled you to National?" he said. "Tell me, are they paying the usual fifty thousand this season? Or does the kiss of death come cheaper lately?"

"Carl's a free-lance reviewer," Peggy said, "so his view of life is misanthropic."

Michael saw that Beth McKay had separated herself from the group near the kitchen and was coming carefully toward them. "Where are you from, friend?" Carl was saying. "And wherever it is, why don't you turn around and go back?" And then Beth had wormed her way between Jean and Michael and had put a hand on Michael's arm to steady herself and was looking vaguely at Roger.

"I want to go home now, Roger," she said.

"Well," Roger said, "I don't. It's early yet."

Beth looked around at them. "Would somebody like to take me home? I'll take care of the cab fare." She waited in the silence for somebody to offer to take her home, and then she looked at Michael. "Would you like to take me home?" she asked. "You don't need to worry about Roger. Roger doesn't care. Not as long as I keep paying the rent. Do you, Roger?"

"All right, Beth," Roger said. "Come on, I'll take you home."

"They say you're a writer," Beth said to Michael. "Maybe you would like to hear a story. Roger can't see any possibilities in this story because Roger has no instinct for—"

"Come on, Beth," Roger said.

"I'm telling a writer a story. Don't interrupt me, darling."

"It's late. It's time we were getting out of here." He took a step toward her and put a hand on her arm.

She stiffened. "Take your goddam hand off me," she said.

"Beth—"

"I'm warning you." Her voice was suddenly cold and quiet and intense, her words no longer thick at the edges. "If you don't take your hand off me, I'll kill you. So help me, I'll kill you in your sleep." Roger dropped his hand.

"It's a story about a woman who went to work so her husband could write," she said, looking straight at Michael. "And she came home early one afternoon and embarrassed him." She giggled. "It's a story with a twist. Usually it's the husband who comes home early, isn't it?" She was looking hard at Michael, watching for a sign of appreciation for the twist in this story, and then the haze came back into her eyes. "Never mind," she said. "It's probably been told before, and anyway it would require a lot of underwriting because the girl didn't

63

make a scene." She was twisting the gold wedding band again. "It wouldn't have been so bad if it hadn't been in the middle of the aftenoon. Can any of you understand how it wouldn't have been so bad if it hadn't been at three o'clock in the afternoon?"

Michael looked quickly, guiltily, at Jean, and then he put his hand lightly on Beth's back. "I'll help you find a cab," he said.

"Never mind. Stick around. Listen to Roger tell some more about how all he wants is his picture on the jacket." She started across the room toward the door. They all stood there, in a semicircle, trying not to look directly at Roger.

The cluster at the kitchen door burst into another roar of laughter. "Does anybody know what's going on over there?" Peggy said.

"Bill Hodges has an idea," Carl said, "for buying up surplus army transports and converting them into flying whorehouses. They have so far recognized the necessity for a decompressor unit so the customers won't get the bends, and they have also come up with fifteen or twenty advertising slogans, including one about sleeping with Alice from Chicago to Dallas. Were you thinking of going over and getting convulsed, Peggy?"

"No," Peggy said. "Can I get you another drink, Michael?"

"I think there's one around I've been nursing."

"Take my advice, friend," Carl said. "Drink it up and let her get you another. You have no idea what this can be like if the alcohol ever goes out of you."

"Let's get out of here, Michael," Jean said.

He looked down at her. "If you want to."

"I want to," she said.

Betty Grigsby was just turning back from closing the door on Beth McKay when they came across the room. After four hours of this she still looked blonde and expensive and glossy, like a woman in a *Vogue* ad. "Not going already?" she said.

"I'm afraid we have to, Betty," Jean said.

Betty looked distressed. "You didn't have any fun."

"Yes, we did. It was a fine party. But tomorrow's tomorrow, you know."

Michael stood at the door, waiting for Jean to get her jacket, while behind him somebody was shouting that the trouble with New York was, everybody was trying to sell everybody something nobody wanted at a forty percent mark-up. Then Jean was back, and they went down the stairs and out onto 67th Street.

She did not say anything when they came out onto the street, and on the way up Fifth in the cab, she kept the silence and the width of the seat stiffly between them, as if she were on her way home with a man who had gotten out of line.

"What's the matter?" he said.

"Use that sometime," she said. "Write a story about that sometime."

"It's been done by better writers than I'll ever be." He reached across the seat and found her hand. "Look," he said, "quit crucifying yourself on my account. Nothing was any of your fault."

The cab pulled up at her apartment, and the driver switched on the light. "Maybe tomorrow night," she said. "Maybe just one night before you go back—"

"Oh, cut it out, Jean."

She smiled at him and it took a while for the smile to reach her eyes, but suddenly the frantic day and Betty Grigsby's party were behind them, were assigned to history, and everything was all right again, everything was fine.

"It's been a fine day, Michael," she said. "Even if it has been terrible."

He remembered lunch with her, and the walks around Manhattan in the sunlight, and dinner in her apartment. "I enjoyed every minute of it."

"Nine o'clock tomorrow," she said. "In Kay's office. For a person who needs his sleep, that doesn't—"

"If you mean am I tired—that's nine whole hours. An eternity."

"Tomorrow will be murderous, too."

"If you are inviting me in again," he said, "I was hoping you might."

"Well," she said, "I guess that's what I'm doing."

In her apartment he took off his coat and loosened his tie while she turned on all the lights. It was a habit of hers with which he was familiar now; it was as if darkness were an enemy she was perpetually at war with. He wondered how much her light bills were and if she slept with a light on, the way his six-year-old daughter did.

She turned the last table lamp on and faced him. "I'll fix you a drink," she said, "if you'll break out the ice cubes."

"Agreed." He followed her out to the kitchen. She poured whiskey over the ice and handed him his drink, and he followed her back into the living room, leaned on her mantel, and looked across the room at her. Even from that distance he felt again that surprise at how small she was, that brief, warm compulsion to protect her.

"You are certainly sunk in thought," she said. "A penny."

"It isn't worth that much. They could convict me of intent to defraud."

"I won't prefer charges. I promise." She waited a minute. "I'll even put it in writing," she said.

"All right." He set his glass carefully on the mantel. "I was thinking about you."

"What about me?"

"No. Never mind."

"Yes. Tell me."

"All right." He spoke carefully and slowly, feeling the breath thin in him. "I was wondering what you might do if I took about two steps and tilted your face and kissed you."

She looked quickly at him and as quickly away again. "What do you think I'd do?"

"I am guessing that you would very politely point out that it is after one and I had better go."

He could see only the edge of her face as he waited. If I leave now, he thought, I will never know, and then he thought of the other things you think about at a moment like this, of the fact of Alice and four children and thirteen years, and then he was acutely conscious of the quiet between them, of the fan in the window, of a compulsion to splinter the silence.

"Is that what you would do?" he asked.

"I don't suppose either of us will ever know, will we? Unless it should happen to happen."

She was the one who closed the space between them. Or most of it—and he did not have to tilt her face up, either. He did not feel any particular surge of passion when he kissed her; he felt only a warm protectiveness, as if he were kissing somebody good-bye. He did not even feel a stir when her fingers moved up into the hair at the nape of his neck and he tightened his arms around her. Because by then he was thinking, I am going to fall in love with this girl. I am thirty-six years old, he thought, and I have a wife and four children, and I am going to fall in love with this girl.

He brushed his lips past hers. "I think," he said, "that I have wanted to do that for a long time."

"I think," she said, "that I have wanted you to do it for a long time."

He held her as tightly as if he were going somewhere and did not expect to come back, his lips on her cheek and the smell of her hair sharp and light and clean, and the whir of the fan off at the edge of the room somewhere, and he wished he knew what you said to a girl when you were married and did not want to go back to a hotel room.

She pulled away and scanned his face. "You didn't want this to happen, did you?"

"I don't know," he said. "I thought I did."

"I suppose it would make things complicated."

"I suppose it would."

"A relationship like this can get very messy," she said, "if you let emotions get tangled up in it."

"I guess it can. Only what is the mathematical formula for keeping emotions out?"

"Anyway, you *are* married."

"Listen, Jean," he said, "one thing I am not going to do.

I am not going to tell you about how my wife doesn't understand me."

"I didn't want you to," she said quietly.

"I don't know how I feel about her. The years get between two people and you don't know after a while." He pulled away from her. "Anyway," he said, "I wasn't thinking of Alice." He moved a hand, briefly and vaguely. "It's just that this is something you only read about. It's just that I don't know what the hell you say next."

She was smiling at him. "What do you want to say next?"

"You know. You know what I want to say."

"I also want to hear you say it."

"All right," he said. "I don't want to go back to that hotel room. I want to stay here. I want to stay the night. Because I think maybe I've fallen in love with you." He had the feeling of burning a bridge behind him. "Is that what you wanted to hear?" he said.

She wasn't smiling now. "Do either of us know what we're doing?" She waited a moment for the answer he didn't offer, and then she turned and started around the room, switching off lights. She went about it very systematically. She left the ceiling lights until last, and then she stood, looking across the room at him, her fingers on that switch.

"Is it all right if I undress in the bathroom?" she said. "Because I'm really a very single girl, Michael," and in that instant he saw her as she really was, standing there with her fingers on the light switch, looking small and uncertain, looking like a child bride on her wedding night.

"Listen," he said quickly. "Listen, are *you* sure, Jean?"

"I'm sure. I have been for a long time. Only I may not be as interesting as you think." She switched off the light then, and he could see her only vaguely, in the light that filtered into the room from the almost closed bathroom door. Then he went into the bedroom.

He lay for what seemed a long time in the dark, listening for her. At a moment like this, he was thinking, the male is supposed to feel triumphant, but he felt only a kind of analytical objectivity, an emotional distance, as if this were not

68

happening to him at all, as if he were rather at a typewriter trying to write a scene in which this was happening to a character of his. Then he was wondering how he would act toward Alice after tonight, and behind that was the nagging fear that he would be inadequate. He heard the bathroom door open, and he watched the quick finger of light reach and then retreat. Then she said, "Where are you?"

"Here. Should I turn on a light?"

"No. Please, no." She was standing beside the bed, and her voice was thin and fast and nervous. He was certain now that although she had lived most of her adult life in this city and had participated in all the conversations which glinted across all the lunch tables, and that although a good many men had told her in taxis that she was a very attractive girl, this was the first time she had ever gone to bed with a man.

He reached out in the dark and touched her bare hip. "It's still not too late, you know," he said. "I can still get out of here."

She sat down on the edge of the bed and leaned over him. Her fingers touched his shoulder. "Who is going to have to seduce who?" she said.

"If only things were different," he said. "If tomorrow we could go down to the courthouse together. Because what the hell is there in this for you?"

"Have I asked for anything?"

"If only—"

She put a finger on his lips. "Have I?" she repeated. "For anything at all, Michael?"

"If either of us weren't us. If afterwards I could just dress and go back to the hotel and forget all about it."

"If you were like that this wouldn't be happening. Not with me."

"If there had been others—"

"Darling," she said, "there have been others. One other. A long time ago. Does that make a difference?"

"No. It doesn't change the picture at all."

"Michael, you aren't taking advantage of me, and will you please stop talking and kiss me?"

69

He stopped talking and kissed her. He was thinking, God, let me be good to her, let me be all right, and then he was aware that nothing was happening to him, and he wondered if this was the way it was going to turn out. So after all the years, he thought, after all the times you have wondered about this, this was how it was going to end? So this is the way the world ends, he thought, not with a bang but a whimper, and he felt a clean, sharp stab of anger because he was the kind of person he was.

"I don't know how to put this," he said, "but I don't think this is any good, Jean. I don't think it's going to be any use."

"It's a long time to morning."

He didn't say anything.

"It will be all right," she said, "if you just stop worrying about it being all right."

"All right," he said. "I'll stop worrying. I'll try."

He lay on his back with his arm around her and her head on his chest, and he could not remember ever feeling exactly like this before. This is the way an animal must feel, he thought, when he has eaten the last acorn and the first snow has drifted down into the valley and he crawls into the cave and works himself down into the warm dark.

She stirred beside him. He traced with one finger the line of her backbone. "Was I all right?" he asked.

"You were wonderful."

"I suppose," he said, "that we really do have to see Kay in another six hours."

"Yes. It means fifty thousand dollars."

"The hell with fifty thousand dollars. Who needs fifty thousand dollars?"

"You can always find a place for it. And there will be other nights. There will be tomorrow night."

He closed his eyes against the dark. He could just make out in the vague distance the faint hum and rattle of a truck, and behind the walls was the feeling, not so much a sound or even a feeling as a guess, of a city turning over in bed and hoping,

70

down in the dark of the half-sleep, that the alarm would not go off for another hour yet.

"Jean," he said, "what is this going to come to?"

"Let's not talk about that. Let's keep our minds focused on now."

"Maybe she'll give me a divorce. Maybe if I can explain to her exactly how it is—"

She propped herself on an elbow. There was just enough light for him to make out the outline of her face and the line of her hair, which was so dark that you could almost see it in the dark. "Did it mean that much to you?" she said.

Lying there, he remembered something that had happened to him a long time ago, back in grade school. "I could tell you what it meant."

She settled back down beside him. "Tell me."

"There was a girl once. Back in grade school. Her name was Mary, and she had long yellow curls, and I was in love with her. Only she liked this Italian kid, this Tony Crossetti." He had the feeling that he was telling this awkwardly, that it must sound silly. "Tony was the best ball player in the room," he said, "and the best marble shooter, and nobody in his right mind would have picked a fight with him. Mary used to let him walk her home from school." He stopped talking. Even today, even twenty-four years afterwards, he could remember how Tony walked across the playground, tall and lean and dark-haired, without awkwardness, with that assurance in his walk you see in natural athletes. "I used to sit in school," he said, "and watch the side of her face and dream about rescuing her from the Spanish Inquisition while Tony stood helplessly by, and I think this is beginning to sound silly."

"No, it isn't."

"One day the teacher called on me to read, and I got stuck on a word." And I can remember that scene like it was yesterday, he thought: Miss Thompson, gray-haired and melon-breasted, calling on him. Sliding out of his seat and standing there in the aisle, too tall for his age and too thin, in the heavy gray sweater with the black leather patches on the elbows. Reading the paragraph slowly and distinctly, trying to

71

slide over the word he did not know how to pronounce. Miss Thompson stopping him and saying, "Well? Well, Michael?"

"Yes?" Jean said. "You got stuck—"

"Miss Thompson told the boy behind me to pronounce it and he pronounced it. I tried to say it after him, but Mary had turned around and was looking at me, and then she covered her mouth and snickered. You could hear it all over the room."

"And that's all?" she said.

"Not quite," he said. Not quite all, he thought, remembering how he had stood there with his hip touching the edge of the desk and the sleeves of the sweater two inches above his wrists and the hair falling over his eyes and the heat in his cheeks and the sound of the snicker still lying in the room, or inside his head. Remembering Miss Thompson looking sharply at Mary and then saying, "Again, Michael."

"I can't say it," he said.

"I don't think I know what *can't* means," Miss Thompson said. "*Can't* is a word we are unacquainted with in this room."

He looked sullenly at the floor. "I can't say it," he said. He brought his head up. "Why did she have to laugh like that?" he shouted. "Goddam it, she didn't have to—"

"*Michael!*"

"I don't care," he screamed. "I hate you! I hate all of you!"

"You're excused, Michael," Miss Thompson said.

He dropped his book on the desk and turned and walked down the aisle, past the blur of faces. It was very quiet in the room. He turned at the door and looked across the seats. He was, at that moment, sharply conscious not of Mary's face, not of all the faces looking white and disembodied across the seats at him, but only of the red book lying on his desk. Then he left.

That had been the middle of the afternoon, and he sat for three hours in the toilet, waiting for the building to empty, before he went back into the empty room for his coat and hat.

Jean stirred beside him, and he tightened his arm around her. "It wasn't much of a story," he said. "Not the way I told it. But I have always thought of it as the parable of my boyhood."

"Did it end in violence?" she said.

"What?"

"That scene on the playground. With the rock."

"Oh," he said. *"The Alley."* He ran his hand along her arm. Her skin felt smooth and flawless, like a patiently sanded maple board. "No, but it ought to have. Because that is the way I felt."

"It's almost morning," she said. "Kiss me good-night, and then let's get some sleep."

She lifted her head and he kissed her.

He lay in the dark, with his arm around her and her face on his chest and a strand of her hair tickling his shoulder. For a minute he thought of Mary and Tony and Miss Thompson, and then he wondered how he could break this to Alice in a way that would not tear her apart, and then he wondered if this girl would make a difference in the way the new novel was going. He had heard a story once about another writer who had gone stale in the middle of a book; someone had suggested that what he needed was a new wife, and he had gone out and acquired a new wife, and then he had not been stale any more. The story had no doubt been made up over a straight whiskey at two in the morning, but he wondered if there might not be a grain of truth underneath—he wondered if this girl beside him might not make a difference.

He lay there beside her, with her breathing quiet and regular, like a wisp of air current moving through time, and that first almost imperceptible lightening of the darkness stealing secretly through the cracks which the drawn Venetian blinds in the bedroom had overlooked, and wondered that. And then, for one brief, vivid second, he saw Beth McKay, standing in Betty Grigsby's living room, twisting the gold wedding band, saying, "Can any of you understand how it wouldn't have been so bad if it hadn't been at three o'clock in the afternoon?" and just before he dropped off to sleep, he had a feeling, like a whisper of intuition, that Jean might not make the kind of difference he hoped she would make.

73

Hyatt Engel   II

6
crossed the reception room Janet smiled brightly and professionally and said, "Good morning, Mr. Engel," and nothing had changed.

"Is Mr. O'Brien in yet?" I said.

"Yes. Did you want to see him, Mr. Engel?" She rested a home-manicured fingertip on the intercom and waited for me to indicate the zero hour.

I let her wait. There was the matter of a fat realtor from Ashtabula to settle with Janet. I walked over and picked up a copy of *Insight* and very deliberately leafed it open to the book page I had already read.

"Should I buzz Mr. O'Brien now, Mr. Engel?" she said.

"Not yet, Janet. I'll tell you when." I dropped the magazine on the stand, sat down on the arm of the nearest chair, and looked across the nine feet at Janet.

"Where did you work before you came here, Janet?"

"In an insurance office."

"Well," I said, "in this insurance office did anybody ever tell you he didn't want to see somebody and to get rid of him?"

She didn't say anything.

"No," I said. "I suppose not. I suppose in an insurance office everybody who calls is a potential customer."

"He was very insistent, Mr. Engel. He kept—"

"No doubt," I said. "But I had no time for Walt Camden

77

Wednesday. I very carefully explained that to you, Janet, before I left for lunch."

"I'm sorry." She was studying that finger as if she had a hangnail that was beginning to fester, and I thought, all right, you have made your point, Engel. Only I couldn't let go of it. Not because Janet had really loused anything up, but because I was sitting on a crucial cover story that refused to get off the ground. Or maybe because two nights ago I had watched Jean Reynolds walk out of a restaurant with Michael Savage, her hand intimately, almost possessively, on his arm. Or maybe just because I was back in the *Insight* building, where you acted as the other Romans acted. Anyway, instead of dropping it, I nodded coldly at the intercom, like the compulsive son-of-a-bitch I couldn't help being for the moment, and said, "See if O'Brien can spare me a minute now."

You could detect the panic in her voice when she put the question to the intercom; give somebody a month or two and a little effort, I thought, and maybe she would last the year out yet. She wasn't much to look at, and she wasn't very bright, but she could no doubt be taught. If somebody would take the pains to put the food in front of her and ring the bell and then slap her across the nose.

"You can go right in, Mr. Engel," she said.

I nodded and started for O'Brien's door.

"Mr. Engel?"

I turned. "Yes?"

"Are you going to tell him?"

I still couldn't let go of it. "I don't know," I said.

"This is a good job, Mr. Engel," she said. "A girl like me doesn't get a chance at a job like this every day in the week."

"I'm glad you like it," I said. "We want everybody on the staff to be happy."

"I didn't intend to tell that man where you were. It just slipped out. I mean I told him you were gone for the day, and then he asked me where you usually ate lunch, and—" Her voice faltered and then recovered. "What I mean is,"

78

she said, "if you didn't have to say anything to Mr. O'Brien—"

"I don't know what I'm going to say to Mr. O'Brien. All I know is, you're in a key position here, and we can't do our jobs if people like you don't give us some cooperation."

She raised her head and looked at me. It was the kind of look that made you wonder if the psychologists sometimes got tired of putting the food down, ringing the bell, and then slapping them across the nose. Then her chin came up another inch and there was another look entirely.

"All right," she said. "Tell him. Go ahead."

"Oh, what the hell, Janet. I never intended to tell him." She studied my eyes a moment, and then she smiled. "Thanks, Mr. Engel," she said quietly.

It was ten feet to her desk and due north, and O'Brien's door was west, but I disregarded the hypotenuse of the triangle and walked over and leaned across her desk and made a fist and jabbed her lightly on the chin. "Forget it," I said.

"Thanks, Mr. Engel," she said again, and I wondered, irrelevantly, if this girl ever prayed. Because if she does, I thought, she had better incorporate a new request—that she never have to take her orders from a bastard like me.

O'Brien was doing something with a set of galleys when I came into his office. When he looked up, his expression told me that the galleys did not represent the faultless and inimitable prose to which he was accustomed. "Come on in, Hyatt," he said, "and close the door."

I came on in and closed the door.

"What's on your mind?" he said.

"A trip to Minneapolis. I'll need some cash."

"All right. Just be sure to keep your receipts." He grinned unenthusiastically. "How's it going so far?"

"It isn't. It hasn't gotten off the ground yet."

"What seems to be the trouble?"

"I can't get anything out of him. He won't talk about himself."

"Tried getting him drunk?"

"He doesn't drink."

He blinked again. "This doesn't sound like you, Hyatt," he said. "A couple of years ago nothing was too tough."

"A couple of years ago I was a couple of years younger."

"You don't sound like an *Insight* man lately. You sound kind of defeated." He fumbled for a cigarette and stuck it in his mouth and waited until I could get my lighter out. Then he lit it for himself. "It happens. We sometimes get men who can't stand the pace." His voice managed to express a profound sadness and regret for all the ex-*Insight* men who hadn't been able to stand the pace.

I straightened up. "All right. If you'll put that call through to accounting—"

"Sure. And don't give up, Hyatt. Keep pitching."

"I know. If at first you don't succeed."

"That," he said, "is the God's truth, Hyatt."

I walked to the door and then turned. "I haven't tried matches yet," I said. "Applied to the soles of his feet."

This time his grin was enthusiastic. "Now you're talking like an *Insight* man, Hyatt," he said.

Savage's wife was waiting for us when we stepped off the plane under a gray, overcast sky. She was pressing against the fence, with a three-year-old boy in her arms and a six-year-old girl clinging to her coat. Visibility under those smoky, scuttling clouds wasn't exactly unlimited, and it was a good fifty yards from the plane to the gate, but still you could make out the relief on her face as she waved. Savage waved back, and then we were pushing through the crowd at the gate and he was leaning to kiss her. You would have thought, the way she brought her face up, that the State Department had just effected his release from a Soviet internment camp.

Savage straightened up from the spousal kiss and took in her emotional state in a single, careless glance. "What were you worried about?" he said. "Statistics prove it's the safest way to travel. Anyway, if anything had happened, you'd have collected twenty-five thousand dollars. For a while there, I was worth more dead than alive."

"Please," she said. "Don't say things like that, Michael."

He reached out for the boy and she passed him over. "Hello, Alan," he said.

"Did you fly in a airplane, Daddy?" The boy had surprisingly clear enunciation for a three-year-old.

Savage said yes, he flew in a airplane.

"Way up in the sky?"

"Yes," Michael said. "Way the hell up, Alan."

Alice Savage looked sharply at her husband and then decided against saying it. Savage said, "Hello, Susy," and the girl looked up and said hello and then looked down at the ground again. Savage asked her if she had been a good girl, and Susy said yes, she has been a good girl. Then Savage remembered me. "This is Hyatt Engel, Alice," he said. "He's doing a story on me. For *Insight*."

She looked levelly at me and said hello. She had very nice eyes, gray and cool but with depth in them. "I've got your room ready for you," she said.

"Listen, if I'm going to be putting you to a lot of trouble—"

"It's no trouble, Mr. Engel." She had passed the age when a woman looks good without working at it. She wasn't exactly matronly yet, but she had probably put on a pound or two since that day when Savage had pushed his two dollars through the grill and they had walked across the street to the parsonage and he had left thirty minutes later with a responsibility on his arm. She had no doubt added something to her hips and bust since that day, and now uplift brassieres and beauty treatments were beginning to count. But she had eyes you liked.

We pushed through the crowd and collected our baggage and started across the concrete. You could tell that she would have put her hand on his arm if he hadn't been encumbered with two suitcases; she was the kind of a woman who would put her hand on her man's arm when she walked across a parking lot. At the car she handed him the keys and he put the luggage in the trunk while the rest of us climbed into the robin's-egg-blue Cadillac, Alice and the boy in front, the girl and me in the back.

Savage slid in behind the wheel. I was watching the side of his face, and I saw something happen to him. He was a handsome bastard if you like them six feet tall, a hundred and eighty pounds, straight-nosed and firm-lipped, but from what I had seen of him that week you would have thought he was going on nine years old and lost in the north woods. But when he slid behind the wheel of that car, he suddenly seemed to find something. I suppose something does happen to a man when he gets behind the wheel of a five-thousand-dollar white-walled job that he has paid cash on the line for. I suppose it is something like what happens to a rookie outfielder when he starts running backward at the crack of the bat and backs up against the wall and jumps and spears the triple with his bare hand and the people up there in the stands get to their feet and let go of the roar.

"Nice car," I said.

"It's all right. It will get you where you are going."

"Also, it wouldn't exactly make your cheeks burn with shame on the country club parking lot."

He laughed. "You stole that," he said.

The gray overcast had turned into a light rain when Savage eased the car out of the airport drive. It was one of those rains you get in Minneapolis in the late summer, and it took me back. What you mostly get in that town is sunlight as brilliant as the glitter of a diamond and just about as warm, but for some reason it was the rain that made me feel suddenly that I was home again.

Alice Savage turned around and gave me an opportunity to admire her gray eyes some more. "I don't suppose you've ever been in Minneapolis, Mr. Engel," she said.

"He went to school here," Savage said.

"Oh. Then you must feel as if you're home again."

"Yes," I said. And I did. I was unacquainted with this section, but in Minneapolis that doesn't make any difference because one section is pretty much like another. So I had the feeling that I was home again, that I was on my way back to the house, and I would take a bath and shave and eat, and then I would pick up Rachel in the Union Lounge and we would probably go to a movie tonight because it was raining.

Alice Savage turned back to the road ahead and sneaked a look at the side of Savage's face. It was a look that told a story. There was pride in it, and possessiveness, and affection—probably as much affection as you have left in the reservoir after fifteen years. "You look tired," she said.

"I'm not. I feel fine."

"You've lost weight, too. You ought to take a vacation, Michael. We ought to go away somewhere and just—"

He turned his head and looked at her. "I'm all right, Alice," he said.

She looked away.

"Anyway," he said, "I may go out to the Coast. Kay says Miller may invite me to work on the script if I'm willing."

"Are you?"

"I don't know. I could use that experience." He braked the car gently for a curve; it wasn't much of a curve, and that car could have taken it at sixty on a glare of ice, but Savage was apparently the kind of driver who would drive you crazy on a thousand-mile trip. And somebody is going to get a buy when he trades this in, I thought. I could hear the salesman explaining how clean it was, and the motor just like the upholstery because the original owner had driven it under sixty the whole twelve thousand miles. "I have to go back to New York again this fall, too," he said.

"Maybe I could get away this time," she said.

"If you want to," he said. "But you'd be on your own—"

"Never mind. It was just an idea."

"If you want to go somewhere, you could go to the Coast with me."

"No. It would be the same story out there."

"What story?"

"Whenever you take a typewriter along. I want to go somewhere sometime when you leave that typewriter behind."

I watched the stone-fronted houses slide by in the rain and

thought about the undercurrents you get when two people have too many years lying between them. Then we turned into a long drive, slid through an orchard, and at the end of the drive was the house.

It sprawled. It was brown shingle rather than stone-fronted, but it would still get by in Minneapolis. It looked like what it had once been, a summer home for one of the Pillsbury executives downtown, with a garage and something that could have been a caretaker's cottage but was probably the retreat where Savage penned his deathless prose. When you got to the end of the drive, you could see where the land at the back of the house fell away, and you could see the valley below, with a river running through it that looked, from this distance, like a highway seen from ten thousand feet up. It was a nice, not-quite-orthodox, thirty-thousand-dollar house and a view thrown in. It was the kind of a place you would expect a successful writer to buy.

Savage got out in the rain and pulled up the overhead door. I wondered why he hadn't had an electric eye installed. Maybe he hadn't thought of it yet. He came back and eased the Cadillac in beside a Packard convertible which, I gathered, was Alice's new birthday present. The Packard wasn't quite as big or expensive as the Cadillac, but it still wasn't a piece of machinery they gave away with nine books of Green Stamps, and it occurred to me that in two months Michael Savage had made some very fancy inroads into that first fifty or sixty thousand. I hoped he was allowing something for tax.

We all piled out. "You go ahead, Engel," he said. "I'll get the bags."

I followed Alice Savage across the yard and into the house, through a General Electric kitchen and a thirty-foot living room with a stone fireplace out of the Arthurian legends and a picture window that could have furnished the glass for a small greenhouse. We walked down a short hall and Alice Savage opened a bedroom door.

"I hope you'll be comfortable, Mr. Engel," she said. There was a coating of pride on her voice.

I looked at the blonde maple Hollywood bed and matching chest, at the built-in bookshelf containing a set of reprints about Sue Barton, Student Nurse, at the pictures of horses and dogs on the wall. "I'm sure I will," I said.

Savage came in and dropped my suitcase. "If there's anything you lack," he said, "just scream. Your bath's across the hall."

Alice Savage nodded at the chest. "The two top drawers are empty," she said.

They closed the door behind them, and I stood there and looked at the room. It apparently belonged to Savage's oldest daughter. It is a symbol, I thought. It was the realization of the American dream of the good life, and for two people who had had money for only a short while, the Savages had, it seemed, caught on quick.

When I came out of the bedroom, the table at the end of the living room was set, and Susy and Alan and a girl of about ten were crouched in front of the television set, absorbed in a piece of elemental drama involving a cave and a lot of men with blazing guns. Savage was standing in front of the fireplace. He had changed into slacks and a sport shirt, and if he had had a straight-stemmed pipe in his mouth and a boxer lying at his feet you could have used the pose on a book jacket.

He grinned at me and asked, over the lash of the guns, if everything was all right. I shouted that everything was fine.

"Cathy," he said, "turn that thing down. You can't hear yourself think in here."

"If I turn it down," Cathy said, "I can't hear it. With you talking."

"You heard me. Turn it down."

Cathy turned it down but not enough to make any appreciable difference, and Savage looked at me and shrugged helplessly. "This is nothing," he said. "Wait until Ellen gets home. I can't understand why Alice doesn't move that thing into one of the bedrooms. Unless it's because she likes to watch it herself. She is rooted in front of it nightly from eight to midnight."

Alice Savage appeared in the kitchen door. She was wiping her hands on an apron. "Tell me," she said sweetly, "how else would you suggest I fill out my evenings?"

He chose to disregard that. "Listen to that dialogue," he said. "The networks are paying over a thousand dollars for scripts, and listen to that dialogue."

I listened to the dialogue and privately agreed with him. I thought of the undercurrents in this marriage and wondered if ethics would forbid incorporating them into the story. "Nice place you've got here," I said.

"We like it," he said. "Except for the mortgage. Like a look around?"

I followed him through the kitchen and had a look at what you buy when you are National Book Club and Century has paid fifty thousand for screen rights. I looked at the two bedrooms on the south wing, both looking like advertisements out of *Better Homes and Gardens*; we toured the basement, with its freezer and automatic laundry; we walked across the grounds to the cottage where Savage churned out the pages that were going to pay the taxes on all this. Out there the hand of Alice Savage was no longer in evidence. The building consisted of two rooms, one of them Savage's study, with bookshelves, a desk, filing cabinets, and a cot; the other a shop with a lot of Delta power machinery and a big workbench. In the gray end of a gray day, I stood in Savage's home workshop and watched him demonstrate the art of tonguing and grooving on a power shaper and wondered if this was the kind of thing our readers would be interested in.

"I bought all this," Savage said, "because somebody once told me it was therapeutic." He smiled crookedly. "I built those bookshelves in the study and roofed the garage. In the midday heat of a July sun. But so far, all I've gotten out of it is blisters."

"Well," I said, "I guess that's life."

"Next year," he said, "I may try gardening. I met a writer once who claimed he did most of his writing in a cornfield."

I had a quick picture of Savage meeting the summer overhead of the local representative for International Harvester. If the money held out. "They tell me travel is a way to fill the well back up, too," I said.

He shot a look at me I couldn't read. "Anyway," he said, "if I've used myself up on *Vine*, I can always start making bids on small defense contracts."

"Hell, you haven't used yourself up."

"You never know. The one-book writer isn't an unknown phenomenon in this century."

"You're out of that category already."

"*The Alley?*" He shook his head. "That was a novelette. I wrote it in six weeks, and it doesn't count." He kicked at a scattering of sawdust at his feet. "They ought to invent a pill or something," he said, "to make you forget what's behind. To forget that the next one always has to be better than the last one. The rules ought to allow you one or two failures, don't you think?"

"What you need," I said, "is a vacation."

"You, too?" he said.

When we came in the side door, Alice was giving the children orders to turn off the TV and get washed. She sounded harried.

"Michael," she said, when we came into the kitchen, "will you see that Alan goes to the bathroom? If you don't, he always wants to go in the middle of the meal."

"All right. Is Ellen home yet?"

"No. I think she's at Scouts."

"She never gets home before six any more. You'd think she was earning a living." We walked into the living room. "Alan," he said, "let's get washed. Cathy, turn that thing off."

"In a minute," Cathy said.

"Not in a minute," he said. "Now." He led Alan off to the bathroom, and I sat down and waited for the invitation to come to the table. I felt the way you feel when you know that people are going to a lot of trouble on your account, and then I was thinking that Americans are a crazy people. An American male, I thought, will knock himself out to buy his wife a lot of labor-saving gadgets, all of them equipped with red lights and warning buzzers and defrosters that work in the middle of the night and sliding shelves to reduce the danger of abdominal twinges brought on by over-reaching and electrical thermostats to eliminate the necessity for memory. The gadgets only made life more complicated, but the American male kept right on accumulating them, and at the same time he would no more dream of hiring a house-keeper than he would of retiring at forty-five. In the barely possible event that man survived his gadgets, I wondered what the anthropologist would make of us a thousand years hence.

Michael came out of the bathroom with Alan in tow, and Alice brought in the ham and the peas and the candied sweet potatoes and the garden salad. We sat down, and Michael began to heap the plates. "Wait'll you taste this," he said. "If there's one thing I married, it's a good cook."

Alice looked pleased and asked us what we had had for lunch, and Michael said roast beef and mashed potatoes and he forgot what else. "It was a lousy meal," he said. "Wasn't it, Hyatt?"

"Yes," I said. What we had really had was ham and peas and sweet potatoes and garden salad.

A door slammed, and then a girl swept into the room. She was just this side of puberty, and she had Michael's black hair but otherwise she definitely belonged to her mother. She stood in the kitchen door a minute, surveying the scene, and then she strode across the room and flung a dripping raincoat across a chair. She had clearly worked out an entrance for this moment.

"Hi, Daddy," she said. "Did you bring me anything from New York?"

"At the moment," he said, "my memory fails me, Ellen."

"He brought Alan a gun," Susy said. "It shoots ping-pong balls."

Michael nodded in my direction. "This is Mr. Engel, Ellen."

"I know it. He writes for a magazine. Don't you?"

"That's right," I said.

"I'm going to be a veterinarian," she said.

"Are you?" I said. "That's fine, Ellen."

"They don't make a lot of money. But that way I'll get to have a dog someday."

"Well," I said, "you don't make any money writing for magazines, either. So you've got everything to gain and nothing to lose."

"I thought you made a fortune. Mother said you probably did."

"Ellen," Michael said, "hang up that raincoat and go get washed. Use our bathroom today. What were you doing at Scouts all this time, anyway?"

"I wasn't at Scouts. Today was dramatics. I'm in a play. I'm Snip, the King's Jester, and it's a corny. I wish we could have a play with a horse in it sometime."

"You mean on that stage at school?" Michael said.

"Where else?"

"I was just checking," Michael said. "I thought for a minute you might be opening in Yankee Stadium."

"A dog, then. You could get a dog on that stage." She picked up the raincoat and flung it across her shoulder. She was very decidedly her mother's child; she had the square face and the firm, wide mouth and the gray eyes. "Anyway," she said, "we get excused every day for practice. We at least have that."

"The school I went to," Michael said, "we never got excused for anything. All we did was learn how to spell and add."

"Gol," Ellen said, "it must have been gruesome." She disappeared into the kitchen.

Michael passed Alan's baby plate down the table, and Alice began cutting up his meat. "We're going to have to take that child in hand," she said. "They don't do anything else at that school, you'd think they could at least teach them a few manners."

"It inhibits them," Michael said. "The theory is self-discipline now. So you don't make them adults before their time."

"Well," Alice said, "I wish they'd get a new theory."

"They will," Michael said. "Give them six months."

Ellen came back and sat down across from me. "Know what?" she said. "Jean's collie just had puppies. She said I could have one. Can I, Daddy?"

"A collie's a big dog," Michael said. "Do you know how much a collie eats in a week?"

Ellen looked at me. "Do you see why I can't have a dog?" she asked.

"Don't get me in this," I said.

"I can see why," Alice said. "Who'd do the taking care of it?"

"I would," Ellen said. "I promise."

"For about three days."

"As a matter of fact," Michael said, "I've been thinking about a couple of dogs. I've got an eye on some Danes."

"No kidding," Ellen said. "Have you, Daddy? Honest?"

"Oh, my God," Alice said. "Danes, yet."

"*Two* of them, Daddy?" Ellen breathed. "You mean a stud and a bitch?"

"Ellen," Alice said. "*Bitch* isn't a very nice word."

"Why not?"

"She's right, Alice," Michael said. "It's a perfectly legitimate word. In that context."

"The first thing you know," Alice said, "she'll be saying it at school."

"That's all right," Michael said. "In that context."

"All right," Alice said, "*you* answer the phone when—"

"No sweet potatoes, Daddy," Ellen said. "Thanks just the same."

"Yes," Alice said. "Sweet potatoes."

Ellen checked to see that Susy and Cathy had sweet potatoes. "I'll eat them," she said. "But damned if I'll like them."

90

Michael laid the meat fork very precisely across the plate of ham. "Ellen," he said.

"You say it," Ellen said. "You say lots worse things than that."

Alice smiled. "She's got you there, dear," she said. "And besides, it's a perfectly legitimate word. In that context."

At the end of the table, Susy, the six-year-old, swam out of her private world and pointed a spoon at her sweet potatoes. "Do I gotta eat these, Mother?" she said.

"Yes," Alice said. "They're good for you." She looked bitterly at Ellen. "I hope you're satisfied," she said.

Cathy, the ten-year-old, said, "I like sweet potatoes. You just don't know what's good, bud."

"You don't like them any better than the rest of us," Ellen said. "You're just trying to get attention. Because we've got company."

"I do so like them. Bud."

"Bud," Ellen said. "Where does she get that 'bud' stuff? Brother, is she ever a goon."

"Ellen," Michael said, "I think you're adopting a very lousy strategy for a girl who wants a dog."

"You mean if I want a dog, I've got to eat sweet potatoes?"

"Yes," Michael said. "Something like that."

"Pass Hyatt the ham, Michael," Alice said.

"No, thanks. Nothing more." I looked at Michael. "You were right about marrying a woman who could cook," I said. "I almost got married once, only the lady wasn't worth her salt in a kitchen."

Alice looked at Ellen, to remind her of an item in the morning's briefing, and they got up and began clearing the table. It was suddenly very quiet, like an inland lake at sunset, and I was wondering how this would read. You would have to cut it, it was like looking for a nugget and uncovering a lode, but . . . Portrait of the Creative Artist at Home, I thought.

Michael was studying my face. "Want paper and pencil?" he said.

"What for?"

"To get this down. Before any of it slips away."

"Oh, you mean the story. I hadn't—"

"Hyatt, you are a bare-faced liar." He grinned at me and I grinned back.

Alice came back and set a piece of pie in front of me. It was a good six inches across at the base, and I looked at it with something like horror. "Look, Alice," I said, "I haven't been out in the open air today, and—"

"You wait till you taste that," Michael said. "If there is one thing Alice is good at, it's apple pie."

I tasted it, and Michael had a point, all right. This was the kind of pie they awarded blue ribbons to, with the September sun beating down on the canvas, and the bawl of the cattle coming at you from across the dust and the stubble, and the judges thoughtfully tasting the final entries, and the Crisco representative standing by with a contract in the breast pocket of his sweat-wrinkled Palm Beach. "My grandmother was good at apple pie," I said. "But not this good."

Alice Savage looked pleased again.

Cathy finished her sliver of pie and got off her chair. "Ellen's turn with the dishes," she said.

"Like so much fun," Ellen said.

"Listen," Michael said, "let's not start this routine again."

"I did them last night," Ellen said. "Remember, Mother? Dinner was late, and I didn't get to bed on time, and you said I wouldn't want to get up this morning. Remember?"

"I remember the part about your not wanting to get up," Alice said. She looked at Michael, and Michael shrugged.

"Don't ask me," he said. "I wasn't here. All I know is, it is certainly going to be hell when Susan gets old enough to start having her character strengthened."

"It's Saturday," Alice said. "And Ellen helped Monday. I guess it's Cathy's turn."

It seemed a complicated way to work it out, but Alice probably knew what she was doing.

"See, bee-bee brain," Ellen said.

"Ellen," Michael said, "it's settled now, let's just let it lie." He looked down the table at me. "Child psychologists," he said. He pushed his dessert plate aside. "You ought to do this for the *New Yorker*, Hyatt," he said. "It's going to go unappreciated in *Insight*."

I said I couldn't write the way they wanted you to write in the *New Yorker*. I said I didn't have the touch.

"Just take it down verbatim," he said. "Or say the word and I'll get a court stenographer out here. Because it will be the same script tomorrow night." He looked at Alice. "I'll wipe the dishes," he said.

She shook her head. "There's no reason why Cathy and Ellen can't help," she said. "You and Hyatt do something. Drive into town or something."

He got to his feet. "You'd better wear a jacket," he said. "It gets cool here after dark this time of year."

When I came back out of the bedroom and started into the kitchen, Alice was at the sink and Michael had come up behind her and put his arms around her. "I feel like a heel," he said, "walking out on you with all this—"

"All this what? This little mess of dishes?" She twisted around and put her arms loosely around his neck. "You developed a conscience on this trip, didn't you?" she said. "What went on in that city, anyway?"

"Nothing." He kissed her lightly. "Tell you what," he said. "We'll drive around a while and then stop back and pick you up. I hear there's a piano player at the Nicollet that's—"

"I get tired sitting in night clubs, Michael. Really, I'd just as soon—"

"Okay." There was a shrug in his voice, and then he saw me and dropped his arms. "We'll be back by ten," he said.

"All right," she said. "I'll be here."

It had stopped raining when we came out into the yard. Off in the west a few final streaks of sunset were coming through the clouds, and the air smelled washed and thin and crisp. Michael said we'd take the Packard this time so we could put the top down.

"I always feel like a heel walking out on her like that," he said.

"She doesn't seem to mind."

He swung the car east onto the blacktop. "Sometimes I feel like a heel, and other times I feel like I'll suffocate if I don't get out of there. But you're not married, so you probably wouldn't know what I'm talking about."

I didn't say anything to that.

"I like my kids," he said. "I really do. But sometimes it doesn't sound funny any more. Sometimes it sounds like a play rehearsal, and then it stops being funny." He eased the car across a wooden bridge and turned south. He wasn't driving so carefully any more. I had the feeling he was trying to put distance between himself and something. I slid down in the seat to get the good out of the windshield and thought, If you caught him in the right mood, a thousand-mile trip wouldn't drive you crazy after all.

"This girl," he said. "This Rachel. I suppose she's the one you almost married."

I smiled into the dusk, thinking of Rachel, thinking of that year in the Village. "I suppose she is," I said.

"A man doesn't give up a girl just because she can't cook."

"There were a couple of other reasons." We came into one of those curves with white posts and glass reflectors, and I watched the reflectors click by. "It clings to the curves," I said.

"Nervous?"

"I like speed. I only get nervous when you crawl." I put my head back on the seat. The clouds were scattered now, and the stars looked as if they had just been polished, and I was remembering those walks through the Village. We used to walk late in the evenings, with the stars out and the sad bars filling up with the lonely men and the Afro-American music that came up the narrow stairways out of the basements. "Rachel was a girl with ideals," I said. "She was always joining youth organizations, and she'd picked up those liberal phrases you hear when you haunt the teas on the third floor of the University Union. She thought prosperous magazines were run by reactionaries and fascists because some bisexual son-of-a-bitch with buck teeth and the Party line had

94

told her so. Also, she had gotten the idea somewhere that Hyatt Engel was the white hope of American letters, and she kept trying to explain to me how I was prostituting my talents."

He was driving very cleanly now. I couldn't tell whether he was listening to this or not.

"At first," I said, "everything was just talk over a dinner table. Then one night the honeymoon was over; I was suddenly tired of the speech, and I told her that for five thousand a year and a future, *Insight* was welcome to my virginity. She didn't say a word. She went into the bedroom, collected some blankets, came out and started making up a bed on the couch. When I got home the next afternoon, she was gone. The only word I ever got from her after that was a wedding announcement. I sent her a Japanese wood block. She was nuts about Oriental art."

"And you never got over it," he said.

"I got over it." I remembered the shape of her face and the blackness of her hair. "All right," I said. "Maybe not. But I'd do it again. Because it was either that or a graduate assistantship at the University and trying to finish a novel I didn't have in me. And because she suffered from myopia. She was incapable of looking life straight in the face. I don't think she knew even the dictionary definition of *ambition.*"

"Like to drive out the River Road?" he said. "It's nice this time of year."

"Sure."

"By the way," he said, "what *is* the dictionary definition?"

We were on the outskirts now, floating past a shopping center, and his question suddenly reminded me of Conneaut. "Rachel's father was a big shot," I said. "Loaded. Owned a foundry in Cleveland. My father was a section hand on the B & O." I looked at him. In that unreal light you get from street lights, his face looked thin and tired and strained, as if it wanted to fall apart and he was holding it together by pure will. "I went into my last semester in high school with a ninety-eight average," I said, "and there was a scholarship each year for the class valedictorian. Christ, how I wanted to go to college. But I got a seventy-eight in English my last semester, and some doctor's daughter beat me out by two-tenths of a point. When I went in to ask that teacher about my final, she claimed she'd thrown it away." Michael leaned and pushed a button on the dash and the lights came on. "She didn't need that scholarship. Didn't even *want* it. All she wanted was to make the speech that night. They say ambition's something that builds up in you over the years, but I think it came to me all at once. That week." I looked at him again, but I couldn't make out his face. "Who's writing whose story, anyway?" I asked. "I'm the one ought to be asking the questions."

He shrugged. "There's nothing to tell, Hyatt. I got married when I was twenty-three, and I spent three years in graduate school learning more and more about less and less, and after that I put in my days teaching freshman composition. Until one day I quit and wrote a book. That's my story."

He swung the car east onto the River Road, and we drove past the thirty-room houses which had once belonged to the lumber barons but were now up for sale, since the state's lumber supply had been reduced to eight-year-old pines artificially watered on the shores of Lake Harriet.

"I've got a favorite spot up ahead," he said. "A sharp curve —the road drops off sixty feet into the River. Sometimes I come out here at night and just sit in the dark and watch the lights on the River." He accelerated up the grade. "It's a really mean curve. Even the Cadillac would have trouble with that curve at more than thirty." He slowed again, and the clay-colored warning sign floated into our lights and out again. Then he pulled off onto the shoulder. "If you see what I mean," he said.

I saw what he meant. It was a nasty curve, all right. Michael had said that the drop was sixty feet, but at night it looked closer to half a mile. When he turned off the car lights, you could see the winking lights, like candles, on the barges sliding up the River, and when the airport beacon twenty miles away swung toward us, I could catch a glimpse of the River's surface in its light, looking like dull silver in candlelight.

"Cigarette?"

I shook my head. He struck a match and bent into the flame. In the flare you could see his nose and mouth, but the rest of his face was in the shadow, like a trick movie shot. "In the daytime this is just another bend in the River. But at night it's something special. I don't know why."

"I do," I said. "It's quiet out here. Out here there aren't any gadgets, any mortgaged houses, any hopes down the drain, any yesterday, any tomorrow, any civilization. Out here the earth has quit turning on its axis for a while. It is a spot half the world is looking for at this particular moment in history."

"Maybe that girl of yours was right," he said. "Maybe you should have written that novel." He flipped the cigarette out of the car. Then he crossed his arms on the wheel and rested his chin on his wrist. "You know," he said, "if you ever wanted to end it all, this would be a place for it."

"I suppose so. Personally, I've never experienced the temptation."

He let the quiet lie uneasily between us for a moment. "One night," he said, "I sat out here and worked it all out. I wanted to use it in a short story. With that stretch behind you you could be traveling eighty before you ever hit this curve, and you could aim straight at the rail and just close your eyes. There isn't a guardrail built that could stop a car with any weight to it, and if the drop didn't do it, you would wind up in twenty feet of water. It wouldn't take ten seconds, and it even figures the insurance angle. No investigator could prove anything but accidental death."

"I trust all this is purely hypothetical."

"Naturally. Just a story I was trying to work out. Because what reason could I have? I'm successful. I wrote a novel, and now I've got all that money." He was tangled in his own thoughts for a moment. Then he said, "Goddam it. Goddam it, anyway," and he might have been talking to himself, and then he said, "I'm going to tell you something. Only off the record."

"Go ahead."

97

"I think I'm going to leave my wife," he said.

I let that hit me in the stomach and settle before I trusted myself to speak. Then I said, "What's the matter between you and Alice? Another woman?" and I think my voice was casual.

"Does it always have to be another woman? Just once couldn't it be the simple fact of thirteen years?"

"All right. Though from what I've seen of Alice, I think you're crazy."

"I suppose," he said carefully, "I suppose this makes me an unprincipled bastard?"

"If it does," I said, "a good twenty percent of the national population falls into the category with you."

"Guess again," he said. "Guess again. I'm in a special class. I am one of those guys who live with a woman when the going is rough, wake up one morning and find myself successful, and then make tracks. The number of people in that category wouldn't fill the boxes in Northrup Auditorium." He slapped the steering wheel with the heel of his hand. "Alice doesn't have this coming to her," he said. "She hasn't earned it. She works hard at marriage, and she never complained, not even when we were so dirt poor that she had to wear a slip around the house because we didn't have a spare two dollars to buy her a housedress. The only thing she ever asked from life was security. Thirty dollars a week, just so it was every week." He studied the end of his cigarette, then flipped it away.

"We never have agreed on what life was all about. She doesn't want to be rich, she only wants something coming in every month. That's why she doesn't approve of writing for a living. She doesn't trust it. It's a gamble. I could write a best seller every two years for the next twenty, and she would still feel the same way. Because people like us aren't supposed to make a lot of money and get our names in the papers. If we do, there is going to be a day of reckoning." He put his head back on the seat. "Or maybe she thinks that if I'm famous every woman in the country is going to have a try at

98

taking me away from her. And she's afraid she can't compete any more."

"I'll take one of your smokes now," I said.

"They're on the dash."

I helped myself. He looked across the seat at me. "I am a bastard," he said. "Aren't I?"

"That's something you have to define for yourself, isn't it?"

"I suppose so." He sat up and started the car. "Remember," he said. "Off the record. Because it would be a hell of a way to break it to her, wouldn't it? On the pages of a national magazine?"

I remembered Alice Savage standing at the sink with her arms loosely around Michael's neck and her face up and the gray eyes smiling. "I guess it would," I said.

When we came into the living room, Alice was sitting on her feet in an oversized chair, watching a couple of TV characters running around on some kind of scaffolding. Alice wasn't exactly fragile, but sitting like that in that chair she looked lonely and forgotten, like a twelve-year-old at a cocktail party. But maybe I was reading into the poem now. Maybe she was just in a new context for me.

"Hello, you guys," she said. "Back already?"

"We just drove out the River Road," Michael said. He had stopped in the kitchen doorway and was looking down at the top of her head. "I showed him my bend in the River."

"What Michael sees in that place is beyond me," she said to me. "You can't even *see* the River. Not after dark."

"Can we turn that TV off now?" Michael said.

"I don't care."

He walked across the room and clicked off the set. Then he looked at me. "What to drink, Hyatt?"

"Anything."

"We're rich now," he said. "We've got anything."

"Veuve Cliquet '29," I said.

"I've got a bottle of Pol Roger, but it isn't iced."

99

"I was kidding. Make it Canadian Club and water."

He looked at Alice. She shook her head, and he crossed the room again. "Be careful what you tell him," he said. "Remember, anything you say may be used in a story." He disappeared into the kitchen. I could hear him going downstairs into the basement.

"He spent a week stocking that cellar," Alice said. "I'll bet he spent three hundred dollars. He's got more variety than a state liquor store."

"Well," I said, "a cellar is part of the secret of gracious living."

"I wouldn't know. I don't drink." Her eyes shifted away from mine. "I suppose you saw a lot of him. In New York."

"No. Only once."

"He never tells me anything about his trips," she said. "It's always like Christmas when he gets back, but he never tells me anything. Personally, I'd prefer a little news to a sixty-dollar negligee. Unless she's in a hard-boiled novel, where can a girl wear a sheer negligee?"

"Maybe he doesn't think you're interested in his trips."

She was looking at her nails. "This editor of his," she said. "This Jean Reynolds. What's she like?"

"She's a career girl. There are two million of them in New York. Jean is just like the ten percent of them who are something besides secretaries."

"Is she bright?"

"In publishing you're either bright or you're fired."

"I suppose she's good at talking about the things Michael's interested in?"

"I suppose she is. That's her job."

"And I suppose she's pretty?"

"I suppose she is. Though I imagine Kay Anderson would beat her out in a beauty contest. Kay's a beautiful woman, if you like your women made out of marble. Why all the questions about Jean Reynolds? What's worrying you, Alice?"

"Nothing." She raised her head, almost defiantly. "What have I got to be worried about? Michael's in love with a typewriter. Sometimes I almost wish it were another woman. An-

100

other woman I might have a chance of competing against."

I heard Michael's step on the stair, and then he poked his head into the room. "Is Seven Crown all right?" he said.

"Sure. You can hardly tell the difference."

"I could have sworn I had some Canadian Club," he said. He looked at Alice. "I trust you kept your lips sealed?" He was smiling.

"I did," she said. "All I told him was what it's like, living with a writer."

"I could have told him that. It's hell." He disappeared into the kitchen, and I sat there and looked at Alice and felt sorry for all the wives in this country who had seen thirty-five and had forgotten what you did about holding a man. If they had ever known. Then Michael came back with the drinks.

"Sure you won't have anything, Alice?" he said. "A Coke, maybe?"

"Nothing." She put a hand up and patted a strand of hair into place, and I thought, the automatic, unconscious gesture of woman everywhere, the left feint of the feminine world. "I'm tired," she said. "I think I'll go to bed. Coming, Michael?"

"Hyatt and I may sit up and talk a while."

"Not too late, Michael. You need some rest."

"Don't worry about us, Alice." He watched her cross the room. Then he sat there, slouched down in his chair, staring at nothing in particular. "You tired?" he asked.

"Not especially."

"I don't feel like going to bed yet. I feel like nursing a couple of drinks into the small hours and talking to somebody."

"I'm a willing listener." I hoped this wasn't going to be off-the-record, too.

"I'm like Hemingway. I know a lot of good stories." He was twisting the plain gold band on his left ring finger. "A man lives thirty-six years, and then he comes to some kind of crossroad in his life, and he feels he has to work things out. In his mind. Only where do you begin?"

I settled back in my chair. "Why not at the beginning?" I said. "That's where most good stories start."

101

Michael Savage   II

7 DURING MICHAEL'S EARLY
boyhood, his father was a farmer, but the farm was slowly
absorbed by interest and drought and market fluctuations,
and in the mid-twenties his parents sold out and moved in
on his aunt and uncle in Schenectady, where his uncle got
his father a job with General Electric. Then they moved to
Columbus, Ohio, where his father went to work for a manu-
facturer of mining equipment. In 1927, when they promoted
him out of the shop and into the accounting department, his
father bought a house on the South Side with a down pay-
ment borrowed from the uncle.

Somewhere along here sharp memory began for Michael;
of this period in his life he could recall the most minutely
painful details. He could remember a question on a math
quiz, the exact color of a teacher's hand, the expression on
the faces of two seniors in the toilet who were sneaking drinks
of Dago red between classes. He could remember the feel of
a seat against his legs (the seats were always too small for
him), and the smell of a crowded school bus. He could remember all the activities he had tried out for and failed at:
how he had stumbled through his lines at tryout for the junior play and been assigned to scenery; how on the school paper they had told him he could solicit for advertising; how
for two years, until he got a paper route, he had reported
faithfully for football in the fall and baseball in the spring
and had practiced grimly for weeks and sat on the bench on

Saturdays and finally, in the middle of each season, turned in his uniform.

He could remember all the girls he had been in love with, though only once had he asked one of them for a date. That once had been in the tenth grade, when he asked a girl named Ina to go to a movie with him. The girl had not even answered him. She just giggled convulsively, and after that he never asked another girl or even spoke to one. Sometimes, at night, he lay in the dark and looked at their faces in his mind, and the ache in him drifted clear into his knees.

The house his father hung grimly onto all those years was buried on a street dedicated to six-room frames, a street owned by bank clerks, vacuum-cleaner salesmen, bookkeepers and school teachers. Michael always thought of that house as a symbol of his father's life. His father bought it in the middle of a South Side real-estate boom, and by October of 1929 he had reduced the mortgage by five hundred dollars and the debt to his brother-in-law by two hundred and forty. But by 1931 payments on the house were taking half his monthly income, and you could rent more pretentious places for twenty a month, and what his father still owed on the place was a third more than he could have gotten out of it.

A bright man would have let it go. His father preferred to sweat out the payments and putter around the place after he got home from work, trying without observable success to prop up the garage or straighten out the warped doors or trim the aphis-infested, scraggly spirea which was all the landscaping on the front lawn; and when he wasn't puttering, he liked to worry about the place going back to the bank. In the evenings he would sit at the head of the dinner table, gray-haired, dry-skinned, stooped, with fear in his pale blue eyes and ink stains on his fingers, and explain to his wife about how they were laying men off at the plant every day. And Michael's mother, short and getting too heavy, with startling black hair piled in a braided knot above her round, shining, Germanic face, would sit at the foot of the table and look worried with him.

And in the bright, naked, painful light, Michael would listen with bent head, feeling something like sadness for his father, and lying beside that sadness a faint, onion-tissue layer of bitterness against something he couldn't identify.

His father worried for several years about getting laid off before it happened.

Michael got home from school very late that spring night. When he came in, dinner was already on the table and his father was sitting at the head, looking thin and tired and worried. In the middle of the meal his father asked if he had delivered his papers yet, and Michael said no, he was going to after supper.

"You are late with your papers too much, Michael," his father said. "People may complain. People like to get a paper in the afternoon."

"Let them. The sales aren't till tomorrow, are they?" The paper he delivered was one of those phenomena of the depression called a shopping news.

"I think you should get home earlier," his father said. "It is important now."

He looked into his father's eyes. "Why?"

"Because it is a rule. If this was not important, it would not be a rule in the manual."

"They've never said anything yet, Pa."

"There are a lot of boys who would appreciate this job. Three, four dollars a week, a lot of money for a boy to be making these days. There are grown men who would be glad to earn three dollars every week."

"Come out with it, Pa," he said softly. "What's happened? Over there at that crummy plant?"

His father's eyes were on his fingers. "They laid me off today," he said.

He felt the sickness hit him in the stomach like a fist.

"All the money we have coming in now is from your paper route," his father said. "So it is important—"

"I know." And that is that, he thought, and now I will have to leave school at three-thirty and walk the two miles home to save carfare. And tomorrow morning he will be up at four-thirty, with a quarter in his pocket for carfare and a newspaper, and he will be standing in the lines by six, and at night he will come home with the tiredness strong enough to kill everything but the panic in his eyes. Now I will never get my hair cut at all, he thought, and Ma will start patching and then repatching this sweater, and we'll struggle along for a few weeks on what I earn, and then we'll go on relief. Ma will be the one to go to the store, he thought, and she will order the cheap flour and the lard and the crackers and the day-old bread. And I can see the face of that goddam clerk while he makes out the relief form.

"I don't like this, Michael," his father said. "Taking money from a boy. It is a bad time when a man is not allowed to earn a living for his family."

"It's not your fault," Michael said. He clenched his hand suddenly. "Goddam them," he said. "Goddam them, anyway."

"Please, Michael," his mother said gently.

"Why does it have to be you, Pa? Seven years you've worked there, why—"

"It is a bad time for everybody. You can't blame the company. They are losing money every day."

"I feel sorry for them," Michael said. "In their big houses, their kids driving cars to school. I am crying for them."

Against the white cloth, his father's hand closed and then opened again, as if, sitting there and looking down at it, he had momentarily lost faith in its existence and had obeyed a compulsion to test it. "Let me help deliver the papers, Michael," he said.

"No."

"I have read the manual. If we are going to live on this money, it is only right—"

He avoided his father's eyes. "No."

His father leaned forward a little. "You are a good son. I am sorry that I should make you ashamed of me."

"I'm not ashamed. It isn't that—"

"You are ashamed of me. It is in your eyes."

He got to his feet. I am not ashamed of you, he thought, I am not ashamed, *I am not ashamed*. He turned and went upstairs to change into the sweater which was not out at the elbows yet. He thought, as he put it on, that he was almost through high school and had never owned a suit in his life.

When he went down into the basement, his father was there folding his papers for him.

"You don't have to do that," he said.

"I am not out on the street. Nobody can see me doing this."

For a moment he almost felt like crying. "You're not folding them right," he said. "Look. Like this."

"This way?" His father folded one clumsily.

"Yes. Something like that."

"If I helped deliver them we could be through in half the time."

"It's a boy's job, Pa."

His father smiled sadly. "I can't afford pride, Michael," he said. "Pride is expensive. You have to be rich."

He reached out, as if to put his hand on his father's shoulder, and then he stooped and picked up the canvas sack.

"When you are older," his father said, "you will learn that because a man does not have a big job and a fine house, this does not mean he is a failure."

"Stop saying that," he said. "I don't think you're a failure." He started up the stairs, leaning against the weight of the papers. On the landing he turned and looked down the cellar stairs. As long as he lived he would never forget the dry, bitter anger, not at his father but at the world, when he looked down on his father, on his knees, slowly, clumsily trying to fold a paper the way Michael had shown him.

That summer he got a job clerking in an A & P. The job paid fifteen dollars a week, and he had been lucky to get it. He knew this for a fact because the manager told him so. The manager made a point at least twice a day of telling his clerks how lucky they were, and one Saturday night, when Michael sat down at eleven at night to the first food he had tasted since a sandwich at noon, his father pointed it out to him, too.

"You are lucky," his father said. "A boy falling into a job like this. It is an opportunity."

"I guess it is." He did not look up from the plate of warmed-up beans. He had been on his feet for sixteen hours; his soles felt hot and itchy, and the calves of his legs ached.

"There are grown men who would appreciate the job," his father said. "At the plant they are standing in line every morning when I go to work. Sometimes they get there at four in the morning."

"I know, Pa," he said wearily. "I'm lucky." He pushed his plate aside.

"Do you see it as maybe a job with opportunity?" his father asked. Without looking at him Michael knew his father was leaning on the answer.

"I see it," he said carefully, "I see it as just another job."

His father sighed. "Would you like another cup of coffee?"

"No," Michael said. "No, thanks. I've had plenty."

"You are almost a man, Mike. You will be meeting a girl soon. It is time you were thinking of how you are going to support a family."

He looked into his father's intent, earnest face, and smiled wryly. "I haven't met one yet."

"But you will. You are—"

He turned in his chair, abruptly, facing into the uncompromising light that spilled down into his father's face. "There are things more important than girls," he said. "Girls can wait."

"For what, Mike?"

"For one thing," he said, "for me to get the hell out of the grocery business."

"A rolling stone gathers no moss, Michael," his father said.

"No crap, either," he said. "Remember that. A rolling stone they don't use while there's a profit in it and then throw out when there isn't. If you're a rolling stone, they don't do you the favor of letting you keep their crummy books four days a week, like they are doing for you now. At twenty cents an hour."

110

"What has happened to you, Michael? What have I done to you, you should be bitter like this?"

"Nothing," he said. "It isn't you, Pa." He reached across the table and touched his father's hand, briefly and tentatively. Then he drew it back self-consciously. "I'm going to college in the fall," he said.

"College is for rich boys," his father said. "Where will you get the money to go to college?"

"The manager said I could keep my job. Part time. I can make it if I live at home." He put a hand in his pocket and pulled out his week's wages, the two fives, the four crumpled ones, and laid the bills on the table. "Give this to Ma," he said.

His father shook his head. "We have taken enough of your money," he said. "I am working again, you keep it. Put it in the bank. Save it for college."

"You're not out of the woods yet. You'd better—"

"Perhaps this is wise," his father said softly. "If you go to the university, you will maybe be an important man someday. A doctor, maybe."

"Maybe."

"It would be nice to have a son who was a doctor. Doctors do well. They make a good living. They are respected."

"Look, Pa," he said, "I don't know what—" Then he saw that his father wasn't listening and he stopped. "Sure," he said, without bitterness. "It would be fine."

For a long time the university was a blur of impressions, a bewildering sprawl of campus where all the buildings looked alike. It took him two weeks to lose his feeling of being lost, and a lot longer than that to convince himself that he belonged here, that he had not wandered into a formal dance without a tie on. The feeling of not belonging went with him wherever he went: into his classes, where the girls wore cashmere sweaters and tiny, jeweled pledge pins, and where the men sprawled in their seats with one foot on the chair ahead and said, "Hey, Jim, gotcher theme today?" or "Wanna write one fer me? There's a buck in it"; to lunch, where he waited

111

in line for milk and then sat in a far corner of the cafeteria, chewing methodically on the sandwiches brought from home, feeling conspicuous among the chattering students, all of whom, it seemed, could afford to buy their lunches except him. Sometimes, waiting in the afternoons for a streetcar, watching the convertibles slide across High Street and up fraternity row, he would ask himself why he did not sell his books, go home, and start working full time again at the A & P.

But in the middle of the loneliness he found out what he could do.

The instructor in his freshman composition course that first term had a new M.A. and a lot of enthusiasm. Like most of the graduate assistants he did not give away A's, but he gave one to Michael. The assignment had been an autobiography, and the writing of it had taken hold of Michael. Maybe because of that (or maybe just out of that ignorance from which courage is sometimes born) he had deserted the formula and had instead seized upon three incidents—a single moment while waiting for a streetcar at 15th and High, another moment outside a class, a third in the cafeteria. He had not known, except subconsciously, what he was doing; he had not known he was writing an impressionistic short story. He only knew when he was done with it that he felt clean inside, as if he had just gotten back from a long, satisfactory vacation.

The instructor was twenty-four, and he was specializing in 15th-Century poetry; he did not recognize the story for what it was, either. Instead he read it to the class and tried to explain, vaguely but enthusiastically, why he had graded it A, while the students looked around and tried to guess who it belonged to and Michael sat in the back of the room feeling warm inside.

When he stopped after class to pick up his paper, there were three girls ahead of him, waiting their turn to argue about grades. The instructor waved them aside and handed Michael his paper.

"Good job, Savage," he said. "Hell of a good job."

"Thank you, sir," Michael said. He felt very friendly toward this young man, and then he was aware of the students grouped around the desk, looking coldly at him.

"Damned fine piece of work," the instructor said. He studied Michael a moment longer. Then he evidently decided that he had nailed his point, and he swung back to the girl.

"Like I said, Professor Stewart," the girl said, "I worked hours and hours on this theme and only got a D. My last—"

"How many hours?" the instructor said.

"Well," the girl said, "five or six. Anyway—"

"How long did you spend on your paper, Savage?"

"I don't know," Michael said. "Quite a while. I got interested—"

"Approximately," the instructor said.

"Fifteen or twenty hours, I suppose. It's—"

"I don't think that's *reasonable*," the girl said shrilly. "I don't think you're being *fair*, Mr. Stewart. I've got three other courses. If I spent that on every assignment, I'd be studying all the time."

"Yes," the instructor said. "You would. A students frequently do." He looked at Michael. "You might give some thought to sophomore creative writing, Savage. You have real ability."

The second girl in line turned and looked Michael full in the face. She was red-haired, a little too thin but calculatingly pretty, and she stared at him as if she were considering an investment. It was as if she were looking behind his cheap clothing and deciding that with a haircut he might not be so bad looking after all. He stood there a moment, hating her for it but letting her look. Then he turned away—but for the first time in his life he sensed that he could have asked a pretty girl for a date without being absolutely sure that she would say no.

It is given to only a few teachers to become campus legends, and to even fewer to achieve this while they are still alive. But Professor Horn became a legend in a surprisingly few years. He was a tall, emaciated man with a long, dour, preacher's face, a violent shock of white hair, hot eyes, and skeletal, blue-veined, long-fingered hands. He had a wide mouth that had once been dryly humorous, but by the time Michael met him it was a line pulled tight across his face and sideways. After you sat in his classes a while, you found yourself staring at the mouth and waiting for something, a twitch maybe. The twitch never came, but you got into the habit of watching for it, of *knowing* that the spastic ripple would occur sometime.

Once Horn had been an energetic, voluble young man with some notions about perfectionism. But by Michael's time English 24 had been his property for twenty years (he had written a novel in his youth and then developed a course which none of the scholars in the department wanted), and in those twenty years he had put his follies behind him. Now he taught with a bitter and accumulated weariness somewhere between indifference and smoldering rage. Now, when he criticized a student's effort, it was as if he carried within him the weight of all the fiction he had never written. Now he was just a man who disliked students in general and journalism majors in particular, and who expressed himself acidly on the subjects of co-eds and Greek-letter organizations and subsidized athletics and his colleagues and slicked-up imitations of Hemingway and first drafts and late papers.

Horn had his bad days, of course, days when the flatness would lie in his voice and he would just be an emaciated figure leaning into the half light with the skin stretched almost translucent across the bony structure of his face and behind the parchment the tiredness in the veins where the blood ought to have been. But he had as many days when he was in form. On those days he would stride into class, dump a stack of papers on the desk, and begin with the observation that America had produced no major writer since Henry James and, if the work in front of him were any indication, he took a dim view of the immediate literary future. Then he would separate a paper from the stack (you held your breath waiting to see if it was yours) and begin to read. He would read slowly and with feeling, lingering over the worst passages, the most obvious clichés, and when he had finished he would stand motionless while the silence in front of him swirled and settled like cigar smoke around a poker table in the back room. Then he would pick the work apart, delicately, and his students would glance nervously at their watches and hope that he would not have time to start on another story.

He was even better in conferences. That was where the polished apple of delusion was sliced for you and the two wormy halves laid neatly out for your inspection. That was where the hole card was turned over and the hand pushed delicately toward the center of the table and there, across the chips, you could have yourself a look at God's bright, irrevocable, and bitter truth.

Michael turned in five stories and got steady B's that term; otherwise Horn ignored him. The day he reported to Horn's office to pick up his final paper, he stood outside for a minute and took a breath before putting his hand gingerly on the doorknob. Then he opened the door. Horn swung around in his chair; behind him the bright, cold light of a December afternoon double exposed the lines of his face, and when Michael started across the linoleum, he could feel his heart in him. Then Horn leaned and squinted up out of the light into his face, and one hand twitched to indicate the empty chair beside the desk, and in that instant Michael felt the nervousness go out of him. For he had gotten the impression —perhaps from the incline of the head—that he was looking at something which had been hung together on wires. The hand, lying against the brown of the desk, looked like a hand out of which the blood has been pumped and that now lies folded against the dark burial suit. When he sat down, he did not feel nervous any more; he only felt a little sad.

Horn pulled Michael's paper off the stack and slid it toward him, and Michael saw the meticulous A in the upper corner. "An A?" he said blankly.

"I was under the impression that the symbol was still drawn in that fashion. Or have we discarded the Roman alphabet along with other conventions?"

"No, sir. I mean, I didn't mean—"

Horn's raised hand interrupted him. "I know what you meant," he said. "But I have been known to give the grade. More reluctantly than my sentimental colleagues perhaps, but—"

"I didn't mean that, either," Michael said.

"Tell me," Horn said softly, "what did you mean?"

Michael looked at the grade again. There was no note under it. "I guess I didn't think this was worth an A."

"Maybe it isn't. Maybe I am just making allowances."

Michael forced himself to look into Horn's pale, hot eyes. "I wonder," he said, "if you would mind explaining what you mean by that, sir? Because I thought my last story was better than this one, and I wonder why you didn't."

"Why do you think your last story was better?"

"I don't know. It just felt better. You know how you feel sometimes."

"Yes," Horn said. "I know how you feel sometimes." He chuckled. "Perhaps you would like me to change that grade?"

On an impulse Michael pushed the paper toward him. "Go ahead," he said. "The grade's not what's important to me."

Horn chuckled again. "Now you are impertinent."

"Yes, sir."

"I believe that you are intentionally impertinent."

"Yes, sir. I believe I am, sir."

There was amusement in Horn's eyes. "You are an unusual young man," he said. "I think that I shall give you an A in this course. Though I'll be doing you no favor since you will then leave here with illusions about your ability."

Michael put a hand on the edge of the desk. "Sir," he said, "would you explain what you mean by illusions? Or allowances? It's important to me."

Horn tilted backward in his chair. "After a man has taught twenty years," he said, "he gives A's for many reasons, most of them irrelevant. Sometimes because he has too many girls in his classes who write glibly about nothing and will someday make fifty cents a word for pieces bought to space the ads in the *Ladies' Home Journal*. Or sometimes because anyone who can write a complete sentence stands out from all our fugitives from trade schools. Or sometimes just because he is tired and wants to give the lie to fraternity-house rumors." He paused. "I gather that you have hopes of becoming a writer."

"Yes, sir."

"Probably you are dreaming of writing the Great American Novel any day now. You no doubt plan to spend all of three hours a day for six months on it. You are sure it will make your fortune, and beautiful women will fall effortlessly into your bed." He swung abruptly out of his chair and walked to the window. "I wrote a novel once," he said. "I was very little older than you, only twenty-seven, and the reviewers said there was some hope for American fiction after all. The novel sold sixteen hundred copies, and I started in right away on another one. I worked very hard for three years on it, and they rejected it." He turned back abruptly, and his lips twisted, as if he were experiencing pain. "I was married by then, and my wife was not happy about my writing for a living." He stood there a moment longer, and then he came back and sat down. "We have a publication on campus," he said. "Called the *Quill*. It has published nothing but bilge for God knows how many consecutive issues, but it might be interested in some of the things you have done for me."

"I'll submit them," Michael said, "if you really think they're good enough."

"They're good enough," Horn said. "Oh, my, yes, they're good enough." He smiled crookedly. "If you can locate the editor," he said, "tell him I sent you over. I understand that the fraternity boys who run the magazine suffer from eyestrain. They have been known to let material lie buried in the slush pile for six or seven months. By the way, do you have a girl?"

"No, sir."

"Very good," Horn said. "If you would be a writer, avoid acquiring a girl."

"I don't think that will be much of a problem," Michael said.

"You have a certain raw talent. Ten years of hard work

117

might develop it into something. You will probably get discouraged and learn a formula and become another fifth-rater, after which you will undoubtedly make a lot of money, but you have something worth working on. Only stay away from women. If you are bothered by natural urges, get thee to a brothel. I am told that any taxi driver—but no, never mind."

Michael decided to obey the injunction. The embarrassed silence hung between them a moment, like smoke.

"If you ever lose your reason and decide to marry," Horn said, "follow Voltaire's advice and marry a peasant girl who will be so eternally grateful for meat once a week that she will never talk you into trying to earn a living any other way." He looked down at his hands. "Such as teaching," he said.

"Is there anything else?" Michael asked.

"No," Horn said. "No, there isn't anything else."

Michael turned at the door. Horn was sitting there, with one hand resting whitely on the desk and the winter light behind him. But Michael could make out the mouth, and just before he stepped into the hall, he saw the twitch. Or thought he did, for it was like the indistinct blur you see when you are looking off across the water toward the reed bed just at dusk, and the insect, traveling fast, draws a tangent along the arc which is the edge of your vision, and after it is past, you wonder whether you really saw something or whether it was just the jump of a tired muscle. And standing there, he knew again that tired anger he had known before in the presence of his father. There, he thought, goes the wreck of a mediocre man. Then he stepped backward into the hall.

A few days later Michael walked across campus to the third floor of the Union and the *Quill* office.

The office was big enough to hold two desks, some typewriters on movable tables, and a big library table, but it looked small because it was littered with galley proofs and layout sheets and yellow dog. The office had a cluttered, weary look; it looked like the editorial office of a weekly with a half-million circulation. Or rather, it looked like a college boy's notion of the editorial room of a weekly with a half-million circulation.

118

And the boy sitting behind one of the desks with his feet up and his hat on looked like a college boy's idea of a big-time magazine editor. He was wearing a sport shirt and gabardine slacks, though it was four months too early for either, and he was chewing gum with a slow, sidewise swipe of his jaw. He did not move when Michael came into the doorway. He did not even open his eyes, for he had probably seen a movie once and now he was under the impression that what an editor did was give his staff hell once a week and the rest of the time sit on his can amidst the clutter of a busy office with his feet up and his hat on and his eyes closed. But he knew Michael was there, all right. He knew because after Michael had stood there for a length of time sufficient to mark the caste distinction between the editor of *Quill* and just one more of the anonymous fees out there on campus, the editor opened his eyes, looked at him, and then closed them again. Then he raised a hand, fumbled in his shirt pocket, came up with a cigarette which looked as if it had been homeless since a week ago Sunday, and lit it, still without opening his eyes. Then he said, "Something for you? A copy of this month's rag, maybe?"

"No," Michael said. "I've got a story."

The editor opened his eyes and then closed them again, quickly. "No kidding," he said. "You mean all written out? On paper?"

"Yes. What should I do with it?"

"How the hell do I know?" the editor said. "I haven't read it. Prob'ly revise it."

"I have."

"Oh," the editor said. "Is it any good?"

"I don't know."

"You're a cautious bastard, aren't you? Do you *think* it's any good?"

"Would I be submitting it if I didn't?"

"Hell, yes. It happens daily. Everybody on this campus is print hungry. They get a C-plus on a freshman theme, right away they want us to give it the lead in next month's issue." He opened his eyes and cocked his head and examined the

119

toes of his tan-and-white oxfords. "Is it funny?" he said. "Is there a laugh in it?"

"No."

"They like humor. They put out two bits, they want cheer. None of this lost-generation crud—despair they can get for nothing these days. How long is it?"

"Three thousand."

"We like them around two. With a surprise ending."

"Well," Michael said, "this one is raw tragedy with an ending you can smell from paragraph one, and it can't be cut. Sorry to have taken up your time."

"Anything can be cut," the editor said. "Nothing was ever written that can't be cut." He said this with great profundity, with that mixture of dogmatic assertion and calm certainty which, if it is not wisdom, can pass for it, and Michael thought, The son-of-a-bitch has heard that somewhere. Or read it. If he can read. "Of course," the editor said, "leave it if you want. I'll try to get to it this week. Don't call me. I'll call you."

"Forget it," Michael said. "I only brought it over because Professor Horn told me to."

"Who? Who told you to?"

"Professor Horn."

"Did he now? What'd he give you on it?"

"An A."

"You're a liar. Horn hasn't given an A in seven years, and there is a rumor that a nationally famous humorist who is considered the second finest stylist writing in English today only got a B out of him, and if you claim an A from Horn, it is a goddam, bald-faced lie."

"All right," Michael said.

The editor let his feet slide off the desk and straightened up. "I took Horn's course," he said. "He gave me a C. A C, and he told me in conference that if I ever published, the exploitation of America's diminishing lumber supply would be on my conscience. Did he honest-to-God give you an A on something?"

"No," Michael said. "It was a goddam, bald-faced lie."

"I've been waiting three years to see what kind of a story Horn would give an A to. You got any more?"

"Five. But he only gave me B's on those."

"Maybe we could use you." He held out a hand, and Michael passed over the manuscript. "They're supposed to be typewritten," the editor said.

"I haven't got a typewriter."

"You can buy one for two bucks down and a dollar a month."

"I haven't got two bucks down and a dollar a month."

"Hell, come over and use the office machines. They're college property, no skin off my teeth." He looked down at the manuscript. "Jesus Christ, an A out of Horn. I can use that in next month's column. I can start it out, 'Michael Savage, our new contributing editor'— You want to be a contributing editor?"

"I don't know. What does a contributing editor do?"

"Writes us four, five stories a year. And reads the slop that flows in here, if he's got no regard for his twenty-twenty vision. And writes my column if he runs out of things to keep him occupied." He put his feet back on the desk and cocked his head. "Interested?"

Michael looked at the manuscript, lying an inch from the editor's heel. "Hadn't you better read that first?"

"Why? I'd run it if it read like Henry James."

"All right," Michael said. "When do I start?"

"Take off your sweater," the editor said, "and roll up your sleeves. There's a pile of slush waiting for you right now, genius."

Michael never had another conversation with Horn. Six months later, Horn stopped meeting his classes. He was out two full days before the chairman tried to get hold of him by phone; failing that, he notified the police, for Horn had been living alone since the death of his wife. Later that afternoon two policemen broke in the front door and cut Horn down from the living-room light fixture. The next day, in a front-page story, an acquaintance of Horn's guessed that the cause had been the death of Horn's wife. Horn had been very hard hit by the death of his wife, the acquaintance said, and he had apparently lived with her absence as long as he could bear it.

8

Alice Graham was listed as assistant business manager, which
meant that in return for manning the homemade stands with
pretty freshman girls on publication days and for collecting
and counting the monthly take, she received forty-five dollars
a year. She was a moderately pretty girl with a square face and
dark hair and a body that was firm-breasted at the moment but
that she had clearly better never let get out of control. She
did not hang around the office much. In fact, she showed up
exactly once a month, coming into the *Quill* office promptly
at one o'clock, carrying the canvas sack the way you might
carry sixty-cent eggs. She did not speak to anyone when she
came in, only nodded vaguely toward whoever happened to be
at Don Burt's desk. Then she would go directly to the library
table, crossing the room as if she were traveling by compass,
and dump out the money. She would count it twice, handling
the coins almost affectionately. She would put it back in the
sack together with the slip on which she had entered the totals
in tiny, meticulous figures. Then she would cross the room
and drop the sack on Don Burt's desk. She would nod once
more, ambiguously, to whoever happened to be in the room
at the moment, and then leave quickly, the way people do
when they have somewhere to go. There was nothing obtru-
sive about the way she would come into the office; in fact,
she always managed to give the impression of walking into a
deserted room in the middle of the night. And yet, whenever

123

she showed up, the conversation would die for a moment and then, when it was resurrected, would be as cautious as if the speakers had just been talking about her. And when she put the money on the desk and nodded and left, everyone would watch her go out. Sometimes, after she had disappeared, they would look at each other, and maybe somebody would shrug or gesture with the palm of a hand.

The first time Michael watched the monthly visitation, he looked at Don Burt and said, "Who the hell was that?"

"Alice Graham. She's assistant business manager."

"What's the matter with her?"

Don shrugged.

A month later, when she came into the office, she was a half hour late. Michael was tilted against the wall behind the library table when she appeared, and he kept his eyes on her when she crossed the room and sat down across the table from him.

"You're late today," Burt said, from across the room.

She did not look up, but her hand, poised over the coins, froze momentarily. "I know." Her voice was cool and distantly polite, like the voice of an experienced telephone operator.

Michael let the front legs of his chair drop. "Why don't I help you with that?" he said.

This time she did look up. Her glance was as brief and as impersonal as her voice. "I can manage. Thanks, anyway."

"You're late. I just thought I could give you a hand."

"It's my job."

"All right."

Her expression relaxed a little. "I have to be sure it's right," she said. "If it doesn't check out, I'm accountable."

"Sure." He looked at Don Burt and shrugged.

He sat in the quiet room another twenty minutes, watching her count and roll the money and then carry the sack to the desk and drop it four inches from Don Burt's shoe.

Don studied the sack indifferently. "Does it check?" he said.

"Yes."

"You're sure?" Don said. "You only counted it once."

Her eyes slid away from his. Watching her, Michael caught the tremor of her lower lip.

Don Burt touched the sack with the toe of his shoe. "I better just leave it out. You can come back—"

"Leave her alone, Don," Michael said.

Don looked across the room at him. He was smiling. "I'm only protecting her interests," he said. "She's accountable; we wouldn't want her shy a nickel, for Chrissake."

"To some people a nickel is a lot of money. Goddam it, Don, leave her alone."

He studied the set of her shoulders when she crossed the office. Then he got to his feet.

She was twenty feet down the hall when he got to the door, and walking very fast. When he called, she turned and waited, one hand resting on the stair railing.

"I'm late," she said. "I have to be at work in forty minutes."

"All right," he said. "I just wanted to say I was sorry. I—"

"Sorry?" she said. "Whatever for?" She turned away from him, and he walked around her and turned and faced her, blocking her path with an arm.

"Don't pay any attention to Don Burt," he said. "Don saw a movie once, and—"

She smiled at him. The smile was tentative, but it was a smile. "I get docked," she said, "when I'm late to work."

"All right." He stepped aside.

But she didn't move.

"Last year," she said, "they claimed I was short and I had to make it up. A dollar and a half. That's a lot of money to me. I'm working my way through, and—"

"I know how much it is," he said. "I'm getting through the same way." He looked up into her face. "Would you be doing anything Friday night?"

"I don't know. Why?"

"Maybe," he said slowly, "if you aren't doing anything, you'd like to see a movie. A neighborhood, because fifty cents is about what I can manage to scrape together."

"A neighborhood is better, isn't it?" she said. "Usually they have a double feature at a neighborhood."

"Seven-thirty?"

"Seven-thirty would be ideal," she said. She started down the stairs. He leaned on the railing and watched her. He liked the way she walked.

"By the way," he said, just before she got to the landing, "where do you live?"

She looked up the stairwell at him. She was smiling. "The Phi Beta Phi house," she said. "On Fifteenth. And if you have any trouble finding any money, we can always take a walk. I love to walk."

He grinned at her. "I think maybe I can manage a half a dollar," he said.

Alice Graham was working her way through school by waiting table at the sorority to which she had pledged—and to which she clung the way people cling to the last splinter of a bitterly remembered and better past—and by clerking in a downtown department store. But that spring and summer she found time to see him once or twice a week, sometimes for a movie, more often for long walks out past the Big Bear. The walks continued into the summer because she did not go home to Elyria in June. She had a full-time job at the department store, at seventeen a week, and by eating on six she could save nearly a hundred and fifty dollars toward her fall tuition.

She had not lived like this always. At sixteen she had come to State with two trunks, a set of golf clubs, a checking account which her father replenished once a month, and an interest in sociology because she was the only child of an Elyria contractor who was doing well and because social work would be a way to fulfill her obligations to a less fortunate economic group. Only Carl, her father, did not continue to do well. He was a master carpenter who could do more with a hammer and jackknife than most industrial arts majors can do with power tools. He went into partnership with a plumber in 1920. They did well during the twenties. Carl got them a reputation for honest workmanship, and the plumber got them the contracts, and in 1926 they developed a subdivision on which the houses sold for sixteen thousand dollars. By 1927 Carl was worth eighty thousand in cash. In September, 1929, he was worth on paper a quarter of a million dollars. In December his paper fortune had vanished but he still had some cash and a business that, if not essential, was nearly so.

The partnership survived the worst and, because of its reputation and performance, struggled into the middle thirties. But as the nation recovered and competition got a second wind, the partners found themselves tired, financially overextended, a little old-fashioned, and suddenly in grave trouble. Carl mortgaged his house, cashed in his insurance and held out for one more year, a disastrous one. Then, with the last dime either of them could lay hands on already borrowed and spent, they filed bankruptcy papers.

Carl did not blow his brains out. Instead he called a family conference in which he told his wife and daughter that there was no more money nor prospect of any, that he was out of business and out of a job and in debt, that there would be no more automobiles or fine clothes or college educations. Then he went back to work at his old trade, hiring himself out to other contractors, content now to get by, at apprentice wages.

Alice dropped out of school, of course, and for three years she worked at whatever she could get, dishwashing, car-hopping, anything there was. Most of what she earned went into the family pool, but she managed somehow to save enough to go back to school. Her interest now was business administration, for she had heard that private secretaries made good money, and, if they were intelligent and ambitious, got to be indispensable in time. She had heard that a job like that offered some security.

Michael did not know all this for a long time; it was June before he knew anything about her family, and midsummer before she told him what it was like to work in a restaurant for thirty cents an hour and tips: how you wore low-cut dresses if you were interestingly developed, for you could sometimes make a quarter tip if you leaned over when you set the pork chops and hash-browns in front of a drummer. Or how the owner would stand in the kitchen door during a lull and chew his lower lip and watch you to see that you kept busy,

127

for you were costing him thirty cents an hour. Or how that same owner had slapped her once for dropping a tray. It was during the evening rush. He had been standing at the range, and when the tray dropped he turned slowly, the forgotten ladle poised in his hand. When she looked into his eyes, she knew she was out of a job.

"I couldn't help it," she said. "I was trying to hurry, and I caught—"

He put the ladle down, very carefully. Then he took one step and slapped her across the mouth. She did not try to avoid the blow. She just stood there, thinking, he is going to fire me now. He is going to give me my money—minus the breakage—and then tell me I don't need to come back. He will be gnawing his lip raw when he counts out my wages, and he will refuse to look me in the face when he tells me.

"You didn't have to do that," she said.

"Get a broom," he said. "Sweep it up."

"It was an accident. You didn't have any call. You could have docked me, or fired me. But you didn't—"

"I'm sorry," he said fiercely. "I apologize. So now will you please get a goddam broom and sweep up the loving floor?"

"There's a customer out there," she said, "waiting for a steak, medium, and mashed potatoes."

"Sure." He turned wearily back to the range.

At eleven that night, with the place cleaned up and the ache in her calves and knees, she stood at the cash register and studied his thin, gray, worried face while he counted out her wages. "Do you want me back?" she asked.

"Sure," he said.

"How much for the dishes?"

"It was only a plate and a glass," he said. "That won't put me out of business."

"How much?"

"All right," he said wearily. "Fifty cents. If you insist."

"I insist." She handed him the money.

He rang it up. "I'm sorry, Alice," he said. "I forgot myself. You know how it is. A man doesn't know if he's going out of

128

business tomorrow or the next day, and my stomach turns at the things I have to do in the kitchen to make out, and—"

"I know how it is." She turned and walked to the front door. Her hand, in her coat pocket, was clenched around her wages.

Michael was ignorant of any of this that first night, when they came out of the State Theater into a three-quarter moon, savagely yellow, riding the tree tops. As they walked up High Street he was wondering what other college boys said to their dates while they were walking them home. You exhausted the possibilities of a double feature in a block, he thought. And then she solved the problem for him. She asked him what he was taking in college, and he told her, automatically and without enthusiasm, for she was clearly just trying to make conversation.

"I took some English," she said. "I could never see much point in it, though. It never seemed very practical."

He looked sidewise at her. Her eyes were on where she was headed. Her gray coat was open, and the dress she was wearing was calculated to emphasize the fact that she had reached maturity. She had done something to her hair since earlier in the week. She did not have the thin, brittle, calculated prettiness of a lot of girls on campus, but she was pleasant to look at.

"You must have your requirements worked off already," she said. "If that's all you're taking. Lit courses."

"I wouldn't know. I never paid much attention."

"Didn't your adviser—"

"My adviser," he said, "is a busy man. He's on a lot of committees, and he's writing a book on the medieval morality play. Last year I had a character who talked a lot about requirements and prerequisites and areas of specialization, and I used to make him unhappy because I kept insisting I wasn't majoring in anything. But everything's a lot simpler this year. Because this one just lets me sign up for courses that look interesting and no arguments."

"It won't be so simple when you have to work off all your requirements in your senior year. So you can graduate."

129

"I'm not working for a degree."

She slowed her stride. "How are you going to make a living? You can't get a job without a degree."

"Write."

"That's romantic. It's like wanting to be a movie star."

He shrugged. "Some people do get to be movie stars."

"More of them starve."

"I won't."

"You will," she said, "if you fail."

"I'm not going to fail. Writing is what I can do. Let's not talk about my future any more." He looked at her. "I want to tell you something," he said. "You're the first girl I ever had a date with, and it's a nice night, and spring is just around the corner, and let's not argue any more."

"All right. Only I still—"

"You are out of order. There's a motion on the floor."

She laughed, and he took her arm when they crossed the next intersection though there wasn't any traffic and the curb was not tricky. Through the trees he could see the moon, riding hot and yellow, almost at eye level. If there were any leaves on the trees, he was thinking, you could use this as a stage set.

"In the last act of *The Merchant of Venice*," he said, "it must have been a night exactly like this. In the seventeenth century you could stage a love scene in a setting like this and the critics wouldn't cut you to pieces. Only you can't appreciate that moon unless you're with somebody of the opposite sex. Preferably a particular member of the opposite sex."

"For somebody who's never been out with a girl before, you have a highly accomplished line."

"You see?" he said. "Lit courses do have some practical value. Because nothing has ever been said that hasn't been said a lot better by somebody else, and if you aren't clever, you can always plagiarize."

They turned into the sorority walk. "You can come in if you want," she said.

"I have a better idea," he said. "Let's stay out here. There's no moon inside."

130

"All right. Only the house mother will be turning on the porch light any minute now. She always turns it on at ten-thirty."

"You girls ought to get up a petition."

"You could call out the militia and this house mother would still turn on the porch light at ten-thirty. She's sixty-two, and she's all out of romance." She had turned on the porch steps, one hand on the railing. "It was a lovely evening," she said. "Thanks for a lovely evening, Michael."

He leaned against the railing. In the shadow cast by the porch roof he could make out only the hazy outline of her face. "You know something?" he said. "You're the first girl I ever asked for a date who didn't giggle or look at me like I was a leper or something."

"All I can say is they weren't very bright girls. That's a personal opinion, of course."

"Maybe there might be other Friday nights when you might not be doing anything?"

"Maybe."

"Say next Friday night?"

"At the moment," she said, "I can't think of anything else I'm doing next Friday night."

He looked up the steps at her. He had a feeling that if he only knew exactly how to put the question, she might let him kiss her good night. "You are very pretty in the moonlight," he said. "You are much prettier than most of the girls around here who think they are very pretty."

She leaned quickly and kissed him fleetingly on the cheek. "All the books say you shouldn't do that on a first date," she said, "but bashful boys have a strong attraction for me."

He moved his hand an inch along the railing. "If the house mother turns that light on in the next five minutes," he said, "I think I am going to develop a strong antagonism."

Behind them the porch light clicked on.

"I have just developed a strong antagonism," he said.

She laughed. He straightened up. "A week from tonight?" he said. "About seven-thirty?"

"All right. And Michael, will you do something for me?"

131

"Anything. Name it. Make it tough."

"It's easy. Just think about—about what we were talking about."

He felt a tiny, sharp twinge in his stomach, like a drop of cold water hitting the stomach lining. "I'll think about it," he said.

"You could have another job and still write. Lots of writers have other jobs."

"The real ones don't. It isn't a hobby, like stamp collecting."

"It's for your own good. I mean, you're going to want to get married someday, and most girls would think twice if you didn't have a steady job. I mean, a girl wants some security."

"I suppose a girl does." He remembered his father leaning into the light, explaining to him about how he was going to find a girl someday, and he knew that what he was going to say was exactly the wrong thing to say, that it was going to ruin the evening.

"A man doesn't have to get married," he said.

Her face stiffened. "I don't suppose he does."

"Are you still interested in next Friday night?"

"I don't know. Maybe you'd better call."

"Sure." He turned partly away from her. "If you should happen to be tied up," he said, "I suppose I'll probably see you around sometime."

"I suppose you will. Sometime."

He did not look back when he walked down the walk. Going home on the streetcar, with his cheek pressed against the glass, he remembered what Horn had told him about marrying some peasant girl who would be grateful for meat once a week. Or, he thought, asking a taxi driver for the address of an alley where sportive ladies left their doors ajar.

He did not call her that week, but he did the next.

"I suppose you're busy tonight?" he said.

"I have an exam Monday."

"The weather report is for continued fair. In case you might

132

be interested in taking a walk." He permitted the silence to hang suspended a moment between south Columbus and sorority row. Then he said, "I was reading the catalogue this week. There's something in it about how you have to take a science to graduate. I thought you might know a good one. In case a man decided to get a degree because he might want to get married sometime."

She laughed, lightly and happily. There was a faint suggestion of triumph in it. "All right," she said. "But not before eight, Michael."

After he hung up, he sat there a while staring at the phone. He had a feeling that in some way he had been betrayed. Or had betrayed himself. Then he shrugged the thought out of his mind because he was wondering instead what area of specialization a girl might like a man to go into.

Now, years later, he could no longer remember exactly when they had decided to get married. Alice claimed that he proposed to her in his junior year, but it was his impression that the knowledge had grown wordlessly between them, that it had been conjured up out of all the movies in which they had held hands, out of all the walks, out of all the evenings on the grass beside Mirror Lake (where the smell in midsummer is inclined to get a little high but where the physical surroundings on a July evening are otherwise romantic), out of all the arguments they had had about what he was going to do with his life, and out of all the concessions he had made. Now it was the arguments they had had and the concessions he had made that he remembered most clearly: the argument about getting a degree, and later, when he had squeezed through geology and economics with D's, the argument about working as hard on his required courses as on his electives, and after that a month-long argument about the advantages of teaching as a career.

There were few enough jobs when they graduated. According to the earlier Fireside Talks, all they had to fear was fear itself, but there still weren't any secretarial openings and no jobs in English departments for promising young A.B.'s. And so both of them went back to school. By that time

133

Michael had decided that he wanted a girl as badly as he wanted fame and fortune, and the path to the girl seemed at the moment to be a Master's Degree. With an M.A., you could get a readership in the department and go on to a Ph.D., and with a Ph.D. you could get the steady job Alice had her heart set on. So by the following June he could add two more letters after his name. He remembered that June all right, because that was when they had gotten married.

It had been on impulse. One early June night they had walked slowly home from a free concert, and there was another moon. He kissed her on the sorority steps, and she caught his hand and held tightly to it.

"Behave, Michael. We're not married yet."

"Well, let's rectify the oversight."

"We will. Just as soon—"

"Now. This weekend."

She laughed. "Don't be silly."

"We could make out. Between the F & R Lazarus Company and the Great Atlantic and Pacific Tea—"

"Be sensible. If we got married now, you'd be stuck the rest of your life in that grocery store."

"Well," he said, "it's probably no more horrible a prospect than writing articles for the *Publication of the Modern Language Association*."

"Please. Please don't do that, Michael. If you can't behave—"

"The hell with behaving. We've behaved for four years. What I want to do now is to go to bed with you."

"I'd better go in now," she said. "It's almost eleven—"

"I saw Myers today. I've got an assistantship for fall. It pays fifty dollars a month."

"Mike!" she cried. "You didn't even tell me!"

"I was saving it. For a surprise." Which was a lie. The truth was that he was still hoping for a miracle, for one of his occasional stories to sell, in which event he would have given up the idea of a teaching career. "I was waiting for a propitious moment," he said.

"Mike! We *can* get married in September, then."

134

"We can get married now. This weekend. Between us, we'll be earning thirty-two dollars a week this summer. Hell, that's an executive's salary. On thirty-two a week you can *save* money."

"I think this is crazy," she said. "Anyway, there's a five-day—"

"The law we'll circumvent. I'll bribe the judge."

"What if something happens between now and September? What if the enrollment goes down, or—"

"Nothing's going to happen," he said.

So they had gotten married that Friday, and they had taken a bus out to a tourist camp, and on Monday they came back and moved in with his parents. And now he could no longer remember much else of that summer. He could not even remember very clearly the three nights in the tourist cabin. He knew that your wedding night was something you were supposed to remember, but all he could recall was that there had been only one window in the cabin and that it had been very warm for June.

For a while that fall, he tried to keep on writing, tried to sandwich in some work he cared about between a memorization of Grimm's Law and a paper on the influence of the Provençal poets on Chaucer. But by the middle of the first term he was behind in both his courses. For three weeks he worked savagely to catch up, and that is how long it took him to get out of the habit. For the first time in his life he learned in those three weeks what it meant to be afraid of losing a job. After that quarter he did not try to do anything except teach with his left hand and pursue scholarship with his right.

Afterwards, he couldn't even remember any very sharp sense of loss when he put writing behind him, for scholarship can be a little like taking drugs. At first his interest was the moderns: at one time he even toyed with the idea of a dissertation on Faulkner. Then he found out that a certain Professor Peters was a power in the department, and so he changed his field to Jacobean drama, and from then on he

135

was lost in Parish Registers and microfilmed first quartos of Middleton. He even bought himself a patented filing case for three-by-five cards, and he did his dissertation on Commonwealth drama. He picked that topic because Peters (who needed the material for a book he was writing) told him that nobody had ever done *anything* with the Commonwealth theater. They were always telling you that nobody had ever done anything with Victorian drama or John Skelton's rime schemes, that you could spade a lot of articles out of virgin territory like that. The fact that the Commonwealth drama was unturned prairie sod because Cromwell had outlawed the theater was the kind of fact you ignore when you are in graduate school.

So he did a thesis on English drama on a period during which there was no English drama. He even published an article on a Commonwealth dramatist whom even the Commonwealth had forgotten by 1658. By that time he looked a little gray around the mouth and eyes, and he wasn't stooped yet but give him five more years, and as soon as the bad light in the library stacks finished the job on his eyes he was going to buy himself a pair of rimless glasses—the absence of which was about the only thing that still distinguished him from the others who had their offices on the first floor of Derby Hall.

If there was any bitterness about the time he was losing, it was buried in his subconscious, and it would boil out only occasionally, in sudden fits of pique in the library stacks, or at home, when Alice would say something to remind him of what his life had become. Meanwhile the A's accumulated on his record, he had gotten his instructorship, and Alice was very proud of him because she had heard around that he was the best of this crop of graduate students.

He was well into his thesis when the Japanese took steps to equalize the balance of naval power in the Pacific, and when Alice came upstairs that Sunday afternoon and told him the news, he pushed his card files and typewriter aside and went downstairs. He sat there all afternoon and evening, listening to the news commentators. It was midnight when

136

Alice came in from the kitchen and asked when he was going to bed.

"Pretty soon."

"Do you think it's as bad as they say?"

"I think it's worse."

"Do you think we'll lose?"

"I don't know."

"We've never lost a war yet."

"Neither have the Japanese." He forced his eyes to hers. "I'm going to enlist," he said.

She stared uncomprehendingly at him. Probably, he thought, this has had no meaning for her until right this moment.

"Don't be ridiculous, Michael," she said.

"They ought to be able to find some use for me."

"You're less than a year away from your degree. You could at least put this off until—"

"For heaven's sake, Alice, they've sunk half our navy, and I'm supposed to put this off to do a thesis on the Commonwealth theater?"

"A few months. What difference can a few months make? When it's your whole future. Listen, Michael, you don't have to carry a gun to be a hero. They've said right along they're going to need teachers—"

"Maybe they are," he said. "But I'll have more self-respect in a uniform."

She put up a hand and brushed uncertainly at a strand of hair. "I guess you've made up your mind," she said.

"I've made up my mind."

"Well, at least you could tell me the truth."

He looked up at her. "The truth? What truth? You heard the radio. The Japs—"

"For the moment, you can spare me the phony patriotism."

"All right," he said. "You tell me."

"I'll tell you. I'll tell you, all right. Because you want to get away. Because you want shut of me. Don't you?"

He didn't say anything.

"Don't you? Isn't that it? Say so."

"There isn't any sense in this, Alice."

"You've resented me from the beginning. You think I'm a millstone. You hate me, and you hate teaching because you think you're a misplaced genius, and—"

"I'm going to bed."

"That's the truth. Isn't it? Say it. Say it's the truth."

He got to his feet. "No," he said. He looked away. "All right," he said. "I suppose part of it is the truth. The part about what I'm doing."

"Go ahead, then," she said wearily. "Join up. Get into a uniform. I hope they give you a lot of medals."

"I hope they put me somewhere where I can earn a lot of them."

"Also, I hope you get a best-selling novel out of it."

"That's a laugh. That's a highly amusing remark. In two years I haven't written a word worth the price of one sheet of watermarked bond."

So he had gone downtown the next morning. But there hadn't been any medals in it. He had stood naked in the naked line, and the fat, wheezing colonel whom he could have taken with one hand had written "fallen arches" on his medical record, and then he had gotten on a streetcar and come back home to Alice and the library stacks and the lectures on the dangling participle. And to the Armed Services Training Program. He had come home to do his bit on the home front, and everybody told him how lucky he was because he could consolidate his position in the profession while other graduate students were taking Guadalcanal. For the next four years, he graded the themes of the bitter-eyed eighteen-year-olds who hated English because it was impractical, hated the maneuvers on the Oval or the Mall with the broomsticks over their shoulders while the girls giggled on the library steps, hated the bleak barracks and the monotonous food and the gray, cold mornings and the gray, lonely evenings, hated themselves because they were Over Here instead of Over There, hated the whole speeded-up, snafued program and all the dry-skinned, dry-voiced 4-F's who stood in front of them in the classrooms and told them about war and democracy and what they would be fighting for once they were given the Word to get the hell out of Here and Over There. So for four years Michael stood in front of them and nursed his flat feet. And Alice seemed to find a plateau of contentment with their first child and Michael's quiet, steady pursuit of a quiet, steady way of life.

Then, the war over, Michael applied for a job at Minnesota because Peters told him that the 17th-Century man up there was retiring in three years and if he would get the lead out and finish his book on Commonwealth drama, he had a chance to step into his place. Only he never finished the book. Because one day in the Minnesota stacks he was seized by an almost uncontrollable desire to hurl the volume he was reading down the length of the dusty aisle. He didn't give in to the impulse, but he got to his feet, collected his note cards, and got out of there. Four months later, in the teeth of the fact that he had been at it over a decade and had learned what scholars think of young Ph.D.'s who desert the monastery for the fleshpots, who decide to try writing literature instead of just writing about it—four months later he finished the first draft of his novelette, *The Alley.*

9 OF THOSE LONG YEARS THAT followed graduation and embraced a war and its aftermath he could remember only a half-dozen sharp incidents like that one; all the rest ran together in his mind, like the impressions you have left when you come up out of the dream, and the only part that remained utterly sharp, that still had acute meaning for him, was the months when he had written *The Alley*, when he had sat up night after night past the quiet of two A.M. and the words had spilled out onto the white paper, coming so fast that his mind was always two paragraphs ahead of his hands. In the quiet he would get the feeling he had learned to crave, the tense exhilaration you get from Benzedrine or creation, and later the slow, dreamlike fall into contentment, as if he had been sitting there alone with the Alone and He had tipped him up and poured out whatever was in him and now peace had rushed in to fill the vacuum. For that is how you feel when the pages are lying on the desk and you know that you have gotten down whatever it is you have to get down.

But a little better than a year ago he could remember. He could remember that year, all right, because that was when he had walked permanently out of Folwell Hall and come home and finished *Some Die on the Vine*.

He could remember the beginning of it and the end, and the beginning had been a cloudy afternoon in February, and the handball court, and Ken Naylor leaning into the serve, and Michael playing it the way you played Ken's serves, turning to face the back wall as the ball went past, watching the ball come off the back wall, then stepping into it like a ballet dancer. His return was too high, but it was hard enough to pull Ken back, and when he moved in toward the service line, the whole court photographed itself on his mind: Ken pulling back, and Strachey still in the box with his back plastered against the wall, and Jim moving across to block Ken out on the left. We have got Strachey pinned against the wall, he thought exultantly, and this one is on Ken. He watched Jim take Ken's return and then crouched on the service line, his eyes nailed to the front wall, watching the ball strike and then disappear for a suspended, anesthetized second and then strike again. Low, Jim, he thought desperately, play it low. And then the ball hit a foot to his left, and he sensed Jim moving over to take it, and he yelled, "Stay on your own side, Jim, don't let him suck you out again." Only it was too late. Because Jim had already pulled too far over and Ken had slammed his return into the left corner, and Jim didn't even try for it. He just stood there and watched the ball hug the distant wall and die.

"That's game," Ken said. He swiped his forehead with the back of his gloved hand. "Another?" He was grinning.

Michael looked at the grin and felt the throb in his throat. "Why don't you three play?" he said. "Jim against you two?"

There was the silence you get when somebody has said something like that, and the grin slid off Ken's face, and in the back court Jim turned around, slowly. And why the hell can't he ever learn, Michael thought sullenly. He walked across the court and picked up the ball.

"Possibly you are dissatisfied with your partner, Mike," Jim said softly. He was leaning a little, relaxed and intent, the smile faint and crooked and thin on his thin, sharp face. "Because if you are," he said.

"No," he said. "I'm happy with my partner. When he plays his own goddam side of the court, I am."

"Oh, for Chrissake, Mike," Ken said, "it's only a game."

He looked briefly at Jim and then tossed the ball to Ken.

141

"Excuse me," he said. He crossed to his corner. "Serve it," he said.

"You three play," Jim said. "I've got to get back. I've got this conference." He did not look at Michael when he said it.

"It isn't two yet," Michael said. "We've got time." And why do I always let it make so much difference, he thought.

"It will be," Jim said, "by the time I get dressed." He tossed his sweat shirt over his shoulder and then stood at the cage door, looking at Michael now, his smile thin and a little sad. "Anyway," he said, "I'm bushed."

"I've had enough, too," Strachey said.

Michael stood there another minute, studying their expressions, wondering whether they were quitting because of him or because they were just victims of a sedentary profession. Then he grinned at Jim. "We've got them worn down," he said. "We could take the bastards on the next one."

"Like hell," Ken said. "We may be pooped, but we aren't dead yet," and then he knew it was all right, and he followed Jim out into the corridor and fell in step beside him, feeling the sweat under his armpits turning cold in the damp corridor, feeling tired and relaxed and grateful for the shower coming up, feeling warm inside because Jim had smiled at him and everything was all right again and this was just a game you played on Wednesday and Friday afternoons.

"That Ken," Jim said. "He was hot today, wasn't he?"

"He can be taken," he said. "If you don't let him outthink you."

"You can never forget there's a score, can you, Mike?"

He glanced sideways into Jim's smile. He is giving me a chance to get it off my chest, he thought. "I'm sorry, Jim," he said.

"Hell," Jim said, "what's to be sorry for? I got sucked out of position, didn't I?" He opened the door at the end of the corridor and then stepped aside. "The only thing is," he said, "I can't make it make any difference. For me, it's just a way to get tired enough to sleep nights. When they made me, they omitted a necessary ingredient. They weren't thinking of the twentieth century at the time. They had their minds some-where else."

Some of the rest of us, too, Michael thought, remembering the conference with Evans that morning. No, he thought, no, don't think of that, think of something else. Think of the weekend coming up, or whether there is enough money to get Alice out of the house—

"College," Jim said. "A college job. The last refuge for all those who cannot do, and the difference between us, Mike, is that the knowledge of that fact frets you."

I suppose, Michael thought, and then the memory was back again, very sharp and clean and not to be denied: Evans leaning toward him through the half-light in the office, his face square and intent and twenty, like the helmeted faces you see on the Sunday sport page, and the question suspended just above the pile of papers at his elbow, and the curious sensation he had gotten just then of standing off and looking at the two of them, at Evans who was not Evans but himself a lot of years ago, at himself who was not himself but some-body else. I suppose, he thought, and made an eye movement calculated to move Jim delicately out of the locker-room door-way. Only Jim just stood there, with his thin mouth pulled faintly to one side, and he thought, *he looks like my father, too.* The resemblance wouldn't show in any photograph, he thought sadly, but Jim looks like my father, too.

He undressed quickly and walked naked into the shower room, on his toes, feeling twenty again and masculine and sure of himself. He always felt this way on his way to a shower; whenever he stepped into the steamy heat, he felt like fifteen years ago, when he would come in from a college gym class, and there would be the hot spray and the sharp, sweet smell of liniment and the careless, profane insults and the flicked towels and afterwards the leisurely dressing, his skin tingling and grateful to his clothes. A shower, he thought, testing the spray with his fingertips, a shower is one of the breaks you can count on. It is one of the compensations for radio com-mercials and unpaid bills and loyalty oaths, he thought, and if I ever strike gold with a novel I am going to devote one wing of my house to a shower room.

He stayed under a long time, washing the years down the drain with the sweat, and when he came back out into the locker room, the blood was pulsing in him, and his body felt sound and fresh and clean, and for the moment it was hard to remember the facts of his existence, the set of unread papers on his desk and the unpaid bills and the conference with Evans that morning. Tonight, he thought, starting up the line of lockers, tonight I could get some work done, tonight I could lick life even if it is in a different weight class.

When he came around the corner, Jim was sitting on the bench; he had already accomplished, in the complex and delicate process of dressing, his shorts and one sock, but now he was just sitting there, staring moodily at the floor.

"Got a cigarette, Mike?" Jim said. "I seem to be fresh out."

"In my coat pocket," Michael said. "Just root around."

"I already took the liberty."

"I just bought a pack this noon," Michael said. "I distinctly remember." He fumbled in his clothes and found the pack and shook one out.

"I started the day with a fresh pack," Jim said. "I'm smoking too much again."

"Medical opinion," Michael said, remembering all the arguments he had had with Alice on the subject, "is still undecided. Now the theory is that it rejuvenates the nerve ends or something."

"Malarkey," Jim said. "The AMA is in the hire of the tobacco cartel." He put the lighted cigarette carefully on the edge of the bench and leaned over and pried on a shoe. "I buy a carton a week," he said. "Eight dollars a month. Eight dollars out of my check is a lot of money. Not to mention what the habit costs my friends."

"There's another theory," Michael said, "about how you can't take it with you."

"Maybe not," Jim said. "But it would sure prove a comfort while you are on the way." He pried on his other shoe and then stepped up onto the bench and slid into his trousers.

It was the way you put on trousers when they are just back from the cleaners and the floor not trustworthy, and Jim's trousers were clearly not just back from the cleaners, and if they had been they wouldn't have betrayed it this late in the afternoon, but in the course of a day Jim went through a lot of motions which wouldn't hold up in the light of reason.

"You on your way home?" Jim asked.

"I'm debating."

"I thought," Jim spoke very carefully, sounding as if he were trying to get an interview with a busy personnel director at General Motors, "I thought I might drop in at your office later. I'll cut this next conference of mine short if I can."

"There's a simple technique for that," Michael said. "Just remind yourself that you're on the staff of a great university, and what you are dealing with aren't human beings, they're statistics. I had a chairman tell me that once. I estimate his advice has saved me upwards of five thousand man hours." His shirt collar felt scratchy against his neck, and he wished briefly that Alice would quit overstarching his shirts. "But that was at another university," he said, "and besides the chairman is dead, and I forgot to ask him at the time what you ever did with those hours after you saved them."

"You devote them to scholarship," Jim said. "You find out in the *Parish Register* that Milton lived three blocks from St. Paul's in 1659, and you write an article for *Modern Language Notes*, and then you get promoted."

"Oh, is that what you do?" Michael leaned against the wall and looked down at Jim. "What's on your mind?"

"It's a long story."

"Well, give me a synopsis."

"A synopsis wouldn't read."

"It wouldn't be a story I've heard before, would it?" Michael asked. "Because I don't want to sit over there in that office another hour just to argue some more about how I'm not interested in getting into the textbook racket."

"It isn't a racket. Why do you keep saying it's a racket?"

"Jim," Michael said, "don't go trying to gild the tar baby." He straightened up. "If that's it, let's let it lay until Monday.

145

Friday afternoon is a hell of a time to be arguing about writing a textbook."

"You stick around another hour. Another hour isn't going to drive you to suicide."

"All right, Jim," Michael said wearily. "All right, I'll stick around."

The main entrance to Folwell Hall always reminded Michael of one of those small Ohio courthouses with the Civil War cannon and the pyramided balls on the lawn beside a stone fountain that had gone dry along with Jeffersonian democracy, and the motto about Justice and Humanity chiseled classically into the sandstone over the entrance. Inside, the fake-marble corridors and the cluttered, dusty rooms should have had signs reading SHERIFF or CITY CLERK jutting out over the doorways. Except, he would think on the days when he had been passed over again in spring promotions or when he had had a bad hour with a student, except that this wasn't a courthouse. This was Folwell Hall, he would think, and Folwell Hall symbolized a great state university. Folwell Hall had been named for a Great Educator who had had a talent for separating land and folding money from legislators, and it was the stronghold of democracy and the guardian of fundamental rights. Folwell Hall was where bright boys sat abstractedly in swivels and meditated about the silent *e* in Chaucer and about Destiny. Folwell Hall was where committees were formed that talked about slum clearance and racial discrimination and proved themselves good, sound liberals. It was where everybody leaned just a little to the left, though they all attached their signatures to loyalty oaths when the chips were down. It was where everybody had a Ph.D. and nobody worried about income tax. And in case you get the idea that they weren't practical, Folwell Hall was the place where, in their spare time, they worked out formulae for atom bombs.

Michael considered the socio-political significance of Folwell Hall while he negotiated the flight of stairs. Then he was walking past the offices where the bright, feverish, but unlucky young men scrawled notes into another learned-journal article and worried about becoming assistant professors, and past the offices where the bright, feverish, and lucky young men speculated on the deaths of civilizations and calculated the time to when they would be full professors, and past the offices where the dry-skinned old men killed another office hour by trying to put liver-spotted fingers on when history had passed them by and why they had never been offered deanships. It would not be hard for a man to get tired of this job, he thought, leaning into the gray light. Not when it is the fag end of a gray month, he thought, and a locker-room mood broken by a reminder of what your life had come to, and you were in your thirties and not getting any younger. If a man could afford to get tired, he thought, and then he was turning into the main office to check his mailbox.

There were quite a few people in the English office for this late of a Friday afternoon. Jorgensen, the linguist, was at the mailboxes memorizing a letter which was probably trying to separate him from a day's wages in return for a membership in the American Association of University Professors. Near the door John Berry was arguing with Jack Munster about contemporary literature. At the counter Jack Eberle was trying to sell Lee Bennett on the latest cause. Michael crossed the room and said "Excuse me" to Jorgensen and resurrected from his box a letter postmarked "New York" and a note from Ken.

"When America learns to distinguish between reporting and fiction," John Berry said, "maybe then it will produce a novel. Maybe."

"I can hear you," Jack Munster said. "I'm not wearing a hearing aid."

Michael wondered how long that particular argument had been going on. Someday, he thought, I am going to ask Johnny Berry why he doesn't try reading a contemporary novel. Just for the hell of it. Just to watch the expression on his face.

He looked down at his mail. The note from Ken said he could pick up his schedule, and the letter was an ad offering, for three dollars less his professional discount, an examination copy of a text which would teach any freshman how to make a lot of money writing articles for the *Saturday Evening Post*. He turned to drop that one in the wastebasket, and then he reconsidered. The book sounded like a good investment. Not that it would teach freshmen anything, but he wouldn't mind learning how to write an article for the *Post* himself. Writing articles for the *Post* sounded like a fine idea, or better anyway than writing novelettes which the reviewers said revealed a fresh, new talent and which sold seventeen hundred copies.

Or maybe I ought to write a text, he thought. Maybe that was what I was born to do, and I ought to resign myself. He turned to Jorgensen, who was still buried in the letter.

"Nils," he said, "does anybody ever make any money on texts?"

Jorgensen gave up the letter and let his eyes focus slowly on Michael's. Jorgensen was a man who had once been stocky but who had lost some weight with the advance of age. He had thin, dry, gray-blond hair and the mouth to go with it. "You've written some texts," Michael said. "Do people make money on them?"

"It depends," Jorgensen said. Jorgensen always put things cautiously; it was a habit you acquired if you expected to get anywhere in linguistics. "Why?" he asked.

"Nothing," Michael said. He straightened up, dropped the ad in the wastebasket, and then crossed the office and opened the door into Ken Naylor's office.

Ken was at his desk, leaning over a large square of cardboard, a pile of green tabs, and a checklist, and Michael stood in the doorway and watched him Scotch tape a tab onto the cardboard and then sway and check off a name. When he swayed like that, Michael could see the bald spot on the crown of his head. He looked up and saw Michael.

"If you're busy," Michael said, "I can drop in later."

Ken grinned.

"Okay," Michael said. "But you sure succeed in creating the impression."

"My boy is probably busy, too. Over at that junior high school. About this time of day they are usually cutting pictures out of magazines. They call it busywork."

"Well," Michael said, "busywork is what they pay us for, isn't it?"

"I guess it is." Ken got a faraway look in his eyes, and Michael wondered what he was thinking about. Probably about when he had been just the department's promising young man, he thought. At thirty Ken published a biography of Debs, and in 1938 he got reviewed on the front page of the Sunday *Times* book section for his two-volume intellectual history of the twenties. Then they offered him the chairmanship, and he put his manuscript on the history of the labor movement in his bottom desk drawer and moved into this office. In the improbable event that his administrative duties ever let him finish it, that manuscript was going to be a standard reference for economists someday, but in the meantime he had traded it in for a car with some guts under the hood, and a brick ranch-type out in the suburbs, and a salary you paid income tax on. And now he did the things a chairman does. Now he worried about getting raises for the deserving out of a budget which hadn't been designed with raises in mind, or about keeping the dean happy, or about breaking in the new secretaries. Or he played at sticking green tabs onto a cardboard chart in such a way as to keep eighty-seven people with, at the outside, seven preferences in courses and hours reasonably happy.

Ken leaned back in his chair. "I suppose you want your schedule," he said.

"That was the excuse."

Ken looked down at the cardboard chart. There was a single tab lying in the wilderness of white, and Ken studied it impersonally. "English A," he said, "Section 5, four to five, and it is a headache to unload. I'd give it to McKinney, except that McKinney has stated a preference for morning classes because he is in the middle of an article about the kind of wrestling hold Beowulf used on the monster." Ken leaned suddenly and flicked the green tab off onto the floor, the way you might flick an ant off the lip of the sugar bowl. Then, carefully and deliberately, he moved another green tab into position. "English X," he said. "Remedial, and when I section them into that, their daddies, who also send checks to the alumni fund, write me long letters, and that course is why we hire graduate students, who are so goddam grateful for their seventy-five a month and the opportunity to memorize the ten classes of Anglo-Saxon nouns that you could give them a four A.M. and never cloud their expressions." He flicked the second tab off the chart, and then he studied the two of them, lying out there in the middle of the dark floor. Then he got heavily out of his chair, walked around the desk, picked up the tabs and put them back on the pile. "I don't know what gets into a man some days," he said.

Michael said, "If you're trying to tell me I've got a lousy schedule—"

Ken opened a drawer, got out a stack of schedule cards, and handed one to Michael. It wasn't a bad schedule—afternoon classes and the course he had particularly wanted.

"Just don't assume that that fiction-writing course is your baby permanently," Ken said. "I'll have to give it to Daddy Barnes once in a while to keep peace in the family."

Michael looked across the desk at him. "That eight o'clock," he said, on impulse. "If you can't find anybody—"

"No. I left you your mornings. In case you decide to finish that novel this spring."

Michael didn't say anything. He was thinking of his novel, lying quiet and neglected in the filing cabinet in the back bedroom. He had worked seven months on it before it had gone sour on him, and he wondered how it would look if he got it out: whether in four months the top pages would have the tired, smudged, handled look that the top pages in manuscripts get, whether the bottom pages, lying down there under the weight, had begun to curl yet. Probably, and then he was thinking again of his conference that morning with Evans, and abruptly he pushed back his chair. "I'd better be leaving you to your administrative duties," he said.

"I have just lost interest in my administrative duties." Ken

150

turned for a look out the window behind him; outside, the first drops of rain were inching down the glass, leaving spots behind them in the dust like scabs of eczema. "Let's brave the elements for a cup of coffee," he said.

Michael shook his head. "Jim wants to see me at three. He wants to argue some more about doing a textbook."

"What the hell would you want to be doing a textbook for?"

"I didn't say I wanted to. I said I was going to argue." He transferred his attention to the pile of green tabs. "Though it might be something to do. In the early spring evenings. Before it gets warm enough to take walks. Writing texts is one of the things you do, isn't it?"

"It is one of the things you do when the ink is still wet on your Ph.D. and they haven't heard of you yet over in the President's office."

"A man can't sit on his can forever. Anyway, I hear you get paid for writing texts. Not that my salary needs augmenting. But you can always stash it away for that rainy day they are always warning you about."

Ken shrugged. "If you've made up your mind."

Michael glanced at his watch. Then he had one more look at the pile of green tabs. "I'd better be getting back," he said.

Ken's eyes had followed his to the tabs. "I guess we both had," he said.

Jim was waiting for him when he returned to his office. He was sitting at Rankin's desk, and behind him the rain was sluicing down the window. Michael dropped into his chair and looked at the set of papers on his desk. Except for one, they were still unread, which meant that he would take them home where they would lie around the house until Sunday night, and he would find himself skimming through them the last hour before bedtime. "I was just talking to Ken," he said. "About textbooks. Ken wanted to know why the hell anybody would want to write a textbook."

"Now just a minute, Mike," Jim said. He leaned an inch or so. "I got a letter from Mattson and Company this morning," he said. "They've just started a college department, and they'd like to see an outline. Only I haven't got one."

Michael shrugged. "You shouldn't be writing to publishers empty-handed. You ought to know better, Jim."

"Listen," Jim said doggedly, "they said they might see their way to an advance. Two-fifty apiece. You could use two hundred and fifty dollars, couldn't you?"

Michael thought briefly of his bank balance and of the garage bill he was going to have to pay this afternoon. "I suppose I could."

"And I know for a fact that you aren't doing anything else right now. Are you?"

"No," Michael said, remembering the novel, then remembering Evans again, remembering exactly how Evans had faced him across the desk.

"Listen," Jim said, "there's a market for freshman anthologies. You can make a fortune. All I'm asking for is a fiction section. I'll do—"

"Ask Munster for a fiction section. Munster knows—"

"Munster doesn't know his fanny from an exhaust manifold. I wouldn't do a title page with Munster. It wouldn't take you three months, Mike. It's a scissors-and-paste job. All you'd have to do is pick out a dozen short stories and knock out an introduction. So why not?"

Michael wondered how you could explain why-not to somebody like Jim, how you could explain this morning, when he had pushed Evans' paper across the desk and Evans had stared at the grade and said, "An A, sir?" How he had felt the smile on his face when he said, "The letter is still drawn in that fashion, isn't it, Evans?" and then the sensation, like dropping through space, which had hit him in the pit of the stomach. "I couldn't explain it to you, Jim," he said. "It wouldn't have any meaning for you." He remembered how Evans had looked up from the A and said that he thought his last story had been better than this one and why had Michael thought different? Michael had said, "Why do you think your last one was better than this one?"

152

"I don't know," Evans said. "It just felt better. You know how a story feels sometimes."

"Yes," Michael said. "I know how a story feels sometimes." He dropped his eyes to Evans's paper. "Maybe," he said, feeling the smile stiff on his face, "maybe I was just making allowances."

"What do you mean by that, sir?"

Looking at Evans, Michael caught a picture of the rest of the students in his classes: the fraternity boys who slouched in a back row, considering boldly the blonde chick ahead, considering slyly the economics assignment for the next hour, considering wearily the weight of abused eyelids, considering anything but the lecture which they would permit to swirl, like fog, around and beyond them; the brittle sorority girls and their superficial, semiliterate, hasty term papers, and their smiles, fleeting and impudent, when the angry D's came back to them; the operators, who crowded around your desk after class and sometimes opened a book if it didn't interfere with the gal they had lined up for the weekend. "I take it," he said, "that you are thinking of being a writer, Evans."

"I'm thinking of writing, sir," Evans said.

"Well," Michael said, "I gave you B's on those other stories so you wouldn't get any illusions about your ability. Though no doubt you are already dreaming about writing the Great American Novel any day now, and after you are rich and famous, beautiful women will fall effortlessly into your bed."

"Not into mine," Evans said. "I'm married. And I haven't got any illusions. I know how tough it is."

"Do you?" Michael said. "Do you now?" He was suddenly sorry for this boy who was ambitious and who knew what he wanted and who was married already. "How are you planning to support this wife to whom you are married?" he said.

Evans grinned. "She's supporting me. She's got a job. Until I can get established. And some writers make a living. The ones who have what it takes."

"How old are you?" Michael asked. "Twenty-one? Twenty-two? I wanted to be a writer when I was twenty-two. Only I got married, and I went into teaching because that was a way to live until I could make a living doing what I wanted to do." He looked into Evans's level eyes; there wasn't any fear or doubt there. "I think you can be a writer, Evans," he said. "I think you have very definitely got what it takes. Only I don't think you will be. You'll probably get a Ph.D. instead, and someday you'll be an assistant professor."

"Is that all, sir?" Evans said.

"Yes. That's all, Evans."

He swung in the chair, watching Evans cross the office in that rolling, loose, insolent way athletes walk. At the door, Evans turned and looked down at him once more. "Thank you, sir," he said.

For what, he wondered, what the hell was he thanking him for? "Evans," he said, "do you want to know something? I wish to Christ I was twenty-two again."

"I'm not twenty-two," Evans said. "I'm twenty-five."

"Well," Michael said, "I wish I was twenty-five again." He looked across the office. The light was bad but he thought he could read something like pity in Evans's eyes, and he put his hand up, in an automatic, subconscious gesture, and covered his lips. It was ten seconds before he realized what he had done.

Christ, he thought. Oh, Christ, Savage.

"Try it," Jim said from across the office.

Michael jerked his hand away from his mouth for the second time that day. "Try what?"

"Explaining it to me," Jim said. "You said something wouldn't have any meaning for me. Try it."

"All right," he said. "For me a textbook is a kind of symbol, the last link in a chain that includes graduate work and dusty articles in learned journals and a steady job and a mortgaged house and the responsibilities of a family and taxes and death. To me doing a text would make me finally and irrevocably a part of something, and if I don't get sucked into that, I can keep hoping I'll escape someday." He looked at Jim. "I knew it wouldn't," he said.

"Wouldn't what?"

154

"Mean anything to you."

"No. The only thing that means anything to me is that five hundred dollars. I was hoping you could use that."

"I could," Michael said, "if I wanted to pay the price." He would have to pay for the car out of a thirty-one-dollar bank balance, he thought, and he hoped there would be something left over. What I would like to do, he thought, is take Alice out to dinner and stop in somewhere for a drink afterwards. She will say we don't have the money, but maybe the garage will leave something. And maybe you are silly, he thought, because what difference will one compromise make after all the other years of compromise? You could use that two-fifty, that's for sure.

He got to his feet. "Give me the weekend to think it over."

"Sure," Jim said.

He watched Jim get to his feet and start toward him. When you think of betrayal, he was thinking, you think of exchanges in secret rooms of blueprints for long envelopes bulging with crisp new bills, you think of slashed mattresses and long, black cars pulling up to the curb, you think of the knife twisting down in the blackness of the alley. But it isn't the major treason, he thought, it is the series of minor compromises. Not the right hook to the midsection, he thought, but the left jabs to the lightly-cut eye; not the armored divisions streaking across a map but the quisling in the capital, and that is a figure of speech to tuck away and remember. It is the story of your life, he thought, and an observation to get down in a notebook, for you might be able to use it someday.

He stepped aside for Jim and then pulled the office door shut behind him. I know already what I am going to say, he thought, but I am at least going to make him wait until Monday to hear it.

10 THERE WAS THE SMELL OF
bleach in the cellar landing when he came in the back door,
not sharp enough to be offensive but enough to tell him that
Alice had done another washing today and would probably
be tired tonight. He kicked off his galoshes and went up the
brief flight of stairs.

Alice was at the sink when he came into the kitchen, and
he did not have to study her face to know she was tired, all
right. "You're a little late," she said.

"Yes. How long before dinner?"

"Not long enough for a nap. How much was the car?"

"Seventeen dollars."

"Seventeen dollars!"

"I was lucky. Seventeen dollars is nothing where that car's
involved." He leaned against the counter and watched her
rinse off a potato and drop it into a battered pan with which
they had started housekeeping. Her housedress was ripped
under one arm, and he suddenly felt sorry for her: for the pan
and the dress and for all the other things he had failed to
give her. He felt, just then, like apologizing to her for all the
omissions, named and unnamed, that can haunt you at five
o'clock of a Friday afternoon.

"Maybe next month we can find two dollars to buy you
something to cover your nakedness," he said.

She smiled fleetingly at him. "There's plenty of wear left
in this dress," she said.

156

"Any mail?"

"Some bills. That one from Dayton's we didn't pay last month. And the electric bill. It's higher this month."

"It's always high in February. February is a gloomy month."

"It's always high when you can never remember to turn off the lights." She carried the potatoes to the stove and lit a burner with a match; the pilot hadn't worked for a year now. "When you go upstairs," she said, "look in on Cathy and Susan. If they've got that room a mess, make them straighten it up before dinner."

Upstairs, Cathy and Susan were sitting on the bedroom floor with a paintbook, water colors, and a pan of water between them. When he opened the door, they looked up at him with the question in their faces kids assume when they are pretty sure they are doing something forbidden and want to check on your mood. Michael studied the smear of paint on the threadbare carpet that had come to them from Alice's parents.

"Hi, Daddy," Cathy said. "We're painting."

"Did your mother say you could?"

"She doesn't care. Last week she let us."

"She'll care," Michael said, "if she comes up here and sees that rug."

"Susan did that," Cathy said. "She won't stay in the lines."

"Uh-uh," Susan said. In five years Susan had learned to deny anything the minute she heard her name mentioned.

"Get a scrub rag, Cathy," Michael said, "and clean it up."

"Why me?" Cathy said. "Why not Susan?"

He wondered why he could never say ten words to his kids without getting involved in an argument. "Because you're eight and Susan's only five."

"Gol," Cathy said, "I've always got to do everything." She scrambled to her feet, hitched up her jeans and walked down the hall toward the bathroom. "Susan has to help," she said.

"Uh-uh," Susan said. She had won one victory, and now she peered into Michael's face to see whether there was any hope of another one.

157

"Yes, you do," Michael said. "Start picking up, Susan."

"Ha, ha, Susy," Cathy said.

Susan picked up a brush and promptly lost herself in a gentler world for a minute while she studied the exact weight and condition and feel of the implement. Then she put the brush in the paintbox and looked up to see if Michael was still watching her.

"The other one, too," Michael said. "And then you can put the box away."

"I gotta go to the bathroom," Susan said.

"After you've got everything picked up."

"Right now," Susan said. "Else I'm gonna wet my pants."

"All right," Michael said helplessly.

When he got back downstairs, Alan was hammering on something in the alcove off the living room and Alice was setting the table. There was a touch of perspiration on her upper lip.

"What were they into this time?" she said.

"Water colors. They touched up the rug, but it's an improvement. Now there's one spot where you can identify an honest color."

"I'd like to see this place if you had the running of it for a week."

He came around the corner of the table and put his arms around her. "Let's do something tonight," he said.

"You'd better let me go," she said, "if you don't want burned potatoes for dinner."

He buried his face in her hair. It smelled faintly of shampoo. "What I would like to do," he said, "is take my wife to a show, and later I would like to drop in somewhere for a hamburger and a beer, and while I was waiting for the waitress to bring the order, I would tell her that she was looking very nice tonight. Not the waitress. My wife."

"I don't like beer but I think I'd like the rest of it."

"And after that I'd like to drive out in the country and park and turn on the radio. And if a township officer happened along, we would explain that it was perfectly all right because we were married and the parents of four children."

She turned around and put her arms up. "Judging from what experience I've had along this line," she said, "it's my guess it would be more comfortable in bed." She smiled at him. "What do you really want to do tonight?"

"I want to get the hell out of here. I want to run away from the day."

"Was it bad?"

He remembered the conference with Evans and the set of unread papers and the talk with Jim. "No worse than yesterday. Just another day."

"It's late to get a sitter. But I'll try. If you really want to, Mike."

"I really want to," he said. "I'll even help with the dishes. And put the kids to bed. Greater love than that hath no man."

So they went downtown to a movie, and afterwards they stopped in for a hamburger. But they did not drive out into the country afterwards. They went straight home because their sitter charged fifty cents an hour after midnight.

And Sunday morning, in the quiet of the back bedroom, with the kids in Sunday School and Alice busy with the chuck roast—Sunday morning he unlocked the filing cabinet and got out *Some Die on the Vine.* He had spent Saturday thinking that perhaps he had just been tired five months ago, that he had been too critical of himself and maybe the thirteenth chapter would hold up on rereading, that he could finish this now if only out of desperation. So Sunday he got out the manuscript, and the first twelve chapters were just as he remembered them, firm and solid, capturing that complexity of real life which later the reviewers were to comment on. The thirteenth chapter was the way he remembered it, too—the characters flat and stale and mechanical, the action as contrived as something by O. Henry.

He finished reading the manuscript at nine that evening, and then he sat another hour in the flabby kind of stillness you get when the kids are finally asleep and your wife is downstairs reading or listening to a radio turned down low and the only sound at all is the whisper of traffic a block away, like the echo of a memory. All the rest of the story of Arthur Miles was there in his mind, the father's failure in his small real estate business, the terrible scene in which Arthur bails him out of bankruptcy, the bitter, ironic final scene in which, with his mind made up, his choice between the principles and the success philosophy he had learned from his father determined now, he coldly and deliberately cuts his partner's throat. The trouble is that I am no longer writing from experience, he thought. I am faking the world of business; I have never really tasted success myself, and maybe I will never write anything from imagination which will truly hold up. Maybe I can never get down anything but autobiography. But there are those early spring evenings ahead, and a man can't sit around on his butt forever and let his hips delicately widen. For the ragged, dusky, nebulous dream can live only so long, he thought, and there comes a time when it is no longer feasible to continue with artificial respiration. He got to his feet then and put the manuscript back in the filing cabinet, laying it gently to rest the way you ease in the box after you have shoveled open the hole, hoisted out the box, unscrewed the lid and, with the sweat cold on your upper lip and the ringed beam of the flashlight blaspheming the dark, you have discovered that it is the wrong body after all. Well, he thought, you can always write textbooks. For what you write textbooks with is a pair of sharp scissors and the sticky, scabby brush from out of the glue pot.

He went downstairs, where some comedian with an audience-participation show was laying them in the aisles again this week.

Alice was sitting exactly where he knew she would be sitting, and he stood in the door, leaning against the jamb and listening to the emcee prove, with the help of a bucket of water and some leading questions about the intimate details of somebody's courtship, that people were funny—that, in fact, they were a goddam riot. Then he closed the door and Alice looked up.

160

"With six radio stations in the area," he said, "is that absolutely all you can get?"

"I have to listen to something," she said. "While you are locked in up there, turning out that virile prose. I have to do something."

He crossed the room and stretched out on the davenport. He looked up at the spot on the ceiling where the water had come through the day Susan had let the bowl run over. "I've changed my mind," he said. "I don't really want to fight."

"I just made mine up," she said. "I do."

"Turn that damned thing off and come over here."

She turned it off but she didn't come over there. "If anybody ever asks me," she said, "what it's like living with a man who's got to get somewhere, I can tell them. The next time Dorothy complains about George not having any push, I am going to tell her she ought to get down on her knees and give thanks."

"You sound like Portia facing life," he said. "Come over here."

"Should I let my hair down? So you can get a better grip?" But she came over, sat down on the edge of the davenport, and looked down at him. Then she reached out a hand. He might have been one of the kids, and she might have been checking for fever. "Why?" she said. "Why are you the way you are? Why do you think you've got to rip the world apart with your bare hands and then wave the pieces in everybody's face?"

"You knew how I was. I never tried to kid you."

"I didn't think it would last. I thought it was just the way you are when you're twenty and think you have to prove something."

"A man's got an itch, he's got to scratch. A man's hungry, he's got to find something to eat. He doesn't try to talk himself out of it. He scrounges around for something to fill the hollow."

She looked away from him. "What's this one going to be about?"

"What one?"

"You started another one today. I can tell."

"What would you say to a textbook?"

She looked out into the middle of the cramped and cluttered living room and did not say what she would say to a textbook.

"Don't you think a textbook is a terrific idea?" he said. "You can do one in three months, and they pay you royalties on them, and maybe next year you can afford to have your hair fixed."

She was still looking out into the room. "I was never any good for you, was I?" she said.

And now he was bitterly sorry for his part in the evening. "It isn't that," he said. "It isn't you, Alice."

"I wasn't right for you, and the kids weren't right for you, and all this"—she swept the overfurnished room with her hand—"all this wasn't right for you. It's what most people want, but—"

"It hasn't got anything to do with you."

"I guess you can't understand a disease unless you've had it." She looked at him. "All I can do is the best I can do."

"We'd better be getting to bed. I've got an eight o'clock tomorrow morning."

She got up. "You go ahead," she said. "I'll turn off the lights."

For the next two weeks Michael and Jim went through the routine you go through when outlining a text. They examined other anthologies, listed tentative selections, and started the card file which, with the limp briefcase, is the identification of the laborer in the academic vineyard. They also threshed out some basic textual principles, for this is the first thing you do when other professors are going to examine your book, and if you do not explain in an introduction that you have modernized Shakespeare's spelling so that he will make sense to a freshman, they will laboriously check your text against photostats of the First Folio and then, over coffee at the faculty club, they will tell each other that you have tampered with the Original and are Unsound. So two weeks later, when Frank Mattson came to town on a scouting trip, they had an outline to show him.

When Michael walked into Jim's office that afternoon, Mattson was sitting at Jim's desk looking over their material. When he got up and shook hands, Michael thought that he looked like a publisher. Or like a successful businessman, a tri-state supervisor for Standard Oil, say. He was six feet tall and thick in the shoulders and chest, the kind of thickness that let you know he didn't deny himself at a table but that he had sense enough to get down to the Club twice a week for squash and a rubdown. He had black, lightly oiled, care-fully parted hair and a square, strong-jawed face, and he wore casually a Brooks Brothers suit which he had hung outside his hotel room last night, and would hang there again to-night. He looked like a man who would get a shoeshine every morning on his way to the office, and who played bridge in the corner of the New York, New Haven and Hartford coach on his way home at night, and who tipped fifteen per-cent in depressions when they expected ten and in good times when they expected twenty.

He also shook hands the way you knew he would shake hands. "Hello, Savage," he said. "They tell me you're a novel-ist."

"I've published a novelette," Michael said.

Mattson almost frowned but he caught himself on the brink. "I haven't read it yet," he said.

"Well," Michael said, "that makes you one of the crowd. The people who have read *The Alley* belong to a very exclusive set."

"Didn't it do well?"

"It didn't exactly put the Rogers Press permanently on its feet."

"Oh?" Mattson said. "Tom Rogers did it?" His tone managed to suggest that that explained everything, that every-body knew that Tom Rogers operated on a shoestring and any book on his list was entirely on its own. "Working on another one?"

163

"I was for a while."

"Troubles?"

Michael said yes, troubles.

"Maybe you need help. A good editor might be able to straighten you out. We've got a couple on our staff. Why don't you—"

"No, thanks. I'm afraid there isn't anything in it for you. Tom Rogers has an option on it."

Mattson dropped his eyes. "Well," he said, "we aren't here to talk about your novel, are we?" He tapped the top page of the outline. "I think this might go. I think Seegar may think so, too." He sat down, leaned back, and talked for an hour about the problems involved in promoting a successful text. Then he tucked the outline in his briefcase and stood up. "If Seegar likes this we'll mail you a contract. And a check." He smiled at Michael. "Sure you don't want me to take that novel back?"

"I'm sure. It belongs to Tom Rogers. If I ever finish it."

"Confidentially, I've known Tom to release a writer if he thought he could do better somewhere else."

"I have no doubt. But Tom took one beating for me, and you don't repay obligations by breaking option clauses." He looked Mattson square in the eye. "You really wouldn't be interested in a publisher jumper," he said. "Now would you?"

Mattson smiled. "If you put it that way."

Michael smiled back. He was thinking that in spite of himself, he liked Mattson. He had read a lot of novels, and he had an abstract picture in his mind of businessmen; Mattson fitted some of the angles in that picture, but he still liked him.

"Well," Mattson said, "when you finish it, keep us in mind. In case anything should happen."

"Sure," Michael said. "If I finish it."

Michael finished his part of the text late in April, on a Sunday afternoon, and when the pages were lying on the table in Jim's living room, looking neat and cold and final, like a blueprint, he tilted back in his chair and watched Jim run uncertain fingers through his long hair.

"Jesus," Jim said, "do you always go at something as if you were killing snakes, Mike?"

"It's the way to get it done." Michael felt very tired; they had been at it for nine straight hours. "How's the coffee holding out?" he asked.

"You better cut down on that stuff. I'll bet you've swilled four gallons since Friday. You can get coffee nerves."

"That's what they tell me," Michael said. He looked at the manuscript in the middle of the table and almost experienced again what he had experienced back when he had been writing *The Alley*, when he would turn from putting the typewriter away and stand at his desk with the exhaustion clear into his blood stream and look down at the pages he had turned out that day. Which was the let-down, completely done-in feeling you get when you have fought with something and made it say papa. Which is how you feel when you have solved the insoluble, and the feeling is as close as man has gotten, since Eve ate the apple, to the peace that passes understanding. Which is the meaning of life and the end of a man, if a man is born lucky. And textbook or novel, he thought, I wonder if it makes any difference just so long as you capture it? Then he pushed back his chair and got to his feet and put his fingertips on the edge of the table to steady himself.

Jim blinked at him. "You've got nerves," he said. "Another five years like this and you're going to burn yourself out, like an overheated motor."

Michael grinned. "It's good for you. It blows out the carbon and eliminates the knock."

"Sure." Jim's eyes wavered. He reached out and touched the manuscript tentatively. "You know," he said softly, "I think it's going to be good, don't you, Mike?"

So Jim feels the same way, Michael thought. Maybe it doesn't make any difference; the object is the mystical experience, and why sleep on spikes when maybe all you have to do is fast? Maybe I have been kidding myself; maybe I ought to stick to writing texts from now on, for they are easier and faster and, no doubt, more lucrative. Then he thought of Jorgensen, who churned out articles on Middle English dialect, and of Karl Dobs, who had spent twenty years trying to find something new to say about Dryden, and then he decided that he was too tired to be thinking very clearly.

"I hope we can turn out three more sections like this one," Jim said.

He was not too tired to notice Jim's use of the first person plural. "I hope you can, too," he said.

Jim's head was bent, and he was playing idly with the corner of the manuscript. "I know it wasn't part of the deal," he said, "but were you figuring on helping any with the rest of this, Mike?"

"I wasn't."

"The point is, I can't make myself work this way, Mike. I need somebody pushing me."

"All right. I'll drop in on you once a day, see if you've turned out your three pages—"

Jim brought his head up. "I don't guess there's any point in trying to kid anybody. Is there?"

"I don't know what you mean, Jim."

"Yes, you do. I can't do the rest of this without help, Mike."

Michael looked at him another moment and then he looked away. He had seen that expression before; once it had looked up a flight of cellar stairs at him, and another time it had been on the face of a man who was telling him about writing a novel. And no doubt that is how I looked to young Evans that day, he thought, and now I know I am too tired to be thinking clearly.

He took his hand off the edge of the table. "I believe I wore a coat."

"I've got to know," Jim said. "One way or the other."

"I'm afraid not, Jim."

Jim got to his feet. "I'll get your coat," he said. "It's in the bedroom."

*

166

It was dark when he got home. The kids were in bed, and Alice was in the kitchen, washing up the Sunday evening dishes, and in the living room the radio was on very loud so that she could hear it while she worked. He hung his coat in the closet off the living room and went into the kitchen.

"You two really made a day of it, didn't you?" she said.

"I didn't come straight home." He opened the refrigerator and stooped, looking for something to eat. Their refrigerator was old and small; no matter how carefully you organized things, you could never find anything in it.

"There's some cold chicken," she said. "On the second shelf. What have you been doing? Since you left out there?"

"Thinking."

"About what?"

"Life."

"Come over here and let me smell your breath."

"I'm sober. I've just been driving around. There's a bend in the river out the River Road. I parked out there and smelled the smell of spring in the air."

"Get much done today?"

"I'm finished with it," he said. He came across the kitchen for some bread.

"Well, thank the Lord for small favors."

He looked at her. "Meaning?"

"Nothing. Just that you're tired out. I don't know why you always have to work at something as if—"

"I'm not tired. I feel fine. But I'm finished with it." He went into the living room with his sandwich and lay down on the davenport. Alice followed him and sat down in the chair by the radio.

"Should I turn it off?" she asked. "There's a good play on at nine."

"Is there?" He wondered why, whenever they found themselves alone in their living room, she always felt a compulsion to turn on the radio. She knew that if he had the operating of it, a radio would stand dusty and neglected in a forgotten corner of the house. He wished that just once when they were alone like this, she would want to do something besides seek

167

refuge behind the wall of a good play at nine o'clock. But maybe she's afraid, he thought. Maybe she knows that if she ever did that, the only thing left would be for us to talk to each other, and neither of us could keep that alive for longer than three minutes. "Turn it off," he said. "So I can tell you what I've been thinking about. Out there in the middle of the smell of spring."

She turned off the radio. "What have you been thinking about?"

He propped himself on an elbow and looked at her. "I could finish a novel in six months. If there wasn't anything else to get in the way."

"Could you? That's fine."

"If there wasn't anything else to get in the way," he repeated.

She looked at him briefly, but she didn't say anything, and then her eyes wandered somewhere else.

"Alice," he said, "I want to quit my job."

Her eyes jerked back to him and froze there a moment. Then she smiled. "Right away?"

"Right away. Tomorrow."

"That would be nice. But hardly practical, would it? Not with seventy dollars in the bank and four children." She might have been talking to a child who wanted a pony for Christmas.

"If we sold the house and car we could realize enough to make out. For six months."

"And if we sell the house, where do we live?" Her tone told him that she suddenly realized he might be serious.

"They advertise apartments every day in the paper."

She straightened up in the chair. "I think maybe we ought to go to bed."

"Listen, Alice, I've lived your way for a hell of a lot of years now. Now all I'm asking is that you live my way for one."

"In a small apartment? With four children?"

"Other people do it."

"I'm not other people. And I think you're just being ridiculous. And what would we live on *after* you finished a novel?

168

Your five-hundred-dollar advance? Until you wrote another one?"

"I don't know. I haven't thought that far ahead."

"You can say that again."

"All right. But it's either that or I walk out of here. Take your choice."

"You wouldn't," she said. "You couldn't."

"Why couldn't I?"

"Because you're Michael Savage. Because you take your responsibilities seriously."

"You think so? Try me." He sat up. "Tomorrow morning I'm going to tell Ken that I'm finishing the term and then he can get himself another boy."

"Mike," she said, "will you do just one thing? Will you put this off until fall? You can have them take your name off the summer-school list—we can probably borrow enough to manage through the summer. But you wouldn't have to resign until fall, would you?"

He didn't answer her.

"What difference can that make?" she said. "If you're not teaching this summer what possible difference—"

"All the difference. I don't want to have a job to fall back on. I want to burn my bridges. I want the pressure on."

She stood up. "It's time we were getting to bed. We want you to be fresh from now on in the mornings, don't we? Because mornings are when you work best, aren't they?"

"They would be if I didn't have classes tomorrow morning."

She walked to the stair door. She stood there with her hand on the knob and her back to him and her head down. "Twelve years," she said. "Three years living on nothing while you get a degree, and nine more getting onto our feet. We were just beginning to get somewhere, and now you want to throw it all away. Just because something went wrong out there this afternoon."

"The only thing that went wrong out there was that I woke up. I realized that it was either now or never, that this is my last chance." He got up and put his arms around her.

169

"We'll still get someplace. Someplace besides an associate professorship and a graduate course in metaphysical poetry. And it won't take me any twenty years, either."

She stood passively, not trying to move, just waiting for him to let go of her so she could open the door and go upstairs to bed.

"All I'm asking for is one lousy year, Alice. If I don't get anywhere in that time, I'll resign myself. But that doesn't seem a lot for a man to ask."

She didn't say anything to that, either.

"We'll make out," he said. "It won't be so tough."

"Of course not," she said. "It will be easy. It's not hard to be hungry. Not once you get used to it."

11 THEY SOLD THE HOUSE LATE in June and moved into an upstairs, west side apartment with two small bedrooms and a pantry off the enormous kitchen large enough for a cot and a desk. They cleared fifteen hundred dollars on the house and car.

For a month the book went well. For a month he was at work by seven in the morning and still at work at eleven at night. Then he struck a snag. He spent a week on one scene, and at night he lay awake with the fear in him that he didn't have it after all. Twice that week, lying there in the dark beside Alice's quiet breathing, he had the feeling, just as he was dropping off to sleep, that the scene he was trying to wrench into shape was sliding across his mind, the lines pure and cold and frightening because they had come so easily. But the next morning they were gone, and out in the hallway he could hear the echo of a soap opera and the kids playing tag around the dining-room table. He sat there with the anger hot and impotent in him because the words would not come and because he should have gotten up the night before and because the fear was in him.

At the end of that week he came out of the pantry one morning, poured himself a cup of coffee, and then stood at the sink, watching Alice iron.

"It must not be going well," she said.

"It's going all right."

She glanced at him. "You don't look as if it's going well."

171

He was suddenly angry, at her cool glance or the indifference in her voice. "All right," he said. "It's not going well. If that's a satisfaction to you. It would be all right if I could just get to sleep nights. But I go to bed and start thinking about what I'm going to write tomorrow, and the first thing I know it's three in the morning."

"Well, don't start thinking about what you're going to write tomorrow."

"You have a great talent. You always make everything sound so easy." He rinsed out the coffee pot, filled it and put it on the stove. "I wish someday you'd make enough coffee to see me through a morning."

"That's probably what's wrong with you. I couldn't sleep either if I swilled the stuff all day long."

"Don't start that again," he said. "Don't start sounding like a goddam medical consultation again."

"Nobody can tell you anything," she said.

"Coffee is what keeps me going. And just once why can't you stop living by somebody's bloody rule book?"

"I made a whole pot this morning," she said. "That percolator only holds six cups, and it's the only one I've got, and—"

"All right," he said. "Why couldn't you just say so?"

"It would take a washtub to make as much as you drink in a day. And I haven't got time in the morning. I've got the kids—"

"All right," he said. "I'm sorry. I apologize." He walked to the stove and checked the progress of the coffee. "Alice," he said, "would you care if I moved into the pantry for a while? To sleep, I mean?"

She raised her head slowly. "Now what would you want to do that for?"

"Because I think I could work better at night."

"I think that's silly."

He had known that that is what she would say. As far as Alice was concerned, the inventor of the double bed had been in touch with God and Absolute Truth. He could have predicted what she would say. He could have given odds.

"You can't sit up all night and sleep all day," she said. "You'd be dead on your feet in a week. And it would make a problem with meals."

"I'll get up for dinner. The rest of the time I'll raid the icebox."

"The rest of the time, you'll prowl around and keep the rest of us awake. Just because you read something somewhere."

"I did not read anything anywhere," he said patiently. He looked down at the dregs in his coffee cup, and suddenly he was filled with a slow anger because she hadn't made enough coffee, because he would sit at the typewriter all day and not accomplish anything, because tonight he would lie awake again and tomorrow morning the kids would be racing up and down the hall and the radio would be on loud enough to crack the plaster. And because Alice had never made any attempt to understand anything. "Just tell me where I can find some bedding," he said. "I'll make up the cot myself."

"I don't think we have any extra."

"Listen, you know goddamned well there's enough bedding for a thirty-inch cot, and what's the point of being bitchy about it?"

"Oh," she said softly, "so I'm being bitchy, am I?"

"You put a name to it, then."

"We've only been married twelve years, and already you want to start sleeping in separate rooms because you read somewhere about some writer who sleeps all day and works all night, and I'm being bitchy. You want to pound a typewriter all night in an apartment with beaverboard partitions, and I'm—"

"I want to work at night because it's quiet then, and because I want to finish a book before we run out of money. To hear you, you'd think I was suggesting a divorce."

"It's early in the game yet," she said. "Give you six months."

"If there are many more mornings like this one," he said, "you can cut that estimate some."

"We're barely in our thirties. We're too young to be sleeping in separate rooms." Her voice was very close to tears.

"That's got nothing to do with it," he said. "Anyway, I haven't gotten the impression lately that it made that much difference to you."

"That," she said evenly, "was a rotten thing to say." She raised her head. "All right," she said. "Move out. Rent an apartment across town if you want to, and visit me on weekends."

"I only want to finish a book, Alice." He spread his hands. "Everything I've ever wanted to do."

"You regret it, don't you?"

"Regret what?"

"Marrying me?"

"Alice, will you please stop it?"

"Answer me. Don't you? If we didn't have the kids, you'd walk out tomorrow. Wouldn't you?"

"Today I would. Whose fault is it?"

"It's not *all* mine," she said. "Am I unreasonable if I don't want to sleep alone for the next six months? How would you feel if I moved out?"

"I don't know."

"I'll make up the cot," she said. "This afternoon." She brushed a hand across her face, the way you do when you have just walked through cobwebs. "How much longer do you think it will be?"

"I don't know. Six months. Maybe less."

"Are you just going to stay in there until it's finished?" Her smile was onion-tissue thin.

"Maybe not. Maybe I won't work any better at night after all."

She looked down at the ironing board. "Never mind. Stay as long as you like. Sleep with your goddam book. See if it's any warmer."

"Alice—"

"Only don't come straying back looking like a puppy with worms. If you move, stay put. If you've got any ideas about—"

174

He straightened up. "If that's the way you feel about it," he said. He rinsed out his cup and set it very deliberately on the drainboard, and then he walked into the pantry and closed the door. Walking past her, he knew she was going to start to cry as soon as he was out of the room, and he felt a brief impulse to put a hand on her shoulder and tell her to forget it, that it was only an idea. Then he had closed the door, and the single sentence he had accomplished since seven that morning was still in the typewriter, and he thought, coldly and dispassionately, The hell with her, I don't want her anyway, I don't think I will ever want her again.

That afternoon she came in and made up the cot. He stopped working and watched her. When she was finished, she sat down on the edge of the cot and looked at him. "There won't be much air in here," she said. "There's only that one little window."

"There'll be enough. I'll leave the door open."

She dropped her eyes. "I'm sorry, Michael," she said.

"So am I."

She got up and came to him and he put an arm around her waist. "I didn't mean any of it," she said. "Not a word."

"Neither did I."

"Is it going any better?"

"No. But it will now." He looked up into her face. "It's just that I can't let it whip me. Because I've burned my bridges."

"I know."

"Maybe it won't make any difference. Writing at night. But I want to find out."

"Well, in any event, come over and see me sometime."

"If you want me to."

She stooped and kissed him. "I want you to," she said.

He reached up and ruffled her hair. "Get the hell out of here," he said. "I've got work to do."

She straightened up and then stood there, looking down at the typewriter. "It would make a girl feel wonderful," she said, "if you thought half as much of her as you do of that."

He grinned up at her. "I do," he said. "In a different way."

*

The money ran out in December.

It was nobody's fault. In September there had been school clothes to buy, and in October an insurance premium, and in December Alice said the kids were going to have a decent Christmas if they had to go on relief in January. By that time Michael was writing on both sides of a sheet of paper and they were eating nothing but casseroles, even on Sunday, but nevertheless the evening came when Alice looked down the table at him and reminded him that the rent was due in another week.

"I know it," he said.

"Michael," Alice said, "will you please pay attention?"

"I am. You just said the rent was due."

"Our bank balance is twenty-eight dollars."

"I know that, too." He tasted the main dish for the evening. If we ever come out of this, he thought, and she serves tuna fish casserole again, I am going to institute immediate proceedings. He looked down the table at her. She was wearing a bathrobe over a slip, and he felt a moment of sharp resentment at the novel because it wasn't going any faster, at himself because he had had to be ambitious. If we ever make it, he thought, I am going to buy her a trunk full of expensive clothes. We'll pack the kids off to a summer camp and go off by ourselves somewhere for a hell of an expensive time. "I can still borrow two hundred on that insurance policy," he said.

"Two hundred dollars. How far will two hundred dollars go?" She brushed a hand through her hair. "I can't stand much more of this, Michael. I just can't live like this much longer. Look at your children. Look at the way Ellen and Cathy have to go to school. If it was just me—"

"Listen, everything's going to be all right. I'll finish in another month, and then I'll get an advance—"

"All right!" she said bitterly. "You'll get five hundred dollars that will have to last until you've written another one, and everything's going to be all right."

Which is without doubt the truth, he thought wearily, and I was probably a damned fool, I should have clung to my job.

176

"More than five hundred," he said. "This one is worth more than five hundred." He pushed back his chair. "I'm going to write Kay. Ask her to get me two thousand dollars. A thousand now, the rest when Tom gets the last three chapters."

"You're daydreaming. Tom doesn't have that kind of money."

"Maybe not. But if he doesn't, maybe somebody else does."

They waited ten days for the phone call.

"Hello," Kay Anderson said when he picked up the phone. "Michael? Tom called this afternoon. He's read the manuscript. If you can get away, I think you'd better come on out here."

"I can get away, but I haven't got any money—"

"I'll wire you a hundred dollars. Can you be here by Thursday?"

"Yes. Is it really any good, Kay? Good enough so that—"

"It's all right. It's going to be fine, Michael."

"More than five hundred," he said. "I've got to have—"

"We'll do everything we can for you."

"I borrowed on an insurance policy this week, and when that's gone, I'm really broke, and I've got—"

"Try not to worry," she said. "Hadn't we better hang up now? This call is being charged to your account."

Kay met him at the bus station. She came across the concrete when he walked through the gate. She said she recognized him from his pictures and had it been a terrible trip? He said he knew how they felt when they had gone ten tough rounds, and she asked him if he'd had anything to eat and how would a steak taste?

"I can't even imagine. I tasted a steak once, but it was longer ago than I can remember."

"We'll make it a steak. On Anderson and Carew."

He picked up his suitcase and followed her out into the whistles and the horns and the shouting.

"We're seeing Tom tomorrow morning," she said. "We'll pick you up around nine."

He looked at her. She walked with a long, clean, easy

177

stride, like a woman golfer. "What's the exact situation, Kay?" he asked.

"It's just around the corner. No atmosphere, but they char-broil a beautiful steak."

"That's not what—"

"It's bad to talk business on an empty stomach. It can do things to your digestive processes."

"My digestive processes are long since down the drain."

She smiled at him. "Don't worry. We'll get you some money, Michael."

An hour later he laid his fork across his empty plate and looked across the table at her. She had been right about the steaks. "How much money, Kay?"

"Enough to see you through those last chapters."

He looked down at the remains of the beautiful steak. "That's not enough," he said.

"It would be a lot simpler if we were dealing with somebody besides the Rogers Press. You have to understand that, Michael."

He watched the waiter lay the check carefully in the exact center of the table. "Exactly how much, Kay?"

"Seven-fifty. Half now, the rest when you're finished."

Seven-fifty, he thought. Six seventy-five when you subtracted Kay's fee—enough to last four months if you were careful.

"Damn it," Kay said, "I wish you hadn't quit your job. It would have made things so much simpler."

"No, it wouldn't. It wouldn't have made things simple at all."

"Universities give leaves of absence. You have a family to support. I can't understand—"

"I didn't want a job to fall back on." He watched Kay glance carelessly at the check and lay a twenty on the tray; the price of this meal would have fed the six of them at home for three days. "You give a decade to a family," he said, "and then there comes a time when it's to hell with your socio-economic responsibilities. I'm not sorry I quit the university. Not a bit. Because I've at least had these eight months. Next

178

year I may be working the swing shift in some factory, or rotting in one of those Ohio colleges that are long on Jesus and short on endowment. But nobody can ever take these eight months away from me."

"I didn't know how you felt about it."

"I'll tell you how I felt about it. I felt like a schoolteacher on her first trip to Europe and a handsome count aboard. The only thing you regret is when it looks as if the trip is coming to an end."

The waiter came back and set the tray of change in front of Kay. "Maybe we can do better than seven-fifty," she said. "It's going to be up to you, of course."

"Goddam it," he said softly, "just once why can't life be nice and clean and simple?"

"I've been in this business eleven years," Kay said, "and this is the second time I've advised a client to beg out of an option clause, and Tom's a personal friend of mine. But this is too much book for Tom to handle, Michael. It could make you a hundred thousand dollars if it's handled right."

"An option is a gentleman's agreement. It's a promise you make, like a marriage vow. Maybe I'd feel different if four other publishers hadn't turned down *The Alley* before Tom saw it. Or if Tom hadn't lost money on it."

She shrugged. "That's the publishing business. Tom didn't expect to lose money on it."

"Yes, he did. He said he didn't expect any more than to break even. He said he was buying a writer, not a manuscript." He picked up a fork and began to draw figures on the cloth. "Most of the sons-of-bitches in this business only want to shoot crap when the dice are loaded," he said. "If they see a sale of fifty thousand, they are very eager. Otherwise, let people like Tom take the beating for them. They figure they can always pick you up after somebody else has made you an asset."

"You've got a lot to learn about people in this business."

"It isn't conscience; it's superstition. I've waited a lot of years for this moment, and now I don't want to foul anything up before I'm started." He raised his head. "I'm not asking for a hundred thousand. All I'm asking for is enough to see me through the next book. If we let Tom have it, how do you think it will do, Kay?"

She was looking evenly and objectively at him. He might have been under a microscope. "He ought to sell six thousand," she said.

Six thousand, he thought. Twenty-five hundred dollars. "No more than that?"

"It takes more than just a good book to sell a good book. It takes promotion." She pushed back her chair. "Let's not talk any more about it tonight. Let's wait until morning. Maybe the light will be brighter in the morning."

He didn't say anything, and she waited a decent interval and then leaned forward and put a hand over his. "It will work out," she said. "Maybe by tomorrow morning he'll have learned how to pull a rabbit out of a hat. Maybe he's remembered some uncle who owns a bank somewhere."

"I hope so," he said. "And I hope the uncle is very fond of him. I hope he thinks of Tom as an only son."

Only the light wasn't any brighter the next morning, and Tom didn't have an uncle who owned a bank, and he hadn't otherwise learned how to pull a rabbit out of a hat. The fact was, he didn't even have a hat.

The two of them were waiting for Michael when he came around the corner from the elevators the next morning. Tom stuck out a hand. "Hello, Michael," he said.

"Hello, Tom." Tom had cropped hair and stocky shoulders, and Michael remembered that Kay had said once in a letter that he looked like a steam fitter. But if he had had the handling of the comparison, he would have said that he looked like a catcher in the International League. Probably Kay had just been trying to say that Tom didn't look like a publisher of thin volumes of poetry and avant-garde fiction. "It's high time I was meeting my publisher," Michael said.

"Second the motion," Tom said. He looked at Kay. "If nobody minds sitting at a counter let's eat breakfast in the coffee shop. They only expect a quarter tip there."

180

"Anderson and Carew is picking up the check this morning," Kay said.

"Like hell," Tom said. "We follow standard operational procedure this morning. So I can put you two under some kind of an obligation."

That was the closest they came to talking business until Tom had paid the check and they had started uptown for Kay's office. It was mild out for mid-December, almost thawing. Michael unbuttoned his overcoat, straightened up in the breeze, and felt that this was all going to work out, that there wasn't going to be any moral dilemma after all. At Thirty-eighth Street he told them something about his plans for his next novel, and at Forty-second Tom was saying that the publishing business had gone to hell. The three of them very carefully avoided the reason for their walking uptown together in the thin morning sunlight.

In Kay's office, Michael looked at the photographs on her wall and wondered what it would be like to know that everything you wrote from here on in was going to be worth thirty cents a word.

Then Kay sat down behind her desk and picked up a pencil. "Michael and I had a talk last night, Tom," she said. "So this morning we've got to have some cards on the table."

Tom slid down in his chair. "What did you and Michael have to say?"

"We just reviewed some of the facts." She leaned forward about an inch. "If this were just another novel—but it isn't. Michael can do very well on this if it's handled right."

Tom turned his head slowly and looked at Michael. The look was very level, very deliberate. "What did Michael have to say? After you'd reviewed some of the facts?"

"I want you to have this book, Tom," Michael said. "But I've got to have some money. Enough to support a family while I'm writing another one."

"How much do you have to have? Right away?"

"I don't think that's the whole point," Kay said.

"What's on your mind, Kay?" Tom said very quietly.

"What I said. I want a look at your hand, Tom."

181

Tom slid down another inch. "I've waited ten years for this book," he said. "I started out ten years ago with next to nothing. For five years I was my own editor and salesman. The going has always been tough, but I've stuck it out. And all the time I was waiting for just this one book."

"I know it," Kay said. "I've known you for most of those ten years, Tom."

"I bought Michael's first novel because I had a hunch, and now I've got something I can sink my teeth into, and how many honor tricks are you expecting me to have, Kay? In this hand you want a look at?"

"About three," Kay said. "And some trump support."

"That's a lot of hand. I didn't invite anybody to any slam."

"I know it. I'm inviting you." Her eyes wavered and then refocused. "I'm only trying to be fair to Michael," she said. "That's my job, Tom."

"Seven-fifty is absolutely the best I can do. I've got at the outside six thousand dollars to put into this until I—"

"Six thousand," Kay said, "isn't even going to pay manufacturing costs, Tom."

"We've known each other a long time, Kay. There's no goddam need to fence like this. What's on your mind?"

"Michael's got to have more than seven-fifty, and *Vine* can be a big book this year if it gets any promotion. If you're in no position to do anything except let it sink or swim, I think you ought to release him."

"I can offer some advantages that Doubleday can't. There are advantages to belonging to a noncommercial publisher."

"There are," Kay said, "when it's a noncommercial manuscript."

"You know what's going to happen? You're going to peddle him to one of the cartels. They're going to read this with a book club in mind, and they're just going to bitch it up."

Kay looked at Tom another minute. Then she laid the pencil on the desk. The pencil made a loud, surprising click when the wood hit the wood. "Now, Tom," she said, "we both know better than that. Don't we?"

"All right," Tom said wearily. Slumped in his chair like that,

182

with his head down and his shoulders hunched, he more than ever resembled a catcher out of Columbus, and at the moment he might have been on the carpet for a batting slump. Suddenly Michael was angry because the morning had started out well and then Kay had found it necessary to maneuver him into a position, suddenly he wanted to say the hell with it and Tom could have the book on his own terms. Then Tom brought his head back up.

"What about you, Michael?" he said. "Is that what you want?"

Michael spread his hands. "All I want is enough money to see me through another novel. I don't want to have to go to work in some lousy factory, Tom."

"No, of course you don't."

"If you could just manage a thousand now, and another—"

Tom turned his attention back to Kay. "You'd better write out that release," he said. "I never did know how you word those things."

"All right. And I'm sorry, Tom. I really am."

"Sure you are." He glanced at Michael. "Good luck, Michael. No hard feelings."

"Listen, Tom, I'm sorry, too. I don't like any part of this—"

"Don't worry about it. Take it over to Random House and get yourself an advertising appropriation—make yourself a mint and don't lose any sleep." He dropped his head. "Kay's right," he said. "I've waited ten years for a book I could get my teeth into, but this one would have choked me. It's all part of the business, Michael."

"Maybe," Michael said. "But I still feel like a bastard."

"Cheer up. You'll feel better when they sell you to National."

"No, I won't."

Tom grinned at him. "You'll get used to the feeling, then," he said. "Give yourself six months. They'll make you a success in six months, and then you'll hardly notice it any more."

When he got out of the taxi, he caught a glimpse of Alice in the upstairs window. He could feel her watching him while

183

he paid off the driver, and when he came upstairs, she opened the door for him. He set the suitcase in the middle of the floor and kissed her.

"It's a long trip," he said.

"It's longer when you don't go," she said.

He dropped his coat on the nearest chair and sat down on the davenport. "Where are the kids?"

"Outside. Building a snow fort in the back yard. They'll probably be soaked to the skin." She sat down beside him. He could feel her eyes on his face.

"There's something for everybody," he said. "In the suitcase. I bought you two house dresses. That's a hell of a romantic thing to bring back from New York, now isn't it?"

"How much money did they give you?"

He got out the check and handed it to her. She looked at the amount a while. Then she looked at him again.

"That's half of it," he said. "I collect the rest when they get the last chapters."

"I never thought they'd give you that much. I thought you were just talking."

"They think it's a good book." He was sitting on the edge of the davenport, with his forearms on his knees and his eyes on the floor. "Tom's not doing the book," he said. "I got a release."

"I don't know much about those things. All I understand is advances and royalties."

"I think I know what it feels like to stab a man in the back. Tom could only advance me seven-fifty, and I told him I had to have more than that, and then he told Kay to write out the release." He opened his hands and closed them again; he thought irrelevantly, that they weren't as grimy as they had been that first night in New York—Pullmans are considerably cleaner than busses. "Mattson's talking about a five-thousand-dollar advertising appropriation," he said. "Frank Mattson said I could make fifty, maybe a hundred thousand on this with any real luck."

"If that's the way it is I don't know why you have to feel

guilty. We have to eat. Even if you did think you owed Tom something."

"The last thing Tom said to me—he told me I'd get used to feeling like a bastard. He said I'd hardly notice it once they made me a success." He got to his feet and began to fumble with the straps of his suitcase. "There used to be a bottle of whiskey," he said, "on the top shelf in the cupboard."

"I never knew you to want a drink before."

"A drink does something for you when you're tired. It relaxes you." He hit the lock on the suitcase with the heel of his hand; if he were going to do much traveling, he was going to have to invest in some new luggage. "Besides," he said, "I've been in New York a week, and a week in New York is plenty long enough to acquire a taste for the stuff."

The lock snapped open suddenly, and he opened the suitcase. The two house dresses he had bought Alice were right on top.

Hyatt Engel III

12

I DIDN'T TAKE A PLANE BACK. I have always thought of trains as the hard way to get from one place to another, but I had a story I wanted written by the time I was sliding past 125th Street. So I cancelled my plane reservation and arranged for a train compartment. I also tried to talk a provincial druggist into an ounce of Benzedrine, but I settled for two boxes of caffeine tablets, and on Saturday I said good-bye to Michael and Alice Savage. I stood on the windy platform and wished him good luck and told him to take it easy. I told him to go off into the wilds and lie in the sun and the quiet, to get reacquainted with his wife and give the battle wounds a chance to heal. I told him to quit knocking himself out, because he was a success and there wasn't any urgency any more, and he smiled at me with a smile in which the eyes took no part of the responsibility.

My compartment window faced the station, and five minutes later, when the train moved out, I could see Michael and Alice standing there. Michael was still wearing that smile. Then he touched her arm, and they turned and started across the platform. There was something sad about the touch. It was tentative and shy and lonely, like the lost, secret signal between two people who are blind. Seeing it, I got the feeling you get when it is Indian summer and the trees are going to be bare in another two weeks and the dusk settles down around another day.

Then I stopped thinking of Michael Savage and shifted my

189

mind back onto O'Brien and the office and a story I had to write.

I was finished with it by the time I got off at Grand Central. At Toledo the story had been smooth, exactly the recommended length, and unsatisfactory, and at Buffalo it had been eight pages longer and rough enough to make an editor quietly unhappy, and when I climbed off the train, it was thirty pages long and I was finished with it. The caffeine tablets had given out by that time, and I was very tired, the kind of tired that is mostly inside. When I walked up the concrete ramp, past the magazine stands and the tobacco counters, I was considering what it was like to be finished with a story. The editor who handled this was going to wince when he saw the length. He was going to read it with a magnifying glass but he wasn't going to find much he could chop out. I wondered if this was the way they all felt when they were finished with whatever it was they were trying to be finished with. I wondered if this was the way Savage felt, as if he were finished with something not just on paper but inside himself, too.

Eighteen is the miscellaneous floor for *Insight*. A lot of it is accounting, with cubicles outlined by veneered panels and frosted squares of glass, and behind accounting is an expanse of green metal desks where advertising does something with those agency layouts that are supposed to sell Old Gold cigarettes and Pontiac automobiles, and behind those is the suite of cubicles which was then Myron Levinski's responsibility.

Inside the main room there were three desks and one man. The man had wavy, neutral hair and shell-rimmed glasses and a shadow which was supposed to be a moustache. He looked like a Ph.D. in history from Columbia and probably was. He looked up from some galleys when I came in.

"Levinski around?" I asked.

"Upstairs."

"Back soon?"

He shrugged. "You've got me. He's been up there most of

the weekend. All of them have been up there most of the weekend."

"All of who?"

"The editors. They've spent the whole goddam weekend riding up to twenty and then coming back down so they can ride right back up again. Something on your mind?"

"O'Brien sent me up. I guess I'm doing a story for you."

"Oh, you must be Engel."

I sat down on the edge of his desk. "I'm Engel," I said.

"We're holding next week open for you. How's it coming?"

"It's finished. What's going on around here?"

He looked blankly at me.

"I've been in the hinterlands a week," I explained. "The riding up and down on the elevators. What's it all about?"

"I wouldn't know. I'm only a year old here. I'm just a researcher who stands inconspicuously in the corners of elevators and tries to piece together snatches of conversation."

"Well, from the snatches you pieced together since Friday, what do you *think's* going on?"

"I think some deadwood got lopped off. I also gather that the Guild's unhappy. That's only a theory, of course."

My heart jumped once or twice and then quieted again. It hadn't been me; there hadn't been any pink slip in my box. "You wouldn't have any theories about who?"

"No," he said. "I'm only on the elevators four, five times a day."

The door behind me opened, and I turned around. It was Myron Levinski.

"I'm Hyatt Engel," I said. "I've got a story for you. I guess you're handling it."

"Oh. Yeah. On that new novelist. How's it coming?" His tone told me that he really wasn't hotly interested in how it was coming.

"I think I'm finished with it." I handed him the manila envelope.

He hefted it. "I'll only need one copy," he said.

"That's how many you've got."

Something that could have been pain flitted across his face.

"I know it's a little longer than most of them, but—"

"That is the understatement of the week." He tossed the typescript onto the desk behind him. "You might as well start making with the blue pencil. You can work down here if you want to."

"Look," I said, "I know most of them are only about four thousand, but—"

"Three. Three is perfect. Any longer than that, we haven't got space left for a picture."

"Look, I know most of them are just long enough to get in the color of somebody's hair and what he eats for breakfast and three pungent quotations which reflect his opinion of why anybody would want to stay alive at this moment in history. But this is something else again. I don't think it'll cut. It may break, but I don't think you can cut it without lousing it up." I had another look into his eyes. "The *New Yorker* runs them this long," I said.

"*Insight* isn't the *New Yorker*. *Insight* is the poor man's *Time*. The reader of this magazine wants news. If he is interested in biography, he expects to go out and buy a book."

I walked over and rescued the manuscript. "I'll take it back downstairs," I said. "I'll ask Jim to show it to Ulrich. I'm not going to have it bitched up just because you never ran one longer than three thousand before."

"All right," Levinski said wearily. He held out his hand and I gave him the manuscript. "I'll look it over the way it is," he said. "If I think it'll run, *I'll* take it upstairs."

"Thanks." I turned toward the door. Then I turned back. "How long before I'll know?"

"I can't tell. We're in a process of reorganization around here. I've got other things on my mind besides a back-of-the-book story." He grinned. "Don't call us," he said. "We'll call you."

I beat everybody else to work the next morning, even Janet. I walked down the empty, echoing corridor of the servants' quarters and sat down behind my cleared and dusted desk and prepared to wait a while.

I waited a while. From eight until eight-forty I sat with my hands folded and tried not to think of anything in particular. From eight-forty until nine I concentrated on the evidences of a building coming to life that drifted in through my door from out there in the corridor. From nine until nine-forty I waited in front of my phone for a call from Levinski, like a college sophomore waiting at the mailbox for his first rejection slip.

At nine-forty the office door opened and one of the copy boys came in. He was a towheaded, sharp-faced nineteen-year-old, and I knew just by looking at him that he was going four nights a week to journalism classes at NYU. He tossed a manila folder and a copy of next Thursday's *Insight* in my general direction, grinned impudently, and disappeared. I sat there and considered the empty doorway and speculated a while about what made Sammy run. Then I reached for the folder and flipped it open.

Inside was a first-draft review of *Some Die on the Vine*. I read the first paragraph. I didn't have to read any farther than that to know that the review was Dave Goldstein's.

He knew how to write a review, all right. *Vine* was a tough novel to approach—structurally orthodox but thematically complex, and the jacket blurb had used the word "levels" advisedly. But Dave had gotten it down. What I am trying to say is, I had sat up until five a.m. one night listening to a man trying to explain himself to me. I had studied him in the bosom of his family and had taken long drives with him in the evenings. Then I had gone to bed one night with his novel. When I dropped it on the floor beside the bed at dawn and turned out the bed lamp, I was thinking that you could not really understand that book unless all the rest of what made Michael Savage tick lay in the back of your consciousness. There was the final third of the book, for example. The first twelve chapters of the story of Arthur Miles—those chapters which took Arthur through adolescence and college—were just what all the reviewers had said, firm and sound and true,

193

a mixture of pity and contempt, love and hate, fear and affection which really captured the complexity of a relationship between a boy with materialistic values and a father who was a failure. But the last chapters didn't ring so true. Because here Michael had been writing something he only half believed. The antimaterialistic theme in those final chapters had a subtly tinny sound, like the notes of a mechanical piano. It was the effect you get when somebody writes something with his head, not his heart.

Two reviewers spotted not just the weakness but the reason for it, in the ending of Vine—and Dave Goldstein was one of them. I could have made a third, but I couldn't have done it without that week in Minnesota. But Dave had managed without any help from anywhere. He had come to the book cold, picking it up during a lull one morning, dropping it for lunch, and then finishing it that afternoon. Then he slid the plastic case off his typewriter and sat there a moment, fingers poised, while he worked out a skeleton outline in his mind. And then he had gone to work. He had started the review at ten and finished it before two, and when he had come out of his office into the silence which is like an echo in a New York office building at two in the morning, with the ache between his shoulder blades and the review back there on his desk, he had no doubt felt the way you feel when you have finished a routine assignment. You could forgive him, I thought, if he hadn't felt that way, but you knew that he had, that he would never feel any other way about anything he would turn out for this publication. You knew that when the night operator let him out of the building all he had on his mind was a cup of coffee and a hamburger before he caught an uptown express.

I tossed the folder onto the desk, and leaned back and looked at my shoes. I still had a chance to beat Goldstein out of O'Brien's job, but I knew now that it would have to be luck, not ability. I knew now that I was competing with a better man. I sat there with that hard kernel of truth in me, like a cold, glass agate in the pit of my stomach.

I could hear their voices when I started down the corridor,

though I couldn't make out what they were saying because Helen's door was closed. When I opened it, Helen was at her desk and Dave was leaning over her shoulder.

"He's important," he was saying. "He's a key man. But he won't listen to me. See what *you* can do with him."

"He's scared," Helen said. "His heart's in the right place, but he owes a lot of money."

I cleared my throat delicately, and Dave turned his head and looked across the office at me.

"Hello," I said.

"Hello, Hyatt," Dave said, without enthusiasm. His eyes flickered toward Helen and came back to mine. "Janet's been trying to get you. O'Brien wants to see you. Right away."

"In a minute." I leaned against the door jamb. "Unless I'm interrupting something."

"You are," Dave said.

"In that case—"

"No," Dave said. "Come on in."

I went on in. I had a feeling that something had been hung quickly and temporarily on a peg. I wondered if it had anything to do with people riding up and down in elevators. "Bill in his office?" I asked.

"No," Helen said. "Not in his office."

"The lion's den?"

"Not the lion's den, either."

"Sick?"

"Yes," Helen said. "I guess you could put it that way."

I dropped into the straight chair beside Helen's desk. "I just read your review," I said to Dave. "Of Savage's book. Good review."

"Thanks. I'm glad you liked it, Hyatt. I value your opinion these days."

I looked from Dave's face to Helen's. Neither of them were going to show anything if they could help it, and it appeared they could help it.

"What's been going on around here?" I said.

Neither of them said anything.

"I've been hearing some rumors," I added.

195

"What kind of rumors?" Dave said.

"Nothing definite. Just something about some people getting fired. And about the Guild being unhappy." I reached into my pocket for a cigarette. "Anybody I know?" Then it hit me, and I straightened up. "Bill," I said. "Bill Servat."

Neither of them said anything.

"When?"

"Wednesday," Helen said. "With the other seventeen."

"Why?"

Dave shrugged. "They need a reason?"

"There must be a reason," I said. "You don't just fire seventeen people without *any* reason."

"If you're Ulrich," Dave said, "all you need is a whim."

"Oh, nuts, Dave." The trouble with Dave Goldstein, I thought, was that everything in his world was either black or white, and he was still fighting the labor-management battles of the twenties. "He must have had some kind of a reason."

"All right," Dave said. "Call it an economic cutback. Say it's in the interests of economy and sounder operations. Say it has become necessary to reduce the rising ratio of editorial expenses in spite of the fact that our gross is now larger than any time in our history." He spread his hands. "To quote the staff directive," he said.

"That sounds like a reason," I said. I dropped my eyes. "If they were all like Bill I could give you another one, too."

"What?"

"Deadwood." I looked straight and hard into his eyes. "Face the facts, Dave," I said. "He never did have it. It was always touch and go with him. It's a miracle he lasted as long as he did."

"Sure."

"He'll recover. He'll get a job on a newspaper somewhere, where the pressure is only fifteen pounds per square inch, and in six months he'll wonder what he ever saw in this job."

"Sure, he will. He only owes around eleven thousand dollars. You can pay that off in no time out of forty a week."

"Well, there isn't anything any of us can do about it."

"Isn't there?"

I leaned forward a little. "I'll put that differently," I said. "There isn't anything *I* intend to do about it."

"That figures," Dave said. He looked significantly at Helen. "I told you, didn't I?" he said. "They can sure become sons-of-bitches in a hurry, once they're started in the direction."

I tilted back in my chair. "All right," I said. "Let's suppose we do start a fight. Get the Guild all stirred up. Organize a walkout. So what happens?"

"I don't know," Dave said. "You tell me, Hyatt."

"First the NLRB steps in. Like over at *Newsweek* that time. It takes six months to a year for them to arrive at a compromise that's halfway acceptable to both parties. Now tell me how I'm supposed to eat for those months."

I waited a minute, but he didn't have any ready solution for that problem.

"So maybe we even pull it off," I said. "Maybe Ulrich finds out he *needs* us, which, given his editors and those lines down in personnel, he doesn't. But he hires back the deadwood. Then what does he do?"

"It's still your story," Dave said.

"If I were Ulrich I know what I'd do. I'd have a careful study made of the enthusiasts in that walkout. And I'd write me down an alphabetized list of the ones who were going to get crapped on from here on in. And speaking personally, I'm not going to be happy being nothing but a lousy writer for the rest of my life."

"Why don't you just pick up and get out of here, Hyatt," he said wearily.

"All right." I stood up and looked down at him. "I suppose I really ought to hope you'll go through with this, Dave."

"But you don't?"

"No. I don't know why, but I don't."

"I don't know why, either. Not if what you've got in mind is O'Brien's job."

"That's what I've got in mind. Maybe it's because it isn't as much fun when you win by default."

He studied my expression a few seconds. "One thing you might like to know," he said. "You're second choice, Hyatt.

197

You're the scrapings off the bottom of the barrel. They offered me the job Friday. For a consideration."

I studied his eyes a minute. "You're a goddam liar, Dave," I said quietly.

"Am I? Ask O'Brien. Or Ulrich. When he offers to buy you with the same proposition."

I turned then and walked across the office and opened the door. After three years it was habit to ask them if we were having lunch together, but habits can be broken and I managed that one between a desk and a door. Because I had a pretty good idea what their answer would have been.

O'Brien was standing at his office window, looking down on 34th Street. He turned when he heard the door open. Beyond him I could hear the murmur of traffic seventeen floors below, and for some reason he looked, just then, small and tired and badly proportioned.

"Hello, Hyatt," he said. "Just get in?"

"No. I've been here since eight."

He came back to his desk. "They tell me you did a job for us out there in Minneapolis."

"Who told you?"

He nodded across the corner of his desk. "Sit down."

"I've been sitting all morning. Who told you, Jim?"

"I don't give a goddam if you've been sitting since a week ago Thursday," he said. "I can't talk to somebody standing in a doorway. You make my feet hurt just looking at you. Come on in and sit down."

I came in and sat down. "Who?"

He leaned back and clasped his hands behind his head. "One thing you're going to have to learn, Hyatt—if you ever want to move up the old ladder—is that when they say *move,* they mean *jump.*"

"Is this what you wanted to see me about, Jim?"

He reached into his shirt pocket and came out with a cigarette. But no matches. He stuck the cigarette into the side of his mouth and sat there, blinking at me. I fought my right

198

hand and thought, The hell with you, you can sit there all morning for all of me.

"Another thing," he said, "you have to develop reflexes, Hyatt. If you expect to do any climbing to speak of." He was wearing a little smile. "I would advise you to light it, Hyatt," he said.

For just a minute I resisted the impulse to stand up and take a calculated swing at O'Brien; then I shrugged, dug for my lighter, and leaned across the desk into that smile. "Sure, Jim," I said. "If this means something to you. If this is the way you get your kicks."

"Sure. I get a bang out of it. A real charge." The smile was gone now, and in its place nothing but a pair of weak eyes set in a face that probably even he didn't remember between one shave and the next. "Tell me something," he said. "What makes a man ambitious, anyway? What is it makes a man get out and scratch?"

"I don't know. Do you mean just any man? Or somebody in particular?"

"You, for instance. You're interested in this office of mine. It can't be the money, because you're old enough to know that you aren't going to be any richer. Just poor on a larger scale. Why, then?"

"Maybe the two windows. Better light. Not to mention the cross-ventilation in July and August."

"The mess of pottage," he said quietly, almost to himself.

"Yeah," I said. "Because birthrights are for those who can afford them. The ones with locker boxes crammed with AT&T and GM Preferred."

"And the rest of us?"

I grinned. "The rest of us learn to lean across desks with cigarette lighters in constant readiness."

He blinked once or twice and then, suddenly, his eyes were as steady as mine. "I guess you'll do, all right," he said.

I didn't ask him what I'd do for. I didn't have to.

"I suppose you know by now," he said, "what's been going on around here in your absence."

199

"Only roughly. I imagine the version I got was pretty slanted."

"Meaning Dave Goldstein?"

"Meaning Dave Goldstein. Dave's got a theory it was just a whim."

"Dave had better keep his theories to himself for a while. Dave's position around here is very precarious at the moment." He untangled his fingers and laid his hands to rest on the arms of his chair. "It was a simple matter of economy," he said. "We've been going into the red for two years now because our organization was loose and sloppy. It was a simple demand for sounder organization."

"You don't have to convince me. I'm not representing the Guild this morning, Jim."

"All the Guild can see," he said, "is our increased gross over the last period. You can't tell any of them that gross is beside the point. They won't any of them listen to you. We had to reorganize from the top down. They gave J. H. all administration, production, and coordination. Behr they moved from foreign affairs to the front of the book. I'm handling the back of the book. After that they took a close look at the rest of the payroll. They found they could eliminate overlapping by cutting off seventeen at the bottom. There's one hole left to be plugged. That's where you come in. The Boss is convinced that you've got the ability. The question is, do you have the other qualifications."

"Such as what?"

"He'll be calling you up there one of these days. When he does, keep in mind that he puts a lot of stock in loyalty. Are you loyal, Hyatt?"

"It depends on his definition. If he means am I willing to cross a picket line—" I shrugged.

"What if he means something on top of that?"

"Like what? What is his definition, Jim?"

"One thing you've got to understand about the Boss," he said. "He's got a 19th-Century mind. He is out of joint managerially with this century. I suppose you'd call him an economic paternalist."

200

I leaned forward a little. "For ten thousand a year I can swallow the divine right of kings. What is his definition, Jim?"

His eyes were firmly on mine, and there wasn't any waver in them any more. "I'd better leave definitions to him," he said. "His command of language is better than mine. He's got that gift of making a vice sound like a virtue. But I guess you'll do, Hyatt. I guess it was carrying coals to Newcastle, taking time out of the morning to test you for the proper reflexes." His eyes started to turn soft again, and then they stiffened, the way they do when they pump some will into them, and for just a moment, and for no reason I could put a finger on, I felt an instant of sadness for Jim O'Brien.

"Thanks, Jim," I said.

"What for?"

"Everything. The advice. The conditioning."

"Forget it," he said. "I'd do as much for any of my enemies."

I stood up, and then I remembered something. "Tell me one more thing," I said. "Am I second choice for this job?"

"Who told you that?"

"Dave. He said they tried to buy him with the job Friday."

"Supposing they did? Would it make any difference, Hyatt?"

"Probably not. I was just curious."

"The first thing I learned after I got this job was that it doesn't pay to ask questions unless the answers make a difference to you." He pushed himself back from his desk and stood up—a short, near-sighted, pot-bellied, gray-faced little man with a nervous stomach and fatigue at the corners of his mouth and in the slope of his shoulders. "Had lunch?" he said.

"I thought I'd just grab a sandwich," I said. "It's going to be a busy afternoon."

He stood there uncertainly a moment, blinking at me. Then he turned away. "All right," he said. "I just thought I'd ask."

I looked at him, turned now so that I couldn't read his eyes, one hand as if for support on the edge of the desk, and suddenly and for no particular reason I felt something in my throat. I had worked three years for O'Brien, and in three years I suppose you acquire the habit of seeing a man not as he is but as your preconceptions tell you he is. Anyway, for a long time now O'Brien had been for me the guy you had to get past with copy, and if he was anything else, it was a bastard who derived a twisted enjoyment out of making you squirm over the syntax of a sentence, or out of instilling the fear of God into the lame ducks like Bill Servat, or out of forcing you, just for the hell of it, to lean and apply the flame of the lighter to the unwanted cigarette. And then one noon he said, quite simply, "I just thought I'd ask," and in that instant he wasn't a bastard any more; in that instant you saw through the preconception to the sad, scared, lonely little man who had, through processes which were no doubt as obscure to him as they were to you, got tangled up in the net. A guy, I thought, who is only trying to escape the pressure by moving closer to its source. A guy who probably lies awake at night and weeps for his sins and worries about the impending coronary and keeps telling himself that in a few years, just as soon as he has saved a little money, he is going to get away from it all and retire to Florida. A guy who no doubt goes home at night and gets into his old clothes and mows the lawn and sprays his roses and maybe plays with the kids after dinner and makes love to his wife when he can keep his mind on it and eats the same toast and cereal for breakfast that you do. Even as you and I, I thought, even as you and I, and if he occasionally delivers lectures on the necessity for developing proper reflexes, it is because once in a while the O'Briens have to let you know what they think of themselves.

That went through my mind while I was in the process of turning and starting for his door, and it is why I interrupted myself in the middle of the motion. "If you're up to a Walgreen peanut-butter-and-lettuce," I said, "I wouldn't mind company, Jim."

He turned back to me. He was smiling faintly. "And a glass of milk," he said. "I've been cutting down on the coffee lately." He came around his desk. "Another thing you'll learn inside the month," he said. "You'll learn that from here on in you don't eat with just anybody."

"Who do you eat with?" I said.

202

"The other bastards in the organization," he said. "The ones who've developed the proper reflexes over the years."

Ulrich gave me a week to think of some new ideas for running the department. I didn't need a week, but he gave it to me. I used half of it to figure out some reasons why a certain Hyatt Engel, with nothing extraordinary on the ball, ought to be an editor on *Insight* at twice his present salary, and I killed another third of it sitting in my office waiting for the phone to ring. Then, at five o'clock Saturday, I gave that up. I went out and had dinner and on the way home I invested in a fifth of Scotch. Back in my apartment I sat down on the bed and studied the label on the bottle. I felt like hanging one on.

I hung one on. When I came to the next morning, I had an enormous head and the light hurt my eyes. I sat up long enough to acquire an impression of an apartment that looked as if it had gone through the worst of the rainy season with a leaky roof. Then I thought, The hell with Ulrich and his editorship, and went back to sleep. I woke up sometime later and managed the distance to the bathroom and splashed water on my face. When I came back, I looked at the telephone beside my bed and remembered, for no good reason, Jean Reynolds' impression of what the nature of a job on *Insight* was. I sat there on the edge of the bed and let my mind dwell on that a spell, and then I thought, The hell with Jean Reynolds, too. I finished the bottle and went back to bed.

I felt that way most of Monday, too. But when, late in the afternoon, I went uptown and the Word was waiting for me and I took the elevator up to twenty, I didn't feel that way any more. I stepped off the elevator and walked past Ulrich's secretary and into that enormous room, and I knew then that I didn't feel that way at all.

I walked across the thirty feet of rose carpeting toward him, toward the neat, middle-aged man in a neat gray suit, with carefully manicured hands and some gray at his brushed temples. A face you would expect to see in the Calvert ads,

I thought, and there is probably some foundation for the stories you have heard about his youth, for he is still a handsome bastard. Then Ulrich contributed a gesture to the atmosphere, and I sat down across from him and had a look into his eyes—and the resemblance to men of distinction went away. There was something too blue and too bright about the eyes; looking into them I thought of men who prayed and fasted under hot, disease-ridden suns, of early Christians who had walked singing to the stakes, of other early Christians who had sent them there.

He pushed an ebony-and-gold cigarette box a delicate inch in my direction. I shook my head. He flipped open the box, and I sprang to life and leaned across the desk with my cigarette lighter.

"Go ahead," he said. "Have one."

"No, thanks. I just threw one away."

"These are filtered. You hardly know you're smoking."

"Not right now. Thanks, anyway."

He leaned back in his chair and acquired an intense interest in the filtered cigarette which you hardly knew you were smoking. "I've been busy this week," he said. "Otherwise I'd have gotten around to this sooner. I might say that I liked that story you did."

"I guess I was lucky on it."

"Not lucky. Lucky isn't the word. When you give a man an assignment that is something besides routine, and he comes up with something good, that's imagination. Imagination is one of the qualities I like in my personnel." His eyes climbed up into mine, and they weren't hot any more; in a 19th-Century novel, I suppose they might even have been described as calculating. "I suppose," he said, "that you guessed that Jim had something besides a story in mind when he suggested that assignment."

"Yes, sir."

"Think you can fill Jim's shoes?"

"I'd like the chance to try."

"I'd like to see you get the chance. You have ability.

There's just one question in my mind. What price are you willing to pay for that job?"

"It depends," I said. "What price are you asking, Mr. Ulrich?"

"Everything you get in life," he said, "has a price attached. An automobile, a corner apartment, a wife and family, a suit that fits, a meal you can linger over. If you want something bad enough, you are willing to pay the price. This is a fact to bear in mind, Hyatt."

The use of the first name did not escape my attention. "I suppose," I said, "that what you've got in mind are Jim's ulcers."

"Partly. In an organization like this, the higher you go, the greater the pressure."

"Or the time element. If so, my day is as long as the next man's."

"Partly that, too."

"What else? What's the carrying charge, Mr. Ulrich?"

"An attitude. A frame of mind." He leaned back and folded his hands over his belt buckle. "You're a writer in this organization," he said. "As such, you bear me a certain attitude, an attitude symbolized by the fact that you pay dues to the Guild." I started to interrupt but he waved a hand. "I don't hold that against you. I expect it. You have to protect yourself just as I have to protect myself. It's a law of life. Only the minute you move into Jim's office, you're an editor. That means you aren't labor any more, you're management. And you have to start thinking like management. Do you follow me?"

"Not quite," I said. "The picture is still a little cloudy around the edges. Unless you are referring to picket lines—"

"No," he said. "Not exactly. Though it does have something to do with the fact that we're on the edge of a little labor trouble right now. A fact which you are apparently aware of."

"I've heard a few rumors," I said.

"I imagine," he said dryly. "About injustice and arbitrary dismissal and the rights of the worker this year, no doubt."

"Something along those lines," I said.

"Something went haywire in this century," he said. "Somewhere we got off the track. Companies kept getting bigger and bigger, and management kept getting further and further away from labor, and now we've got battle lines where we ought to have communication lines. Between forces that ought to be cooperating because it's to their mutual advantage." He leaned slightly. "I didn't do what I did because I wanted to. Christ, don't you think I know what it means for a sixty-dollar-a-week researcher with a wife and kids and rent to pay to come to work some morning and find he's just joined the ranks of the unemployed? But what the Guild won't understand is that I'm not a free agent. Hell, I haven't got as much freedom of action as one of my own linotype operators."

He paused, but I didn't offer to comment on that generalization. I had my own opinion about its validity, but I didn't express it. I didn't see this as the propitious moment.

"*Insight* is a corporation," he said. "I don't own it. I'm responsible to other investors. Being responsible means just one thing; it means my job is to produce a profit. The system may be all wrong, but as long as we're stuck with it, I have to play by those rules. And for almost two years now we've been operating in the red. That's in black and white, on the books. Our circulation has gone up, sure, along with our advertising rates. But so have our manufacturing costs and our overhead and our labor. We couldn't raise our rates again because we'd have priced them out of the competitive market. Our only choice was a drastic cutback right here, a surgical job on an organization that was sloppy, that was overstaffed."

His eyes stayed on mine another ten seconds; they reminded me, just then, of the eyes of an experienced salesman who was determined not to let this customer switch to another brand. Then they fell to the onyx ashtray. The cigarette he had ground out a while back was still smoldering, and he picked up a burned match and began poking at the ash. "I started this magazine in 1935," he said. "I sunk an inheritance into it, and it took me two years to make something besides a subsidized plaything out of it and five to make it a paying proposition. When I started it, I had three staff members, and as late as 1940 I was still writing half of every issue and editing the other half. I worked twenty hours a day those first years, and then one day *Insight* wasn't just a business any more. It was a creation. It was *me*, something I'd made. And it's something I'm not going to let be destroyed. Not without a hell of a fight."

His eyes came back up unexpectedly and caught my look of surprise. "Are things that bad?" I said.

"I'll put it this way," he said. "When you think of the American newsstand, you think of perhaps ten magazines. Well, two of those ten are almost certainly going to fold within the year because they can't keep abreast of increased costs."

I didn't reply to that because for a moment there I was busy on a quick job of mental arithmetic. Those seventeen researchers and writers had probably been costing *Insight* a hundred and twenty thousand or so in salaries and expenses, and if they spelled the difference between red and black, then we were skating a hell of a lot closer to the thin edge than showed on the surface. I thought of that a moment and then I leaned. "All right," I said. "But what has this got to do with the price of an editorship?"

His eyes weren't hot any more. His eyes were suddenly cool and level and distant, as though they had come to some kind of a decision, and the smile below them made me wonder if an Ulrich smile would ever have any warmth in it. "I suppose," he said, "that they're talking downstairs about organizing a walkout."

"I don't know," I said. "I haven't been around much since this came to a boil."

"Labor-management," he said, "is like a chess game. Half the victory lies in anticipating your opponent's moves before you have to face him across a conference table. The trouble is, the organization has gotten too big. I'm up here and they're down there, and what I need is some way of keeping in touch. If you follow me."

I followed him, all right. And whatever else you had to say about him, I thought, you had to admire his neatness. He had pulled out all the stops on me, from the lecture on economics that would have done Adam Smith proud to the financial report that made you imagine for a while there that you were a member of the Board and not just a two-bit writer scrambling for a four-bit editorship. He had been very goddam persuasive and confidential, and then he had read your eyes and decided you were sufficiently softened up, and then he had handed you the book open to the page and the letters writ large.

Only I still didn't like the plot.

"What I am in the market for right now," he said, "is a man who can learn in a hurry to think like management."

"I think," I said, "that I'll take one of your cigarettes now."

He pushed the box in my direction and then he got partly out of his chair and held a light to the cigarette. His smile, I decided, could have warmth in it; at the moment it could have been lavished on a woman on whom he had been spending a great deal of time lately. I let myself bask in the glow of it a minute. Then I tried erasing it.

"What you are in the market for, Mr. Ulrich," I said, "is a company spy. That's putting it bluntly, but I never did care much for euphemisms. And if this is the asking price for O'Brien's job, and I decide to pay it, I want to be able to look at the title on my door and know exactly what it means."

"So you're going to prove a disappointment, too," he said.

"I don't know. For the sake of discussion, let's suppose I'm not, that I can be bought. What makes you think it'll work, Mr. Ulrich?"

"What makes you think it won't?"

"For one thing, because by eight tomorrow morning the Guild is going to know that I've been closeted up here with you this afternoon. They can add two and two, Mr. Ulrich. They can even manage three and three, once my promotion is announced."

"It isn't going to be announced. Not for a while. As for being closeted up here, they'll open their arms to you. If you leave here mad."

"Mad?"

"Because of the proposition I just made you."

"That's very cute," I said. "It would be even cuter if you hadn't made Dave Goldstein the same proposition."

"Who said I made him the same proposition?"

"He did. At least he said you tried to buy him with the job."

"But not with the same proposition." He waited a moment. "Well?" he said.

"I don't know. When I came up here, I wanted this job. I *really* wanted it, Mr. Ulrich. But now I don't know." I shifted in the chair. "Can I have a little time to wrestle with my conscience?"

"Sure," he said. "Take all the time you need. Take a couple of days."

I got onto my feet and walked across the hundred yards of carpet to the door. When I turned to close the door behind me, he seemed very far away, like somebody seen through the wrong end of a telescope. "One more question," I said. "If I should happen to win the wrestling match, what happens to Dave Goldstein?"

He smiled. "Mr. Goldstein is a man who would make the most of martyrdom. So we'll keep him in the family. For the time being."

"He's a good man. You don't just flip a card down there in personnel and come up with a Dave Goldstein every time."

"I have no doubt," he said.

"I could use Dave if I were running the department. And I think maybe I could keep his wings clipped."

"I'll devote a little thought to it," he said.

I closed his office door and walked past the receptionist who, as befitted the difference in status between Ulrich and O'Brien, was a considerable improvement over Janet. There was a water cooler beside the elevator—probably a memento from Ulrich's early days, I thought, when he had had a staff of three and no reception room with rose carpeting—and while I was waiting for the elevator operator to make up his mind, I drank some of Ulrich's flat, distilled water. I drank four or five paper cones of it, and on the way down to seventeen I could feel the water

209

sloshing around down there in my stomach, like cold, liquid rubber.

On seventeen, I picked up my brief case and started for my office. I didn't do anything about Janet's exploratory smile. If I took this job, I was thinking, I was going to do something about Janet. I was going to have a receptionist like Ulrich's, and maybe her duties would not necessarily end at five in the afternoon. And Dave was right, I thought, a man can certainly become a son-of-a-bitch in a hurry once he is started in the right direction.

I could hear voices in Goldstein's office. I suppose I should have stood there a while and eavesdropped, but I didn't. Instead, I walked on by and into my office. I sat down at my desk and looked at the three copies of the little magazines that contained the first four chapters of a novel in progress by Hyatt Engel. Then I opened my bottom drawer and dug out the picture of Rachel and set it on the desk beside the magazines. I sat there and studied it, and it seemed to me that she was looking at me out of the corner of her eye. I let her look while I thought of a David Bernard Goldstein, who was an idealist, and of a Hyatt Engel, who could be bought for ten thousand a year, and of what it took to get ahead nowadays.

And the hell with that, I thought. I don't owe Dave Goldstein anything. If he chooses to play the Knight on the White Horse, Enemy of the Strong and Champion of the Oppressed, it's his battle and his wounds. If every job in this country went to the best man, there would be a lot of majority stockholders standing around in the unemployment lines. Besides, if I played Ulrich's brand of ball, maybe I could save Dave Goldstein from striking out.

And the hell with that line of reasoning, too. If you are set on arriving somewhere, I thought, you can manage it without rationalizing—you can call a third-class passage a third-class passage. You are a single man, I thought, and young, and you don't need this job. You could walk out of here this afternoon and stroll downtown and land a job on a newspaper. With three years on *Insight* you could get a job on a newspaper.

You could get a job where what they pay you for is your limpid prose.

I gave some thought to a job on a paper. Outside, a day was beginning to die, and I witnessed the death scene and thought about the kind of suits you wear when your salary is seventy-five dollars a week, about living in a third-floor walk-up over some Village bar, about coming home on the subway at six in the morning with ink smudges on your last clean shirt, about waking up someday and discovering you are fifty and tired and still bucking for a desk job in somebody's City Room. From where I was sitting, I couldn't work up any enthusiasm for that kind of job.

I turned to look at Rachel. All right, I thought, so you were a prophet.

Then I picked up the phone and dialed Ulrich's extension. Her voice was exactly like her face, cold and regular and distant, like something done in marble. "Hyatt Engel," I said. "I was just up there. I want to leave a message for Mr. Ulrich."

"He's still here. One minute—"

"No. You can just deliver this to him."

"Certainly."

"Tell him I said all right provided I can have Dave Goldstein. Otherwise he'll have my resignation in the morning. Got that?"

"Yes, Mr. Engel. Anything else?"

"No. Nothing else."

I dropped the phone and took one more look at Rachel. Then I turned the picture face down on the desk. It was better that way. That way a man could have a little privacy.

211

Michael Savage   III

13

HE LIFTED THE FLY OFF THE
surface of the water, over his shoulder watching the line S
and then straighten out, pressing his right elbow against his
hip the way the fellow at the sports shop had showed him, this
time laying the lure within two feet of the reed bed. In three
days, he thought with satisfaction, you can get pretty good at
this. He hadn't caught a fish yet, but in two hours he hadn't
snapped off a fly or snarled the line. He let the fly rest a minute, and then he brought the line back in with the brief jerks
which were supposed to simulate insect life on the surface of
the water.

Through the T-shirt he could feel the sun, warm on his
back and shoulders, and across the water he could hear the
shouts of the kids in swimming. He smiled, remembering how
they had warned him that it would be colder than the devil
up here in October. I am going to try casting a couple more
times, he thought, and then I am going in. Maybe if I go in
before she gets back, I can get a little work done. A page or
two, he thought, knowing he couldn't, remembering yesterday and the day before yesterday, knowing that the minute he
got the typewriter out of the case, the mood would go away.

Across the water he could hear one of the kids yell, "There's
Mother," and he glanced toward the shore and saw the car
moving around the bend in the lane. When she got out of the
car, she was waving something at him, a newspaper. Standing

there beside the car, she looked small and far away and somehow very alone.

"Hey," she called. "You're third. You moved up from ninth to third." Her voice, floating across the water, sounded distant and hollow, like an echo.

"Which one?" he called. "The *Times?*"

"Yes. They didn't have a *Tribune.*"

He brought the line in and hooked the lure into the cork handle. As he brought up the anchor, he thought, I don't believe there are any fish in this lake. The tourist folders are a snare and a delusion, he thought, and we drove across two states for nothing. He started the motor and swung the boat in toward shore. Across the bow he saw Alice turn and walk across the grass and into the cottage. I am going to have to tell her pretty soon, he thought. I am going to wait until Saturday, he thought, remembering ten days ago in New York, remembering the night at Frank Mattson's and the two nights with Jean and the lunch with Kay Anderson, and then I am going to have to tell her.

That first night in New York he spent at Frank Mattson's place on Long Island. Just before the war, Mattson had bought two acres near Port Washington and put up a house. It meant spending half your waking hours on a train, he explained to Michael, but it was like being in the country and you got to bed at a decent hour because there wasn't anything else to do.

They rode out on one of those commuter trains which leave Penn Station at four-ten or four-forty or five-fifteen. The men from the Street read the financial pages, the conductor knew Mattson's name, and there was a bridge foursome in the front of their coach. It was a train out of John P. Marquand. On the way Mattson talked idly about how inflation was murdering the book business.

When they got off the train, Mrs. Mattson was waiting for them in a new Buick. She drove them efficiently and without undue conversation the seven miles to a house that looked like any fifty-thousand-dollar ranch type in any suburb north of Knoxville and east of Denver—a house with a brick front and a lot of thermopane and an attached two-car garage and a few scattered maples which might provide a little shade in another ten years.

Inside, in a study which Michael had known would be knotty pine with a matched-stone fireplace and worn leather furniture, Mattson watched his wife reflectively until she had settled on the davenport. Then he opened the liquor cabinet.

"Drink, dear?" he asked.

"A light one. Then I'm going to have to go and superintend dinner. Mary's having trouble with the stove again. We really are going to have to do something about that stove, Frank." She was a very good-looking woman, fifteen years younger than Mattson, with hair that looked naturally blonde and a tranquil face. She smiled at Michael. "Excuse us for being domestic, Michael."

Mattson was looking across the room at her. "It's a perfectly respectable stove," he said.

"Frank, darling," she said, "I know some perfectly respectable women, too. But a lot of them are a long way past any further usefulness."

Mattson took her drink gloomily across the room to her. "Drink, Michael?"

"Not right now, thanks."

"Sure?"

"Sure," Michael said. "I'm on the wagon these days."

Mrs. Mattson got reluctantly to her feet. "I'd better explore the kitchen. Stick to your guns, Michael. If you don't want a drink, you don't want a drink." She disappeared into the hall. Mattson poured a stiff shot into a glass and siphoned some soda into it. "I went on the wagon once," he said. "It lasted two months."

"I'm on it for good," Michael said. "I got scared a while back. I tried a drink one morning out in my cottage, to see if it might help, and then I sat down at a typewriter and wrote eight pages before I ran dry. The next morning the pages didn't read, but they had seemed good at the time." He ran his fingers through his hair. "In ten days a drink before starting work and a pint before noon had become a necessity."

Mattson took a long pull on his drink. "Ever been to a psychoanalyst?" he asked. He was trying to sound casual.

"I'm not going berserk." Michael tried to match Mattson's tone. "There's nothing the matter with me that another novel won't cure."

"I think you take all this too seriously," Mattson said.

"All what?"

"Getting words onto a piece of paper. Being a writer."

"How else can you take it? If you want to be good?"

"Who's talking about being good?" Mattson said. "Look at it this way. You happen to have a skill for arranging words in an order that'll suck a reader into wanting to read them. So you arrange a hundred thousand of them, and we print them and bind them and sell them to a retail outlet. We pay you fifty-five cents a unit for peddling something we can't originate and you can't manufacture or distribute, and everybody's reasonably happy."

"There's more to it than that."

"There's not a damned bit more to it than that. It doesn't make a bit of difference whether you're Ernest Hemingway or Kathleen Winsor. Not a loving bit."

"Maybe not, but you have to think it does, Frank."

Mattson shrugged and settled back in his chair. He looked prosperous and fit and satisfied with life. "I am not going to advise you to lock up that typewriter and go away somewhere and get a long rest," he said. "We've been preaching that gospel since February. But I am going to tell you this. You had better get the idea of deathless prose out of your head, Michael. Otherwise you're going to wind up in somebody's sanitarium."

Michael didn't say anything.

"I am talking to you like a Dutch uncle because I like you and because you are a valuable asset." He fumbled in his pocket for a cigarette. "The best thing you could do for yourself at the moment would be to sit down and just write a story. Nothing symbolic or pregnant with meaning. Just sixty thousand fast-paced words. Something to give you back your perspective, stop you from thinking you have to be Shakespeare on every page."

"I can hear the critics now," Michael said.

"So can I. The hell with the critics." Mattson got to his feet and walked over and stood at the fireplace, his hands in his pockets. "Or maybe your trouble isn't that. Maybe it's Jean Reynolds." He turned and looked calmly into Michael's stare. "Slept with her yet?" he asked pleasantly. "Or is it so far purely a meeting of the minds?"

"I don't think," Michael said carefully, "that it's any of your goddam business, Frank. Or that there's any call—"

"The trouble with people is that they have to make everything tough on themselves. They don't come by enough grief naturally, they have to invent some yet. So the churches tell you how marriages are made in heaven, and the sociologists correlate broken homes and juvenile delinquency, and the female contributors to the slicks spread the myths around where people can read them. A piece of tail is a piece of tail, but since the human race stuck its nose out of a cave, it has conspired to pretend that it really isn't, that it is something else instead." He leaned lightly against the mantel. "When I got my divorce I sweated and fasted and wept and prayed and got drunk and otherwise tortured myself for six months. Then I walked out. No backward glances. Which is what I should have done in the first place."

"I don't suppose you figured you owed her anything."

Mattson looked puzzled. "I put a roof over her head," he said, "and fed her three times a day. And while it lasted, it was as much fun for her as it was for me. I paid her a very generous alimony until she could find another husband. What more did I owe her?"

"Or that there were any children," Michael said.

Mattson looked off into space. "I'll admit that's the tough part," he said softly. "But tearing out your heart and eating it raw isn't going to sop up any spilt milk."

Michael looked steadily at him. "I don't believe you're really a bastard, Frank," he said. "You just talk like one."

Mattson smiled. "Okay. Believe half of what I tell you. Believe a third of it." He walked across the room and laid a hand on Michael's shoulder. "A man has to try to do what he can," he said, "to protect his investment."

"That's right. The business of America is business."

"That," Mattson said, "was the most profound statement of political philosophy in our time. And don't you ever forget it."

"I think," Michael said, "that I could use that drink now."

"I think I'll join you," Mattson said.

Mattson shook him awake at six the next morning, and after breakfast Mrs. Mattson drove them to the station through air that smelled clean and crisp, like the beginning of winter. On the train he read the paper that Mattson bought him. When they got to 38th Street and Michael drifted into Jean's office, she was just hanging up her coat.

"Hi," she said. "How was Long Island?"

"Fine. I'm glad I went."

"It must have been. You look alive this morning."

"I feel alive. We had a fine dinner and took a fine walk. I went to bed at ten and got up at six, and I feel as if I had been reborn." He sat down on the edge of her desk. "Frank Mattson is all right," he said. "Intelligent. Realistic. He looks steadily at the problem."

"What problem?"

"All problems. Employee morale, for instance. He agrees with me that my editor ought to have the day off."

"I'd like to, Michael, but—"

"I've got news for you. I'm an important figure in Mattson and Company. The book business is always uncertain, and I'm a selling writer. I'm money in the bank and equanimity at the Board of Directors' meetings, and while I'm in town I'm your most important job, and you'd better never forget it."

She laughed. "I capitulate."

"On the way in this morning," he said, "I worked out a schedule for the day. I want to go to the Museum of Art and

220

look at the 16th-Century nudes and feel sorry for the painters because they didn't have you for a model. I want to take you to Cartier's and buy you something expensive and unnecessary. I want to lunch at Keen's, where I hear the steaks are six inches thick, and I want to neck with you in the back row of a movie, and tonight I want to order the twenty-six-dollar dinner at the Stork Club. That isn't the full itinerary, but it hits the high spots between now and midnight."

"You really are alive this morning."

"I got a lesson in the art of living last night. The gospel according to Frank Mattson."

"What about after midnight?"

He smiled at her and she smiled back. "I wish it were after midnight," she said.

He helped her on with her coat, and they rode down in the elevator and walked uptown in the morning crowds and the smell of exhaust fumes and the bright October sun. They did not do all the things he had planned to do that day, but they did a lot of them. At midnight he leaned on her mantel and looked across the living room at her. She was opening the cigarette case he had bought her that morning.

"It's a lovely case," she said.

"It isn't enough. You should have let me spend more than twenty dollars while I was in the mood."

"It's a lovely case. And it was a lovely day, Michael."

"Jean," he said. "Jean, hadn't we ought to get this settled?"

"What?"

"This. You and me and Alice."

"Why? Aren't you happy the way we are?"

"No. It's no good the way we are." He watched her face for a change of expression, but there wasn't any. "I'm going to tell her," he said. He ran a finger along the edge of her mantel; his finger came away dusty, and he thought of Alice, who dusted twice a week and worried about cobwebs in the corners. "Will you marry me?" he said. "If she'll give me a divorce?"

"I don't know. It will take some thinking over, Michael."

"You love me, don't you?"

221

"I think so. That's why it will take some thinking over."

"You'll have to go on working for a while. I'm going to be pretty broke until I can finish another book. Because I'll have to settle about everything I've got on her."

"I'll go on working even after you finish another book. Did you think I wouldn't?"

"I didn't know. Whatever you want to do, Jean."

"What made you think I'd stop working?"

He opened and then closed his right hand. "I didn't think much about it. One way or the other. Except that Alice has never worked. And I thought you might like some kids. Later."

She was looking across the room but he couldn't tell whether her eyes were precisely on his or not.

"I just thought you might. A lot of women do."

"I'd better tell you something, Michael."

"Not that it makes any difference to me," he said. "It's what you want, Jean."

"Listen to me, Michael."

"All right. I'm listening."

"When all this started," she said, "I didn't know where it was going. I mean I didn't know whether it would last a week or a month or a year." She gestured vaguely, groping for exactly the right words. "What I am trying to explain is, it was just one of those things that happened one night. With a stranger, somebody I'd only just met." She brought her eyes up and this time she was very definitely looking at him. "If I should say yes," she said, "what is all this going to do to you, Michael?"

"I don't know. I don't know what you're talking about."

"You believe things. Loyalty, duty, responsibility, things like that. Things people used to believe but don't any more."

He straightened up. "I'll tell you what I believe," he said. "I believe in you and me."

She snapped the cigarette case shut. It made a loud, surprising noise in the room. "You sound very sure," she said.

"I am."

222

"I hope you are. Because I don't want you blaming me for anything. Afterwards."

"I'm sure. Aren't you?"

"If you are, Michael." She came across the room to him. "If I'm what you want, then that's what I want, too." She came up on her toes and he leaned down and kissed her. She smiled at him and then turned her back. "Unzip me?" she said.

"The lights are on. I thought you were a very single girl."

"I was," she said.

He had lunch with Kay Anderson the afternoon he left. At noon, in Jean's office, with the door closed discreetly behind them and his arms around her and his face buried in her hair, he said for the tenth time that morning, "I'm going to tell her. As soon as I get home. I'll let you know."

"Be very gentle with her, Michael."

He kissed the tip of her ear. "As a kitten," he said.

She pulled away from him and smoothed her skirt down around her hips. "It's after twelve. You'd better be getting out of here."

"I guess I had." He kissed her once more, and then he straightened up and took a last look at her. Then he got out of there.

It was raining when he came out on the street, one of those cold, steady, gray rains you get in New York just before winter. He had trouble getting a cab, and it was almost one when he walked into Kay's office. She was waiting for him, with her hat and coat on.

"I'm sorry I'm late," he said. "I had—"

She was looking narrowly at him. "I know," she said cheerfully. "Cab trouble. It's a terrible day, isn't it?" She glanced at her watch. "I thought we'd eat at the Biltmore. We can get there without having to stick our noses out into the weather for longer than a brief dash." She looked at him again. She was smiling, but it wasn't exactly a smile of approval. "You didn't quite get all the lipstick off," she said.

The balcony of the Biltmore was crowded but the head-waiter found them a table. Over coffee and dessert he lit her cigarette and then planted his elbows on the table.

"Kay," he said, "Frank says *Vine* is selling about nine hundred a week. Do you think that's all it's selling?"

"If it's selling that many it's doing very well. Why? Money troubles?"

"Not yet, but I was wondering how much I could count on."

"I can tell you that. About eighty thousand."

"That's how much I *have* made."

"In this business that's how much you can count on."

He pushed his coffee cup aside. "I can expect to make *something* from the trade sale, can't I?"

She shrugged. "I can name thirty titles that were book-club choices and didn't sell thirty thousand in the trade. I hope to God that you haven't spent it *all*, Michael."

"That's not what I'm worried about." He let his eyes fall away from hers. "I'm going to leave my wife," he said.

"Are you?" she said politely. "Who for, Michael?"

"I'm going to ask her for a divorce. But I've got to have enough money for some kind of a decent settlement."

"This goddam town," she said, without bitterness. Then her tone was suddenly businesslike again. "How much have you had so far?"

"Seventy thousand. Fifty from Miller, twenty from Frank."

"Spent it all?"

"No. I've got twenty-one thousand left."

She spread her hands, in a gesture of despair. "Your taxes will come to better than that."

"Not if I file a joint return and spread it over three years. That way it comes to a little better than sixteen. If I sell the Cadillac, that will give me pocket money until I can finish another book. Everything else I want to sign over to her. The question is, will it come to enough?"

"Your guess is as good as mine."

"Well," he said, "could you do some checking and let me know?"

"Sure." She ground out her cigarette. "I hope you know what you're doing," she said.

"I know what I'm doing."

"I hope you do. I hope the girl's worth it, Michael."

He began to draw circles on the tablecloth with his spoon. "I think we'll go away for a week. The weather's still nice. I think I'll take her and the kids to some lake. That's where I'll try to explain it to her." He glanced at his watch. "It's after two," he said. "And I have to pay a hotel bill and get out to La Guardia before five. I'd better be shoving."

She pushed back her chair. "Luck, Michael," she said.

"Thanks. You sound like you think I'll need it."

"The way you're built," she said, "I think you are going to need all you can get of it."

Ten feet offshore he throttled down and aimed the boat diagonally at the point where the dock joined the shore. Then, just as he shut off the motor, Ellen appeared from nowhere and caught hold of the side of the boat.

"Hey," he said. "Cut it out, Ellen."

"Catch any fish?" Her face was wet and she was laughing.

He leaned over the side and put a hand on her head. "If you don't let go, I'll duck you."

She made a face at him, and he pushed her head under. She was still laughing when she bobbed back up. "How many fish?" she said.

"Sixteen. But I threw them all back."

"I'll bet."

"That's right. I was out there just for the sport."

She got a firmer hold on the side of the boat and hooked a heel over the side. "Take me for a ride," she said.

Alice came out of the cottage with Alan in tow. "They had a paragraph in that 'In and Out of Books' section," she said. "About how the reviews have been. Eight raves, twenty-one favorable, seven unfavorable. Is that good?"

"I'll settle," he said.

"Come on, Daddy," Ellen said. "Take me for a ride. Like this."

225

"I'm tired." He was smiling.

"You've got a motor."

"Okay. Just a short one, though." He started the motor and circled out into the lake again. She hung on with one hand, her body gliding on the surface, the water breaking off her feet in a brief, white wake. She was wearing one of the two-piece suits even the five-year-olds wear; it would be another year before she would really need the halter to it, but looking down at her, he was aware of the fact that she was growing up. She is going to look like her mother, he thought, and at nineteen she is going to be a very pretty girl. And I hope she will not marry some son-of-a-bitch, he thought. Like me.

"Faster," she yelled, above the chug of the motor.

He grinned and pushed the throttle up an inch. Looking down at her, he remembered a day last summer. She had been eleven that summer, and she had lost her heart to a tall, pimply male. The boy had asked her to go to a movie with him one Saturday afternoon. She had spent the week deciding what to wear and the Saturday morning getting into it. At one that afternoon she came out on the porch and settled down to wait. She waited a long time. She waited until four-thirty, and then she went up to her room and cried for an hour. When she came down for dinner, he put his arm around her and told her no guy was worth crying over; at that moment he knew that given the opportunity he could have strangled the boy.

He began to bring the boat around in a wide circle. He was remembering that afternoon, thinking of her face when she had come down from her room, thinking that of the four she had always been his favorite.

"Don't go in yet," she yelled. "Take me out in the middle."

"Can't hear you," he said.

She yelled louder. "Don't go in yet."

He pointed to his ear. "Stone deaf. Can't hear a thing."

She stuck out her tongue, and he grinned at her and headed into shore. She had always seemed to learn faster and think straighter than the others, and she had always been his

226

favorite. He wondered how she was going to take it. It will probably hit her where she lives, he thought. He wondered if she would shut herself in her room and cry for an afternoon. Or if she would just hate him, without ever showing it, without ever showing anything in her face for him again.

Well, he thought, it is one of the prices you apparently have to pay.

When he swung into the dock, Alice was standing there in the sun, holding Alan's hand, and Cathy and Susan had come around the corner of the cottage and were running toward him.

"Hey, Daddy," Cathy called, "look't, we caught a turtle, and I named him William. Can we keep him?"

"William's a fine name," he said. "Just right for a turtle. Nothing fancy about William."

"Can we?" she said. "Keep him?"

"That is a problem to bring to the attention of your mother. That is in your mother's department." He looked at Alice, standing there in the sun; she was dressed in slacks and a T-shirt, and he wondered why she looked more desirable that way than in a brief bathing suit. "Like to go for a boat ride?" he asked her.

"I'd better be thinking of getting us something to eat."

"Maybe after dinner we can go fishing."

"I'd like to go fishing after dinner," she said.

Alan pulled away from his mother. "Take me a ride, Daddy," he said.

"Okay."

"I get to steer."

"Of course. Naturally." He held out his arms, and Alan came to the edge of the dock, closed his eyes, and jumped. Michael caught him and set him on the back seat.

"Watch him," Alice said.

"I'll keep my eyes glued."

"Can Cathy and I go?" Susan said.

"Not this trip. This trip is just between us men."

"Later?"

227

"Later, we eat. Then your mother and I are going fishing. Then it will be dark. When it's dark, it's time for six-year-old girls to be in bed."

"You gotta take us tomorrow, then. Turtle hunting."

"It's a solemn promise. We'll start early in the morning. Make an expedition out of it."

Heading out, he looked back once at Alice, standing on the dock with the sun behind her and her face in the shadows. Then he put an arm around Alan.

"Lemme steer now," Alan said.

"Okay. Take over, Captain. Only keep it straight."

"You gotta get in the other seat first," Alan said.

"That's right. I almost forgot that." He inched back to the middle seat and sat on the edge of the seat, looking over the stern, squinting into the sun low on the horizon. A year ago this time, he thought, I had my mind on the things you have your mind on when you are the father of a son: on taking him fishing or teaching him how to catch a baseball or buying annuities for his college education. He wondered if he would miss bringing up a son. He supposed that that was one of the prices you had to pay, too.

It was dark when he came out of the cottage and it had gotten chilly; it was going to be a night for extra blankets. He sat down on the ground and leaned against a tree. Ten feet from him something squeaked, a mole or a chipmunk or a field mouse. There was no moon, but the stars were out, and the lake looked black and mysterious and limitless.

Inside the cottage, the last light went out, and then she was a shadow in the doorway. "Boat unloaded?" she said.

"No." At the moment the boat seemed remote and unimportant. "Kids in bed?"

"Yes. Alan's exhausted. He was asleep before I got him undressed."

"He's having himself a time." He remembered how she had wanted a boy all those years, and how proud she had been when Alan came, as if having a son was some miracle cement which would bind them a little more closely together.

She came out of the cottage quietly, and sat down beside him. "Are you?" she asked.

He turned and stretched out on the ground and put his head in her lap. "A million stars," he said. "You wouldn't think that a guy could live half a lifetime and never know the name of one of them. Now would you?"

"Are you?" she said again.

"I suppose so. As much of a time as you ever have when you've lived half a lifetime." He could feel her body, warm against his cheek, and he felt drowsy and relaxed. "I wonder what it would be like living up here the year around?"

"Lonely," she said. "And cold in the winter."

"You could build right over there on that point. Not a cottage. A house. With all the modern conveniences except daily mail delivery and a telephone, and you would be isolated by snow in the winter and rain in the spring, and maybe, given time, you could forget there was any other world. Maybe if you really forgot it, this would turn out to be a good place to write. Maybe you wouldn't feel drained any more."

"Poor Michael," she said. "My poor, ambitious Michael."

"You would have to forget it, though," he said. "Completely. Really put it out of your mind."

Her hand was resting lightly on his forehead. She was playing with his hair, twisting a strand of it around her finger. "Would you think I was awful," she said, "if I wondered if it was time yet to go to bed?"

"It's early. It isn't ten yet."

"I know. Would you think I was awful?"

He lay there with his head in her lap and listened to the frogs in the reed bed along the shore and the crickets and the stirrings in the grass that could have been anything. "I think I ought to tell you something."

"What? That you love me?"

"No," he said. "Something else."

"Do you?"

"Yes," he said. "I think so. Yes."

"Then I don't want to hear it. Not tonight." She moved

her hand to his cheek and pressed his face tight to her. Through her jacket, he could make out the beat of her heart. "You could see the stars from in there, too," she said. "Through the window."

"It's about that other world. The one you could maybe forget if—"

She put a finger over his lips. He reached for her hand, and then he gave up inside, and when he pulled her hand away, it was very gently.

"Okay," he said.

Later, he lay in bed in the almost dark and watched her shadow as she undressed. She had never conquered her modesty, and usually when she undressed in the same room with him, she went through an elaborate ritual, pulling the straps of her brassiere off her shoulder, then slipping on her night-gown before she stepped out of her underclothing. But to-night, when she sat down on the edge of the bed, she did not have a nightgown on.

"It's going to be cold tonight," he said.

"Not for a while."

He reached out and touched her shoulder.

"Was it important?" she said. "What you were going to tell me?"

He turned his head and looked out the window beside him. He could see the shadow of a tree outside, but he couldn't see any of the sky. If you moved your head, he thought, you might be able to make out the stars, but you would have to crane your neck.

"It must not have been," he said. "Anyway, I've forgotten what it was."

14 WHEN THEY GOT HOME, the country mailbox at the end of their lane was stuffed with mail. After he had unloaded the car, Michael sat down at the dining-room table with it. Most of the mail was fan letters, forwarded to him through Mattson and Company; without variation the letters began by saying that the writer had never written a fan letter before, and seven offered him an opportunity to discover an unpublished manuscript. There were also invitations to join the National Writer's Club or to address County Library Association meetings, and there were letters from Kay Anderson and George Miller. The letter from Kay hoped he had had a good vacation and gave him an unofficial report on sales to October 1st. The letter from the Coast was an invitation to come out in January to help on the screen treatment.

He was doing some figuring on the back of an envelope when Alice came out of the bedroom.

"Anything interesting?" she said.

He pushed Miller's letter across the table toward her. "They want me to go out there to help on the screen treatment."

"Going?"

"No. I'm going to stay right here and write another novel." He looked down at the figures on the envelope. "Kay checked the sales to October 1st. So far, *Vine* has made me ninety-six hundred in the trade."

"Is that good or bad?"

"It's no figure anybody is going to retire on."

"Maybe," she said, not looking at him, looking instead at the letter lying between them, "maybe you ought to go out there, Michael."

"No. There isn't anything in it for me. All the good Hollywood novels have long since been written."

"I know he's only offering you two hundred a week and expenses, but maybe if you learned how to write a script, it would be something to fall back on. Just in case."

"In case of what?"

"We could go along. If you wanted us to. We could take the kids out of—"

"In case of what?" he said again. "In case I'm written out?"

"No. I didn't—"

"I've got something to fall back on. Frank Mattson told me I ought to quit trying to be Shakespeare on every page. He said I ought to just try telling a story."

She let her eyes fasten on his long enough to interpret the tone of his voice. Then she leaned forward and put a hand over his. "Michael, do we have to make a lot more money right away? Haven't we—"

"I am going to capitalize on four years of graduate school. I am going to write an historical. About bosomy heroines and duels and midnight rides and intrigue in the dissolute court of Louis the Fourteenth and Merrie England in the year 1658. Highly recommended for light summer reading."

"Do we? Do we have to—"

"Yes," he said. "Yes, I've got to make a lot more money."

"Why?"

"Because after the first of the year we aren't going to have ten thousand dollars left in the bank."

"We've lived on less."

"But not in the manner to which we have recently become accustomed." He patted her hand. "Maybe Frank's right. Maybe I do have delusions of grandeur. Maybe if I tried an historical, I'd get back something I left lying around somewhere." He picked up Miller's letter and pushed back his chair. "Miller will want an answer to this," he said.

Outside, the grass in the yard was beginning to look brown and thin and tired, and the color was almost gone from what leaves were still left on the trees. The cottage looked plain and white and simple, like a chapel or a monk's cell, and when he crossed the yard, breathing quickly and lightly, he could definitely smell winter in the air. Inside the cottage, he tossed Miller's letter on the desk and then lit a fire in the oil Heatrola. He was running over in his mind the possibilities of an historical novel, and when he had the stove going, he walked over to the row of reference books from his graduate-school days. He hadn't looked at these titles for years now, but suddenly they seemed familiar and friendly to him, like the faces in one of those group pictures of a high-school graduating class. Standing there before the histories and bibliographies, he began to get back the general outline of the period: the names—Ashley Cooper and Vane and Haselrig and Fleetwood and Lambert and George Monk; the events —Cromwell's death in September, 1658; Richard Cromwell's dissolution of Parliament in April, 1659; the Royalist uprising in August; Lambert's escape from the Tower in April, 1660; the last fight between Roundhead and Cavalier at Daventry; Charles II's landing at Dover in May. He would call the novel *The Courier*. His hero would be Lord Mordaunt, who in the contemporary oils was hawk-nosed and swarthy and had a lean and hungry look but whose name sounded romantic. The heroine would be the daughter of the Presbyterian who had fallen heir to Mordaunt's sequestered estates. And wasn't it Hemingway, he thought, who had said something about how, if you ever sold a piece of your integrity, you never got it back? Well, he thought, the hell with Hemingway. The hell with you, Mr. Hemingway.

He sat down at his desk. On the green blotter was the folder containing the first hundred pages of the novel he had started last March, *The Suburb*. It was to have proved that he could write about somebody besides himself, and it was to have been his answer to all the young novelists since the

233

war who had written their one novel and then called it a career. Or had closed the garage doors, taken a long drink and then turned on the motor. And *The Suburb* was some answer, he thought. He pushed the folder to the back of the desk.

His new IBM electric was on the typing table, but he moved it and got the portable out of the corner. It was the machine on which he had written *The Alley* and *Some Die on the Vine,* and maybe it had another novel in it. He rolled a yellow second-sheet into the machine. At the top of the page he typed, "OUTLINE FOR *The Courier.*"

It was when he reached for the carriage return that the pain caught at his heart. He had been getting the pains for two months, and he had been dismissing them as heartburn or a muscle cramp. But this time the pain was sharp enough to make him catch his breath. He sat there a moment, with his right hand cupped over the quick, eager stab. Then it was gone, and he shrugged his shoulders in a brief circle and began to write a tentative synopsis of the story about My Lord Mordaunt and the golden-haired daughter of the whey-faced Roundhead who had seized Mordaunt's sequestered estates, about the not-so-Merrie England of the time of Oliver and Richard Cromwell.

So in November he found himself back in the library stacks, with his patented filing case and his note cards and the collections of three-hundred-year-old letters and diaries. After the first week, he felt at home again among the rows of books and the dust. At night he would go home and work until eleven, and then he would go to bed and dream. Sometimes he dreamed that he was being chased by something; the something was never more than a shadow in the shadows behind him, but he was always terrified, and he would wake up in the mornings as tired as if he had walked for miles. Or he would dream about falling, jerk awake in a cold sweat, and remember that Freud had written somewhere that dreams of falling were a sign of basic insecurity. But in the dream which recurred most frequently, there was a stage with a lectern

234

standing bare and final in the middle of it, and he was walking out from the wings with a book under his arm; across the footlights was a sea of white, middle-aged, feminine faces, the faces one sees at the afternoon teas of the American Association of University Women. He would walk across the long stage and look down into the faces, and then he would glance at the book. Until that exact moment he never seemed to know what the book was, and he would look down at the jacket, and it would be *The Courier*. He would know an instant of surprise because he could not remember the book's having been published. Then he would look across the painful lights again, where the faces were all nodding and smiling, and he would smile back and open his mouth. Only he would never say anything because it would be then that he would hear the titter. At first it was a single voice somewhere in the back; then it would begin to grow; and then all the hundreds of faces were laughing, their mouths gaping and tears streaming down the powdered cheeks. He would stand there, wondering why they were laughing at him, and then he would realize, in the instant of knowledge that is purely intuitive, that he had gone out there without any clothes on.

The first time he awoke from that dream, his heart felt as if someone had taken hold of it and squeezed. He lay in the dark beside Alice, sweating, breathing deeply to rid himself of the cramp. He wanted a drink suddenly, very badly. Maybe I *had* better see an analyst, he thought. In the dark, carefully so as not to wake Alice, he reached out and fumbled on the bedside table for the sleeping pills he had bought a week before.

The lightning struck in December.

He was finishing up the sixth chapter of *The Courier* at the time. The work had gone well that morning, so well that he had returned to it after lunch. Only after lunch it had not gone so well. He had spent the afternoon trying to whip a single paragraph into shape, and he had just ripped a sheet of paper out of the carriage and inserted another when he became aware of the spot of heat in his chest. He sat still for a moment, waiting for it to go away. But it didn't go away. He sat there, his jaws locked against it, his hands gripping the sides of the typewriter, feeling it grow, feeling it begin to travel, following it as it burrowed into his shoulder and started down his arm, feeling the nausea and the sweat breaking on his forehead and upper lip, thinking, *It is the genuine article this time, Savage, it is exactly the way the book described it. Keep breathing,* he thought, *you have got to keep breathing, you aren't dead until you have quit breathing. Thirty-six,* he thought, *you are only thirty-six, whoever heard of anybody dying of coronary thrombosis at thirty-six.*

Then it was over. The tension went out of his wrists and jaw, and his lungs relaxed to accommodate the air he was sucking into them, and the relief was like a hole in his chest. He rested his forehead on the typewriter for a moment. Then he got up, cautiously, and started for the house.

Later, with his head back against the car seat and Alice driving hell for election for town, the realization hit him that he had felt everything except fear. There had been pain and nausea and cold sweat, and the instinct, the reflex, to keep breathing, and the knowledge, like quiet anger, that he was having a heart attack at thirty-six. But no fear. At ten minutes after two on the first Friday in December, he thought, you knew suddenly that you were a dead man, but you hadn't been afraid. If you felt anything at all, it had been only a weak and tired relief.

Their doctor was named Davis. His waiting room was miraculously empty when they got there, and he smiled professionally at them when the nurse ushered them into his presence.

"What's this I hear?" he said cheerfully.

"I'm afraid I've had it this time," Michael said. "The genuine article."

"What makes you think so?"

"A sharp pain in my heart, the size of a quarter. It traveled down my left arm, and I couldn't breathe." He leaned forward. "Symptoms of a coronary. Aren't they?"

"Possibly."

"I know," Michael said. "I did some research on coronaries. A couple weeks ago."

Davis gestured toward the cot in the corner. "Take off your shirt and lie down. We'll have a listen."

He listened a long time, and then he strapped the rubber tube around Michael's arm and took his blood pressure. When he straightened up from the reading, his face was expressionless. "I think we'll send you downtown," he said. "Borgson or Harvey. I think Borgson on this case."

"Tell me something," Michael said. "Why is it you people will do anything except tell a patient what the score is?"

"I'm a general practitioner," Davis said, "not a heart man. I've got nothing except your blood pressure and what I can hear through this stethoscope to go on. I could tell you what I think, but it wouldn't mean a thing without an electrocardiogram, an X ray, a blood count, a urinalysis, and maybe five or six other checks."

"Tell me what you think. I'll make the allowances."

"Your blood pressure is one thirty over eighty-five, and if there is any irregularity, I can't hear it through this." Davis smiled dryly. "I think you'll make it downtown. I even think that if you take it real easy, you'll last the week out."

Michael waited thirty minutes in the city clinic where Borgson was a staff member and then went obediently downstairs and had an X ray and an electrocardiogram. Back upstairs in Borgson's office a nurse led him down a maze of closet-sized rooms and sat him on a stool, and he settled down to wait some more.

It was almost an hour before Borgson came in. He was one of those abnormally tall men who have learned to walk with a stoop, and his face wore the expression of a man whose wife had just died in an automobile accident. He sat down on the edge of the hospital cot and looked moodily at Michael.

"Well," he said, "what's the matter with you?"

"I'm the one Davis called about. I just had a heart attack. Coronary."

"Did you, now? And what medical school did you graduate from?"

"I've done some reading on heart diseases. I know what the symptoms are."

"All right," Borgson said wearily. "Take off your shirt."

For the fifth or sixth time that day Michael took off his shirt. "The T-shirt, too?" he asked.

"Please," Borgson said.

Michael took off the T-shirt and stretched out on the cot and Borgson bent over him with the stethoscope. Then he sat down on the stool. "What's your business?" he asked.

"I'm a writer." Michael wondered if Borgson had an idea what kinds of incomes writers made.

"A writer? What do you write?"

"Fiction. Novels."

"How long has this been bothering you?"

"About three months. Not bad. Like a muscle cramp. Until today."

There was a knock on the door, and the nurse came in and handed Borgson a set of X rays, still damp from the developer. Borgson walked to the window and studied them. Then he turned around. "You can put your clothes back on now," he said.

Michael sat up. "How bad is it?"

Borgson leaned back against the window sill. "How successful are you? At what you're doing for a living?"

"I get by."

"Don't hedge," Borgson said irritably. "The fee for this has already been determined. How successful? Worried about a lot of bills?"

"A sixteen-thousand-dollar one for income tax this year. Otherwise, I don't owe a dime."

"My God. That's as much tax as *I* pay. Do you make that much *every* year?"

"No. This year was a good year."

"Do you *like* what you're doing?"

"It's the only thing I ever wanted to do." Michael stood up

and slipped on his shirt. "I don't see what all this has got to do—"

"Any other worries? Domestic, maybe? Do you get along with your wife?"

"I came in here to find out about my heart. What has my domestic situation got to do with a coronary?"

"You haven't got a coronary," Borgson said.

"What then?"

"Nothing. Nothing organic."

Michael's fingers paused on the button he was fumbling with. "Are you trying to tell me," he said, "that I didn't have a heart attack this afternoon? That—"

"I could make you happy," Borgson said. "I could tell you that there is a splintering of the QRS wave on the electrocardiogram, which there isn't. Or that X rays reveal an accentuated aortic, which they don't. Or that your blood pressure is 170 over 95. Or I could find minute traces of albumin in a urinalysis. I could put you to bed for six months, take you off alcohol and tobacco and sex, and favor you with a twenty-dollar house call once a week. I could—if I weren't too busy already with patients I can maybe do something for."

"If I follow this, what you are saying is that I am gifted with a vivid imagination."

"Don't misunderstand me," Borgson said. "Hypertension, hypochondria, whatever you want to call it, can be dangerous. People have died from psychosomatic coronaries. All I'm saying is, I'm not a psychoanalyst."

"I don't believe you. You can't tell me—"

"I didn't think I could."

"You boys aren't infallible," Michael said. "You have been known to make mistakes in diagnoses."

"I admit it. Maybe you better try Harvey. Maybe he isn't too busy this winter."

"If you *are* right, if that's all that's wrong with me, what can I do about it?"

"Lie on a couch for a year," Borgson said, "at fifty dollars an hour. Find out why you subconsciously hate your wife, or feel insecure in your work, or what guilt complexes you developed at the age of three."

"What can I do that won't cost fifty dollars an hour?"

"Quit reading medical books. Resist the temptation to memorize the symptoms of angina pectoris. Otherwise, come February you are going to be paying Harvey sixty dollars to tell you that you haven't got that, either."

"All right," Michael said. He walked across the room to the mirror and smoothed down his hair with his fingers; at that moment, he almost hated this man. "How much do I owe you?"

"Sixty dollars," Borgson said gloomily. "Just leave it with the girl on your way out."

Except for insisting on doing the driving, he did not say anything to her when he came out of the clinic. Behind the wheel, he drove recklessly out Hennepin and savagely once he was clear of the traffic.

When they got out of the car, they heard the whine of power machinery through the garage partition. He went into the garage and opened the shop door. Ellen was working at the belt sander.

"What are you up to?" he said.

She turned and smiled happily at him. "I'm making Mother a magazine rack. For Christmas. I found the plans in my Scout magazine."

"Turn that off."

She stopped smiling. "Why? I know—"

"You heard me," he said. "Turn it off. You've no goddam business messing around on that machinery."

She turned it off. "Jeez, Daddy," she said, "it's only twenty days to Christmas. I can't sand all these boards by hand in—"

"You can't go through life with only eight fingers, either. Not and expect to pass arithmetic."

He walked out of the shop and across the yard, across the brittle grass. In the living room, Alice had taken off her coat. She said, "Are you going to tell me? What's the matter with you? And how bad is it?"

240

"Nothing's the matter with me," he said. "Everything's fine."

"I'm your wife, Michael. I've got a right—"

"I'm telling you what he said. He said it was my imagination. He said I probably hate my wife or the way I make my living, and I'm a goddam hypochondriac."

"That's ridiculous. I saw you when you came in here. You looked like a corpse." Her eyes drifted away from him. "They make mistakes," she said. "Maybe you ought to see another—"

"According to Davis," he said, "Borgson is the best heart man in the city." He threw his overcoat on the davenport and sat down. "He could be right. I remember a story about Flaubert. Right after he'd finished *Madame Bovary* they took him to the hospital for arsenic poisoning. He had all the symptoms except one. He didn't have a trace of arsenic in his system." He leaned back and closed his eyes. "I'm going back to New York," he said.

"Now?" she said. "This week?"

"Yes."

"Why? What can you—"

"I want them to see those first six chapters. I want to know if they're any good."

"Couldn't you mail them?"

He sat up. "Damn it, Alice," he said, "don't start an argument. I don't feel like arguing."

"I'm sorry. I just thought it was so close to Christmas—"

"I'll be back for Christmas." He ran his fingers through his hair. "I want the verdict face to face," he said more gently. "I need the encouragement. I am going to give up unless I get the encouragement." He got up and shook a cigarette out of the pack on the stand and then looked down at her. "I always knew before," he said. "I didn't have to ask anybody, I knew. I knew with *The Alley*, I knew with *Vine*. But I don't know about this one."

"It's an historical. You've never written an historical before. That's probably the reason."

He didn't say anything, and she sighed. It was a very gentle

241

sigh; he wouldn't have caught it at all if her lips hadn't been parted slightly and if he hadn't had his eyes on her face. "When do you think you'll leave?" she asked.

"Now. Tomorrow, if I can catch any kind of transportation out of here."

She got up. "You call and find out," she said. "I'll pack your bags."

15

THE MINUTE HE CLIMBED off the plane, he got that feeling of excitement, of energy under pressure, that he always got in New York. It was like being charged with a spiritual dynamo, and as he hurried through the gate and across the crowded waiting room, he wondered whether this wasn't the town you ought to live in if you wanted to write. Even if they did say that towns didn't write books.

In his hotel room, he stripped to the waist and went into the bathroom and splashed cold water on his face and shoulders. Then he stretched out on the bed with the telephone.

"Surprise," he said when she answered.

"Michael!" she said. "What on earth—"

"How've you been?"

"Fine," she said. "I was just taking a shower. I'm standing here dripping water all over everything."

"I'd like to see you. At this exact moment, I mean."

"You're not alone," she said. "Where are you?"

"At the Prince George. I just got in."

"Well, give me an hour, darling. I'll throw something on and—"

He wanted to see her. He could feel the subtle ache in him, and he wanted very badly to see her. "I don't think tonight," he said.

She gave herself ten seconds to mull that over. "Is something wrong?" she said.

243

"No." He paused. "I've got a manuscript with me," he said. "The opening chapters of a novel. I want you to read them tomorrow."

"All right. We're swamped over there, but I'll push everything else to the back of my desk."

"The thing is, I don't want anything to get in the way of an objective opinion. That's why I'm going to dig in my fingernails and practice self-control tonight."

"All right. Though I don't think—"

"It's an historical," he said. "I started it six weeks ago. It's a portrait of pre-Restoration England. About a Cavalier named Lord Mordaunt and a black-haired, black-eyed daughter of a dour-faced Presbyterian. She started out to be golden-haired, but I guess you must have gotten in the way. Anyway, she's black-haired now."

"Well, there's nothing the matter with a good historical. A well-written historical is nothing to be ashamed of." She allowed ten seconds of silence to take over the wire between uptown and 32nd Street. "You haven't told her yet, have you?" she said.

"No," he said. "No, I haven't told her yet, Jean."

"Listen, darling," she said, "you don't have to think that just because you lost your nerve or something—"

"I haven't told her," he said, "because I had to get your opinion of this manuscript first. I had to know whether I have an outside chance of paying my share of the rent."

"You don't have to worry about that. You *know* you don't have to worry about that, Michael."

"I am probably on my way downhill," he said, "and it may be on a toboggan. But I'm not to the bottom yet. I am not far enough gone yet to be willing to be kept." He rolled over on his back. "I'll see you tomorrow morning. I'm going to sleep until I wake up, but it ought to be by ten."

"All right. I'll be there at ten, Michael."

The next morning, coming out of the Mattson offices, he ran into Tom Rogers. Tom spotted Michael first and called to him. When he came up, he was smiling and his hand was out. "In town for the holidays?" he asked.

"No. Just for a couple of days." Michael felt embarrassed, the way you might feel if you ran unexpectedly into your ex-wife.

"I'm Christmas shopping," Tom said. "What can you get a thirteen-year-old boy?"

"I don't know. My thirteen-year-old's a girl. All she wants is a dog, but Alice won't hear of it."

Tom was looking narrowly at him. "If you're not doing anything," he said, "why don't we go somewhere and have a cup of coffee and talk about your successful novel?"

They walked north together, two men with the wind in their faces and not much of anything to say to each other. Over the toast and coffee, Tom looked across the table into Michael's face, the same look he had bestowed on him out there in the street. "You're a lot thinner than when I saw you last," he said. "You look like success has been giving you a hard time."

"I'm sorry, Tom."

"What for? What's to be sorry for?"

"I didn't *have* to do it. I *could* have let you do the book, Tom."

"If you had, it would have sold six thousand and I'd still be in the red and you'd be behind in the rent again."

"Sometimes," Michael said, "I almost wish I were."

Tom leaned forward. "What have they been doing to you, Michael?" he said softly.

"Nothing. Who, Tom?"

"I don't know. All of them. The promoters, the advertising agents who buy full pages in the *Times* under the delusion that that proves something, the editors who read a manuscript with a book club in mind, the publishers who would rather have Yerby than Faulkner. All the sons-of-bitches in this town who do things to people."

"Nobody's been doing anything to anybody."

"All right. What have you been doing to yourself, then?"

245

"Working. I'm six chapters into a new novel. An historical."

Tom set his spoon carefully on his saucer. "Now, who talked you into that? Mattson? Or that glamour-girl editor they assigned you?"

"I talked myself into it," Michael said. "I've got to make some more money, Tom."

"You must have made a hundred thousand on *Vine*. What the hell did you do with it all?"

"Bought a house. And went hog-wild on automobiles."

"An historical," Tom said. "An historical, for Chrissake."

"That's nothing to be ashamed of, is it? There's no damned law, is there?"

"No, I guess there isn't. Excuse me, Michael."

"You're all alike. The bunch of you."

"Who?" Tom said. "And how are we alike, Michael?" His voice, lying beside Michael's, was very quiet.

"You long-hairs," Michael said. "You *Kenyon Review* boys. If a writer tells an honest story and fails to load every page with Freudian symbols, he's an object of derision, he's somebody to spit on."

"I didn't mean anything like that."

"The hell you didn't."

"An historical's all right. I've got nothing against historicals. Just as long as you believe in what you're doing."

"I believe in what I'm doing," Michael said evenly.

"All right. Just so you don't let the bastards with their success philosophy get to you, that's all." He tasted his coffee and then spooned more sugar into it. "So far," he said, "you've got nothing to be ashamed of. You've got your name on the title page of an honest novel, and you can look any of them straight in the eye. It's just that I hope you never have to be ashamed, Michael."

Michael dropped his eyes. "I'm sorry, Tom."

"Forget it."

"I don't know what's the matter with me. I never used to jump down throats like that."

"Forget it," Tom said. "Let it lie." He glanced at his watch. "If I'm going to find anything for my kid," he said, "I guess

I'd probably better get started." He pushed back his chair. "You're in a jungle now," he said. "And don't you forget it for a minute."

"I'm a big boy now," Michael said. "I can take care of myself."

"You aren't very big. You aren't very big at all, sonny." Michael grinned at him.

"Anyway," Tom said, "luck on the new book. I hope it's an exciting story about the Revolutionary War."

"Why? Do you like stories about the Revolutionary War?"

"No," Tom said, "but they tell me stories about the Revolutionary War sell better."

He lost track of time at the Museum of Art, and when he hurried out into the dusk, it was the rush hour and no cabs; he had to settle for a Fifth Avenue bus. It was dark by the time he climbed off at 38th, and there was the smell of snow in the air and a Salvation Army Santa Claus on the corner. He dropped a quarter into the pot for luck and then hurried across town. When he got off the elevator, Mattson's office door was closed and the receptionist was gone for the day. As he walked down the passageway to Jean's office, his steps echoed in the empty building, like loneliness or sadness or doom.

She was at her desk putting on a new face when he came into her doorway. She looked up at him and smiled, quickly and a little shyly. Looking down at the smile, he felt the vague, familiar ache of desire and affection.

"I thought you'd stood me up," she said.

"I forgot the time." He leaned against the jamb. "My standing you up is one thing you never have to worry about," he said. "Not ever."

She snapped her compact shut. "What did you have in mind for tonight?"

"Anything. You name it."

"I just woke up to the date. Would you mind very much taking a girl Christmas shopping?"

"No. I'd like to."

She gave him a quick, sideways glance. "What would Michael want for Christmas?"

"That's easy," he said. "You."

"I mean something you haven't already got."

"All right. A kind word about a manuscript."

Her eyes came up to his, as if by an effort of will. "I have a confession," she said. "I thought I could get to it. Then these galleys came in—a week late already—and it was a rush job, and—"

He felt the disappointment. He had counted on telling her sometime tonight what had been on his mind for three days, and he had wanted the verdict on those chapters behind him when he did. "It's all right," he said.

"One thing—we can go through the evening now without talking shop. Can't we?"

"I guess so." He held her coat and when she shrugged her shoulders down into it, he touched the collar tentatively, straightening out a fold. Then he put his arms around her from behind and buried his face in her hair.

"Christ, you're beautiful," he whispered.

She took hold of his hands, almost fiercely. "Don't," she said. "Please don't. You make me want to cry."

It was ten-thirty when they got to her place. His arms were full of packages, like one of the abused husbands in cartoons, and they were both laughing when they entered her apartment. While he dumped the packages, she went around the room, turning on lights. When the place was ablaze, she turned and faced him, her hands behind her on the edge of a table. Her face was still flushed from the cold, and her eyes were black and liquid and alive. She might have been a little girl on Christmas morning who had found a life-sized doll under the tree.

"Well," she said, "take off your coat and stay awhile."

"I'll do that. It was exactly my intention to do that."

"You can fix some drinks while I change into something more comfortable, like one of those delinquent girls in one of those hard-boiled novels."

248

"Toms and Jerrys," he said. "I'm pretty good at Toms and Jerrys."

She had changed into a robe and slippers when he came out of the kitchen with the steaming toddies. He handed her one, and she tasted it critically. "You *are* pretty good," she said.

"I told you. I'm going to make some lucky girl an exceptional husband." He set his cup on the coffee table and stretched out and laid his head in her lap. Looking up at her, he could follow the fragile line of her jaw; he had always known that she was small-boned, but until this moment, until he could follow that delicate line from exactly this angle, the knowledge had been remote, like a theory you learn in a classroom. He reached up and ran a finger along her cheek.

She looked down at him and smiled. "A penny," she said.

"I am lying here," he said, "in a kind of wonder that even two or three million years of evolution was time enough to create something like you. I am also lying here weighing a desire to kiss you against the effort it would require to raise my head."

She slid a hand under his head. "I'll meet you halfway," she said.

He raised his head and kissed her. "As usual," he said, "you are the one who does most of the giving, and I am the one who does most of the getting."

"It is more blessed to give than to receive. They say. Happy?"

"There is only one thing missing. If you had read that manuscript. And agreed with me that it is going to be a Guild selection in the fall."

Her eyes strayed out into the room.

"I had it all planned for tonight," he said. "I was going to meet you at six, and you were going to be enthusiastic about those chapters. Afterwards we were going to be very carefree and irresponsible, like Scott Fitzgerald on a pagan holiday in Paris. And about this point in the evening, I was going to tell you that I wasn't going back home. That this trip was permanent."

Her eyes flicked back to his face, but only for an instant. "I guess I'm going to have to tell you," she said.

"You see," he said, "I wasn't telling the strict truth last night. The manuscript wasn't the only reason I haven't told Alice about us."

"Listen to me—"

"The fact is," he said, "I couldn't. I tried, but I just couldn't do it—not there, not then. So I drew out four thousand dollars before I left, which I figured would see me through this novel, and I put everything else in her name. I'll tell her in the letter—"

"Michael," she said, "will you please listen?"

"All right," he said. "I'm listening."

"What if those chapters aren't any good?"

"I'm not even considering the possibility. They've *got* to be good." He shifted his weight. "What did you want to tell me?"

"I was going to," she said. "I had myself steeled, and then you stood in the doorway back there and—"

He looked into her face and felt the cold suddenly in him. "What?" he said.

"Because I wanted tonight," she said. "I don't think I could have stood it if I couldn't have had tonight."

"Goddam it, what, Jean?" He came up onto his elbow. "You *did* read it," he said.

"Yes."

"You read it, and you're trying to tell me it wasn't any good."

"That's right. It was pretty bad, Michael."

"Well, I'll just have to rewrite it, then."

"I'm afraid it's worse than that, Michael."

He tried to force her to meet his eyes. "If you're trying to tell me I *can't* write an historical, I'm not buying that, Jean." He sat up. "I know what's the matter," he said. "You're expecting one thing and getting another. You're expecting me to still be the white-haired boy. Only I'm not trying for immortality with this one. All I'm trying to do is follow Frank

250

Mattson's advice, to tell a workmanlike story. Literature is for my next trip, after I've made some more money."

"Frank ought to know better. There has to be something else. There has to be some belief in what you're doing."

"Look, I've read Yerby and Costain—"

"They believe in what they're doing. That's why people read them."

He got to his feet and walked across the room. "Even if it's as bad as you say," he said, "I'm betting Frank will publish it. My name's worth something. Maybe it isn't Pulitzer, but plenty of second novels are lousy. Every writer takes advantage of his prerogative to one or two failures."

She shook her head. "It doesn't work that way, Michael. You have a reputation now. Every critic in the country is sitting on the edge of his chair, waiting to see if you've got what it takes to protect it."

He leaned against her mantel, his left arm resting on it. He opened and closed his left hand, slowly, the way you do when your fingers have been cramped around a pencil for a long time. "Is it really terrible?" he said. "I mean leaving *Vine* out of the picture—"

"It is really terrible." She pushed a hand vaguely out into the space in front of her. "It reads like a doctoral dissertation."

"It was going to be perfect," he said. "I was going to meet you tonight, and you were going to tell me I had a future in this genre, and I was going to tell you that I wasn't going back, and it was going to be so damned perfect. Why couldn't you have told me this back there? At six o'clock?"

She looked very steadily at him. "Because I wanted the evening. I haven't ever asked for very much, Michael. I thought I had a right to that."

"Sure you did." He turned and hit the mantel lightly with his clenched fist, though he was conscious, even as he did it, of the histrionics in the gesture. "What's happened to me, anyway?" he said. "First I can't get it down; now I can't even look at it and see what I've written, and what the hell's happened to me, anyway?"

"I did," she said quietly. "I happened to you. And I wasn't any good for you."

"Oh, for Chrissake, Jean."

"I suppose," she said, speaking slowly and carefully, "I suppose you're in love with both of us. Your wife and me. Anyway, you're tearing yourself apart inside. How can anybody write if he's tearing himself apart inside?"

What she was saying didn't penetrate for a minute and then it did. He waited patiently for her to go on with it, like a fighter with his instinct for self-preservation gone and his left arm hooked over the ropes.

She stood up. "I'm giving you back to her, Michael. Because it's the only way I can think of to give you back to yourself."

"I wouldn't have put it in exactly that way. But I'm probably not as civilized as you are."

"Please. This is the hardest thing I ever had to do, Michael, and please—"

"Not that I blame you. After all, I *don't* have it any more. Do I?"

"Please, Michael," she said. "That's not the reason—"

"Sure it isn't." He walked over to the chair where he had thrown his coat and hat and scarf. He shrugged into the overcoat and turned the collar up. She stood, a foot from the davenport, her arms stiffly at her sides, watching him. "Don't you see, Michael," she said. "Don't you? How impossible it would be for me—"

"Look. I am trying to do this very quietly. Very goddamned sensibly and maturely and civilized."

She stopped looking at him. "All right, Michael."

"Before I go," he said, "I want to thank you. For three months of your life. I also want to apologize. For taking up so much of your time."

"Will I see you again?" she said. "Before you leave?"

"I doubt it."

"What about the manuscript?"

"Just drop it in the nearest wastebasket."

She turned then and walked ahead of him to the door and

stood aside. He turned on the threshold to look at her just once more.

"It was a lovely evening," he said. "For a while."

"Please," she said. "Please, won't you just go now, Michael?"

She was standing in the doorway, her hand on the knob, and he could not see the delicacy of her cheekline from that angle, but he knew the line was there and he knew it could break a man's heart. "I love you very much," he said. "I loved you before I ever loved anybody else, and I'll never love anybody else."

"If you don't go," she said, "I'm going to start to cry."

"Don't do that, darling." He reached out and touched her cheek, lightly, with two fingertips. Then he stepped backward into the hall.

"Merry Christmas," he said.

He had the slight, nagging headache you get after a sleepless night. He turned down 41st, found a bar, went in and had a drink. He had, in fact, three drinks, very quick ones. Then he went out into the thin, winter sunlight and walked up to the offices of Anderson and Carew.

Kay was bent over her desk when he opened her door, and he stood there and watched her at work. Even with nothing more animate than a batch of letters she looked efficient and orderly and capable of driving a bargain with a sharp horse-trader without winding up on the short end of the stick.

"Hello, Kay," he said.

She looked up, and then she pushed back her chair and got to her feet. "Michael! When did you get in town?"

"Tuesday."

"Three days. You've been in town three days and you didn't even call me."

"I couldn't think of anything important to call about."

"You could have just said hello."

"All right. Hello, Kay."

She smiled, and he went in and sat down. He noticed his picture on her wall. It looked glossy and neat and successful,

253

like the picture of a man who makes thirty cents a word. "How have I been doing?"

"Not bad. National's sold a hundred and seventy thousand, the trade not quite thirty. It comes to about forty-five thousand. You've drawn twenty of that."

"Is that going to be the story?"

"More or less."

His eyes moved back to the picture on the wall. He was wondering how long another twenty-five thousand would last him.

"Tell her yet?" Kay asked softly.

"No."

"Twenty-five thousand plus the property. That's not too bad a settlement. She could have gotten a rawer deal."

"I'm not going to tell her." He wasn't looking at her, but he could feel her eyes on him, cool and objective, only faintly puzzled. Then she changed the subject.

"How's the work going?"

He considered telling her about the historical, and then decided that water under the bridge was water under the bridge. "I don't think Mattson can count on a title for their fall list," he said.

She tried once more to get underneath his expression, and then she gave it up. "Oh," she said, "I almost forgot. There's a letter here for you. I won't have to forward it now." She sifted through her wire basket and found a long, official-looking envelope. The return address was an FRS at the University of Louisville. He tore open the envelope and pulled out the letter. It was two pages long, but the substance was that Louisville was starting a writing program in the fall and would he be interested in an associate professorship at sixty-five hundred? He read it through slowly, and then handed it to her.

"I guess I finally got my promotion," he said, and then he began to laugh. It was in the beginning only a chuckle and he thought it would pass over, but it didn't. He could feel it in his stomach when he tried to swallow it, and then he gave up trying to control it. He was conscious that the sound of the laugh was subtly hysterical, but he couldn't do anything about it.

254

When he straightened up, Kay was staring at him. "Are you all right? Are you all right, Michael?"

"I'm all right." He gestured toward the letter. "Read it."

She read it. Then she looked at him again. "I fail to see what's so funny."

"I finally got promoted. I finally arrived." He swallowed another laugh. "I thought it was funny," he said.

She was still looking narrowly at him. "You aren't all right. You aren't all right at all, Michael." She glanced at the letter. "It might not be a bad idea for you to give this some thought," she said.

"Oh, for Chrissake, Kay."

"A hundred and twenty a week isn't bad. Lots of people live on less. And it's not a bad life."

"I know what kind of a life it is. I've been there." I know exactly what kind of a life it is, he thought. For the first five years I would be a writer, somebody to be excused from committee work because I was a Creative Artist, somebody for the Writers' Group of the AAUW to collect on Friday afternoons. For the next five years I would keep telling myself that I was going to get down to work on another book as soon as the pressure of classes and student manuscripts and informal Friday-afternoon talks permitted me. For the next five years my colleagues would ask me how the New Novel was going, their eyes shifting the way they do when they already know the answer. After that my students would begin asking me if I had ever published anything, and could you still buy it in a bookstore anywhere?

"I've been there," he said. "Thanks just the same but no thanks, Kay."

"You're no wolf-at-the-door writer, Michael," she said. "You're helpless when you're trying to fight worry. And this could take the pressure off. So I don't see why not."

"I'll tell you why not," he said. "Because I'm never going to be bored again. A drunk on skid row, maybe. Frustrated, maybe. Desperate, maybe. Dead, maybe. But not bored. Not full up to here with a sense of my own insignificance and the unending progression of infinite days. Not again." He made a brief, uncertain gesture in her direction; it would have been reaching out to her if he had finished it. "Where did it go, Kay?" he said. "I had it once. I had it in the palm of my hand once, and where did it get to?"

She didn't try to guess where it had gotten to.

"I was going to be important," he said. "I thought I'd found out what I could do, and I was going to be so goddam important."

"Michael," she said, "it's like luck. When it turns you have to wait it out—"

"Is that why you lose it?" he said. "Because you are going to be so goddam important?" He dropped his eyes. "I'd better not be taking up any more of your time."

"Tell me," she said, "what are you doing tonight? I've got a pair of tickets to 'My Fair Lady.' We could have dinner—"

"I'm afraid I'd make a lousy dinner companion. I'm full up to here with self-pity this week." He stood up and looked down into her eyes; he read worry in them. "Thanks just the same," he said, "but I think I'll get to bed early tonight. I wasn't sleepy last night, and it's too early in the afternoon to tell, but maybe I can sleep tonight."

"Well," she said, "take care of yourself, Michael."

"I'll do everything I can," he said.

Hyatt Engel   IV

16 MY PHONE WAS RINGING when I let myself into my apartment. It was no time of night for a phone to be ringing, and I wasn't in any mood for conversation if it had been, but my conditioning betrayed me, and I answered it. It was Michael Savage.

"Where you been?" he said.

"Working."

"At one A.M.?"

"I'm an executive now. It says 'Associate Editor' on my door now. I work all hours now. Where are you?"

"I'm in a bar, a crummy bar on Eighth Street, and I'm going to get drunk. Come on over and join me."

"It's late and I'm tired. Some other time, Michael."

"This place is on Eighth Street," he said. "Just east of Third."

"I know where it is. I've been there."

"Listen," he said, "you come over here, I'll give you a story. A goddam exclusive. For that magazine of yours."

I started to say no again, and then I thought of Goldstein facing me across my desk two hours ago, and of the resignation, neatly typed and lying in the center of the green blotter. I thought, Maybe that is what I need, too. To get drunk. In a crummy bar on Eighth Street. "All right," I said.

It was still snowing when I came back out onto the street. It was one of those soft, damp snows where the flakes are the size of dimes and if they don't melt the minute they touch the street, it is hell to pay in this town, and I turned my coat col-

259

lar up against the weather and started across town. On lower Fifth, the street crews were out with the trucks and the shovels, and I knew the city was going to be tied up by morning. In the pale, futile street lights, Washington Square Park looked like the Almighty had spread an unbleached cotton blanket over it, and the wire fence around the playground looked gaunt and stark, like a concentration camp. And I guess it is going to be a white Christmas, I thought. With a vengeance.

Down on Eighth Street there was still some life left in the city, and I walked through the tinny, mechanical music floating out of basement joints and past the lonely people huddled under the lights on the street corners. The place was just the other side of Third, and inside, I stood with my hands deep in my coat pockets and the brim of my hat dripping and took it in. All of it, the gaunt floor, the bitter overhead lights, the scarred bar with the wire-legged stools lined up along it, the half-dozen tables scattered along the wall. The last time I was in here, I was thinking, it had been with Rachel, and that afternoon the place had seemed like something you stumble onto when you are looking for atmosphere. But the circumstances had since altered, I thought. For that had been the quiet end of an April afternoon, and I had been two months old at *Insight* and a young man with a future. For that had not been one o'clock in the morning, and a snow storm outside, and the young man with the future fresh from a bitter hour with a colleague. And now the place looked exactly like what it was, a tired dive on the wrong side of Third Avenue. Now it looked like a place where you could find an empty table in the corner and meditate on your sins and get quietly and effectively drunk.

I didn't see Savage right away. I saw the established quota of tired men in heavy overcoats lined up on the stools, and at two of the tables a couple of hard-looking, ageless men making plays for hard-looking, aging women, and behind the bar the kind of bartenders who tend bar in a place like that. Then I spotted him, at the far end of the bar, and I made my way to the empty stool beside him.

"Hello, Hyatt," he said. The light from the overhead bulb

behind him spilled down over his shoulders. He looked thin and white and sodden, like somebody walking in his sleep or just rounding the first turn into a three-day binge. "How's our news analyst?" he said.

"I'm not a news analyst. I'm a critic."

One of the bartenders came up the counter. His flat eyes were on my coat and what he could see of the suit underneath; he was no doubt wondering why the two of us weren't uptown, in one of those places with chrome edging around the bar stools and waiters in black ties. "Another one?" he said to Savage.

"Two," Savage said. "One for me, one for my friend here."

The bartender had a craggy, unvarnished face that didn't want any trouble, and the kind of eyes that can study you narrowly without appearing to be on you at all, and for just the flick of an eyelash they studied Savage. They weren't worried yet, but they were calculating the distance to possible trouble and matching it against the minutes left to closing time. "I'll have to have a look at some money, Mister," he said.

I was about to say that this round was on me, but Michael's hand was already in his pocket. It came out with a twenty. "That enough?" he asked.

"Plenty."

"Lay it over there on the register," Michael said, "where you can rest your eyes on it every four or five minutes. And put your goddam mind at ease."

"Sure," the bartender said. "No offense, Mister."

"Naturally," Michael said. "No offense."

The bartender set two almost-clean shot glasses in front of us and slopped them level full. Michael set himself and then raised the drink and tossed it off. A drop ran down his chin. He swiped it off with his coat sleeve, set the glass back on the counter, and made a brief gesture. The bartender slopped it full again, and as Michael looked at it, I caught the shudder.

"Why don't we sit at a table?" I said. "Where we can look each other in the face while we perform the operation?"

"Sure." He maneuvered himself off the stool, and I picked up the drinks and followed him to a table. He kicked out a chair and sat down, and I set the drinks on the table and faced him.

"Well," I said, "what's the story?"

"What story?"

"The one I was going to hear. As a reward for braving storm and sleet to come over here at one in the morning."

"Oh, that story. That was a lie. A goddam ruse. I just needed somebody to see I got home without getting rolled." He cocked his head and looked foggily at me. "So you got a promotion," he said.

"That's right."

"Imagine that, now. That sounds like news a man can drink to. There's nothing like getting on in the world, Hyatt."

"That's right." I looked around at the rocky-faced bartenders and the two tired people at the table behind Savage and the naked lights. "And this is a place to drink to it," I said.

He took time out to drink to the news. Then he pushed his hat back off his forehead, put his forearms on the edge of the table, and leaned his weight on his shoulders. His eyes were black and dead, like buttons that had been left out in the weather. "Maybe," he said, "maybe you could get me a job over there. Since you are a VIP now."

I thought he was joking. His lips weren't trembling exactly, but they were on the verge, and his expression wasn't the expression of a man who is trying to be funny, but that is the way I interpreted the remark. "I could probably put in a word for you," I said.

"Could you? Could you do that, Hyatt?"

I took another look at his expression. "I don't believe you're kidding," I said.

"No, I'm not kidding. Why should I be kidding?"

"You aren't broke, are you?"

"Not yet."

"If you're not broke, you wouldn't want a job on *Insight*. Believe me."

He gestured toward his empty glass. "If you've got any reservations about this, put your mind at ease. I can take this stuff or I can let it alone."

I thought of Ulrich, who, thanks to me, was going to win his fight with the Guild, and I thought of Dave Goldstein, who had had his resignation on my desk six hours after my promotion was announced. "That's not what I had in mind," I said.

"The way I figure it," he said, "if a man got a job like that and kept his eyes open, he might get material for a novel out of it. If he were the kind of a writer who couldn't write about anything unless it had happened to him. And if he couldn't write books any more, he ought to at least be able to write *about* books. He ought to be able to do that, hadn't he?"

"Do you know what it's like?" I said. "A job over there?"

"I am not asking for a dissertation," he said. "Just a simple answer to a simple question."

I watched the man at the table behind Savage help the woman on with her coat. When they do that in this section of town, I thought, the arrangement is probably without benefit of clergy. Then I looked at Michael. I was thinking of Goldstein's resignation. If I hated Savage, I thought, it would be very simple. But I did not hate him. "I could get you a job over there," I said. "In my department, because we are going to have an opening come tomorrow. Only you wouldn't be interested in it."

"Try offering it to me."

"I could do that if I hated your guts. Because you wouldn't get any novel out of it. And in five years you would be another second-rate bastard beating better men than you out of jobs. Like me."

"Have you ever been to Louisville?" he said thickly.

Oh, God, I thought wearily, he is sodden drunk and you are just wasting your breath, Engel. "Yes," I said. "It's a pleasant town with wide streets and a lot of trees, and they make whiskey there. Why?"

"That's right. I guess I knew that. I guess that just slipped my mind." He opened and closed his right hand. "You think I'm not paying you any attention. You think I'm drunk and Louisville is without relevance. Well, I'm drunk, but Louisville is not without relevance, and I guess Housman had the right idea, at that."

"What idea was that?"

" 'Smart lad, to slip betimes away, from fields where glory does not stay.' That's Housman. 'Now you will not smell the rout of lads that wore their honors out, runners whom renown outran, And the name died before the man.' That's Housman, too."

For a minute I didn't know what the hell he was talking about, and then I did. I felt that cold emptiness in my gut like when you have just come over the brow of the hill and the jungle is down there below you, and then you hear the click of the bolt, and you know, even as you start the dive, that it isn't going to buy you anything, that the sniper is tied up there in one of those trees somewhere and he has got you dead in his sights and you have had it. No, I thought. No. He is just a guy in his cups. He has been cooped up in a hotel room all day, with time on his hands to brood. They never do it when they talk about it, I thought, and where the hell did you read that, Engel, and I hope to Christ that whoever it was knew what he was talking about.

" 'Grow old along with me,' " I said. " 'The best is yet to be, The last of life, for which the first was made.' That's Browning. And quit talking crap, Michael."

"Sure," he said. "Crap. I'm only thirty-six, and I've got a devoted family, and I'm rich and famous, and I've got my whole goddam life ahead of me. Haven't I?"

I didn't say anything.

"Let me tell you about a writer I met once," he said. "My first time in New York." He leaned toward me. The brim of his hat cast a shadow across his forehead and eyes. "Five will get you ten, you never heard of this writer," he said. "Hell, I have talked to specialists in contemporary American lit who never heard of him. But thirty years ago they had heard of him. Thirty years ago he was the fair-haired boy of American literature. Hemingway was a young man with one successful novel, Fitzgerald was selling to the *Post*, Hergesheimer commanded front-page reviews, Faulkner was chummy with Sherwood Anderson but elsewhere unheard of, and this writer was the boy to watch. This boy had it made. For he was Living Literature." He dropped his head, and his hand went out to the empty shot glass. "Now," he said, "he's an old man who sits in a crummy walk-up here in the Village, somebody no one has ever heard of. Except me, on whom he made an impression." He looked up suddenly. "The hell with forgotten old men in lonely cold-water flats. A simple answer to a simple question. Yes or no?"

"No," I said. "Not a job on *Insight*, Michael."

"That's what I asked for. A simple answer to a simple question." He turned in his chair. "Bartender," he said loudly.

The bartender came around the counter and slopped Michael's glass full again. He looked at me. I shook my head.

Michael peered up at him. "How's my twenty holding up?" he said.

"There's a piece of it left, Mister."

"I have a suggestion. Why not just set the bottle on the table?"

The bartender shook his head.

"If what is left in the bottle is worth more than my balance," Michael said, "just name the figure."

"Sorry, Mister."

"I am only interested in saving you steps. I am asking you very patiently to name your price and set the bottle on the table."

"I'm not looking for trouble, Mister," the bartender said. "Don't give me any."

I reached across the table and put a hand on Michael's sleeve. "Maybe he can't. Maybe there's some kind of a law, Michael."

"There's no law," Michael said. "And I am asking the son-of-a-bitch to set the goddam bottle on the goddam table because I am interested in saving him steps and because I am going to kill it before I leave anyway and because I am tired of waiting fifteen minutes between drinks."

The bartender looked over his shoulder. His buddy came up the bar a few feet and leaned on it, his right hand out of sight.

265

The bartender looked at Michael and then at me. "You'd better get him out of here, Mister," he said. "If he's a friend of yours."

I still had a grip on Michael's sleeve. I could feel the pressure in my throat; I knew what it could be like if you ever started anything in a place like this. "Let's get out of here, Michael," I said. "Maybe somewhere else they will sell us a bottle."

"Sure." He got to his feet and stood there a minute, his fingertips on the edge of the table, swaying slightly. His eyes were trying to focus on the bartender. Then he took his fingertips off the edge of the table, and then he swung. It was the swing of a drunk, telegraphed forty miles before it even left the hip. The bartender didn't even bother to move out of his tracks. He just tipped his head an inch to the right, and when Michael fell into him, he put one hand on Michael's collar and the other on his coattail.

"You better open the door, Mister," he said to me. "If he is a friend of yours. Because I am heaving him, and I ain't in any mood to bother."

I opened the door and watched the bartender maneuver Michael toward me. I watched the heave, and then the door closed behind me. Michael crawled to his knees and then swayed to his feet. His face was a blur in the dim light, but I could hear him sobbing.

"I'll kill him for that," he said. "I'll kill the bastard for that."

I grabbed his arm. "Stay out of there."

"Let go. I only wanted to save him steps, and he put his loving hands on me, and I'll kill him for that."

"Listen, there are two of them in there. If you stick your head in that door again, you are going to get it split open with the business end of a sawed-off baseball bat." I swung him around. "I'm six inches shorter than you," I said, "and forty pounds lighter, but if you don't settle down, I'm going to clip you myself. And in your condition I can get away with it."

Suddenly the rage went out of him. At first it was all there, in the white, set face and the tensed arm, and then he sagged inside his coat and started to tremble. At first it was just a slight tremor of his arm under my hand, no more distinct than a strong heartbeat, and then it began to grow until he was shaking all over, like a man with malaria. In the light that splintered out from the doorway behind us, I could see that his lips were trembling too, and I didn't realize right away that he was trying to say something. It took him two or three tries.

"What's going to happen to me?" he whispered. "Oh, my God, what's going to come of me?" He wasn't talking to me, but he wasn't talking to himself, either. Not exactly.

Up the street half a block, a street light was a nebulous, ragged circle of sick yellow. Behind us, I could hear the muffled sound of a bus going north on Third. I stood there for the space of a dozen heartbeats, with my hand on his arm, and had myself a look at the face of a man who has fallen apart inside, and if that description is inadequate, it is because you have to see the face of a man to whom that has happened before you can know exactly what I mean. I began to brush him off, and then I started fumbling at the buttons of his coat. He tried to help on the bottom button, and then he gave it up and just stood there, like a kid getting dressed to go outdoors and play. When I reached up to pull his hat down, I had one more look at a face that was on its way from uptown to skid row. You poor bastard, I thought, you poor driven son-of-a-bitch.

I touched his arm again. "Let's get you home," I said. "Let's find a cab somewhere and get you home."

Michael Savage   IV

17 BY THE TIME THE PLANE
set down at Minneapolis, he knew what was going to come of
him.

The knowledge had not come suddenly. For a long time,
months maybe, the idea had lain down there in the dark, like a
piece of waterlogged driftwood wedged under a boulder; then
something, the jar of an explosion upstream or the weight of
silt piling up against one end or maybe just the inexorable
nudge of the current, had loosened it and it had swirled dreamlike up to the surface. For there had now been one novel he
knew he couldn't write and another he thought he could but
didn't believe in; there had been a moment when he knew he
was going to die and had known peace; and another in a New
York apartment when ultimate self-knowledge had been born,
and still another in a Third Avenue bar, with his soul on the
operating table and a New York newsman in attendance to
administer the anaesthetic, and the operation not a success.
Not exactly.

Now there lay behind him all the slow accretion of events
and emotions and self-knowledge and despair, like the imperceptible growth of a coral reef, and then he knew what he was
going to do and suddenly life became simple again, became
clean and neat and uncomplicated and almost comfortable,
all the complications of choice and chance and desire and
frustration erased for him between here and God knows
where.

Alice was waiting for him at the gate. She looked anxiously

271

into his expression when he came through, and he smiled re-assuringly at her. He felt a kind of subtle cunning in him when he smiled like that. He leaned down and kissed her, and for an instant it was just the greeting of a husband and wife who have been apart for a few days. Then he was conscious that she was conscious of his breath.

He straightened up. "We put down at Cleveland. There was an hour stopover and nothing much else to do."

"I didn't say anything," she said.

Sometimes, he thought, it is not necessary to say anything. He took her arm and started toward the baggage counter. She did not ask the question that was on her face until they were in the car and turning out of the airport.

"Well," she said then, her voice tentative and diffident, her voice preparing to skirt the subject cautiously, like a kitten stalking a spool of thread, "well, did they like it?"

"They think it's going to be all right."

She sighed. "I suppose that means you'll be working night and day for the next twelve months."

"Not until after Christmas. I'm going to lay off until after Christmas. Help Ellen build you a magazine rack. And teach Alan to dribble a basketball." He eased around a curve and faced the car down a mile of straight and level highway. At the edge of his vision he could see the telephone poles sliding by, and he tried to calculate roughly the distance between them. Say fifty yards, he thought, and eased up on the accelerator, watching out of the corner of his eye for the next pole. As he drew even with the pole, he tramped down on the accelerator savagely, feeling the car lurch ahead, hearing the scream of the tires, counting the poles as they flashed by, glancing at the speedometer as they passed the fourth one. Eighty-five, he thought with satisfaction, eighty-five in two hundred yards; it is going to be a cinch. Then he remembered he wasn't alone in the car. He slowed down and turned his head.

She was staring at him. "How many drinks did you have during that stopover in Cleveland?"

"I'm not drunk. I was just wondering if a car with this tonnage really did have pick-up."

272

Her expression relaxed a little, though underneath he could still see fringes of concern. "The next time you decide to check," she said, "give me a little advance warning, will you? Unless you *want* me to die from heart failure."

"Sure. Sorry." He transferred his eyes to the road ahead. He held the car to fifty, driving sedately home through the cold, thin, winter sunlight, with the whiskey he had drunk in Cleveland wearing off and the nagging headache still lingering from the night before and the dull ache in his heart which a specialist had said was imaginary. And there was a quietness in him, like rested muscles, because he knew now what he was going to do and how he was going to do it.

He waited a month before he bought the insurance policy. Thirty days before, lying awake beside Alice, he remembered the family in the upstairs apartment where they had been living this time last year and the fact that Mr. Nestor sold insurance. So he waited a month, with that sense of peace like quiet exaltation in him, and then he drove into town one afternoon. The stretch into town was level and straight and four lines wide, but he drove cautiously, thinking, You don't want to be taking any chances, not until it is time to take the final chance. He smiled inwardly, almost with pleasure, at the irony of that thought, and pulled up cautiously in front of the house. After a year the house still needed paint and the front porch still sagged, and he thought, There are some things in life that do not change. And maybe I would not have changed either, he thought, if by necessity I had stayed here. Maybe they are wrong, all the people in all the books who tell you that a room or a house or a town does not write a book.

Mrs. Nestor answered his ring, and she hadn't changed, either. "Well, for heaven's sake," she said. "Mr. Savage."

"Mr. Nestor home?"

"He just drove in. Come on in."

He went in and sat down. Mrs. Nestor came back from hanging up his coat. "He'll be in," she said, "as soon as he gets the garage doors closed. It always takes him a while to get those doors to close. How's the family?"

273

"Fine."

"We were downtown just before Christmas and we saw your book in the window. I said to Alfred at the time, I never met a writer before. Until you." She sat down and laid her hands in her lap. "I guess you make a lot of money on books," she said.

"I made out on that one."

"I've often wondered what it would be like if Alfred ever made a lot of money, and I could have a cleaning woman once a week—" She turned her head to watch her husband come into the room. "You remember Mr. Savage, Alfred," she said.

"Sure." He nodded at Michael. He was a slight man with graying hair and the kind of a face that is usually tired from worry but not strained by ambition. A man, Michael thought, who would always manage to have a meal on the table but who would never be out of debt. "I hear you're a pretty important man now, Mr. Savage," Nestor said.

"Is that what you heard?" Michael said. "Where?"

Nestor put his thin insurance case on an end table and wormed out of his coat. Mrs. Nestor was searching his face. "Any luck?" she asked.

"He wants to think it over," Mr. Nestor said.

Michael watched the disappointment settle onto Mrs. Nestor's face and tasted a mild pity for Mr. Nestor, who had fumbled his chance again to sell somebody something, who had gone through another day without making a lot of money. Well, he thought, before the afternoon was out, the hope will have come back into their faces again.

Nestor said, "How's your family, Mr. Savage?"

"Fine." Michael straightened up, no longer feeling pity, feeling only tension, like a man on a tightrope, thinking, If I do not introduce the subject, he will spend half the afternoon creeping up on it. He would make it a lot easier, he thought, if he were any kind of a salesman. Because they will be asking him some questions in a few weeks. I am going to have to be on my guard, and I wish I had a drink. "My family's why I'm here," he said. "I've been giving some thought to my insurance program lately."

274

Mr. Nestor's tired eyes brightened a little. "Well," he said, "insurance is my business."

This is going to be like a chess game, Michael thought, and oh, Christ, but I would appreciate a drink. "I've only got twelve thousand," he said. "When you're twenty, you never think of dying. It's only after the rates have gone up that the possibility occurs to you."

Nestor smiled grayly. "That's a good one," he said. "I'm going to have to remember that one." He focused his eyes somewhere on the space between them. "How much did you have in mind?"

Lying in the dark the night before, Michael had thought a long time about the answer to that one. He had worked it out carefully, the reasonable amount, thinking, You have got to be careful not to kill the goose. "I don't know," he said. "I was just thinking the other day, if something hap—" He stopped abruptly, thinking, That was almost a fool thing I said; that is exactly the kind of remark that insurance adjustors . . . He leaned forward, breathing thinly through his nose. "For a man in my position," he said, "how much insurance would you say I ought to have?"

"That's a hard question to answer. I don't know how much you can afford. For a family the size of yours, though, I'd say you ought to be carrying twenty more. Anyway."

Like a chess game, Michael thought, and you have sucked him into moving into the covered check, for twenty thousand was exactly the amount he had decided on. He concentrated on keeping his voice casual and steady and cautious. "That would come to quite a bit, wouldn't it?"

"We've got ways you can handle it. Term insurance, for instance. You could—"

Michael shook his head. "No, thanks. I know about term insurance. You've got no loan value on a policy, your payments are down the drain." He settled back, feeling fine now, the way you feel when you are in control of a delicate situation. "Let's say thirty pay. How much would twenty thousand, thirty pay cost me?"

Nestor zipped open his case and checked his rate book. "About six hundred a year." His eyes were trying very hard not to hope for anything yet.

"That's not too bad," Michael said. "I could probably handle that. I guess you can write it up." Nestor let his lids drop over the triumph in his eyes. He probably thinks he has sold me this, Michael thought; no doubt they will go out and celebrate tonight. Give him two weeks and he will be prepared to testify under oath that I didn't come to him, he came to me. "I'll write you a check," he said. He got out his checkbook, and then he remembered a detail he had worked out the night before. "I had a good year this year," he said, "and I may not have another book written for a long time. I'd like to pay this up for three years in advance. If I can do that."

"Sure," Nestor said. "Of course, you understand we can't issue a policy this size until you've been checked by our company doctor."

"I understand." He felt tired now that it was over. He wanted to get out of here and go somewhere and have a drink. "Just give me what it'll come to," he said.

Nestor told him the amount and he wrote out the check. The last cast of the die, he thought, the crossing of the Rubicon. I hope Alice doesn't look at this checkbook until this is over and done with. He passed the check across to Nestor.

Thirty minutes later, after he had answered the questions and signed the application, Nestor walked to the door with him. "If I can do anything more for you," he said, "just let me know." His eyes still did not believe that this stroke of luck had fallen on him.

"I'll do that. How soon will I be getting the policy?"

"About three weeks. If it goes through. I'll mail it to you. No particular rush, is there?"

"No," Michael said. "No particular rush."

He felt a sense of exultation when he got back to the car. He felt empty and weak, as if he had just been sweated by an investigating committee, but he felt exhilaration, too. I guess I did one thing right this year, he thought. He sat in the car a

276

while, going over in his mind the hour with Nestor, trying to think of any slip he had made and not thinking of any; thinking, I feel fine again; thinking, I feel like I used to when I had just finished a scene and knew that I didn't even have to read it over; thinking, How long since I felt that way, how long? I guess you have just earned yourself a drink, Savage. No, he thought, No, you can't afford to be taking any chances until the policy is issued and in your hands; you are going to have to let the stuff alone until you are home and this car is safely in the garage. He sat behind the wheel, tasting a drink on the back of his tongue, trying to remember how much whiskey was still left in the cellar at home.

He had to drive two miles before he found a liquor store. "Whiskey," he said to the clerk. "Seven Crown. A case, I guess."

"You must be throwing a party."

"In a manner of speaking. I suppose some people would call it that."

Outside of town he turned east and drove two miles and turned into the farmhouse. McElroy came out of the barn, and when Michael started toward him across the frozen sod, the dogs inside the barn set up a furious barking.

McElroy squinted and then grinned. "Hello, Mr. Savage," he said. "I ain't seen you in quite a spell."

"I've been commuting back and forth to New York this fall," Michael said. "How'd that litter of Danes turn out?"

"Fine. Want to have a look?"

"Yes." He followed McElroy into the barn, into the furious barking. When McElroy opened the cage, the puppies came out like water boiling through the gap in a bombed dam.

McElroy leaned against a post. "Good papers on this litter," he said. "The grandsire took best in his class at the Westminster a few years back. And Bea's got two champions in her own pedigree."

Michael sat down on his heels, and one of the puppies bounded up on him, stretching his neck, trying to lick Michael's face. Michael scratched him behind the ears, feeling as he always felt around dogs, a kind of warm fullness as if he wanted to cry. "This one likes me," he said. "How much for this one?"

McElroy shifted his position. "That one's the pick of the litter, Mr. Savage. He's gonna be his grand-daddy all over again. That puppy's gonna carry off a goddam slew of cups. I gotta have two hundred for him, Mr. Savage."

"That's a lot of money."

"I could get twice as much if I wasn't stuck up here. In the East, I could double that. Pick any other one, it's yours for a hundred fifty."

Michael stood up. "This one likes me. I'll take him. They ready to go?"

"He oughta be wormed. And he ain't had shots. You leave him a couple weeks, I'll—"

"I'll see to all that. I'd kind of like to take him along today. I might not be around in a couple weeks."

"Sure," McElroy said. "Whatever you say. Where you going this time, Mr. Savage?"

"I'm not sure," Michael said. "West, I think."

He came out of the garage and looked across the yard toward the house. The house looked deserted, like a summer place closed for the season. Which means that the kids aren't home from school yet, he thought, and Alan is still deep in sleep, and Susan is playing in the basement, and Alice is lying down for fifteen minutes, her hand over her eyes. He got the puppy out of the car, carried him across the yard, and deposited him in the shop. Right after dinner, he thought, watching the dog sniff out the mysteries of workbench legs and piles of wood shavings, right after dinner I'll lure Ellen out here on some pretext. I'll let her open the door and go in ahead of me. He smiled to himself, imagining her face when the puppy bounded across the shop at her. She will probably cry, he thought; she will no doubt throw her arms around my neck and burst into tears.

He slid out the door and made another trip to the garage. He shielded the case of liquor with his body when he came back across the yard. I am going to have to do something with these, he thought, when he set the case on the shop floor; I am going to have to take precautions. They are my courage for the next three weeks, he thought, and leaned against the bench and gave some thought to where he could hide the bottles. Behind the books in the study, he thought, no one would ever think of looking there, and then his eyes fell on the box under the workbench where he tossed scrap lumber. He pulled it out, unloaded it, put the case in the bottom, all except one bottle, and piled the lumber back on top. I could even knock out the end of that box, he was thinking, hinge it back on; that way I wouldn't have to paw through all that wood every time I wanted a fresh bottle. I might just do that one of these days, he thought; it would be something to take up the time some long and empty afternoon. He pushed the box back under the bench. Then he walked into the study with the bottle he had saved, the taste of the drink he was going to permit himself already heavy and thick in his throat.

His hand was shaking when he pried his penknife open, and he had to force his nerves quiet before he could run the point of the knife around the coating. I'm scared, he thought, I'm scared to death though I don't know what of. Then he had the bottle uncapped, and there was the thick, sweet, heavy odor of the liquor, and he felt his stomach turn over. As long as I live, he thought, I will never get used to the taste of this stuff. As long as I live, he thought, *as long as I live.*

He took a long drink and then he sat down. I could get drunk, he thought; I could sit here and drink myself sodden. He felt a cramp of fear at the thought of going into dinner like that. I am going to have to discipline myself, he thought, and I wonder how much you can drink in a day without showing the effects? He considered that problem. Then he got a ruler, a roll of scotch tape, and a pair of scissors out of his desk and measured the level of the liquor through the am-ber—eight inches of whiskey in a full bottle. He peeled off a strip of tape and stuck it three inches from the bottom of the bottle and then stuck another two and a half inches above it. I will allow myself this much before noon, he thought, this much in the afternoon, this much in the evening. He leaned back in his chair, admiring his handiwork, thinking, Very pretty, Savage, very goddam neat and pretty.

On the shop side of the door the puppy began to whine, and he got up and opened the door and then leaned there, watching the dog pad around the room. In a few minutes the dog went to the outside door and sat down and whined again.

"Sorry," Michael said.

The dog looked at him and wagged his tail and whined again.

"Can't do it," Michael said. "You're a surprise, and the one you are going to surprise is probably home by now." He snapped his fingers and the dog came to him. He nudged him through the shop door with his toe and reached for the knob.

It was in reaching for the knob that he first missed the pain in his heart. He had lived with it so long now that he would sometimes go for hours without noticing it. Unless he reached for something; there was always a stab when he reached. But this time there wasn't. He realized it even before his hand touched the knob, and he wondered how long he had been living in comfort without knowing it. I do not remember any pain this morning, he thought, and I do not remember any yesterday afternoon, either. He sat back and then reached again, not really convinced, prepared for a twinge at least. There wasn't any pain at all.

I suppose that proves something, he thought. His eyes strayed around the study. I wonder what would happen, he thought, if I touched a typewriter. He had a reflective drink while he turned that question over. Then he sat down and rolled a sheet of paper into the machine and rested his fingers on the keyboard and began to type. *Chapter One*, he typed neatly in the center of the page, and then he hit the carriage return with the heel of his hand and sat there a moment, thinking. *The quick, brown fox jumped over the lazy dog*, he wrote, and *Now is the time for all good men to come to the aid of their party*. After that what is there to get down?

He leaned back in his chair. There was still no hint of any

palpitation or pain or flutter. He reached for the bottle and drank to that mystery. He could feel the effects, the lightness, the sense of confidence and well-being. *When you think of betrayal,* he wrote, *you think of exchanges in secret rooms of blueprints for long envelopes bulging with crisp new bills, you think of mattresses slashed and long, black cars pulling up to the curb, you think of the knife twisting down in the blackness of the alley. But it isn't the major treason, it is the series of minor compromises. Not the right hook to the midsection but the left jabs to the lightly-cut eye; not the armored divisions streaking across the map but the quisling in the capital. . . .*

Two hours later the door opened behind him. He had filled six pages by that time, typing the same paragraph over and over, and he had just leaned back and reached again for the bottle. He twisted around in the chair, and she was in the doorway.

"I'm working," he said. "What do you want?"

"I called you to dinner." Her eyes strayed once to the bottle on his desk and then moved somewhere else, as if by the simple act of not looking at it she could deny its existence. "Are you at a stopping place?" she added.

"I guess so." He straightened the pages on his desk and then swung around. "I was tired," he said. "I've been working hard since three, and I was tired. That's why, Alice."

"Why what?"

All right, he thought, all right, goddam it. "I bought Ellen something today," he said. He got up and crossed the study; his head felt light and abstract, and he had to concentrate on what he was doing, but he was sure his walk was steady. "After dinner," he said, "I'm going to lure her out here on some pretext." He opened the shop door and the puppy wriggled into the study and across to Alice.

She stood stiffly in the doorway, looking down at it. "How much did you have to pay for a dog like that?" she said.

"He's a good dog. His grandsire was a champion."

"How much?"

"I promised it to her. A long time ago." He sat down again, grateful for the chair under him once more. "Two hundred dollars," he said.

"We've got to stop spending money, Michael. We've got to start saving somewhere."

"Quit worrying. Everything's going to be all right, Alice."

She turned away. "Dinner in five minutes," she said.

"All right." He started to swing back to the typewriter, and then he put a hand on the edge of the desk and interrupted the movement. "Listen," he said, looking up at her, straight into the light of the open door in front of which her face was an etched shadow, like the face on an overexposed negative. "Listen, Alice, I had a drink because I've been working all afternoon and I was tired. You don't have to act like I was a candidate for AA."

"Do you know what you're doing to yourself?" she said. "Do you know, Michael?"

This time he completed the swing. "I'll be in in five minutes," he said.

He heard the door close, and he touched the typewriter keyboard, idly, with one finger. *paragraph two,* he wrote, not bothering to capitalize because it was too much trouble when you were typing with just one finger like that, *i am not doing anything to myself i am not doing anything im not im not i am just waiting. there are four thousand plays and stories about people who discover that they have a year to live it is what is referred to in the craft as a formula and sometimes the people go temporarily to pieces but only temporarily they always surmount the knowledge in the last act the plot is a convenient vehicle for the depiction of the potential nobility in man. i give to whoever wants it the story of a man who has three weeks but all the difference it makes to him is that he has to learn to wait.*

He stopped pecking at the keys. In three weeks, he thought, they are going to be pawing through the desk and filing cabinet, and this is the kind of evidence that adjustors use to cancel policies. You are going to have to destroy this, he thought. Remember, he thought, to take this out to the trash

282

burner and touch a match to it. First thing in the morning.

He hit the carriage return once more, *paragraph three, insurance adjustors can't read insurance adjustors are perfectly adjusted and can't read anything tougher than a business letter and you ought to keep a diary of the next three weeks.* He paused a moment. *You could preserve the document,* he wrote then, *for the bewilderment of posterity. . . .*

The policy took eighteen days after his medical examination to arrive. At first he was impatient, waiting for it, and then that passed and it was like living on the waking edge of a dream, the act he was going to commit indefinite and unreal, something he was not going to do this afternoon or next week but just sometime. He spent the days pecking idly at the typewriter or playing with the dog or just lying on the cot waiting for morning to merge into afternoon and afternoon to fade into evening.

Then it was there. Then one morning he opened the mailbox and it was there, a heavy, brown envelope. He did not have to pull the envelope out and look to know what it was.

And I am not afraid, he thought, walking back to the cottage through the morning that was not sun nor even light, exactly, but just the absence of rain, like the light in a forest. By God, I am not afraid. In the cottage he dumped the rest of the mail on the desk and opened the brown envelope. I have been afraid once or twice these past weeks, he thought, not of dying, not of that, but just afraid that at the moment before the final moment I would find myself afraid. But now I am only a little excited, as if I were boarding a plane for some place I have never been to.

And there are the things I still have to do, he thought. He sorted through the rest of the mail, thinking, when he passed over an airmail letter, I will have to read that before Sunday, it might be important. And I am going to have to sort through the filing cabinet again. And I will have to mail off that letter to Jean. He lifted his desk blotter and read through the undated letter he had written a week ago, through all the lies about how the work on *The Suburb* was going fine again and how her criticism of *The Courier* was the luckiest thing that had ever happened to him, through the phrases he had worked and reworked and added to and subtracted from until everything but optimism had been ironed out of them. You can at least still write an Exhibit A in an insurance investigation, he thought with satisfaction. Standing there with the letter in his hand, he felt again that sense of fullness, of completion, of creation that he had lost months ago and only rediscovered the afternoon he had bought an insurance policy.

Then it was Sunday. Then it was the introduction to Sunday afternoon, and he was walking across the yard to dinner. When he came in the side door, the dog bounded up the basement steps to meet him, and he crouched to wrestle a moment with the puppy, thinking, I am glad I got it for her. No matter what Alice says.

They were all at the table when he came in. Alice was fixing Susan's and Alan's plates when he came into the dining alcove, and Ellen looked up at him and smiled with excited satisfaction.

"Hey," she said, "you know what he can do already? He can heel. I taught him this morning."

"I'll bet."

"I did. I'll show you. This afternoon."

"Hey, Daddy," Alan said, "you know what gets clothes cleaner than any soap?"

Michael looked down the table at Alan. "I know," he said. "Water."

"No, sir," he said.

"What, then?" Michael said. He filled his plate with roast beef and Yorkshire pudding, thinking with surprise, I am even hungry.

"Tide," Alan shouted triumphantly. "T-I-D-E, Tide."

"Than *any* soap?" Ellen said. She looked up the table. "Hey, Daddy," she said, "Mother says we can't take Prince on our vacation next summer. She says he's too big. Can't we, Daddy?"

"Why, I really don't know," he said. "I'll have to think

some about that, Ellen." He spooned gravy over his Yorkshire pudding, thinking, My favorite meal; thinking, Judging from this meal, you would almost conclude that she knew. "We may not take a vacation next summer," he said. "I spent the vacation money on that dog."

Cathy had her eyes on Michael's face. There was a weighty problem in her expression. "Ellen says Prince is her dog," she said. "She says you bought him just for her. Did you, Daddy?"

"I did not," Ellen said. "I never said any such thing."

"If she did," Michael said, "she shouldn't have. I bought him for all of you."

"Hey, Daddy," Alan said, "you wanna hear a funny story? See, there was this little boy, and he fell in a mud pud—"

"What was his name?" Ellen said.

"Shut up, Ellen," Alan said. "See, this little boy fell in a mud puddle, and his mother said, Did you fall in that puddle with your new pants on, and he said, Yes, I didn't have time to take them off." Alan began to laugh, hard, with his face and shoulders and stomach. "Isn't that a funny story?" he said.

"It sure is," Michael said. "I don't think I ever heard a funnier one. I'm going to have to remember that story."

"I want to know what the little boy's name was," Ellen said.

Michael pointed with his fork at the pudding. "Wonderful Yorkshire pudding," he said. "I had Yorkshire pudding in New York once. Made personally by a twenty-thousand-dollar-a-year chef. It couldn't touch yours."

Alice smiled.

"Listen, Daddy," Ellen said, "I know what we could do. We've got two cars, Mother could drive one, you could drive the other, that way we could take Prince—"

"Now listen, Ellen," Alice said.

Michael moved a hand. "Every girl has a right to take her dog on a vacation," he said.

"I thought you said Prince was *our* dog," Cathy said.

"Well," he said, "he is, Cathy. I just meant—" He stopped

285

talking. She has always known that I preferred Ellen to her, he thought, and he suddenly felt ashamed that he had never treated Cathy as fairly, or anyway as affectionately, as he had Ellen. If I had ten years to live over, he thought, I would try to do something about that. He felt a brief regret that he did not have ten years to live over.

Alan looked up at his mother. "Is this Sealtest milk?" he asked.

"Yes," Alice said. "Let's take a big drink of it. And I think we'd better be getting to work on that plate."

"I'm not hungry," Alan said.

"Yes, you are," Alice said. She filled his spoon with beans, and he turned his face away. "You have to eat beans, if you want to grow up to be a ballplayer."

"I don't wanna be a ballplayer. I wanna be the Lone Ranger."

"I'll bet the Lone Ranger eats beans."

"Uh-uh. He eats Cheerios."

She put the spoon down. "Well," she said, "if you're not hungry, I guess Daddy can have your apple pie."

"Apple pie?" Michael said. "You mean with ice cream on top?"

"I want it," Alan said.

"You're not hungry," Michael said. "I distinctly heard you just say that you're not hungry."

"I'm not hungry for beans," Alan said. "But I'm hungry for pie."

Ellen began to giggle. Alice looked sharply at her. "Don't laugh at him," she said. "It only makes him worse." Then she laughed, too, and Michael turned and began to help Susan with her plate, feeling content that if he were going to do it, he had picked this day, this afternoon. As he watched Ellen and Alice clear the table, he thought that if he were writing this, this would have been the ending he would have chosen. . . .

Alice watched him finish his pie. "Going to work all afternoon?" she asked.

"No." He got up and came around the table and rested a

hand on her shoulder, briefly. "I want to finish a chapter. But it shouldn't take the whole afternoon."

It was four o'clock when he came back in. Alice was in the kitchen, popping corn. "Finish the chapter?" she asked.

"In rough draft." He crossed the kitchen and looked into the living room. Alan was sitting in the TV chair they had bought him for Christmas, and Susan and Cathy were in the big chair behind him. They were all absorbed in the flickering on the screen, and he felt an impulse to go in and play with them for a moment or two. That way, he thought, I could kiss them good-bye without it seeming suspicious. "Where's Ellen?" he said.

"Outside. Somewhere. Probably playing with the dog."

He experienced an instant of panic. I have to see her once more, he thought. I cannot bear it if I do not see her one more time. "I have to run into town," he said. "I have to mail a letter."

She looked over her shoulder at him. "Important?"

"Not very. But Kay asked for a quick answer." He glanced at the cupboard door, remembering the bottle that was on the shelf. You are going to have to allow for it to take effect, he thought. He walked across the kitchen, opened the door, and got down the bottle, thinking, I don't want a drink. I have needed it to live, but I do not need it to die. He could feel her eyes on him when he unscrewed the cap, though he knew that if he turned around, she would shift them back to wherever they had come from. I've got that bottle in the car, he thought; if I waited until I got out there, that ought to be time enough. He studied the amber of the liquor sitting there against the bright yellow of the workshelf, wondering how long it took a drink to get into your blood stream in sufficient quantity to show in a lab analysis; thinking, This is a hell of a last memory to leave her; thinking, Goddam it, I do not have to do this to her. He picked up the bottle and tilted the whiskey into the sink.

When he turned around, she very definitely had her eyes on him. The little pucker she got between her eyes when she was puzzled was a sharp crease this time. "See?" he said. "It's like I keep telling you. I can take it or I can leave it alone."

"Dish of popcorn?" she said.

"Not now. Later. When I get back." He looked firmly at her, wondering if he dared permit himself this final indulgence. Then he closed the space between them and leaned down and kissed her. "So long," he said.

He experienced a rush of relief when he came out of the house and saw Ellen rounding the corner of the garage, the dog at her heels. "See," she called to him. "I told you he could heel."

"Darned if he can't."

"Where you going?"

"Into town."

"Can I go?"

I wish you could, he thought. I wish this were just a normal Sunday afternoon drive and you could ride in with me and tell me what the dog can do already. "You'd have to leave Prince behind," he said. "He's all muddy."

"Oh. Then I guess I'll just stay here."

He put his arm around her. "Take care of everything," he said. "While I'm gone." He brushed her forehead with his lips, and then he dropped his arm and started for the garage. He did not look back.

In the garage he shot another five minutes wondering whether he should take the Packard or the Cadillac. The Packard cost less, he thought, but they are both insured, and I might as well make this privately symbolic. He climbed into the Cadillac and uncapped the bottle and had a long drink. He recapped it and laid it beside him on the seat. He sat there a few minutes, giving the drink time to begin to take hold. Then he backed the car out of the garage.

He drove a cautious fifty into town, waiting for the drink to hit him. When he got to the first cluster of stores, he stopped and deposited the letter in a mailbox; then he drove on. A mile from the place he was going, he pulled off the highway, beside a sign that read SPEED LIMIT 35, and had another drink, thinking, If they don't find it in my blood stream, at least there will be a puddle in my stomach. He

288

pulled out onto the highway again, driving faster now, anxious to get it over with, thinking, I am not afraid, I am not afraid, Oh, Christ, do not let me be afraid. He was going sixty when he started up the hill.

That was when he heard the siren behind him. An ambulance, he thought, there has been an accident out here. He glanced into the rearview mirror and saw the black Ford rounding the curve a quarter of a mile back, coming fast. State Highway, he thought, the realization still unrelated to him, State Highway boys out for a Sunday afternoon and opening up the new model just to see what it will do. Then he remembered the curve behind him and just before it, the dirt road dissecting it, and he thought, *They are after me.* Speed limit 35, he thought, and they were parked behind that billboard back there, their motor idling, *and they are after me.* If they catch me, if they cut me off with this liquor on my breath. . . . He tramped down hard on the accelerator, feeling the horsepower under the hood take hold smoothly. They will have themselves a goddam picnic, he thought, trying to catch this baby with a souped-up Ford, and then his mind was suddenly cold and distant and objective, as if it were engaged in a problem of some kind. It is perfect, he thought exultantly; it is as if I had planned it this way. He slowed a little, his eyes moving back and forth from the road to the mirror, the crest of the hill just ahead now and three hundred yards beyond the curve. It is perfect, he thought, for they are going to be eyewitnesses.

He came over the crest, still slowing, watching for the Ford to show, seeing it when he still had better than two hundred yards to go, his foot tensed over the accelerator and ready to tramp down when they were close enough; thinking, I will swerve to the left and then I will jerk it hard to the right; thinking, I am going to be going a hundred when I hit that rail; thinking, On the police blotter tonight it is going to read *Driver attempting to elude pursuit, car out of control, accidental death.* He felt no fear but only the exultation, feeling the way he used to when he was coming fast into the end of the book and the wrestle over, the plot all straightened out at last, the story neat and tight and strong and inevitable at last. The Ford was close enough now so that he could make out the blurred face of the driver, the black bill of his cap slanting across the line of his eyes. Then the Ford started to swing out, and Michael put the accelerator to the floorboard.

At first it seemed as if he were already on the curve, the guardrail close enough so that he could have tossed a rock and hit it; and then it seemed to be taking a long, long time to get there. He did not look at the speedometer again, but he knew the needle had crossed ninety. He waited another second, trying to judge the distance exactly, and then he flicked the wheel to the left. He was surprised at the distance the car traveled before he could wrench it back; for an instant he thought he wasn't going to make it, that he was going to plow off the road to his left. Then he wrenched the wheel hard to the right, the car swaying but still upright, still clinging to the blacktop, and he thought, Jesus, but these are sweet automobiles, and then the guardrail was straight ahead and a hundred yards away.

At a hundred and ten miles an hour, which it was later ascertained is what he was doing, it takes a car sixteen seconds to cover a hundred yards. But to Michael it seemed like a long, long time. He could see the rail, dead white in the overcast, coming at and at him, and then he could see the cable, looking black and very strong, looking strong enough to hold him even if he broke off a post. And he thought, *You are afraid now; now you are afraid, all right. You are going to die and you have left undone those things which you ought to have done, and you have done those things which you ought not to have done, and you could have written this, this is a story you could have written.* That is when he hit the brake pedal, hard. But on a road surface providing seventy percent coefficient of friction, it takes four hundred feet to stop a two-ton vehicle going a hundred and ten, and, allowing for reflex time, he had given himself a hundred at the outside, and so all the reflex accomplished was that he had slowed down enough, by the time he hit the guardrail, so that the impact felt surprisingly light, no harder than if he had run into a sack of melons. Then the front end of the car was hanging out in space. He could feel it hanging there, suspended in time, like an action caught frozen into the shadows of a snapshot, and he thought, You aren't going over. Something has caught hold of the rear end, and you aren't going over, you are just going to hang here until they can get to you. In that instant he experienced a great flood of relief and behind it a kind of bitterness that he had botched the last thing he had wanted to do right, that the last story he had tried to write had turned sour on the final page. Then the car began to tip. It was at first very slow, like the sensation of just starting down the first slope on a roller coaster, the river below beginning to roll now, like a geographical surface in one of those camera shots taken from a rocket. He could see the horizon sway, as he had seen it sway from a banked plane, and he could see the river come up to meet the sky and then disappear and then come at him again at an angle, and there was the sound of metal ripping loose, and he thought, You did catch hold of a post and you have ripped the whole damned bottom out of this car. Then the river was coming up fast to meet him. For a single, sharp instant, just the onion-thin shaving off the edge of time, its surface was very sharply defined; he saw the ripples on it, and the limb of a tree caught in a crosscurrent and just beginning to swing, and five feet beyond the limb a shaft of light spearing the black water. Then he took his hands off the wheel and covered his face with his arms.

That is probably the last thing he remembered.

Hyatt Engel   V

18

THE DISPATCH CAME ACROSS
my desk at ten o'clock on the morning of February 27th. Janet
brought it in and stood in front of my desk while I read it. It
said that five miles southeast of Minneapolis, Michael Savage, the novelist, had been trying to elude pursuit by two
State Highway police, and had come into a curve too fast; his
car had crashed through a guardrail into the river below; an
autopsy had established the fact that he had been drinking;
the absence of water in his lungs indicated that death had
been instantaneous; he was survived by his wife and four children.

I read the dispatch through twice. So he did it, I thought,
so the poor, driven, frustrated, mixed-up bastard really did
it; and then I thought, why, *why*; and then I was thinking, I
wonder if he really thought he could get away with it.

I looked up at Janet. "Call upstairs," I said. "See if Mr.
Ulrich is in yet. Find out if I can see him."

Up on twenty the receptionist gave me a bright, cold smile
and said that Mr. Ulrich was busy but only for a few minutes,
and I sat down across the room and tried to focus my attention on her cool and classic brow while my mind drifted to
that sharp curve on the River Road. I waited fifteen minutes,
and then Mr. Ulrich wasn't busy any more, and I went in
and laid the dispatch in front of him.

He read it. Then he looked up. He was frowning slightly.
"Well?" he said.

295

"I think I'd like to take another trip out there," I said.

"Why? It doesn't look like much. A forty-line obituary, maybe. The accidental death of a promising young—"

"He was a friend of mine," I said. "I'd like to attend the funeral. I'll settle for a week without pay if—"

"That all?" he said.

I lounged against the edge of his desk and looked him square in the eye and fed him the bait, the deliberate and calculated lie. "I think there might be a story in it," I said. "Something more than an obituary. I've got a hunch."

His eyes warmed and then went cold again. "If you're thinking what I think you're thinking," he said, "what there is probably in it, Hyatt, is a nice fat lawsuit."

"It depends. On what you can make stick."

"It will take some real adhesive. Look at the picture. He was only thirty-six. He was a successful novelist. He had a nice family and the world at his feet. And if you can get around that, why would he pick this way? Why not sleeping pills or carbon monoxide? It would have been a lot surer and less painful."

I held onto his eyes another heartbeat or two and then I let mine drift. I was thinking that maybe he was right, maybe I ought to just forget it, maybe there wasn't enough there for anybody else to go on. I had liked Michael, and I liked Alice, and I didn't want to go out there and poke around. I didn't want to ask Alice Savage a lot of questions at a time like this and maybe stir up muddy waters just as they were beginning to settle. I wanted to let Michael rest in peace, and to give Alice the chance to bring up four kids without anything more coming down on her. Except that I couldn't be sure. Except that the story was there to be gotten, and plenty of bright young men in this town who would welcome the opportunity to get it, and only one person in the world in the position to tie up the loose ends. It wasn't a matter of doing it or not doing it; it was a simpler matter of who got there first.

I straightened up and forced my eyes back. "I can't answer

296

any of those," I said. "I can't even answer simpler ones than those. All I've got to go on is a hunch."

He considered that another moment. Then he smiled. "Okay," he said. "Go ahead."

"Thanks."

He let me get almost to the door. "Good hunting," he said.

"Yeah," I said. "Keep your fingers crossed."

Downstairs, I put a call through to Mattson and Company. When Jean answered, her voice sounded vibrant and light and alive.

"Hello," I said. "It's a hell of a morning, isn't it?"

"I think it's a beautiful morning," she said.

"You won't when I relay some news I have to relay." I waited a minute. "It's about Michael Savage," I said. "I'm afraid you people just lost a novelist, Jean."

"I don't know your source, but I'd double-check that, Hyatt. Because I just got a letter from him. Saying that the book is finally going fine again, and there isn't anything in it about his being unhappy with us—"

"It isn't publisher-jumping," I said.

Over the phone I could hear a sharp intake of breath, like the rustle of paper.

"They got a car out of the Mississippi River," I said. "Yesterday afternoon. He was in it."

"Oh, my God," she said.

"I'm sorry. We just got the dispatch, and I didn't want you coming cold to it—"

"Oh, my God," she said again.

"I'm going out there," I said. "But I'd like to see you first. Could we have lunch?"

"Please," she said. "Oh, God. Oh, Michael, Oh, my God."

"Look, get hold of yourself. There isn't—"

"I want to hang up now."

"Listen," I said, "I have to ask you some questions. Maybe you might know—"

297

"Some questions," she said. "You want to ask some questions. I just this morning got this letter, and he was dead already, he was lying dead while I was reading it, and what kind of questions did you have to ask me? While we were very calmly eating lunch?"

"I've got a theory. I don't think it was an accident. Maybe in that letter you've—"

"I'm going to hang up now."

"Listen," I said, "I was a friend of his, too. But if—"

"Good-bye," she said.

I heard the click. I put the phone back, very gently. I allowed myself ten minutes, and then I called La Guardia.

I checked into the Nicolet at five in the afternoon. By seven I had the story from a police captain. There had been a puddle of whiskey in his stomach but none to speak of in his blood stream, which could mean that he had gone over that drop cold sober. And three weeks before he had taken out a twenty-thousand-dollar, double-indemnity insurance policy. Put those two facts with what I had come out here with, and you just about had a case. Except for one troublesome detail—a good fifty yards of burned rubber. He had known that that curve was there, all right, and he had come hell-for-election over the crest of that hill knowing it, but why, if he had had the intention, had he then hit the brake? Panic? A sudden failure of nerve? Instinct? Window dressing maybe, one more detail calculated to make it look good? Or had the beginning of this just been idle talk after all, the wishful thinking of a guy in his cups and at the bottom of the emotional curve?

Well, I thought, whatever the answer, you will play hell getting possession of it. I went on back to the hotel with that thought lying comfortably in my mind.

It was just nine when I called Alice. Her voice was cold and controlled and unemotional; I got a picture of her holding herself together by digging in her fingernails. "This is Hyatt," I said. "How is everything out there, Alice?"

"Hyatt?"

"Hyatt Engel. From New York."

"Oh. Oh, yes. I'm sorry."

"Are you all right?"

"Yes. I'm all right. I'm fine."

"If there's anything I can do—"

"Are you in New York?"

"I'm at the Nicolet. I flew in this afternoon. For the funeral."

"It's Wednesday. Two o'clock. At All Souls' Church. Do you know where that is?"

I didn't, but I said I did.

"You knew him," she said. "Do you think he'd want the funeral there?"

"Sure. I guess so, Alice."

"He hasn't been inside a church since we were married. I didn't know whether a church was how he'd want it or not."

"I think a church is exactly how he'd want it," I said.

"I remember he said once he didn't want a funeral—that funerals were barbaric and he wanted his body turned over to a medical school. We had an argument about it. We were always having arguments about things." She paused briefly, the way women do when they are on the edge of tears.

"Listen, is there anybody out there helping you, Alice? Because I could—"

"Everybody's been very kind. His old department chairman is taking care of everything."

"Well, I wanted you to know I was in town. In case you needed me for anything."

"Thanks," she said.

I hung up, and then I sat there a while and looked at the phone and wanted a drink. There are times, I thought, when this is a job for the birds, and someday, when I have a bank balance and a few bonds in a locker box, I am going to give it back to them.

There were a lot of flowers, and the kind of casket you get with the twelve-hundred-dollar deal. The minister read a service which Alice sat through with a paralyzed face, and afterwards I got in line and filed past the casket. They had done a very good job on him, all things considering. They had stuffed his broken nose and parted his hair ingeniously over the crushed head, and underneath the undertaker's rouge he looked distant and unreal, like a product out of somebody's factory. Afterwards, I stood aside and watched the rest of them take a look. There were four or five faces that apparently belonged to people at the University; there was one which could have belonged to Michael's father; and there was Jean Reynolds. She was at the end of the line, and she had a handkerchief over her mouth when she stopped and looked down at him. She glanced at Alice, and then she turned away. It was, I am sure, the first time she had ever set eyes on the legal Mrs. Savage, and I don't think Alice even noticed her. Alice was standing off to the side, still wearing that paralyzed face. She was hanging onto the boy with one hand and the youngest girl with the other. The two oldest girls were behind her, both of them crying, bitterly and silently. The boy was primarily interested in the scrollwork on a pew. The youngest girl was cold and excessively bored.

Then there was the procession to the cemetery, and they were lowering the casket into the raw hole, and the boy was asking something, and his mother, still with that concentrated, terrible control in her face, was trying to force her mind onto an answer, and the crowd was drifting toward the cars, and I walked across the twenty yards and touched Alice's arm.

"I've got a car," I said. "Why don't I take you home?"

"Thanks, Hyatt. But Mr. Naylor drove me out, and—"

Her eyes were paralyzed, too. I dropped mine, and discovered that the boy was studying my face.

"My Daddy had a accident," he said.

"Yes."

"My Daddy's in heaven now."

"Yes. He sure is." I looked back into her face. "Let me take them off your hands. Just for the ride back."

She shook her head.

"Well," I said, "is it all right if I come out for a while?"

Something that could have been suspicion flitted across her face. "What's there to come out for?"

I dropped my eyes again. "I've got to ask you a few questions," I said.

"Can't you let him alone? Not even now? Haven't you done enough to us already?"

"I haven't done anything to you, Alice. He's a celebrity. He's news. And there's nothing either of us can do about it. Except see that the right story gets printed."

"What do you mean by that?"

"I mean the facts," I said. "I mean the way it was."

She let go of the little girl's hand and grabbed my arm. "What do you mean?"

I looked at the two oldest girls behind her. "Why don't you send them home with somebody else?" I said.

"All right," she said.

We walked back to the road. She put the four children in the Packard and told the man at the wheel she was driving back with me. Then we climbed into the rented Buick.

I headed the car down the incline and out through the square stone pillars, and then I stole a look at her. She was sitting stiffly on her side of the seat, her eyes nailed to the windshield. "I'm going to give this to you straight, Alice," I said. "No babying."

She didn't say anything. She didn't turn her head, either.

"I'm out here," I said, "because sooner or later the possibility can occur to a few people that this wasn't necessarily any accident."

Her head turned slowly, as if it were operated by remote control. "I don't think I can stand much more of this," she said. "I really can't."

"In a couple of days there is going to be an insurance investigator around asking a lot of questions. And if he should put the right questions to the right people, he is going to have a hunch, too."

"Please," she whispered. "Please, I don't want to hear any more."

"I don't want to tell you any more, but I haven't got much choice." I took a breath, and then I laid it out neatly for her inspection: the analysis of his blood and the insurance policy and a few other facts. I skipped telling her about the night he had told me that this curve would be a place to commit suicide, and the night in the bar when he had quoted Housman, and the rest of it that only I knew. "If they want a motive," I said, "they can find that, too. In some letters in the files in New York. Letters which tell how he was running out of money and the next book not going anywhere—"

"It was an accident," she said fiercely. "The police *saw* it happen and they can't prove—"

"All right. It was an accident. Only there is this insurance policy and this investigator, and for forty thousand dollars a company will go to relatively distant lengths—"

"Do you think I care about that? Do you think I care about anything any more except the children?" She turned in the seat and looked fiercely at me. "If you write that," she said, "and my children have to live with it the rest—"

"I'm not going to write it."

"If you do. If you so much as hint—"

"I'm not going to write it. For one thing because those skid marks don't fit the rest of the theory. But they aren't going to stop an insurance company from taking this to court. Not if they dig up the rest of it."

"I'll tell them I don't want the money. I'll—"

"You think that would call off any dogs?" I said. "You think a big company wouldn't think it bad business to welsh on a claim? You think any of them will rest easy until they've come to a conclusion, one way or another?"

She put a hand up to her face. "Oh, God," she said. "Oh, God, I don't know what to do, and I haven't got anybody—"

"You've got me."

She studied my face. "No," she said, and turned away. "No."

"Yes. So why don't you just tell me how it was? That afternoon."

"I don't remember. It was just another Sunday. I remember

the kids were watching TV, and I was popping corn, and he came in and said he was going into town to mail a letter. I don't remember—"

"Who was the letter to?"

"Kay Anderson. He came in with this letter, and he said it was to Kay."

"That's one thing to check on," I said. I fumbled in my pocket for a cigarette. "What else? How'd he act at dinner?"

"He joked a lot. With the kids."

"And later?"

"We had this bottle in the cupboard, and he came in with this letter and got the bottle out and looked at it, and then he looked at me, and then he—he poured it down the sink."

I looked sharply at her. "Have you told that to anybody else?"

"He poured it out and then he looked at me and said, 'See, it's just like I told you. I can take it or leave it alone.' Those were his exact words, and then—" She put her hand over her mouth. "Oh, God," she said.

"Go on. Give it to me. All of it."

"He kissed me," she said. "He came across the kitchen and kissed me and then he said, 'So long.'"

"Jesus," I said.

"It wouldn't *have* to mean anything. He might—"

"Maybe not," I said. "But you are still going to permit that detail to conveniently slip your mind. No matter how many times you tell the story, you never tell that. Have you got that?"

"I've got it," she said.

"We could even dress it up a little. You could tell them he asked you to go along, and you said you couldn't because of the kids. Then he asked you if you wouldn't like to take in a movie that night. He said there was a good one downtown, and—"

"I couldn't. They'd know it wasn't true. They'd know I was lying—"

"They had better not know you are lying. Anything else?"

"No," she said. "Except when he went out, Ellen was out

there, and he put his arm around her and told her to take care of everything while he was gone. That didn't mean anything to me either, until—"

"You see what I mean, though."

"Yes," she said.

I made the last turn toward her place. The snow beside the road looked blue-white and freshly fallen, and the air fresh and crisp and clean. I pulled into the drive, stopped the car, and leaned across her and opened the door.

She got out of the car. "Wait here," she said. "I'll be right back."

I watched her cross the yard and disappear into the cottage. I was thinking that Michael hadn't known when he was well off, that he had never appreciated what he had in this woman. Then she came out of the cottage with a manila mailing envelope. She came back to the car and laid it on the seat beside me.

"It's the novel he was working on," she said. "I haven't even looked at it. But I don't know what else to do with it, and maybe he'd have liked you to have it."

I didn't know what I'd do with it, either, but I didn't say so. "Thanks," I said. "I'll look it over. Maybe under the circumstances it might publish. Somebody might be interested in a fragment—"

"If you want to." She looked, standing there, like a small, lost child. "Thanks, Hyatt," she said. "For everything."

"Forget it. I'd have done the same for anybody." I smiled at her. "Keep your chin up."

"Sure," she said.

I backed the car around and drove out the gravel lane. I didn't glance into the rearview mirror but I didn't have to to know that she was still standing there when I turned into the highway. I aimed the car down the highway and felt, suddenly, like opening it up, and I did. I was thinking, while I watched the needle climb toward seventy, that they ought to be very proud of me at *Insight*. I was thinking that it had taken me only six months to master the technique of the interview.

Back in New York I made a couple of phone calls. From Kay I found out that there wasn't anything in the letter from Michael that an insurance investigator could make anything of. Then, on the chance that Jean Reynolds was back in town, I called Mattson and Company.

She was. "When did you get back?" I said.

"Oh, it's you." Her voice was low and vibrant. It was also cool. "What's weighing on your mind?" she said.

"I've still got some questions."

"You've got the wrong party."

"I'm not playing games. These are questions I have to have the answer to. How about lunch? Tomorrow?"

"I'm on a diet," she said.

"Listen, Jean," I said, "these questions are a lot more important to you than they are to me." I waited a minute. "They are even more important to Michael's widow. I think the least any of us who bitched up his life can do now is—"

"All right. I suppose I have to eat lunch somewhere. But I'm warning you, Hyatt—"

"Twelve-thirty," I said.

I went out and told Janet that if anything short of the opening of World War III came up this afternoon, I wasn't around. Then I went back into my office, closed the door, undraped my typewriter, and put about a hundred sheets of yellow dog on my desk. I felt as if I were going to need that many.

I don't know what time it was when I finished it. When I came out of my office, there was a single lamp burning near the elevator. I waited for the night operator to make up his mind and thought that I had a story that would go perfectly beside all those journalistic triumphs framed on the wall there. I had just finished a story that three years ago I would have given a right arm to have written. I felt the way you are supposed to feel when you have just seen a Greek tragedy. I wondered if I would ever write anything else which would make me feel like that.

I paid the cab driver and followed her into the restaurant.

305

I asked the headwaiter for a place where we could have it quiet, and he led us somewhere in the back. She sat down and threw her coat off her shoulders, and I dropped the two manila envelopes on the table and sat down across from her. I told the waiter two martinis and he went away.

"You look good in black," I said.

She looked across the table at me. "You had some questions to ask me," she said.

"Let's make it later. Let's drink our drink first."

"Let's make it now," she said.

I shrugged and pushed one of the manila envelopes in her direction. She fingered it idly. "What's this?"

"A story I wrote," I said. "You might call it a study of an American phenomenon. I'm in need of an editorial opinion."

"I've had no experience with nonfiction."

"Read it."

She didn't shrug exactly, but she gave that effect, and then she extracted the manuscript and read the first paragraph. Then she put it back down. "I really don't think I'm interested," she said.

"Read it," I said again.

This time she did shrug, but she picked it up and began reading again. She read it clear to the end and she did not even notice when the waiter set our orders in front of us. When she was through with it, she laid it quietly to rest between us. Her eyes were black and limpid and oblique. She was a very beautiful girl, and I wondered if I was in love with her.

"You son-of-a-bitch," she said softly. "You unprincipled son-of-a-bitch."

"I'm a reporter," I said.

"There are some things you don't have to be," she said. "Even when you are a reporter. Even when you are a reporter on *Insight*."

"There was a story to be gotten," I said. "And I was elected the one to go get it."

"Any way you could," she said. "No holds barred, and I hope it gives you a feeling of satisfaction when they refuse to pay her that forty thousand dollars and she runs out of money before those kids are through school—" She broke off and then she pulled her coat back over her shoulders. "I'm not hungry any more," she said.

I took hold of her forearm and pressed down. "It figures," I said. "Doesn't it? Except for the skid marks, it—"

She looked down at my hand on her arm. "Take your goddam hand off me," she said.

"All the answers but one," I said. "The one I wasn't sure enough of to mention any names." Her eyes were still black, but they weren't limpid any more and they weren't oblique. I explored under the table and found the rung of her chair and hooked my toe through it. "What did he tell you?" I said. "That he was going to leave his wife? Make an honest woman of you?"

"I'm giving you thirty seconds. Then I'm calling the management."

"You were in the clouds the morning I broke the news to you. What was it he wrote in that last letter?"

"Twenty seconds," she said.

I let go of her chair. "Okay," I said wearily.

"I hope she sues you," she said. "I hope she takes you for your next ten years' salary." She pushed back her chair. "Do me a favor," she said. "Mention my name in this. So if she doesn't sue, I can have the pleasure."

"She won't sue me. Neither will you." I opened the second envelope and pulled out the six yellow sheets and handed them to her. "Read these, too. Especially page six."

She read page six. Then she looked up. "What's this supposed to prove?"

"For Chrissake, it's his suicide note. How could he make it any plainer? It's the detail that wraps it up—"

"What? That he was messing around with an idea for a story? If every writer who kept a notebook—"

"Nobody's going to sue anybody," I said. "You can't sue somebody for a story that never gets into print."

Her eyes twitched. "You're lying. This is another scroungy trick to get me—"

"Guess again."

"Why, then? Why did you write it, then?"

I could have told her. If I had known myself. I could have said that a woman back in Minneapolis had asked only for the chance to bring up four children without a shadow over them, or that once in his lifetime a man had felt a compulsion to do something which would leave a decent taste in his mouth, or simply that yesterday I had thought that maybe by getting it down I could understand Michael's motives myself. I could have told her that, even if I didn't think that those were the real reasons. Except that telling her wasn't going to help. Because I knew now what Michael and she had been to each other, and nothing I could say was going to perform any miracle. For it is not true that the living can replace the dead.

"Why, Hyatt?"

I do not have any luck with the women I fall in love with, I thought. I looked down at my untouched plate. "I don't know. Maybe because I had to. To kill it. To kill all of it. Maybe because I had to let you know all that I know, so I could ask you what was in his last letter?"

She shook her head.

"Listen, I'm an amateur investigator and I came up with this. What do you think a trained one could accomplish? What was in that letter, Jean?"

"Nothing anybody could do anything with," she said.

"For forty thousand dollars they can do quite a lot with not very much. Where is it?"

"Where nobody's going to find it."

"Do something," I said. "Not for me. For him. Go through your files over there and burn every letter you've had from him. Every last one."

She looked down at her hands. "All right," she said.

I pushed back my chair. "It was a good story," I said. "I dug up the facts and got down the answers. I'll probably never write another one that even comes close."

"It's very neat," she said. "It probably proves that he could have committed suicide. But if he did, I don't think it explains why." She drew a little circle with her hand, a circle that included me and the restaurant and herself. "You're the answer," she said. "You and me and the rest of us are the answer to that. One-book novelist, worry about money, domestic problems, the compulsion to stay on top once he'd smelled the rarified air up there, the inability to write about anybody except himself or anything unless it had happened to him, those aren't the answers. You're the answer. You and me and Kay Anderson and Frank Mattson and success and this goddam town."

"Everybody's always blaming everything on New York. This town didn't do anything to him. Except get his name in the papers. And give him a hundred thousand dollars."

"Maybe that's what I mean." She drew that vague circle again. "He was different. Maybe all the good ones are different. Maybe you could call it innocence. But it is innocence which is most susceptible to moral disease. We're immune because in this world you catch it and get over it and that's that. But we are also carriers."

I shook my head. "That's like blaming it on Hollywood. The eternal scapegoat for the second-raters, the haven't-got-it-but-once-or-twice guys, the ones who want to be writers but don't really want to write."

"Sometimes Hollywood can do it to you," she said. "Sometimes your name in the papers, and the awe of middle-aged club women, and more money than you've ever seen in the rest of your life put together—sometimes all that can get to you, change your values, rob you of—"

"It can, if you've got something wrong with you to begin with."

She smiled. "You and I," she said. "I don't suppose we have anything wrong with us."

She hunted in her purse and found her gloves and put them on. I reached across the table and retrieved the envelope with those first chapters of *The Suburb* in them and laid them in front of her.

"Take it home with you," I said. "Burn the yellow pages. But read the first hundred pages of what was going to be the next Savage novel."

"Why?"

"For the sake of knocking a romantic theory in the head. Remember what Dave Goldstein said about the ending of *Some Die on the Vine*? How it was faintly mechanical, though the first two thirds manage to carry the ending? Well, that's what those pages read like. Because he was trying in this one to write the story of a middle-class street. Not himself or his family but the story of a grocer and a time-study man in a factory and a teacher and a drug jobber and some woman who moved in among them and who wasn't middle-class." I caught the eye of our waiter. "He would never have brought it off," I said. "Not as long as he lived. Because he wasn't writing about Michael Savage this trip, and do you know what those chapters read like? Like he'd been separated most of his adult life from the human race." I looked at her. "Maybe he had," I said.

Her eyes were on the envelope under my arm. "You never did answer my question," she said. "Not satisfactorily. Why did you write it, Hyatt?"

I looked a long look at her. I had been right, black was certainly her color, and there was very little possibility that I would ever see her again.

"Maybe I just wanted to fix it in mind. Maybe I'll write a novel someday."

"Be careful. The same thing could happen to you."

"Not to me," I said. "I've got no itch left for success. I've got my belly full of it. That's one lesson I've learned that life never got around to teaching him."

Back in my office, I dropped the manuscript on my desk and then went up to twenty. This time I didn't have to wait. This time the receptionist with the cool and classic brow told me I could go right on in.

I went right on in. "I just wanted to let you know I was

310

back," I said. "And that there isn't any story. I'm afraid it has to go down as accidental death."

He looked narrowly at me. "I'm sorry to hear that," he said.

"Yeah. It would have been a good story." I concentrated on keeping my eyes on him. "I ran down every lead I could think of. There's circumstantial evidence, all right, but there was also a fifty-yard skid mark that all the circumstantial evidence in the books is never going to get around."

"Well," he said cheerfully, "you can't get them all. Just send your expense account down to accounting."

"If it's all right with you, I'll pick up the check this time."

He waved a hand. "You did what you could. We expect to pour a certain amount of money down the drain."

"If it's all right with you," I said.

He leaned forward a little. "Why?" he said.

I could tell you, I thought. It would be a pleasure, I thought, if I just had a few bonds in a locker box. "Because my hunch was bad," I said. "Because I failed. Because—"

"Why, Hyatt?" he said again, very softly. "Why the gesture?"

I couldn't keep my eyes on his any longer. "Skip it," I said. "I'll make out a voucher."

He smiled faintly, and I walked back to the elevator and pushed the button. While I was waiting, I looked at Mr. Ulrich's private water cooler, and remembered what Michael had written about betrayal, and wanted a drink of Ulrich's private water and didn't allow myself the indulgence.

Back in my office, I sat down at my desk and contemplated the yellow manuscript, lying neatly in the precise center of the desk. For a minute my mind was on the fact that I would probably never see her again, and then I was asking myself why I *had* written this, and then I was wondering what Michael would have done, if he had faced Ulrich across that expanse of desk and Ulrich leaning, the suspicion bright in his eyes suddenly, and the question, "Why, Hyatt?"

Only I didn't have to wonder that. The world had perhaps conspired for a while to mix Michael up, but I knew what ultimately he would have done, bonds in a locker box or not. Only Michael Savage was not Hyatt Engel, and what Michael would have done was now irrelevant. For Hemingway had been right, I thought: they threw you in and told you the rules and the first time they caught you off base they killed you. Only sometimes they did not even bother to tell you what the rules were. They had never told Michael what the rules were. They had never told him, for example, that when a man's reach exceeds his grasp, he can get his arm chopped off. They had never told him that it is not wise to try to put your scratch on the face of anonymity with a penknife, for the granite is hard and the blade untempered. They had never told him that man was not born to go out too far. They had not told him that the struggle naught availeth, for all is vanity and the discoverer of fire and the inventor of the wheel are nameless, even as you and I. They had not told him that the object of life is life, and the secret of life is to learn to live with the eternal compromise.

I had gone to search out the answers on Michael Savage, but all I had brought back were the answers on Hyatt Engel. And the only question that remained was the question of which one of us deserved pity. For sometimes the taste of self-knowledge is neither bitter nor sweet.

I did not pursue that line of speculation long. There was no profit in that line of thought, and instead I leaned and drew the oversized ashtray at the back of my desk toward me and consigned Michael's story, page by page, to the flame of my cigarette lighter.

At five Janet appeared in my doorway. She had her coat on, and she was pulling on her gloves. "Is that all for today, Mr. Engel?" she said.

"I guess so," I said.

"Well," she said, "I'll see you Wednesday morning."

She finished with her gloves. I sat there and watched her. For a moment my mind had slid into its old familiar grooves, and I was comparing Janet to the paragon in Ulrich's office and reminding myself that someday I was going to have to do something about Janet. And then, quite suddenly, I knew I never would. For I had sat here an hour on this Monday afternoon, with the magazine put to bed for the week and the high-speed presses spinning out the verbal patterns somewhere else and the lights in the editorial offices flicked off, and here, in the shadows and the quiet, I had had a look at myself and I had come to terms.

"Tell me," I said. "What does a girl like you do in this town on her night off?"

"Nothing," she said.

I watched her smooth her plain, black coat down around her hips. Her teeth were still the teeth which ought to have been straightened when she was twelve, and her hair would have proved a challenge to any beauty expert in town, but so far as I was concerned, she had no further worries. She had it made. You do not know it, honey, I was thinking, but you are a lucky girl, for you have just become a symbol. You are the vague dryness of ashes in the mouth. You are the fruit that has soured on the vine. You are the bitter almond on the tip of the tongue, which is the taste of self-knowledge, and doubtless most of us would prefer the cool and marble brow, but the cool and marble brow is something that fits into the landscape of only certain lives.

I shifted my weight in my chair. "I guess you're not alone in that," I said.

"Pardon?"

"In doing nothing. On your night off."

"No, sir," she said. "It can be a lonely town. For some."

I pushed back my chair and got to my feet. "Sometime," I said, "maybe we can do it together, Janet."

10.00 av 91